GEARED TO SELF-DESTRUCT

Hoping they had also turned off the mines, Trennt cut back hard for the barrier wire. But his swing went wide in the soft loam and the Chevy slid outside its tight umbrella of supporting fire. He felt the vehicle buck and nose with hits from his own people. Through the dusty swirl of his dashboard, he saw the oil gauge bolt, tremble, and plummet. A quick gush of rank steam licked over the windshield. One of the big farm rounds had split the night pony's engine.

"Not now," he pleaded. But the Chevy's hurt was too big to cure with a wish. She was fast going lame.

Trennt managed to straighten his broad, shearing turn and throttled hard, back toward the farm. His engine now groaned with slapping pistons and dry, hammering valves. Beneath the hood a speeding tick sprouted, quickly growing to a chorus of screaming metal.

SKYLOCK

PAUL KOZERSKI

A Baen Books Original

Baen Publishing Enterprises
P.O. Box 1403
Riverdale, NY 10471
www.baen.com

ISBN: 0-7434-3570-2

Cover art by Gary Ruddell

First printing, November 2002

Distributed by Simon & Schuster
1230 Avenue of the Americas
New York, NY 10020

Production by Windhaven Press, Auburn, NH
Printed in the United States of America

This book is dedicated to
JIM RENNECKER

Moses then told Aaron,
Take an urn and put an omer of manna in it
Then place it before the Lord in safekeeping
for your descendants.

—Exodus 16:33

CHAPTER 1

June 24, 2050. What remained of California had been written off as frontier. Too little American influence. Hardly anything left recognizable or worthwhile after the Quake. In this, the midpoint of its first century, the new millennium held little in common with all the technological greatness which had preceded it.

Far up here though, all the tragedy and ruin seemed part of some other world. Lost to view from the great wretched masses, a tiny bit of rare technology tracked silently along the border of near-space, headed toward a far distant Midwestern retrieval site and the complex network of couriers waiting to deliver it into anxious scientific hands.

Accompanied only by the low hum of its motor, Solar High Altitude Powered Platform 216B6 and a dispersed fleet of its siblings cruised the thin North American air nonstop. Some performed the routine daily function of measuring ozone concentrations and dust content of the upper atmosphere. Others gauged the polar magnetic shift or the growth of unexplored quake rifts some twelve miles below. But certain units, like 216B6, were dedicated specifically to watching the sun itself for the dreaded signs of its healing.

Bursts of intense solar radiation had long ago fried all spy, weather, and communications satellites into useless orbiting junk. So this type of inexpensive vinyl glider had become the government's feeble eyes to the outlands of both space and ground.

Powered by a toothpick prop and pusher-type electric motor, SHAPP 216B6 ran directly off the harsh sunlight during daytime hours and a bank of lightweight membrane batteries at night. The SHAPP's optic orange color had long been faded to a pale yellow. Made brittle by constant immersion in lethal ozone baths and high-altitude acid sleets, its fuselage and wings were riddled with pinholes from micrometeorite hits and passage through volcanic dust clouds.

Still, the glider doggedly held to the 100 mph pace programmed at its launch those many weeks ago. Leaving the NASA/Crop Research Division research station at Fort Collins, Colorado, 216B6 traversed the great wasteland of America, spread dimly out 60,000 feet below. It crossed cities broken down to kingdoms, towns fallen to clan rule, regions sterilized by the North American Flu epidemic—or worse.

Ironically, none of the damage had resulted from war. Not a nuke had fallen. Not a gun had been fired. All the ponderous volumes on nuclear winter were just so much idle trash, for after a couple million years of putting up with mankind's antics, it seemed Mom Nature herself had finally decided to intervene. Realizing her error in sparing the rod, she now meant to yank the rug from under her sloppy tenants through the simple, but effective, mechanism of global hunger.

Politically, Washington had held out the longest among its worldwide counterparts. Then it too followed the rest of the world in closing down its bankrupt central government. But where even the Wall Street crash of 120 years prior had at least left a rubble pile from which the nation could rebuild, here now was only a smoking crater. The grand experiment was over; Uncle Sam, dead—and left unburied.

A hasty bureaucratic reorganization was devised that split the country along supposedly more manageable, regional lines. Blocks of states were cleaved from their federal union and turned back to the cloisters of their decentralized origin. A series of smaller governing offices were temporarily opened throughout the land. And a reunification was planned after the crisis had been stemmed. So, at least in concept, the nation survived.

But all that was meaningless to the SHAPP. Flying solo so far above the ruinscape, its own life was nearly over. Earlier, 216B6 had banked away from its outflight over the California peninsula. It departed the distant rubble of the Great West Coast Quake and left behind the tricky wind patterns flushed upward by the recontoured land.

Obeying the final orders of return and descent geared inside its old-fashioned clockwork brain, a dozen hours from now, the broad-winged glider would begin a prescribed aerodynamic death ritual of gentle, descending corkscrews. Its valuable data would be wrenched free and thrust into the waiting hands of a complex courier network.

CHAPTER 2

Trennt watched from the spartan back seat as his driver ran an adjusting hand over the crackling radio monitor. He then checked his own obsolete, mechanical wristwatch. The hands showed 3:50 glowing in silent, lime urgency on its dim face. Dawn was too near, safe haven too far off. Trennt looked again to the darkened radio, wondering himself what was wrong with the thing. Northern lights were a continual and understandable signal interference these days. But the month-end clear window still had another twenty-four hours before it closed. The night sky was obligingly clear and reception should be good. Yet, it wasn't so. The driver gave his receiver another rap of knuckles, then wrote it off.

"No more friendly voices guiding this ride," he offered soberly. Glancing from radio to horizon, he appraised his rider. "And a hijacker's moon due up, to boot."

But if the wheelman expected any show of nerves from this particular passenger, he'd be sorely disappointed. That part of Trennt had dried up long ago, making him so effective at what he did today.

Trennt was a prized member of the government's twenty-first-century express relay system. His job was assuring the personal transport and delivery of priority communiqués between Midwestern pickup and drop-off points. It was a vocation he handled with total unquestioning professionalism and personal indifference to the cargo he carried.

The work had taken Trennt across great stretches of Midwestern desert and through crowded city ruins. He'd escorted cargo midday to midnight, horseback to hotfoot; through a latter-day Pony Express gauntlet filled with primitive dangers, both backwoods and open highway.

Understandably, a courier's life didn't boast of longevity. The stable's mules mostly did it for the common macho-jock reasons of tech village status and perks. And the cheap thrill of pressing their luck and daring to yank the devil's tail.

Reasonable precautions were afforded their ranks in issues of shirtweight body armor, scrip money, and medicinal goodie packs. But anything more was strictly self-provided. It was a job for the fearless and foolhardy. Or for those like Trennt, who simply needed the penance.

He'd done well, having started in the bowels of Chicago as a black market runner for Fat Manny, the local neighborhood boss. During his two-year apprenticeship, Trennt had proven his mettle regularly, hauling premium canned goods and bootlegged medicines in a car much like this.

Two wounds and no hijacks brought a notoriety that eventually ushered Trennt into the big league transports of "most favored" status. And here he thrived.

Gravy runs were done in daylight and sometimes

under escort. But tough, demanding ones like this were what he craved. For unchaperoned travel after dark meant covert goods and rewards worth very big risks to the daring opposition. Any solo car with wheels and gas was priceless in itself, not to mention the black market value of whatever illicit freight it happened to carry.

As expected, competing forces of random bush-whackers and organized crime felt the challenge worthy enough to subsidize their own fleets of midnight cruisers. And they loosed them to roam the old blacktop in search of just such booty.

Tonight Trennt was tired. Having personally escorted this particular cargo pouch the full six hundred miles from its South Dakota origin was his biggest run ever. Thankfully, the base leg from Milwaukee to her atrophied twin sister, Chicago, had been uneventful and chauffeured, and the courier thought to allow himself the luxury of a cigarette.

He studied the driver's ancient, grime-shiny Green-bay Packers windbreaker.

"Okay to light a smoke?"

The man spoke over a shoulder. "Sure. But keep it real low. The auto-dim system on my night specs ain't working right."

"Okay."

Trennt dipped his head and drew a quick hit off the harsh, hothouse tobacco. He knew to keep the smoke cupped. Night drives were done in total darkness and blackout specs a delicate commodity. The quick flare of a nearby match might be enough to burn out an older, ailing pair, the mere glowing tip of a cigarette, enough to damage hard-to-replace circuitry.

Trennt tossed the remaining pack ahead to the car's dashboard in good will. The driver nodded and glanced back amiably.

"Thanks, man. I'll save 'em for later. Coming into some crowded overpasses on the homestretch. Need to keep my eyes open, ya know. How 'bout you? Long trip?"

"The longest," answered Trennt.

"I know it's not smart to ask, but . . ."

Trennt finished the all-too-familiar question, "But what's in the bag?" He glanced at the dark, battered pouch. "Never really sure myself. Coming from NASA's Dakota recovery site, I'd guess some kind of high-altitude data."

"But that's just low-priority stuff, ain't it?" The driver sounded disappointed.

Although he'd wondered, himself, Trennt gave his stock answer. "This must be different."

"Yeah."

Both knew to end the shop talk there.

Trennt took another ragged puff off his smoke and, with a mechanic's appreciation, scouted the car's dim instrument panel. Tach, oil, boost, and amp gauges all rode at contented midrange readings.

He hadn't really seen much of the car's exterior at the Milwaukee relay station, but he'd guess her to be an old '06 Chevy Impala. Stripped of reflective trim and dolled up in high-tech options, ancient sedans like it were the last production-bred heavies reliable enough to meet the challenge.

Whatever family had once tooled to soccer games and shopping malls in this old sled would sure be surprised by it now. Its current occupants rode sandwiched between window glass of impact resistant acrylic sheeting and a body layered with the plastic mesh of armorlite fragproofing.

The interior was gutted and reworked with a low-riding, back-seat cargo sump. The trunk held a self-healing fuel cell and everything was set atop priceless solid core tires—hard as a rock, but never a flat.

The old civilian colors were long gone from this night pony, replaced with the modern wonder of stealth antiradar paint. Equally sophisticated bad guys still might find you up close with their own night specs. But they'd never see you on a green screen. In the midst of total social ruin, science marched proudly on.

Trennt popped a side window and rested an elbow on its edge. A flood of warm air rushed in. Above, distant worlds softly twinkled their lover's light. It might have been any other sultry night in any other year. Only the sluggish drone of a billion fatted locusts, singing lazily after their day's pillage, would forever set it apart.

Trennt remembered happier late night rides of bygone years: coming home from Dena's folks in Los Angeles, kids tucked away in the back seat. Her, asleep and cuddled against him, up front. Bright stars and empty interstate, just like now. He moved a hand toward her image but touched only sterile sheet metal and pop rivets in the darkness.

She had seen the truth, right from the start. No fooling that woman with threats of terrorist missles or warlording anti-Christs. She'd known better than to believe in some grand, flaming extinction for mankind. God worked in subtle and poetic ways, she'd advised. And the medium of His glorious, life-giving sun proved just fine.

Trennt was too far removed from either science or religion to really understand the genesis of it all; something to do with a freakish outbreak of sunspots was all he knew. Whatever, it was enough to put the screws to humanity, big time.

He puffed his rough smoke, remembering the first days of this mess. Winters got glacial and long.

Summers molten and short. Weather jumped track everywhere, disrupting growing seasons, creating mutant crop blights, defiant insect strains, and the steady decline of mainline food harvests.

Four seasons of major crop failures had seriously drained worldwide grain reserves. Led by dollar-bloated desert oil countries and Asian manufacturing giants, a struggle for control of the world's grain-producing regions mounted.

Offshore investors each hoped to create their own farms on foreign soil. But great stretches of Canadian ground had succumbed to drought. South American bottom land sank hopelessly beneath the constant flooding of a perpetual El Niño. So, the ragged American turf caught in between became the big prize in a worldwide tug-of-war.

Hundreds of thousands of American acres were simultaneously claimed by Middle Eastern, Oriental, and European deed holders. The Breadbasket of the World became their weakened hostage, paying out corn, wheat, and soy ransoms from its own diminished output to a frenzy of foreign foreclosures.

With the calling in of a century's notes, a financial panic also ensued. The dollar collapsed. Toppling headlong into a black hole of bankruptcy, it dragged world finance and trade with it. Global industry and commerce locked up. Civilization ran aground in a worldwide famine and depression that now approached its ninth year.

The situation had leveled off somewhat, giving scientists hope for an eventual "solar recovery" and likely return to a normal existence. But it didn't much matter to Trennt. His life was long over.

He took another hit from his smoke and spied the first fingers of dawn prying under the black eastern sky. A familiar scent was growing in the mucky breeze.

Chi-town. He'd recognize that cheesy puke smell anywhere. Home. Like hell.

"Heads up!"

On the car's dash, a tiny red LED flickered. Their scanner had picked up another mobile electrical source. Still distant, but by the increasing pulse, closing fast.

Trennt squinted about. The surrounding highway loomed empty and still. A couple of junk cars lay sprawled across the median. A broken-backed semi and some other trash with them. Then, up left, bingo.

Tucked neatly in the crotch of an approaching overpass sat another car. Two murky figures shone dimly inside and the muggy air carried a heavy whiff of its rich, idling exhaust. The night was about to get interesting.

Trennt's driver yanked on the floor shift. He dropped back a gear and broke the rear wheels loose with the power surge. The tachometer peaked out as they blew past the now rolling interceptor.

"Too easy," he muttered over a shoulder. "It's a good bet they've got someone else, waiting ahead. You hang on to your cargo and hug the floor. If it looks bad, I'll try to slow down some place soft, so you can bail out."

Trennt knew the routine. Elbows in, chin down, tuck and roll. He'd done it a few times and didn't like it. Still, he got into the preliminary crouch, tightened his shirtweight armor against friction burns, and braced a foot low on the door in preparation.

Their second opponent cruised a half mile beyond. It was a faster wagon, already rolling at intercept speed. And merging from their right were two more bandits. The robbers had planned their ambush well. There was no crossing the garbage-strewn median strip anywhere near here. No way off I-294 for several more miles.

From his hiding place, Trennt heard the other cars bracket them. He felt their testing fender bumps and his own driver's NASCAR-like taps in return. A satisfying crunch vibrated and Trennt heard one opponent fishtail away on crying tires.

"Hang on!"

His wheelman cut a hard arc away from the second pirate, adding a squirt of nitrous oxide to the engine. The Chevy chirped its tires and leapt ahead of its pursuer. But at that same critical moment, the car's interior exploded in a grating halogen brilliance. Hot, white, and loaded with candlepower, the cruel radiance instantly bleached away all color and shape.

The opposition had hoped to blow out their night goggles with a spotlight overload and force them into an easy collar. Set low in the car, Trennt's own battle damage amounted to only a faint, red afterimage that quickly dissolved with a few blinks. But the driver wasn't as lucky.

"Dammit!" he bellowed. "The light got through my specs. Grab the wheel, man. Quick!"

Trennt sprang from his crouch and lunged halfway over the seat back. He grabbed the steering wheel as the driver leaned aside, ripping off his night goggles and jamming clenched fists to his scalded eyes. The man's throttle foot instinctively stayed mashed to the floor though and Trennt was left guiding a runaway missile from an impossible angle.

"I can't keep on like this," he gasped. "Can you take her back?"

The driver held spread hands before his dim, anguished face.

"No, way! My eyes're on fire! Crawl on over!"

He scooted aside, but still kept his throttle foot jammed as Trennt plunged over the seat's rock-hard bulletproofing. Quickly settling in, Trennt familiarized himself with things.

"Okay! I've got her. Give me your specs."

Trennt one-handed the electronic glasses about his head and jabbed the temple reset button. But as he dreaded, nothing happened.

"No good," he snapped, peeling them back off. "They're fried. If this rig has headlights, we've got to use them."

The driver spoke through gritted teeth. "Low right, by your knee."

With a single toggle flip, the dead night erupted to a brazen, polished steel glare. Trennt hunkered behind the steering wheel in a squinty grimace.

"Might as well add a siren!"

"Shouldn't be too far from the I-55 cloverleaf," encouraged the huffing driver. "Concrete's too bad to chance holding a car anymore. But we can take the far side embankment up. Just keep heading south. You'll see the overpass."

The blinded man licked his lips and drew a pained breath.

"By your seat," he added. "Taped to the runners; a starburst grenade. Tear it off and pass it over. If they get too close, yell out and I'll give 'em one back."

Trennt felt low in the blackness. There, by his left ankle, was a beer-can shape. He yanked the device free and milked its safety spoon, eager himself for a quick payback. But the bandit car had fallen off, satisfied to merely tag along—or to keep herding them ahead.

Trennt saw the blockade with only seconds to spare. A half dozen more cars sat parked and ready. Their crews, all armed with 1000-watt light guns, patiently awaited his arrival.

The dim glint of all those shot-ready chrome reflectors stole Trennt's breath. No way could he dodge a barrage of that magnitude. But, he also wondered, were the bandits really intent on blinding him and chancing a high-speed wreck that might ruin both car and cargo? Or was it just part of some grand diversion?

The forty-foot-wide median strip was weedier here than other places they'd passed, yet strangely unbarred and inviting. Then Trennt spied slivers of black quicksilver wavering through its concealing growth.

Natural or engineered, the median was simply a bog. And the bad guys just out for an easy collar. Let the driver try a stupid dash across and trap himself. Then bust his head, grab the loot, and call it a night. The old caveman and mammoth routine. Hardly original, yet well proven.

But one thing Trennt had cultured early in his lost California home was a knack for off-road driving. He called to his blinded chauffeur.

"Can this thing mud?"

"Mud?"

"Yeah, run the bogs."

"How deep?"

"Don't know yet. But I wouldn't say we have much choice."

"Try it. Drop her down a gear when we hit. Keep the tach riding high."

The driver yanked the safety pin from his light grenade and clamped hard on its spoon. With his other hand, he reached over and took hold of the nitrous oxide knob between them.

"I can still run the joy juice. Say when!"

Trennt aimed the old beast for a straight shot through the dividing strip and gave it open rein. It hurled itself across like a champ, not even touching ground until halfway through the mire. Boring the rest aside like a high speed snowplow, it mounted the opposing concrete mud drenched, but hardly winded.

"Now!"

Back on solid ground, Trennt's passenger let the

starburst grenade roll out his window. A split second later the night sky lit to a brilliant false dawn.

The ploy worked. Their own teams blinded, only a couple of the parked cars were able to start after them. But the tone darkened as the first weapons barked in the Chevy's wake. Bullets slapped its rear flanks, thunking hollowly into the fuel bladder. Tire hits vibrated and jerked the steering wheel.

The loose weave of interior frag netting popped and whined as it trapped and smothered more wild slugs. Even so, occasional bullet slivers did get through. Whizzing about the passenger compartment like mad hornets, one ricocheted off the dashboard and bit Trennt's thigh. The chase drew its first blood.

Trennt angrily yanked open the car's exhaust cut-off and pegged the gas pedal. His Chevy squatted low and keen, easily outpacing the hounds.

"Should be coming up on the Central Avenue overpass," said the sidelined driver. His voice was suddenly sluggish and oddly braced.

Trennt checked his flanks and rear. The on-ramps were indeed too crumbled and dangerous to risk. But the night pony had all the heart it took for hill climbing. The rest didn't matter.

He doused the headlights, pumped his unlit brakes, and slowed enough to tackle a crumbly slope face. The tranny clicked back to low and was joined by a couple notches of parking brake to balance the rear wheels' grip. A nice, even sip of nitrous oxide coaxed more torque from the old V-8 and the car lugged on, heavy but confident.

Once over the crest, Trennt left his car and rider to creep back and watch the highway below. Through the quarter light they came. Full bore and bent on revenge. Their own headlights now brazenly lit, they roared beneath, shaking the weary overpass with their

harsh, blatting exhaust. Four, five, six—that's right, boys.
Keep on going. All the way downtown.

Trennt rolled to his side and drew a deep relaxing
breath. About him, shapes were condensing from the
thinning night. Here was the somber gray outline of
another trashed suburb. Marked by a half-fallen water
tower still carrying the weather-beaten township name
of Berwyn-Stickney, it was the carbon copy of so many
other outlying Chicago spots: littered with stripped and
torched cars, paved with buckled, pockmarked streets.
The area's huge and abandoned sanitation plant loomed
as a silent, hulking derelict in the murky distance.

Ironically, the desolate landscape also sat dotted with
cheery strips of fluorescent rag—fresh surveyor stakes,
marking off more of mid-America for razing. Sometime soon, lame duck President Warrington's army of
farm contractors would commence grinding this wasteland into another fortressed brick-dust farm, vying for
any extra measure of grain to channel into the sorry
regional harvest.

Trennt started back for the idling car.

"Well," he asked the napping driver, "where to from
here?"

With no answer, he called again.

"Hey."

Still there was no reply. Then he inhaled the
sweet-sour pungency of blood and adrenaline—that
old familiar battlefield scent of the badly wounded.
Trennt quickened his pace and found the man half
conscious, glazed in a chocolate-syruplike sheen of
heavy venous blood. Regardless of cargo priority,
Trennt owed him some tending.

He carefully nosed the tired Chevy through the
weedy rubble of old Pershing Road, past gutted Geor-
gian houses, through ghost neighborhoods where kids
once played hopscotch and street football, where

housewives had gossiped and soap operas played. Now all that was a memory, skinned out by salvagers and torched by crazies. America's essence had become a home for bats.

In a makeshift lair, Trennt turned off the car and carefully rolled the driver to his side. A golden BB had gotten through the frag netting. It had managed a path up through a tiny gap in the man's armor vest, to where the shoulder parted for movement, past his armpit and into a lung. He was still alive, but not much more.

Trennt dug out his own medical goodie bag. He cleared a spot for it on the car's dash, amid the scattered clutter of good luck mojos, wild-haired troll dolls, holy medals, and assorted charms—none of which had offered their owner enough protection tonight.

He sprinkled out his pills, sweeping fingers through the cellophaned variety of hunger and thirst depressants, energy tabs, and vitamins; searching for those priceless blood thickening gel caps. Someone had wisely devised a liquid medium to contain the powerful coagulant, figuring rightly that an injured person might have problems contending with anything more.

Trennt raised the wounded man's head and punctured a pair of capsules. He gently squeezed their dark syrup between the driver's parched lips.

"Swallow this," he encouraged. "It's for the bleeding."

The weakened driver nodded slightly and slowly worked his tongue about the thick liquid. Setting the man's head back, Trennt offered a promising smile.

"Good. Take a couple minutes' rest to let that stuff bind you up. Then we're out of here."

But Trennt climbed out from the car, himself unconvinced. His shoulders ached and eyes burned. He set a probing finger to the slash in his pant leg. No serious blood from the bullet graze, but it was dirty and seeping, could probably stand some stitches.

He'd been hurt worse in the course of his work. This stuff was all minor. Though, suddenly, nothing seemed minor anymore. A power deep inside Trennt was calling it quits. Urging him to cash in his chips and give up this silly-assed cowboys-and-Indians life for the bullet he might finally be worthy of. He silently gazed skyward. Dena, have I paid enough?

A low moan oozed from the car.

No. It was time to get real. He had a wounded man and priority cargo in tow—charges beyond just himself. Trennt leaned against the car's warm fender and looked to the brightening east. He drew a slow breath and listened. Through the heavy dank air he heard the sound of their returning engines. The bad guys would know where he was now and they wouldn't be forgiving.

Trennt fished about his shirt pocket. Out came a pear-shaped lump of crinkled black foil—his own lucky piece. Inside sat an old hunk of rock candy—Mother's little helper. He twirled the nugget speculatively between his fingers.

From kitchen labs all over greater Chicagoland came simmering stews of low-grade amphetamines. Alcohol was too expensive for the modern despairing masses; religion, unbelievable and abandoned.

But synthetic bulk chemicals had long since become a cheap, state-funded substitute. And the crock pots of a million orphaned grandmothers, forever empty of prime meat cuts, now held new and much more enterprising personal recipes. Conscientious product served up with the same loving care as ancient Sunday roasts.

Trennt had never subscribed to the chemical confederacy. Too many zombies out there already. And he didn't deserve the raw edge of his memories being falsely dulled. But Mama Loo, the resident chemist of his old neighborhood, had coaxed him into carrying a single tab as a sort of combination lucky piece and emergency mind fuel.

For more runs than Trennt could remember, that same tab had ridden quietly forgotten in his pocket. Wonderful Mama herself was long gone, another victim of the deadly ozone inversions which fell unannounced over the sluggish downtown area. But her spirit lived on in this tiny piece of cottage chemistry. And to that memory, Trennt now surrendered.

He reverently peeled off the old foil. The pearly rock inside was gummy with age, melted by sweat and re-formed in that same battered wrap a hundred times without ever seeing the light of day. It might not even carry a punch anymore. Still, Trennt raised it in salute, then slipped its metallic bitterness under his tongue and began the wait.

In a couple of minutes he felt the change. His exhaustion flaked off and fresh juices of optimism soared up inside like sweet springwater. Thank you, Mama.

Okay. The bad guys would have them zeroed before long, set for a last-ditch try at his car and cargo. Sunrise was working against him. But, there was also a satellite farm due south of here, just a few miles cross-country. Several thousand acres Trennt recalled from the times he'd worked the ration trucks as a "Common Displaced" person.

He knew sector farms had their own police forces— and electric minefields surrounding. The good guys wouldn't know he was coming. If they misunderstood his charge into their defensive perimeter, he could expect even less mercy than from the mobsters. But waiting here longer only gave the hijackers their own private hunting preserve.

"Okay, sis," Trennt encouraged the idling night pony. "One, the hard way."

The gas pedal went flat and the Chevy burst in the open. Squirting twin rooster tails of orange brick dust high into the clammy dawn air, it vaulted the ruined crown of Pershing Road like a hot black missile. And as expected, a half dozen pursuit cars bored in, snapping at its flanks.

The prairie was hard going. All potholes, stumps, and weeds. The floorboards banged. Trennt's teeth chattered. His hands looked transparent on the gyrating steering wheel and, across the car, his silent passenger rattled with a brutal palsy.

Still, he forced more gas to the thundering pony. Cresting 100 miles per hour over terrain that would have tested the best dirt bikes, Trennt's 3800-pound car blitzed like a rocket—wide open, on the deck, and below radar.

The bandits were now tired of all the effort they'd invested in their quarry and wanted a quick end. Bullets again peppered Trennt's fenders and roof. They stitched trails across the resistant window glass and punched into his doors.

But ahead, his distant target also appeared. A teasing green mirage that rose and sank in the thick dawn air. A dusty emerald crowned in flickering pearls of stainless razor wire, it cycled in and out of a heat-soaked pulse that seemed to mock his efforts to reach.

Then, it burst upon him. The farm's minefield materialized so abruptly that Trennt barely swung away in time. He glanced longingly beyond, through the deadly twinkling coils of heaped barrier wire and broad irrigation moat, to the safety of the farm's thick-packed rampart walls.

Inside, they'd heard him coming. From behind a line of automatic weapons, a cluster of armed men appeared. Atop an earthen parapet, they curiously watched him approach.

Trennt veered hard and raced parallel to the deadly earthwork, hoping to show his plight without forcing a test of their hospitality. But the farm cops were slow at taking the hint and the bandits were not about to give up. Still closing in, enemy gunfire came thicker with each new second.

Hundreds of yards flashed by without any sign of invitation from the farm. It was down to crunch time. Trennt's gas gauge now tickled empty and no other evasion was possible. Desperation fueled a reckless plan.

He'd make his own entrance. A low spot in the glinting lacework showed itself. A gate. At this speed, it'd be the weakest link. But he was at the wrong angle to channel his full momentum into piercing it. He'd have to loop back and gain speed—right through the snapping hounds.

They momentarily gave way to his surprising charge, though quickly recovered, dousing the Chevy in even more concentrated gunfire.

A determined bandit car cut in from the right. Trennt countered with a quick tap of his brakes and hard right turn. His opponent spun off through the dirt, tail first.

A second tried forcing him over from the left. Trennt reversed his first maneuver, easily twirling the car amidships and away to his rear. With all their high-tech engineering, newer graphite-composite autos just didn't have the spunk to go one-on-one with an old hunk of Dee-troit iron. A strange and heady euphoria grew from Trennt's mix of adrenaline and meth cocktail. All the danger was almost becoming fun.

Then above the engine roar and popping weapons, friendly fire announced itself. The slow, throaty clap of armor-piercing slugs came arcing in from the farm's fifty-cal. The good guys finally understood and were trying to cover his escape.

Hoping they had also turned off the mines, Trennt cut back hard for the barrier wire. But his swing went wide in the soft loam and the Chevy slid outside its tight umbrella of supporting fire. He felt the vehicle buck and nose with hits from his own people. Through the dusty swirl of his dashboard, he saw the oil gauge bolt, tremble, and plummet. A quick gush of rank steam licked over the windshield. One of the big farm rounds had split the night pony's engine.

"Not now," he pleaded. But the Chevy's hurt was too big to cure with a wish. She was fast going lame.

Trennt managed to straighten his broad, shearing turn and throttled hard, back toward the farm. His engine now groaned with slapping pistons and dry, hammering valves. Beneath the hood a speeding tick sprouted, quickly growing to a chorus of screaming metal.

The car barreled across the deactivated minefield. It springboarded off the thick dirt ramp and launched with a rolling *CRUMP!* Connecting rods and scalded oil blew from the engine compartment as the auto spiked the gate dead center, exploding the barrier in a spray of shocked glitter. Coils of lethal razor wire sang invisibly by, clawing both roof and floorboards a time each in passing.

Trennt felt a momentary nothingness under his wheels; the brief peace of a quick heavenly passage. Dena and the kids filled his windshield. Then the Chevy impacted, plowing itself a watery grave in the deep muck of the farm's irrigation moat.

CHAPTER 3

Clinical experts had long claimed that extinction through starvation was simply the natural avenue man was choosing for himself. His persistent meddling in the earth's basic crop stock through splicing, hybrid development, and chemical dependency had diluted rudimentary genetic codes in each succeeding generation of foodstuffs.

Of equal consequence was a secondary trespass into the arena of socioeconomics. For hybrids meant higher yields from less ground. Higher yields insured a mounting birth rate with more need of land dedicated to housing, education, and commerce; and a natural reduction of the ground reserved for farming.

And so, a mighty doomsday machine was born. One which grew larger with each new decade, until civilization's entire presence came to hinge on a collection of high yield, fertilizer sensitive weeds—themselves existing in an ever narrowing band of production and fertility.

Warnings of potential catastrophe had surfaced periodically throughout recent years of industrialization. The Irish Potato Famine of 1845, the corn leaf blight of 1970, the worldwide wheat smut and soybean leaf rust epidemics of the late twentieth century all hinted at a mounting likelihood for disaster.

With each new growing season, the firing mechanism of the great doomsday machine drew a little tighter. At the turn of the new century, it was finally set fully cocked and awaiting just the right trigger to start it in motion.

That trigger arrived by way of chance solar convulsions early in the new millennia. Fickle spasms of mass and energy in earth's distant benefactor that bombarded the solar system with immense gravitational, magnetic, and ultraviolet fluctuations. Given the innocuous nickname of "Skylock," the event itself would not be anything as trivial.

A consequential fluxing of its poles resulted in a minute reduction of the earth's rotational speed. The varied densities of planet crust and core fell ever so slightly out of synch with its atmosphere, rattling tectonic plates worldwide and giving rise to a subsequent increase in earthquake and geothermal activity.

Erratic and violent weather grew commonplace. Besides obvious land damage, resulting high-altitude soot layers also changed the specific light bands necessary for proper plant growth. Radical ozone generation at ground level impeded crop ability to absorb nutrients, making root systems easy prey for disease and hearty droves of mutant insect strains. Contagion ravaged the planet and worldwide crop harvests fell off by forty percent.

Enter the Manna Project, a global research campaign created by the United Nations and run under license of its Disaster Relief Foundation. It parceled out assignments in plant genetics and was regulated by a world governing board with total project sovereignty over all governments and powers.

But too many jealousies had been fostered for too long a time. And even united in the starkness of their common need, what surfaced among countries was a gaggle of uneasy alliances, which held little trust in their counterparts and gave birth to the inevitable secret societies.

Royce Corealis pumped through the last of his midmorning push-ups. He drew a deep breath and snapped to his feet, savoring the exhilarating rush of fresh blood through his system. Eighty hard ones, like clockwork. Just the right finish to his daily regimen of weights, running, and bag time.

Checking his profile in a gym mirror, the USDA director and head of American Grain Studies was well satisfied with what he saw. At fifty-six, Director Corealis still cut a dynamic figure. Steel gray eyes set in a square, powerful face returned his stare. A set of broad shoulders, firm arms, and flat stomach boasted a man willing to expend whatever personal exertion was required to achieve his goals.

As appointee to the American chapter of the Manna Project, Corealis proved as hard a charger in his professional labors. Under his capable direction, the main research station at Fort Collins, Colorado, and a smattering of contributing countrywide sites delved headlong into their world-class assignment.

Through their studies of plant cloning, cell fusion, and gene splicing, the Crop Research Division of the USDA searched for the isolated traits which would strengthen the UV and ozone resistance of cereal grasses.

A spartan life had toughened Royce Corealis and

forced him to achieve things in the old-fashioned way: with smarts and drive.

The eldest of a struggling Iowa farm family, Royce had had nothing else to help him along. No godfathers or family-paved avenues waiting in business or politics. Just a harsh awareness of economics made early in life, on those humiliating Saturday trips to town. Hellish little journeys from near poverty to a voyeur's world of new bikes, clothes, and treats; all belonging to other, more prosperous children.

The message burned bright to the gawking nine-year-old standing empty-handed in his tattered bib overalls. One which became his fuel and rose as his herald: Success was what you clawed out for yourself.

Scholarships got Royce started and personal savvy held the compass for his upstream fight. In 2021 he became a grain broker for the Japanese, eventually gaining exclusive rights to procure all the American buckwheat so craved by that wealthy island nation.

But these current global hard times proved Corealis' best working medium. His business savvy helped penetrate the newly formed CRD. There, he maneuvered himself with timely favors and adroit flanking moves, eventually standing as chief of the restructured USDA itself; a force to be reckoned with and—once federal decentralization had taken place—a position grown to parallel the very presidency itself.

At first, only the power was his motivation. But, slowly, a greater feeling of responsibility awakened in the man: accountability of what he controlled and stewardship for his country's best interest. So driven, the director shouldered a total patriotic acceptance which made him expect no less from his peers. In mind as now in body, Royce Corealis was a force nothing would be allowed to obstruct.

Today found the director far from his Fort Collins

home base. He was in Illinois, attending a quarterly staff meeting at the regional capitol and interim White House. Along with the other regional governors and various department heads, Corealis spent the three-day assembly delivering progress reports to the president-in-exile and compiling notes for distribution through subordinate channels back at home. Unknown to the majority, however, another private order of business still remained for Corealis and a select few.

Through a scattering of other exercisers, the director caught sight of his executive assistant. Toweling off, he awaited the man's approach.

"Morning, sir," said the aide quietly on arriving. "The latest encrypted progress report from the country club was finally deciphered. Also, a special SHAPP update arrived by courier this morning."

"How do things look?" asked the director.

"The final steps in the catalyst rendering process are nearing completion. Keener reported station personnel to be condensing the first sample batches from prototype refining equipment. They should be completing all their process documentation for actual production manufacturing in the next couple of days. Then it's just a matter of striking camp."

Corealis nodded pleasurably. He added a guarded sigh of relief.

"Excellent, John. The uncertain pace out there lately has had me a little concerned. For all his whining, it seems maybe Doc Ashton has been on the mark all along. The project's ending just when things are starting to get a little too spooky with Keener." Corealis searched the young man's eyes. "What about the SHAPP data?"

"Mixed news there. The report confirms a big EM storm brewing up over the North Pole. Its projected pathway is still holding steady across the Midwest and out over the country club, as we'd hoped. But its ETA has been moved up appreciably."

"How much?"

"Nominal projections are revised to thirty-six hours."

"I assume solar recovery is also still proceeding."

"Unfortunately. And with an accelerating pace."

Corealis pursed his lips. "We were banking on the pre-storm margin for a gradual shutdown. But we'll just have to expedite things. Do you have a list of finalists for an extraction team?"

"Yes, sir."

Corealis swept his eyes about.

"The time's also come to bring the president in on this. Guess I shouldn't really mind that part so much. It's been a long three years, keeping things secret. I'll be glad when he's finally on the inside. Sometime after tonight's dinner I'll get him alone and break the news."

At that point, the aide conjured up a sheepish grin.

"One other thing I have to report, sir. Seems there's been a minor change of plans regarding the normal send-off dinner."

A note of special attentiveness rose in Corealis' voice. "Change?"

"Yes, sir," replied his aide. "The regular dinner is still on. But the president has sent word of a meeting he wants to schedule with the regional governors and staff directly beforehand. In advance of that, he also sent word he'd like to see you alone in his private study."

Reading the young man's face, Corealis huffed self-consciously. "Those tired old rumors again?"

His aide shrugged coyly.

Since Royce could remember, there'd been noise of filling the empty vice president's slot. His loss to the N.A. Flu had left the unmarried President Warrington with no executive backup or personal sounding board.

And though decentralization of the federal government had reduced the presidency to a shadow of its former self, Royce knew reams of due-process laws still had to be reviewed before any could be modified to fit the circumstances. That would not only take time, but a gathering of lawmakers reluctant to invest it outside their own devastated state sectors.

Besides, Royce Corealis was far too busy with important matters to spare much thought of appointment to the second-highest office in the land. Still, something struck him.

"I will admit that personal audiences are a little out of character for our Commander in Chief."

The aid dropped his facade and stepped closer. "So what else can it be, 'Mister Vice President'?"

Corealis smiled uncertainly. "You never know."

His invitation for cocktails that afternoon took Corealis deep inside the president's mansion. Eugene Warrington's study and private domain was a cavernous affair. Rough hewn, ancient native timber rose up the textured plaster walls to brace and cross the lofty, cathedral ceiling. Thick glazed tile ran cool and solid underfoot. At strategic points sat a thousand-gallon aquarium, a broad tapestry depicting a medieval boar hunt, and a glassed walnut case of assorted long guns. Everything was engineered for his comfort and tailored to project exactly what a proper, refined leader's abode should be.

The president was preparing gin and tonics as Corealis entered. He looked up from his bartending to present a cordial smile. But something in his over-precise manner seemed preoccupied and distant. His greeting offered little more.

"Rest easy, Royce," said the man in a neutral tone. "Just us and a couple drinks. No fanfare, no charts.

Nobody else. With our jobs taking us in opposite directions so much of the time, we seldom talk these days. And we need to. Please, have a seat."

Doing so, Corealis was reminded of just how much an unlikely team they made: he, with his blue collar, mechanic's approach to work, and Warrington, with his cultivated presence and progressive views. They stood galaxies apart in background and social ranking. But together, the pair gave order to and aligned everything in between like the poles of a singular guiding force.

Corealis settled in one of the plush leather reading chairs. He quietly followed the vintage green bottle pouring hefty dual shots of juniper. A squirt of lime impregnated them and a splash of tonic made their universe. A clink of ice topped off the effort.

The director received one of the drinks. Its light steel color held murky, ancient visions as the president raised his glass in a toast.

"Better things for our people—quickly."

Corealis nodded and touched glasses. His eyes stayed on the lean man, though, who didn't sit. Rather, after a perfunctory taste, the president abandoned his drink entirely.

"Royce," he began, "one of the big failings in my life has been a lack of complete faith in those around me. Throughout, I've relied on too few people or councils to help me properly shoulder my tasks. That same lack of proper utilization has penalized me and our country. And especially, that means in regard to you.

"You're a human bulldozer, Royce. A heads-up taskmaster that takes a job by the horns and doesn't let up until it's done. No one or no thing stands in your way and that's what I'm badly going to need shortly. Because I'm about to undertake a new burden, which I can't possibly shoulder alone.

"I've asked you here as the first person I want to share some momentous news with."

Ablaze with sudden anticipation and his own purpose, Corealis felt himself eager to reciprocate. "Very well."

Warrington raised his face to a run of UV-screened French windows. He surveyed the sprawl of the regional-capital grounds silently, as if looking miles beyond. The muted light colored his face a cadaverous gray and Corealis was suddenly made starkly aware of just how much the man seemed to have aged.

"This poor country's been through so much," began the president. "Dealing with its own ruin. Adjusting to all the new burdens placed on it by the world board. So much has forever gone away from what we thought we knew, myself included.

"It was five years ago today that I was evicted from our bankrupt capital and brought here as a charity case. My office was removed from any active diplomacy or practical policy-making to endless days of confinement in this"—his tired eyes swept shamefully about—"this wonderful house arrest I've endured. With no election to remove me and no vice president to share in my predicament, I began seeing myself as the last curious zoo specimen of a dying species. But it doesn't have to be so. I realize that now."

His own drink went forgotten as well as Royce listened uneasily to the man's strange and evangelic tone.

"Adam and Eve were expelled from the garden because they chose knowledge over life," Warrington continued from across the room. "The exact thing mankind—our very own society—has blindly done time after time since. And maybe through the ages we have been punished deservedly with wars and pestilence.

"But even as horrible as they've all been, has anyone really seen what those, or more importantly, these

newest hard times might actually be? Just another
pointless tragedy in a chain of events that happens
along every so often? Or, a God-given chance to start
over and make things right? As countries and men.

"Amid all the current global destruction and chaos,
I see that opportunity for America now, Royce. A time
for us to come clean from everything done wrong in
the past and make a new start.

"I hope you might stand with me to see it, too."

The director nodded hesitantly, perplexed and lost
as to what he was actually witnessing.

"I'd like to, Eugene. But I'm not sure I do see it."

Warrington finally took a chair. He leaned forward
as he sat, hands wrapped about each other, in the
posture of someone giving deep council.

"America used to claim that it set the standard for
the world, though maybe 'dictated' is a better word.
In the past, our nation forced changes on fellow countries that they didn't need or want. It justified its
power-hungry greed with the simple-minded claim of
eminent domain. Balanced the scales between acceptable losses and worst-case scenarios, instead of pursuing
what was truly right. Or disarming what was truly
wrong.

"Then Skylock settled in. Shook America like it's
never been shaken. And Royce, things are going to be
forever different.

"Just like the times, the power has shifted and to
exist now we've got to adapt. We're not the big dog
on the block anymore. From the food crisis, global
destruction, and depression has come a new world
order, like it or not. The consortiums. United Europe;
the South American Federation. The African Order and
the Asian Alliance. Any one of them alone dwarfs our
place on this planet.

"Our own state of Alaska and the slivers remaining

of Hawaii have, for all intents and purposes, quit the union. And who can blame them? What's left of the West Coast states is nearly open frontier since the Quake. And we stand powerless to correct or help in any case."

The president drew a slow breath.

"Royce, I want to believe that it's all part of a long deserved wake-up call, which will only do us future good. Force us to concentrate more on our own problems and quit meddling in foreign matters. Make us do with less, instead of monopolizing and squandering world resources on some snobbish whim of manifest destiny."

President Warrington nodded woefully.

"For so long I was no better than the rest. I came into this position thinking that public office was just a sales pitch; no matter where you went or who you met. Try to do some good, sure. But more importantly, exploit whatever personally profitable avenues might materialize.

"I was supposed to be the country's leader. And yet when hard times hit, I abdicated. I was disgusted to look at the nation's wounds and wouldn't tend to its injuries. When the offer came, I gladly took up residence here. Hiding out amid all these illegitimate trappings as if they were something my position automatically deserved.

"But, through the grace of God, instead of languishing on in such a wretched condition, my eyes were gradually opened to what I can and must do."

Warrington rose from his chair. Again, gazing beyond the compound walls, his voice rang in a vigorous oath.

"No longer will I stay dormant, biding my time in unqualified comfort with my books and memories, while an entire population does without, just miles away. No longer will I wait for the old government to be reinstated—if that day ever comes—only to have it return to its sorry old path of compromise and favoritism. No. No longer for any of it.

"True leadership isn't making promises that die on the vine. It's not just rubbing elbows with those few clean and well-fed audiences still to be found. It's giving justice to and caring for the real majority—those faceless voices I've heard begging for help so many times over the radio late at night. The ones with their dirty faces and ribs showing.

"Leadership is making decisions that matter in their regard and following through on them. It's sidetracking the lip service and doing what's truly in the best interest of those who might never even know I was behind it."

Even the battle-hardened Corealis began feeling uneasy in the obscure and growing vacuum of the president's rhetoric. Tiny cold fingers played up his spine as he listened further.

"We owe the American people decent care, Royce. Things we can no longer supply or afford on our own. So after months of personal agonizing, I've decided to convene the regional governors here in the next few weeks and tell them of a plan I've developed.

"I'm going to start by paring this whole bureaucratic mess down to the thin veneer our forefathers originally meant it to be. We'll knock down the walls of our separatist mentality, enter into and really share in the global community. Submit to a world government, if that's what it takes. No longer will we be satisfied by setting a standard, but for once and all, by setting an example.

"I'm then going to make a bid to the World Finance Council for help in restructuring our land. We will recant our nationalization of worldwide holdings. Ask forgiveness for the bad manners of all those before us and implore combined global assistance in taking care of our people. Our meager coffers, as well as our bankrupt ideals, will be offered to their total management."

Royce Corealis felt his wind leave him in a ragged puff.

Bowing to the project's scope, Warrington's tone softened. "Yes, I know," he said, reading his colleague's mind. "It will be humbling beyond belief to the memory of such a once proud and mighty nation. And overwhelming for myself alone to bear.

"That's why I'd like you by my side, Royce, when I reveal my plan. And afterward, to help me orchestrate whatever mechanics are required to make it happen. Become my vice president, and partner, for as long as either one of us is truly needed.

"Will you?"

Corealis fought to regain control of his swimming senses. Just finding his voice took a Herculean effort.

"I . . . don't know what to say," he mouthed in a near whisper.

" 'Yes' is all I need for now," encouraged the president. "Please."

The director swallowed a hard, rough knot.

"Something this drastic . . ."

Warrington vigorously nodded. "I know and agree. But together, the two of us can make something good happen. And it would be the two of us. Side by side in joint leadership. No longer would the vice presidency languish in a pointless role."

Royce blinked. "I'm not even sure how such a plan could come about. With the Fed broken down and so many congressmen and senators lost to the Flu, could any kind of proper quorum be reached? Or even be legal?"

"We'd call together whomever we could," said the president. "Try to do things by proper procedure. But, if not possible, it might very well boil down to invoking Emergency Order 8D966; allowing my final decision on all matters of national emergency."

"Maybe," Corealis suggested cautiously, "there're other . . . avenues."

The president paused, his voice spent and dry. "If you know of any, please tell me now, because I've searched long and hard without success."

Corealis wet his lips. His next words came calmly.

"The slot you've asked me to fill is the greatest honor, Eugene. And I agree in part with what you say."

"But?" asked Warrington.

"But this country is not alone in any of its so-called sins. We joined the Manna Project of our own volition and in good faith. And even as its largest single player, we did not force our dominance on the leadership.

"Instead, we submitted to a project steering group comprised of countries with the least funds or technology to contribute. We pledged ourselves to abide by any and all decisions made by that group in the name of our common survival. And we've stood by that pledge, even as the marginal integrity the project's governing board had at the outset was eroded further by bias, favoritism, and pure conniving."

"Only years of greed by our wealthy citizens put us in bad stead to begin with," Warrington declared. "Long before times ever got bad, they were let run wild like spoiled children; selling off their companies and private land. Taking foreign money indiscriminately with no qualms of conscience or thoughts of patriotism. Nationalizing property which was no longer ours only brought on the financial censure we rightly deserved."

Corealis gently shook his head.

"I don't see it that way, Eugene. And I certainly

don't see us as having cheated on our pledge to the global program.

"We nationalized foreign holdings, yes, but only after the closeout of accounts by overseas holders made doing that our only means of survival. And how did it vary from what the U.N. ultimately did itself? The only difference was their pseudo-parliamentary approach to make the maneuver look legal.

"Coincidentally, those same funds we 'commandeered' were dumped right back into the common pot by way of USDA contributions to the Manna Project. So we haven't shortchanged anybody."

The president sighed. "Like it or not, Royce, the alliances you object to are now, and possibly forever, in control of all meaningful finance. We can only hope they'll be willing to step in and help us out."

"Of course they'd bankroll us," retorted Corealis. "Only a fool wouldn't. Question is, what do we have left for collateral? Terra firma. If we'd throw wide our doors, we'd be parceled out and turned back into the very colonies we started out as.

"Look," he continued. "You mentioned foreign legion outposts currently established on our West Coast. That's correct. Between the South Americans, Orientals, and Soviets, it's open season out there, already. Could this not only make things worse?"

"I am aware too," replied Warrington, his voice slowly filling with iron, "that they're doing the only real job of tending our people. I certainly haven't heard of anyone on the receiving end complaining. Have you?

"In addition, can you tell me when was the last time anyone from back here even made an effort to venture forth and dialogue with those folks? Never. They were just written off and put out of mind. But not anymore. Because I intend to go out there and do just that.

"Furthermore, if we were to be 'parceled out,' as you claim, would the pride of a starving so-called free man be better than the full stomach of a colonist? Which would the average Common Displaced family just outside these fortress walls rather have—a foot of earth or loaf of bread?"

The president drew a bolstering breath.

"My mind is set. If a world government is what it takes to finally put mankind on a level playing field, then I say let all countries tear up their flags and truly become one under God. And by that same God, let us lead the way."

Straining to preserve his last threads of objectivity, Royce dared to contradict one final time.

"That's a grand notion, Mister President. But there's more to life than scraps from a master's table. There's dignity and pride of independence—also God-endowed traits."

"Again," countered Warrington, "values mattering only to those with full stomachs."

A leaden, icy silence wedged between the men. Feeling its heavy chill, the president sought to mitigate the distance separating them. "I so wanted this to go easy and well between us, Royce. Hoped you'd embrace my concept outright and pave the way for converting other department heads. But I also understand what impact such a strategy must have when dumped unannounced on the table."

Warrington reconsidered his glass. He didn't drink, but slowly spun its condensation into wet circles on the polished surface beneath.

"Do me one great personal favor," he asked Corealis. "Don't make any decision on the matter until you've at least had time to sleep on it. Take more time if need be. I do need your help on this."

Warrington dropped his gaze and turned away,

ending the talk. But recalling an earlier item, he swung back with renewed vigor.

"Royce, a moment ago you mentioned the possibility of alternatives. Do you have any such in mind?"

Corealis looked up, then away. "No," he said quietly and left the room.

CHAPTER 4

Fifteen hundred miles to the west Doctor Martin Keener sat alone at his lab desk. Struggling with both his composure and handwriting, the bioengineer swiped again at bunched tears of frustration. He braced himself with yet another deep breath and refocused on setting his coded script to the coarse yellow pages before him.

The frivolous adolescent behavior of keeping a secret diary was decidedly out of place for a man of Keener's educational stature, position, and clinical logic, not to mention just plain risky. Yet the nightly ritual he'd taken up in these last months offered the single vent to all his years of scientific captivity; the old-fashioned method of putting pencil to brittle pages became the sole confessor he dared share a desperate prisoner's deepest secrets with.

Even so, limiting himself to just this secondary exercise was no longer possible. A bizarre fury had grown within the soft-spoken man, one gone beyond the simple restraints of such a passive avenue. The stark truth of his labors had swelled to a boiling rage, which now demanded a much more radical and total closure.

Like so many researchers kept in governmental harness, Martin had for years turned a blind eye to the reality of his work. Leading a handful of learned disciples who had unquestioningly accepted him as their shepherd, Keener had slogged the way through scores of military-interest projects.

In the name of so-called national security, the doctor and his loyal troop had developed plant forms ranging from the very strain of antipersonnel thorn barriers encircling this camp, to crop poisoning viruses capable of starving whole nations into submission.

For three decades the plant geneticist had labored solely on dark government projects, hoping someday for a truly noble cause to materialize and be his ransom. The horror of global starvation arrived to grant just that wish.

But even mankind's threat of total annihilation couldn't disrupt military scrutiny of Keener's work. And eventually an object of covert value was detected in his reports—something powerful enough to forever divert and sequester his team from a key Manna Project conference trip those many months ago.

Given the simple explanation of having been reassigned to new and alternate duties, Keener's squad was severed from all further contact with the Manna Project and plunked down here, wherever this place was. And again, his obedient, if typically naïve team, followed Martin in complying.

But the doctor could stand no more. In his diary, he'd detailed the truth of his work. Subtly coded in the dog-eared commonplace notebook, he hoped, like a message in a random bottle, it would somehow be discovered by an honorable person, who would carry the truth forward. Yet, even if that never happened,

Martin felt somehow cleansed by the exercise, purified for his next and final step.

Martin closed the book and spared a moment to reflect on the quiet night about him. He'd given his life to his work, forsaking even marriage in its name. Never sparing the time for anything remotely like love, until Geri happened into his life with her beautiful smile and gentle ways.

It was her presence here which gave him the focus to finally devise a stern course of action. Yet a gnawing wave of regret washed over Martin, as well. Regardless of the years separating them, given the means, he'd have grabbed her hand and abandoned everything familiar to run just as fast and far as he could. But there was no escape from this remote prison. And nowhere to run to. He'd been over that element too many times.

The doctor capped his thoughts and straightened. His task was at hand. Important work to be done. No longer in the devil's fashion, but finally an honorable, God-fearing kind.

For some time Keener had been intentionally altering and omitting key bits and pieces of data in his reports, dragging out the work here as best he could to help make time for his plan. With him gone, the records destroyed, and no product to reverse-engineer, the power structure sustaining this work would simply have to admit defeat and recall everyone to more ethical enterprises. There'd be no practical reason to retain the team. It would work, he assured himself for the hundredth time since morning. Yes. It had to.

Martin's plan was simple and direct, bold and irreversible. Wait until everyone was asleep. Gather up the electronic and hardcopy research files, along with the rendered catalyst samples. Place them all in the central vault storage, then smash and set fire to the whole thing.

Yet again, his thoughts slipped to Geri. His only regret was in keeping the truth from her. She at least deserved to know why. But he couldn't tell her for her own protection. Not to mention weakening his resolve.

Martin listened to the night. The research station was quiet about him. With everyone in bed he could start his chore.

The young woman leaned against a low, prefab building in a different part of the same lab complex. She drew another puff, indulging in her single camp vice, a late-night cigarette. Though the others never openly criticized, she knew they disapproved of her habit and honored their feelings by smoking privately, only at certain times of the day, and only at this place.

Tonight, though, there was another reason to be here, a deep and smothering gloom. The research program was fast winding down. And with that thought any hope of sleep was lost.

Geri exhaled another puff, gazing forlornly after it. From the darkened camp to the azure and vermilion waves of silent northern lights washed across the corrupted sky. Somewhere beyond loomed invisible Chicago and a return to her hated old way of life.

She so loved it here. As odd and isolated a place as it was, Geri had grown to prize the secluded tableland site as her refuge. After nearly two years, everything about its small cluster of camouflaged labs and living quarters had come to represent all things good and honorable. Her simple "housekeeping" chores for the group had gone on to offer so much personal reward.

Genuine friendship had been extended to Geri from the outset by this very exclusive fraternity of researchers. They had easily accepted the pretense of her arrival as a cook and housekeeper after she had struck up a premeditated friendship with Martin during a brief R and R recess those many months ago.

Unaware of her true purpose as a sentinel, they'd quickly come to enjoy Geri's cooking and conversation as a relief from their otherwise humdrum existence. And she had strangely found herself eager to reciprocate, furiously supporting a project she could never hope to understand, simply because of the eight wonderful people invested in it.

Then there was Martin. No more gentle-hearted, giving man had ever existed in her life, certainly no recent client. Had he asked, she'd have given herself over to him in total. But he wasn't the kind. So they shared a special love in subtle, platonic ways. But now that was unraveling as well. No, he wasn't the kind to lament. Yet Geri had felt Martin's melancholy grow as certainly as her own.

Geri drew a deep, slow breath of the cool, open country air. Out here, everything from before seemed part of someone else's life: the shattered society, the suffering, violence, and despair—her own degrading life as a tech center VIP "hostess." Now, though, it was all coming to a certain and quick end. With the work here complete, her separation from the place, her adoptive family—and doubtless return to the hostess "stable"— were inevitable.

Geri had suffered privately through each dwindling day, clinging to the fragile, impossible hope of some last-minute program extension. But in this eleventh hour, no such relief seemed likely. So she sat, helpless to change any of it.

Until maybe now.

Geri felt about her throat for the special necklace

and chrome key given her those months ago. She
remembered the specific instructions on its use. Using
it now was still far premature. But her desperate fingers
clenched its hard, tiny outline as the only life preserver
she could find in her vast, churning sea of despair.

Geri crushed out her cigarette. Clasping the key
tight, she started a determined pace toward the night-
shrouded battery of humming camp machinery.

The post-dinner meeting convened in a comfortable
guest bungalow. No introductions were required of its
gathered members. Through allegiance and necessity,
they knew each other too well. Their faces belonged
to a tight-knit group of conspirators.

Staff economist, Hampton. Chief meteorologist,
Shields. Medical officer, Ashton. Transport manager,
Clausen. Quinsel of Census and Demographics.
Marquart of Communications. Security head and chief
intelligence officer, Welton. All reliable and efficient
to a fault, they were the nucleus of covert power in
modern devastated America.

Sitting in their midst, Royce Corealis never felt he
could truly call any one of them friend. But that
seemed a fair enough compromise for the monumental
task they'd shouldered together in the name of their
country—a task which now teetered, pointless and
floundering.

"Just like that?" protested the first voice to thaw.
"Warrington decides to surrender, so it's all over?"

"He can't!" joined a second. "It's . . . unconstitu-
tional."

"The Constitution is a tired old piece of paper
without much current relevance," snorted a third. "Like
the man said, Emergency Order 8D966 puts him in
the driver's seat on any decision of national concern
he chooses to orchestrate. That includes surrendering

the entire country for its believed betterment, unless somebody cares to stop him."

"Regardless of what he wants—or thinks he can do," returned the second, "ours is a project that doesn't officially exist in the first place. So he has no control over it."

"Maybe. But surrendering national sovereignty to the World Finance Council is something he has plenty of control over. There's no dedicated Congress or Senate to oppose things anymore. All the regional governing groups have gravitated to practical matters closer to their own homes—and that's their individual survival.

"Face it, through disregard, the presidency has reverted back to its original father figure supremacy. Just like a monarchy, with all the now tragically obvious potential for dictatorship."

"Wait a minute," said the meteorologist, Shields, walking over.

"Royce never really did bring up the project, did you, Royce? So maybe we're just getting the cart before the horse. If we take Warrington aside and explain things as a group, he'll see it our way. He's an objective person and, deep inside, still every bit a politician."

Welton, the intelligence man retorted. "Objective? Objective enough to have been totally bypassed up to now for the sake of project security. He's always been a borderline progressive. And from what Royce says, he's gone over all the way now.

"What happens if we do take the chance, show our cards, and can't bring him into the fold? We stand to lose a lot more than just wasted dollars and a lost cause if this comes to light.

"The world court is always looking to make public examples of covert actions detrimental to the Manna Project—let alone what might be considered an entire secret society like ours."

Clausen spoke up. "If we're really committed to this program, we can't allow either possibility. Until the opportunity presents itself for an organized election or some chance for us to replace him with a more agreeable successor, the man is in power indefinitely. We need to face the plain fact: If Warrington can't be brought in, he needs to be diverted."

"How?"

"By any means required."

"And what do you suggest, lock the President of the United States in his room like some naughty little boy?"

Clausen's blue eyes iced over. "If it can be done simply that way, yes. If not, whatever it takes."

The implication smothered further talk.

Outside the debate to this point, Corealis' eyes rose slowly in the heavy silence. Looking back, Quinsel gave voice to the wall of flushed faces encircling the director.

"Royce? What do you say? You've spearheaded this project from day one. How do you call it?"

"Yes," Shields chimed in. "You know him better than the rest of us. You're the only one who he's ever gotten close to. Is he actually serious about this nonsense?"

The director nodded soberly.

"Blame me. There simply wasn't enough busywork to keep him occupied. It left him with too much free time on his hands. All his reading and radio room eavesdropping seemed a harmless enough diversion and it kept him from being underfoot. Who could've guessed where it would lead?"

"So, we have no alternative then," said Shields, spreading upturned palms and walking away. "No matter how close we are to the end, for the sake of our own skins we'd better just pull the plug on the program here and now, count our blessings, and not look back."

"And what about the country club members?" added another voice. "What do we do with them?"

"Same thing that's been planned all along. Parcel off the team and bury them in isolated labs."

"Uh-uh. That was the plan only once the work was successful. Think it over. If we abandon this thing now, we'd have a handful of people thought dead for three years just reappear. Regardless of where we put them, word would get out. Sure, we can stop, all right. But we can't quit."

There Corealis finally entered the fray. "The first thing we do is keep our heads," he declared. "It's a matter of finding some quick means to get and keep the upper hand in this problem. And we start by forgetting our individual emotions and remembering our pledge—to the project and each other."

His tone braced the group's flagging mettle.

"Okay, Royce," agreed Clausen. "What do we do?"

"The same as was planned all along. We let the team finish up their work. In the meantime, we make preparations for the close-down of the base."

Thom Ashton, the team physician, up to now removed from the discussion, spoke up.

"Once again, from a purely medical point of view, I vigorously emphasize the need for an immediate removal of the station personnel—regardless of how close to finishing up they are."

Marquart looked over impatiently. "You're not going to drag on again about their sniffles, are you, Thom?"

The medic kept an even tone in spite of the familiar antagonism.

"Minimize the situation if you like, Brad, but my primary responsibility has been to ensure the project's success by maintaining the physical and mental well-being of its researchers, not to mention their basic value as human beings."

The doctor's eyes moved accusingly about the room.

"I also remind everyone here that it's been anything but an easy chore monitoring those people long distance, like I've had to do. A smattering of periodic saliva dabs and respiratory felts is no way to do business.

"That research team has been working with very potent plant toxins out there. Their so-called 'sniffles,' Brad, are—again—elevated blood allergens. Trace alkaloids are present in many of the exotic grasses they've been blending; not to mention all the synthetic concentrates and extracts they've been subjected to.

"The heartiness of Sudan grass alone has made it a keystone in their studies. Yet, immature plants have toxic levels of naturally occurring prussic acid—cyanide. The country club has been distilling and genetically altering great quantities of that same grass extract since the start."

A couple of members groaned over the well-covered ground. But the medic continued: "Even with adequate safeguards, you cannot simply leave people continually immersed in an adverse environment. Minute amounts of compounds, as they've been working with, are bound to get absorbed into their systems. The body can flush out a certain amount of contaminants on its own, sure. But even so, trace levels have a cumulative effect. And after three years, those people have crested the limits of acceptable tolerance. For their own good, they must be removed from that environment and detoxified immediately."

Corealis exchanged a sidelong glance with Welton, the security man, then drew a breath, addressing the doctor.

"Thom, once again, I appreciate what you're saying. But you've just agreed yourself that this project has been an arduous maneuver. We've made the best balance possible under the circumstances facing us."

The security man joined in reassuringly. "That's right. We're so close to wrapping this whole thing up, surely a few more days can't matter. Besides, they're the experts who better understand what they've been dealing with than we ever could. Has anyone heard complaints? When they're done we'll give them all a nice long vacation."

The doctor wasn't swayed. "A few days lounging about some R and R center won't fix things. Long term, they may already be in line for a degree of irreversible liver or kidney damage."

Abruptly matching tones, Corealis cut to the chase. "And short term?"

Realizing his disadvantage, the medic remained determined. "At the very least, the distinct possibility of mental impairment, hampered decision-making—confusion. After the withering momentum and complete isolation of their last thirty-six months, it's not too late in the game for some sort of individual—or even group—mental breakdown."

"You're saying that this close to the end, they might actually become dangerous; destructive?"

"Unintentionally, yes; possibly. Anyone familiar with the psychological profiles of hard-core researchers knows they are a narrowly focused bunch, individuals who have to be handled in a very sheltered and kid-glove sort of way. Most aren't equipped to deal with issues as commonplace and practical as food and shelter—let alone ever being confronted by the potential for a dark side of their work."

Economist Hampton muffled a snort.

"That's part of the reason they were stuck out in the middle of nowhere to begin with. We'd feed them. We'd clothe them. They'd have each other, but be totally dependant on us.

"Be realistic, Thom. These are lab nerds for Pete's

sake, not dock workers. Keener's breed doesn't walk off the job or revert to savagery. If you know their kind as well as you claim, you'd also know the one thing they'd never do is abandon or sabotage their work. It's all they have in life. It *is* their life.

"Hell, if you pumped that whole garden party full of LSD I still doubt they'd know how to get rowdy. And remember, we threw in a 'housekeeper' to sweeten the pot. That fact alone has got to knock your data off kilter."

Nervous grins flashed around the room as Hampton finished.

But the doctor maintained his dignity, adding a final declaration. "Exhausted people in normal, healthy surroundings make catastrophic mistakes when pushed. We've taken already-spent persons and turned the speed up on them."

"Only through necessity," countered Quinsel. "You know Skylock's breaking, same as the rest of us. We're in a race to finish the product, get it in a can, and on the shelf."

There, the doctor jabbed an emphasizing finger to the table.

"The facts of what I say remain and I'm telling everyone here. Either we get them out now, regardless of how close the project is to completion or I swear I will quit this program and personally go to Warrington to get them out."

Brows raised and bodies stiffened.

"The hell you say!" challenged one voice. "You signed in on this thing, same as the rest of us!"

"In for a penny; in for a pound!" joined another.

Corealis got to his feet, diplomatically intervening.

"Easy, everyone, easy. Going at each other will serve no purpose. Let's all take a deep breath."

He patiently addressed the defiant medic. "No one

is criticizing your ethics, Thom. I personally appreciate your professional concern and frustration. It means you care and that's the glue that's united us from the start. But we have to stay realistic, if we hope to finish.

"I also applaud what you speak of from a personal level. Doctor Keener has indeed undergone some obvious attitude changes, turned somewhat critical and antagonistic. I've had my own hands full trying to keep him on track."

Feeling the medic settle back, Corealis offered a morsel of indulgence.

"Would you be satisfied if someone was sent out to babysit them, Thom? It's the best I can offer."

The medic mulled it over, giving a reconciled nod. "That's a start, yes. But right away. Someone who could issue concentrated diuretics to start flushing their renal systems. And I personally don't care what kind of excuse is made for his appearance there."

Corealis nodded in return. He looked about the group, agreeably. "For starters, how about yourself?"

The doctor's eyes flared in surprise. But he didn't object.

"We need field agents to chaperon the base shutdown anyway," reasoned the director. "If you say we should have someone out there, okay. And I have no problem with sending people a little early—including you as the man best equipped to treat our scientists."

Royce watched a dazed sort of vindication settle over the now quiet medic. He then looked to the meteorologist. "Ryan, I understand the latest SHAPP data confirms that the ion storm we banked on is brewing prematurely over Greenland?"

Shields nodded. "It's also grown to a number ten magnitude cell that will slide right down over the east-west corridor in the next twenty-four to forty-eight hours. The usual high power EM forces will be dumped all along the route. But this one will also carry a lot of supplementary weather which will come down hard in the far west. The lead elements will definitely mask an excursion. But if your team can't beat it back, they'll have to find some place to weather out the secondary effects. And they will be rough. There still is some time left in the clean air window. But that's also closing fast. So any radio transmissions you might want to send in advance had better go soon."

Corealis shook his head. "Better that our people show up unannounced." He turned to Clausen, the transportation manager. "You're certain your special bird can handle something this strong?"

"In its stride," replied the lean hawk-faced man. "When we christened it an all-weather flier, we meant it. Including the worst-case EM hurricane. No need to risk a crew at all if you don't want. With its self-contained decision making, we can key in its flight parameters from here, let her go out empty and bring the people back. That bird is the closest thing to perpetual motion any of us will ever see."

Corealis had heard the proud litany before. But this time something new struck him. He tabled the notion for later, addressing the chief of security. "Refresh my memory on the base dismantling, Dick. Precisely, how is it to be handled?"

Welton, a stocky crewcut man, paused in lighting a cigarette. Their eyes touched speculatively before he spoke. "Nuclear clean sweep. A small fusion device was implanted to scour the area after the team extraction."

"How small?"

"A plum-sized chunk of Californium 252 packed in a conventional explosive tamper. Typical neutron-type result; total vaporization of a few hundred yards with little detectable radiation afterward. The magnifying effect of the upward sloping canyon walls about the station will act like a naturally drafting chimney. Complete incineration of the site.

By the time atmospherics would ever be normal enough for free travel, all anyone would see would be just another barren hunk of table ground somewhere out west."

"And you're sure this device is safe?"

"Buried beneath the foundation of the main storage vault. Safe as a baby. And to keep the research team from being nervous about it—completely unknown to them."

"But it does need to be triggered by an outside source?"

"Correct. A matching pearl of 252 set inside a mechanical detonator is to be brought in by an army ranger team when it's time to close up shop."

Corealis brightened. "Maybe we can kill two birds with one stone. Send out the detonator with Thom and the chaperones. But without a special forces team."

"It's their mountain."

Corealis shook his head. "Not anymore. Warrington's decision has changed the flavor of this whole thing. I want those teams disbanded and separated. Any files or records on them, regardless of how innocent, need to be destroyed."

Welton nodded. "I'll see to it personally. But non-military personnel means civilian field agents, correct?"

Concerned eyebrows raised about the room.

"Freelancers?"

"Contract mules," Corealis replied. "From the courier stable. People with good track records, some military history, and no previous knowledge of the project. We'll keep them in reserve right here until the final details are ironed out, then fly them in to chaperon the extraction. I've taken the privilege of having a check made through our database. The field is narrowed down to some impressive semifinalists."

Corealis pointed to the crisp personnel folders held underarm by his aide and glanced about: "Everyone is free to examine the dossiers and cast their vote for a selection."

But spurred by his renewing shot of confidence, group members settled back wordlessly, Doctor Ashton included.

The director purposely singled out his security man. "Dick? How about you?"

Welton declined. "Royce, I don't think there's anyone in this room who doesn't have complete faith in your choices. I'll have my inside people keep their eyes and ears open. Just let me know if there's anything special you need help with."

Corealis smiled. He patted the man on a shoulder, signalling him to remain, after the meeting's adjournment.

"We will proceed in our more public tasks as if this gathering had never occurred," Royce declared to the group. "In the name of our continued work, I will accept the president's appointment to the second office."

The director glanced at Doctor Ashton. "But we must keep our poker faces at all times."

The doctor lagged behind the others in leaving. His agressive tone was now flavored with contrition.

"I apologize for seeming harsh in front of everyone, Royce. My frustration got the best of me. But I do have a job and oath to uphold. And we all need to remember, that long after this project is over, those same people are still going to have years of life to live. They shouldn't be ones destined for crippling ailments or a bed-ridden existence."

Corealis nodded his concurrence. "Yes, Thom, I understand and agree. No hard feelings."

The doctor hesitated still. "What is our plan, Royce? We can't hope to keep Warrington in the dark forever. And those team members—they . . ."

Corealis clasped the man's shoulder with practiced ease.

"In all honesty, I haven't quite figured the answer out yet. But I promise, I'll come up with something quick and workable—on all counts. Meanwhile, you can get a bag packed and be ready to pitch in."

The director solemnly studied the physician's departure, coolly making an observation after the door closed.

"Our good doctor's reliability has become highly suspect. He seems bent on needlessly complicating matters at a time when we certainly don't need it."

The security man nodded. He knocked the ash from his cigarette in an empty coffee cup and asked, "We planning to stay with the girl for shutdown?"

"It's the best way."

Corealis pointed to the personnel records. "Since you're here, Dick, let's see what kind of candidates John's found us."

The aide offered two manila folders.

"The list came down to seven finalists. Of those, one's missing, another's dead from job-related injuries, and three are out in the field on extended assignment. Fortunately, that leaves us with the two probably most skilled."

Corealis shrugged. "As long as they're top mechanics."

"Best of the litter," pledged the aide. "Survivors and mechanics, both. One's a courier; the other, an expediter. Talked to the second already and, interestingly, they go way back. So they already know each other's personal ins and outs."

"Background?"

"Army infantry trained. Served together on long-range recon missions in the Peru-Ecuador police action of 2034. Both decorated for bravery. Neither has family. The courier saved a district boss's nephew from a mob beating during the big city riots and was rewarded with an entry level slot in the city messenger network. Worked his way to 'Special Ops' status in less than a year."

Corealis nodded, appreciating go-getters like himself.

"The other?"

"An efficient and methodical expediter. He's reliably handled a number of delicate personnel 'retirements' for other jurisdictions without any fuss. A trouble shooter in every sense of the word."

"How soon can you get them around for an interview?"

"Immediately. Both happen to be on the compound grounds this very moment. One is in the hospital, though."

CHAPTER 5

Pans were clattering. Juices were being mixed. The smell of frying potatoes, sausage, and eggs came to Trennt. Breakfast. He swept a hand across her side of the bed and came away empty. She was already up. Just as he should be. But the covers felt extra inviting this morning, comforting in the security of his own house after all those crazy dreams.

Then she was there, calling to him. "Hey, sleepy head."

Lustrous red hair and liquid green eyes loomed in the bedroom doorway. Valleys and rises flowed in just the right spots of her silky nightgown as she breathed. Trennt ached with longing; like he'd been away for ages. He reached out, beckoning, needing to draw her in, to touch and be assured.

She came to him in that familiar, fluid glide. Smooth arms going about his head, drawing and cradling his ragged breath to the creamy warmth of her bosom.

"Say, Pard."

Trennt jangled awake.

57

There was no perfumed skin. Just the harsh clinic smells of rubber and carbolic. And again, as always, there was no Dena. Only a fast-fading image in the back of his eyes.

Looking about, Trennt discovered himself in a hospital bed. He ached all over. His teeth felt too big for his desert-dry mouth, and his head, somehow not firmly screwed to his shoulders. He tried to lift a bracing hand, but found it wired to an intravenous bottle. At the foot of his bed a familiar, spare figure had materialized—Baker.

Trennt settled back, reality sifting down through his cobwebs at an aggravating, molasses-like rate.

"Take'r easy, Jimbo," said the slim visitor with an unabashed Oakie twang. "You been through a heap."

Trennt licked crusty, swollen lips and closed his eyes.

"Where the hell am I?"

"Base hospital. Been zonked out for the last couple days."

"Huh?"

"Car wreck, 'member? Took a fair crack on the head. Mild concussion. Needed some stitches on your leg, too."

The lean man smiled with a hint of worship, exhibiting square white teeth as he spoke.

"But you still brought home the bacon."

A plotter's grin spread across Baker's narrow lips as he leaned toward the bed.

"In perfect timin', too. Cuz, you and me got us a meetin' with the man—Corealis, hisself."

"Who?" Trennt asked, still groggy.

"Royce Corealis. Head of the U.S. Manna Project. Second highest fellah in the country, I understand."

Baker slapped the bed frame, jarring the patient.

"Come on now, up and at 'em. I'll get someone in here to lend a hand." He started for the door.

Trennt watched him go, suddenly remembering the courier run.

"Hey," he asked wearily. "What about the driver? The other guy with me. How's he?"

Baker shrugged. "Dead, I guess. Why?"

He waited at the front desk. Trennt's few belongings tucked under arm, his usual impatience was set a notch higher than normal.

"Got a jitney parked outside, Pard. Ready to drive us on up to the big house. Don't wanna keep those folks waitin'. Let's get a move on."

But Trennt stood focused on the late afternoon sun, streaming in blue rays through the solar-screened lobby windows. His destination still didn't register—or matter. He only knew he needed some fresh air. "Let's get a couple sun ponchos and walk over."

"It's a cooker out there," protested Baker. "And almost a mile walk. Nuthin' to take lightly in your condition. Besides, we got our own ride on call. And your leg . . ."

"You ride. I need to walk."

Baker gave a nod to the lobby clerk. "Rustle us up a couple sun ponchos and some UV specs, huh, sis? The man needs to work his legs."

Trennt donned his wispy tinted poncho with some effort. Sliding on the almost comical cellophane UV glasses, he exited the hospital door looking the part of some stiff, surreal scarecrow. But once under way, Baker struggled to keep pace.

Ivory Baker was a commodity the civilized world needed, yet wasn't really comfortable with: a back alley mechanic required to handle its dirty work, but never thought of as kin.

Teethed on cordite, Baker had a knack for weapons,

explosives, and orchestrating key moves in those trifling and non-patriotic skin games that kingdoms wanted won by proxy. So while friendships were few, business was always good.

Quickening his pace, Baker spoke again of their good fortune.

"Pard, I got a good feelin' on this un. We done made the top ten list. Something big is in the wind and us two boys're on the cuttin' edge."

But with the sprawling capital grounds of State Sector Three spread free to his view, Trennt was too occupied to hear. The murky blue distance marked the boundaries of a latter-day fortress—one designed to billet the core of administrative, technical, and military power drawn from its six-state realm.

This was the Midwest's governmental seat, storage site for all worthwhile plunder—and residence of the U.S. president. Made self-sufficient with an on-site nuclear powerplant, parts of the immediate grounds included a disbanded Catholic seminary and the University of Illinois campus. Both properties, as well as an additional 50-square miles of land had been appropriated and consolidated under the Decentralization Act of 2044.

Though the roads could obviously handle much larger conventional vehicles, more efficient motorized carts and economic tricycle mopeds comprised the bulk of daytime traffic. Functioning as personnel jitneys and freight haulers, they parted around a smattering of prowling staff cars like minnow schools about random whales.

Trennt's eyes roamed lustfully over a colossal motor pool. Gleaned from confiscated personal estates and bankrupt companies, acres of seized cars and trucks rested in outdoor cold storage, blocked and draped in protective styrene cocoons and awaiting their call to serve. Those already in use sat sheltered inside a run of pole-style buildings, prepped for their next assignment.

Equally impressive was the distant flight line of hangared tilt wing and ducted fan aircraft. Air travel was a rare commodity these days. Avionics required fantastic amounts of ion-deadening material above a few thousand feet; crew and passengers, even more. Only ultra-priority persons and goods moved at all by air and even less during high magnetic or UV daylight hours.

Farther off rose the silvered tops of huge geodesic farm domes. Heaped above the stunted treeline, they sat clumped like gigantic metallic mushrooms. Each was a separate miracle of terraced, germ-free hybrid farming. Covering a hundred acres apiece, their combined indoor output supplied all the crop and livestock needs for the compound's 25,000 personnel.

Trennt walked on in silence, also watching its people. In the harsh, direct sun there were few actual pedestrians. Most were mechanics and tradesmen moving from one repair job to the next. A few lab-coated technicians, sporting appropriate ID tags, scurried among adjacent research buildings.

With each passerby, Trennt felt a growing touch of anger, for every face was clean, rested, and well fed. All eyes were blissfully ignorant of the absolute despair piled high just outside their walled fortress.

His parents had been hard-working, simple country folk, who seldom ventured from their upper California home. Only once did they leave the state in the new century and that was just for a rare family reunion back east. His mother, near term with Trennt at the time, had had the incredibly poor sense of timing to deliver her baby during a layover in the Windy City.

It was as brief a visit as possible and an innocent enough remembrance, one of those recounted lightly at many future holiday gatherings, but also a fact forever stored in some vast, indifferent government computer bank.

For the first time Baker's voice registered.

"I don't know 'bout choo,' Jimbo, but this is the only time I've ever really been inside this place. You know, some service entrance job stuff, tradesmen parties a time or two, but never a full, front door walk-in like now."

He looked at Trennt, but Trennt was silent.

"Here's one ole boy who could sure get usta' this style of living—in a hurry. You and me play our cards right and I believe we just might find ourselves full time management jobs right here in gravy city."

At this Trennt glanced over at Baker, unimpressed.

They passed before the president's trilevel mansion. Its many windows were sun-screened to near-blackness and the lot was patrolled by a select group of casual looking, yet formidable, military police. Considering its obvious importance as the acting White House, a forlorn simplicity still mingled with its grandeur.

Arriving at the admin building, clearance tags were assigned the visitors. The pair were then transferred to a civilian page, who wordlessly led them through priceless air conditioning, beyond numerous office cubicles, to an elevator and an electronically secured VIP meeting room two levels lower.

They passed through a range of comfortable smells: dim hints of cooking from some unseen private cafeteria. Leather, paint. And print. Side glimpses flashed rooms with books. Hundreds of volumes lined thirty-foot runs of floor-to-ceiling shelves. Research and records as well as history, philosophy, and science.

Enough material to flood several small town libraries. A sight Dena would have loved.

An anemic administrative type impatiently awaited them in a lower level anteroom. Obviously uncomfortable with such coarse outsiders, he dared to chide their tardiness.

"Where have you been? You should've been here twenty minutes ago. The director is waiting!"

Baker and Trennt exchanged a glance as the aide ushered them into an adjoining meeting room. He swept a hand forward, indicating another man seated directly beyond.

"This is Royce Corealis, director of the American Manna Project."

The man made no effort to rise, and offered only the slightest of cordial nods. It was an exercise all too familiar to Trennt: checking the candidates' reach, setting a quick pecking order—the gambit never changed and whenever the game was played, big stakes were at risk.

Meetings such as this happened only when commoners were thought worthy of some lofty task, one where anonymity was crucial to top management and the agents generally expendable. The key in passing muster was to remain emotionally detached; impassive to the point of denying your very presence.

His genuine lack of concern made Trennt a formidable player. Focusing on a neutral point between them, he freely left himself open to scrutiny, yet peripherally scanned his captor in return. His assessment was unfavorable. The seated man was a whipping storm flag if ever Trennt had seen one.

Scouting his guests like a horse trader, the man's eyes stayed nonbetraying and impenetrable. But when a final try at overpowering Trennt failed, his stone face relaxed a bit. Quick fissures of amusement sliced the far corners of his hard gray eyes and the room's heavy mood thawed.

"I trust you gentlemen have been treated properly during your stay?" inquired Corealis in his rich baritone voice.

"Mister Trennt," he started, not waiting, thus staking his immediate claim to superiority. "You've recovered well enough from your car crash to consider a return to duty?"

Trennt shrugged, unaffected. "Yeah."

"And, Mister Baker, you're feeling properly?"

Baker nodded curtly, anxious to please. "Always ready."

The director settled back in his chair. "John, my friend, our guests might like some drinks."

He motioned the visitors to chairs. "Gentlemen?"

"Whisky and ice," gushed Baker, eagerly taking a seat.

"Water," Trennt muttered.

The product was offered him in a crystal glass with brutally clear ice. As a "Cee-Dee" family, his had once existed on bug-filled runoff, while here was a personal bar with its own ice cubes. A quick resentment of his hosts boiled up and out.

"Why are we here?"

The aide bristled at his forwardness, but Corealis welcomed the tone as a quick preamble to his subject matter.

"To perform a special, patriotic duty for your country. These times are different from any other in Mankind's history. Freak weather. Worldwide hunger, starvation, dead economies. Whole governments dead, for that matter. A large number even claim we're in the throes of heaven's own Armageddon.

But you know all that from personal experience. What you don't know is the broader picture of the biased political climate, which has put our nation at a serious disadvantage among its so-called allies. This has forced us to take certain drastic steps in the name of future self-preservation; not if, but when, Skylock comes to an end."

The director gave his aide a nod.

"Set on a remote plateau," continued the younger man, "is a covert research station operating outside the conventions of the global Manna Project. Shortly, we will be concluding its work and closing that station, removing and relocating its personnel. It's been decided to add some non-military specialists to the site as camp overseers—operatives, if you will, to expedite the final evacuation. That decision has put us in the market for skilled and reliable agents to handle the task. You gentlemen come highly recommended for just such an undertaking."

"For obvious reasons," interjected Corealis, "it's best not to give too many exact details. But I will tell you that the guardianship of the work being conducted at that station is of utmost value to the future autonomy of this country—and yourselves.

"If you're willing to accept the job, you'd be inserted by air, assist in the shutdown of the base and departure of its people. That will likely occur in a few days. Until that time, you will be our guests here in the regional center with all executive privileges."

Baker glowed comfortably, sipping his drink, but Trennt never relaxed as the director went on.

"Also understand that the mission requires strict secrecy. No flight plan would exist for your trip, nor any record of you. In the event of an emergency, you could likely find yourselves left to your own devices for survival. But you do seem to be thorough experts in that field."

"Be also advised," said the aide, "that if at any time

during the course of the project—for whatever reason—
it is deemed that the integrity of your work is jeopar-
dized or compromised, or your relationship to it judged
to have become a liability, you could be subject to
termination."

Corealis scrutinized his candidates. But the only
reaction came from Baker, who regarded his whisky,
then huffed behind a bored smirk.

"Been there before, sonny. Ain't no big deal."

Corealis took back the reins. "On the other hand,
your success would guarantee you substantial and
permanent privileges higher in the organization."

Baker's glow heightened, but Trennt looked away.

"The entire task should be handled easily by men
of your caliber," said the director from behind another
sweep of calculating eyes. "Will you do it?"

For the first time, Trennt showed a sign of interest.

"How many people are on site?"

"Nine."

He set his water glass aside and stood. "No thanks.
Bye."

Corealis blinked. His aide was staggered. For the
first time, their authority was in question.

"Why not?"

Trennt hovered impertinently between them.

"Because I shepherd hard goods. Livestock is delicate and demanding. Intellectuals are worse; clumsy.
They get afraid and lack survival skills. Makes extra
danger for them and me, both."

"But we wouldn't be herdin' 'em, Jimbo," interrupted Baker hurriedly. "Just sharin' their bunkhouse
and ridin' home on the same bus. Besides, it's our
patriotic duty."

Baker faced his hosts, deciding for both men in a
broad, honeyed smile.

"We'll take the job."

Trennt drew a measured breath, but did not object.

The aide offered up a photo package for inspection. First from the folder was an aerial view of a rugged, tree-covered mesa.

"The place you'd be going is this particular Wyoming tableland. Originally the site of an old Special Forces training camp, it was converted for the current research work. It's been made totally self-sufficient by its own power systems. Nine tenths of its diameter is sheer rock face and impossible to scale."

"And the rest?" asked Trennt.

"A very narrow band that was designed as an emergency evacuation route. It can be traveled upward in reverse, but not easily. The circumference is layered with an independent defense system, a mix of natural barriers and passive booby traps that are ringed and overlapped at various separate levels. Near the summit, an intruder alert system constantly monitors things through a laser gridwork, which is plumbed into a series of electric mines and an automatic gunnery system."

Trennt interrupted again. "What kind of gunnery system?"

The aide fumbled with his folder, annoyed and obviously unfamiliar with the mechanics of weaponry.

"Ah, 40-millimeter grenade dispensers and overlapping 7.62-millimeter machineguns."

"I want specs on the mechanism," declared Trennt brusquely. "Setup, range, and fields of fire. And whatever maps and pictures there are to detail every square inch of the terrain."

Corealis concurred with a benign nod.

"You'll have them. One other thing. You'll also be carrying a trigger mechanism to arm a small on-site nuclear device for neutralizing the grounds once you've departed."

Trennt gave the footnote a cursory shrug, then moved over to sift through the mug shots and attached bios. All those pictured were plant geneticists, but from the pile one photo stood out. A slim, middle-aged man with thick salt-and-pepper hair. He gazed out from intelligent, yet heavy-laden, brown eyes.

"This the top dog?"

"Correct. Doctor Martin Keener, project team leader. A humanitarian individual who has answered a personal call throughout his life to abolish world hunger. Much of the Manna Project's core effort was based on his wealth of studies on drought-resistant grains for the old Third World.

"One of his products you may have had practical experience with is the V3A barrier thorn-bush. A quite impenetrable living organism meant to contain livestock or prisoners of war."

"And what's he doing now?"

"Keener and his people are the best we have at plant cloning, cell fusion, and gene splicing. Early on in the Manna Project, they mutated a very critical amino acid-protein link that helped develop a saline tolerance for the world's inundated, rice-growing coastal areas. They're been working on it since."

Baker leaned over with a bolt of stirred personal interest.

From the packet he slid out a woman's partially exposed picture.

"Say now, who's the honey?"

Corealis exchanged a furtive glance with his aide. "The group's housekeeper, Geri Litten."

Baker lingered a moment on the photo before returning it to the pile. "Sure looks familiar."

Their meeting concluded and Baker and Trennt were dismmissed. Back outside, Trennt drew a worn breath.

"They're lying about something. Big time."

Baker shrugged it off in typical nonchalance.

"Shoot, Jimbo, all staff level folks do. What's it matter?"

"So why us?"

"Our track record!" cawed Baker self-indulgently. "They know who's good, when they see 'em. And, baby, that's you an' me!"

Still, the gunman scouted his cohort with bewildered concern. His words came solemn as the grave. "Jimbo, I know you're prob'ly still shook up from that wreck an' ain't thinkin' too straight yet, but listen to me; this here is our big score. And I say don't look no gift horse in the mouth. We ain't marryin' those folks back there. Just contractin' a job for 'em. Straight talk or no, the payoff's all that counts for us boys. And this 'uns gonna set us for life."

The gunner's smile returned as he glimpsed the area.

"We finally got us the brass ring, Pard. And what sounds like a couple solid go-to-hell days in this here kiddie park before we even need to dirty our hands. Let's us find those guest cottages and get started on some serious R 'n' R.

Back in the meeting room, Corealis settled deep into his overstuffed chair, rocking gently with pleasure.

"Excellent candidates, John," he complimented. "Commendable work in locating them so quickly."

The aide received the praise tentatively.

"Thank you, sir. I didn't feel it was my place to object at the time. But the abrasive one, Trennt—I may have been too hasty in nominating him."

Corealis dismissed the notion with a slow head shake.

"His aloofness? That's the ultimate sign of professional confidence. Besides, your report on his handling of that car chase tells me we definitely want him in on this project."

Corealis touched a thoughtful finger to his lips.

"Before I forget, make an appointment for Clausen and me to speak in private sometime tomorrow. I want to better understand the exact capabilities of his special airplane. In the meantime, see to it that our new agents are treated well while they're here. The best of everything—like you would any condemned men."

The expediters hopped aboard a courtesy jitney and rode out to a small neighborhood of private guest bungalows. There they matched housing assignments with numbers of newly received electronic security cards.

Trennt swiped his card through a computerized door slot and stepped into the narrow hallway. As was his habit, he lingered a few moments, comparing, recalling all the different places he'd weathered in. Some, just a pile of chilly straw in a long forgotten barn, his express pouch for a pillow. Others, like Mama Loo's old courier station, sparse in accommodations, but rich in a furious notion of family.

Then there were those rare spots like this—a wealth of sanitized booty and comfort, all waiting freely for his use or abuse. There'd been too few of these in his travels. But for all their warm showers, clean sheets, and precise comfort zones, they were indifferent places, which always seemed to solicit more than they offered.

The customary enameled shapes waited further on: efficiency fridge and stove, frosty air conditioning. Trennt ran a hand over their cool, clean surfaces and felt the uncommon pulse of electricity humming deep inside.

He followed his usual ritual whenever camping in

rich digs. Both kitchen faucets were turned on full and left running. Water roared out, clean and fresh. No murky, half-pressure rations here. Maybe the clean flow would somehow flush into a faraway ditch and help a Cee-Dee family struggle through one more day.

Trennt wantonly flipped on every light he could find and cranked up a wall-mounted stereo. Cable music filled the air. Next came the bathroom. Piled thick with towels and scarce toiletries, an indoor crapper all to himself seemed vaguely obscene. Still, Trennt eagerly peeled off his threadbare duds and tossed them in a trash can.

He touched tender fingers to the bug bites and bumps from his crash, checked the stitching job on his thigh, still smeared bright orange with dried surgical soap. The ugliness of wounds had long ago ceased bothering Trennt. But what always would bother him and could not be avoided was his reflection in the mirror.

Looking at himself had become a stark confrontation Trennt abhorred. No longer did he see any face he knew; instead, one of a callous and indifferent stranger. A man bent on his own slow destruction.

Beneath the bleary, unshaven mess still lingered origins of a face once called handsome. Now though, his blue eyes, once said to have sparkled, shone back flat and drained of vigor. His skin had grown stiff as old jerky; his disposition, stiffer yet.

Trennt brushed an idle hand across his mandatory health department crewcut. Bits of dried turf skipped comically free of his dishwater blond hair, like fleas abandoning their dog in an old cartoon. Somehow, he still found the ability to grin.

A long scalding runoff did wonders for his aches. Minutes were spent soaking in the shower before Trennt even cared to soap up. Afterward, his skin blushed comfortably with the result. A couple aspirins fixed the rest.

On an adjacent table waited several full changes of clothes, casuals to relax in and, to the side, a separate packing of new field utilities and boots, made ready for his eventual trip. At the same time, his nose caught the unmistakable aroma of roast beef.

Sometime during his shower a stainless dinner service had arrived: tossed salad, heaped with shredded lettuce, tomato chunks, sweet onions, red cabbage, and green peppers. Hot biscuits, whipped butter and the pièce de résistance—a steaming, two-inch-thick slab of prime rib. Perfectly marbled and set in just the right shade of pink, it alone oozed more calories than an entire Cee-Dee family might see in a month.

German chocolate cake, coffee decanter, brandy flask, and after-dinner cigarettes were included. The only thing absent was a mealtime companion, but even that was covered by a small envelope tucked subtly between the dessert and smokes. Inside, was a business card offering a phone number for the "conversational companionship" of a VIP hostess. Though he wasn't at all comfortable with Corealis, Trennt admitted a true respect of the man's well-oiled operation. He devoured the meal.

Sometime after, a nap followed. Trennt woke about dusk, aware of the low, mellow sound of old fashioned citylike traffic. Outside, a splendid burble of expensive internal combustion engines had replaced the lesser whine of daytime electric carts.

He peeked through the curtains and down the street. Sure enough, heavy cars were about. A legion of old Caddys, Buicks, and Lincolns filled the pavement, all polished like brand new.

Suited doormen and elegant nightwear abounded. Calling to mind an old-fashioned Hollywood gala, the air was a spray of flashing sequins and crisp taillights, fine machinery and well-tuned female hindsides. Pretentious as hell, yet intriguing. A world of chemical suntans and healthy teeth, soap and perfume, square jaws and plenty of cleavage.

Thousands of families were living in stripped-out cars, thankful to be eating stale ration crackers and hoping just to survive the next ozone inversion. Yet here was a chunk of ancient society, its gold and diamonds undimmed by all the suffering just beyond these tidy grounds.

In the distance, Trennt recognized Royce Corealis, in the midst of a greeting line, pumping hands and grinning with heaps of plastic good cheer. Rubbing elbows with elitist strangers held no interest for Trennt. Neither did the invitation for an evening's personal female companionship. He had his work to fill the void. And strict penance to maintain.

Letting the curtain drop, Trennt lit a cigarette and spread the contents of his mission folder on the room's coffee table.

CHAPTER 6

Atmospheric anomalies had become commonplace during the nine years of Skylock. Whipped into a frenzy by a continuous spectrum solar flare, cantankerous skies chewed away at both wireless and cable-strung communications. Also stalling all commonplace electronics, Skylock had generally ended Mankind's grand dominion over electricity.

But throughout the event, a tiny spot of the sun's exterior remained oddly uncontaminated by the churning disturbance around it. That same calm eye orbited continually within the solar storm, never dissipating and offering a brief window of electronic stability that fell on the earth with a tidal rhythm.

This "clean air" window ran on a 21-day cycle, allowing a nominal 72-hour period free of EM interference. In its eclipse, everything of electromagnetic origin functioned normally. Pocket compasses to computer circuitry came back on track. Earthbound radio signals shot as far as their surviving transmitters could hurl them. And listening posts worldwide eagerly trained on the sky, gobbling up news, scientific updates, and just plain eavesdropping.

Then all too quickly, the tide of interference would rise. Radio receivers would once more clog with white noise. Compasses would grow confused. Electronics would stall.

As expected, that familiar monthly window was again drawing shut. Yet in these early morning hours one faint distress signal struggled among the thickening static waves. Aided by fluke solar currents, it hopped about the atmosphere, was magnified and reached out to any and all listening ears.

Director Corealis had lain awake for hours. But his sleeplessness went leagues beyond the simple strangeness of a guest-room bed. His mind was in high gear.

Even with adequate babysitters on line, he still wasn't comfortable rushing the camp shutdown. Time was against him. There wasn't enough to iron out details—or devise an adequate reserve plan. And too many bodies, too many trails, too much evidence. How to contain Warrington's new utopianism—or Doc Ashton's weak knees?

Royce had spoken with Clausen in depth on the nuclear airplane's intriguing capabilities. Its blending of self-contained intelligence and unlimited flight potential were priceless commodities, but its best employment hadn't yet come to mind when he finally dropped off from pure fatigue.

Even so, the director's sleep was anything but restful and he bolted fully awake when the phone rang. Three-forty shone on his bedside clock.

He rolled to its shrill buzz and grabbed at the receiver.

"Yes!"

On the other end was Marquart, the communications manager. His voice sounded recently raised from its own sleep, but also tense and frazzled.

"Royce, we've got big trouble. Something's come in over the radio that sure sounds like a mayday from the country club."

Corealis shot erect in the darkened bed. "What!"

"About fifteen minutes ago."

"Are you sure?"

"Not absolutely, no. It was fragmented and not in any wording they were instructed to use. But team members were mentioned by name in a woman's voice screaming for help."

Ashton's words rang cruelly prophetic.

"It can't be. We're too close!"

"The ion wash did smother it," added Marquart. "But even worse trouble may be right here. Warrington's damn insomnia was acting up again. He was camped out on the radio room graveyard shift with my boys tonight. He heard it come in, same as them, over an open speaker."

The director felt an icy grip take hold deep in his gut. "He did."

"My guys didn't even know what they were hearing. So there wasn't a thing they could've done to conceal it."

Corealis felt the ice climb up his chest. "Did Warrington?"

"The names clinched it. He ordered my boys to make a tape copy and stormed out of here with it a few minutes ago. I wouldn't be surprised if he shows up at your door any time now, wanting answers."

Corealis nodded uncertainly. "That's okay. Might be the best way to finally bring this whole thing into the open."

The director hung up and waited. Within moments a hard rap of knuckles rattled his door. Outside was the president's voice: Curt, firm.

"Royce, wake up. I want to see you."

"Just a minute."

Corealis grabbed his robe. Opening the door, the president brushed passed him. A cassette player was clenched tightly in his hand.

"What's the problem, Eugene?"

Warrington tossed the player onto the director's bed.

"I had insomnia again tonight. So I sat in with the night shift radio boys. Not long ago, pieces of a message came in. One you should find interesting."

The president keyed the machine and a hysterical female voice filled its speaker.

" . . . you . . . please hurry . . . ible acciden . . . plosion in . . . Carringer, Vonchek, Keener . . . may be dying . . . please! . . ."

Even somewhat prepared, Royce flushed as the voice faded. Most of the words were garbled. But every syllable of the researchers' names had come across clear as a bell. The two men stood in stark silence as the tape ground quietly on.

"That's it," said the president. "A grand total of seventeen seconds. Just a voice in the middle of the night, coming from nowhere, addressed to no one; accidently heard by a casual listener with insomnia.

"Not much different than any number of distress calls heard by any number of listening stations— except for the names in this one. Knowing them and looking at you now makes a lot more sense of your demeanor in our talk yesterday, doesn't it?"

Corealis settled back. A bit frayed by his sudden unmasking, he also welcomed the sudden opportunity for full candor.

"All right, Eugene," he began. "Maybe this is the

best way to bring the matter to light. Lay out the truth, here and now. No pulled punches."

He pointed to the silently turning machine.

"I can't imagine how this message was sent or what, if anything, it really means. But yes, the names you heard are true. Those people . . ."

" . . . were supposed to have died three years ago in a plane crash!" snapped Warrington. "On their way to a Manna Project summit meeting!

"The whole world, including myself, knows of and grieved at their terrible loss. Now, that doesn't seem the case at all. And I demand to know what is going on!"

Corealis stood rigid to the truth.

"The crash was a ruse, the personnel diverted to a secret location to work on a project dedicated strictly to the future welfare of this country."

"Project!" bellowed the president. "On whose authority . . ."

But throwing his spread hands between them as a quick barrier, Warrington stopped Royce before he could answer. "No! I don't want to know. Good god, I can't know! I'd be going to the World Finance Council aware that my country has been part of a covert operation entirely opposed to the Manna Project!"

The president's hands wilted and plopped to his sides. A weariness stole his wind as he gazed at the director, disbelieving and totally deflated. "But what does that matter now? Just knowing those people are alive makes me and the whole country an accomplice. Royce, how could you, above all, ever be party to something like this!"

The director gazed back candidly.

"I could because I saw how that self-righteous U.N. steering committee was selling out on their pledge to this same country. And yes, to answer your next question, I'd do it again."

Warrington stood looking on, mute and pale. Without invitation, Corealis expounded.

"Shortly before the summit they were off to, Keener and his team stumbled on a unique alkaloid property in their work, blending Sudan grass with sorghum. Trying to merge the heartiness and saline tolerance of one with the millet production of the other, they inadvertently uncovered a whole new vista in population control.

"Just a couple of innocent paragraphs scribbled in a call report spoke of an unbelievable attribute: the likelihood of producing a grain catalyst which could, at will, be blended into select generations of cereal grasses and command the first ever workable balance of a country's birthrate.

"But maintaining Keener's team was essential to preserving and continuing the work. And they were marked for reassignment by the global board. So I took some drastic steps."

"Yes!" roared the president. "By staging their deaths, lying to the steering committee, and making this country party to a wholesale criminal action!"

Corealis matched stares with the man. His explanation marched on in a calm, reasoning tone.

"There's no call to go over the edge on this, Eugene. It was a brief message that we can investigate easily enough. No one knows what it regards or who even may have heard it."

Corealis shrugged indifferently. "From the start I've known that the existence of those researchers might become common knowledge. And when that happened the world alliances would certainly censure us. Considering their mentality, it's inevitable and expected. But a small price to pay and nothing to concern ourselves with—if we stick together on this and see it through. This undertaking has been methodically planned out from square one, Eugene. Certainly it's radical. Economic tactics are cutthroat by virtue of expediency."

"The world court—"

"Be damned!" snapped Corealis, barging forward to take the offensive. "That phony high and mighty rabble has no claim to any loftier moral ground than we do! Our researchers have dutifully submitted every nutritional benefit they've discovered. So we found a little something extra in the works to save for ourselves. So what? If we were discovered and refused to allow our own prosecution by their kangaroo court, what could they do? Blockade us? Cut off our foreign holdings? Refuse us aid?

"All the forfeitures imposed on us as so-called Manna Project support payments have already siphoned off a king's ransom in technology and scientific expertise. The truth is we've been nothing but a cash cow and sorry stepchild to that global clique since the beginning. And it's damn well time we stood up for ourselves!"

Corealis looked Warrington hard in the eye.

"Has it ever occurred to you why they've been so continually tough on us, Eugene?"

Somewhat cowed, the president stammered indignantly. "B-because we were the most affluent of the pre-crash nations and should rightfully bear the heaviest taxing!"

Corealis shook his head woefully. "Open your eyes, Mister President. They're jealous of us. And have always been. Their only real hold was through our own volunteer subscription to the almighty Manna Project. If we broke that, what would they have?

"We enlisted in what was to be a noble campaign. Instead, we made ourselves prisoners to our own oath for a cause that was soured by petty greed and outright hatreds from the start. But if we cancel our membership and don't yield to their pressure for selfprosecution, we can stay solvent and in control of our own existence when Skylock relaxes."

Corealis drew a resolute breath. "Our SHAPP reports continue to indicate a steady decrease in the rate and intensity of the solar storm. Skylock is showing the first real signs of weakening. They're staying mum on the fact. But the U.N. Disaster Relief board knows it too. That's what has them keeping the screws so tight on the old USA, because they want us under their thumb completely before things clear up. And asking their financial help now would only make it that much easier for them."

Warrington fell quiet, drawing Corealis closer with a softer, conspirator's tone.

"Eugene, I've studied this thing from every angle. With a population staying regulated by this new discovery, we could live indefinitely within existing, domestic resources. Think of it. Enough food and jobs to go around. Comfortable living, adequate petroleum, and technology for everyone to share in.

"No one is asking for an indiscriminate, mass sterilization of any one group, just a tactical application when and where future projections dictate the need.

"For a time, no action at all would even be necessary. Heaven knows, as ghastly as it was, the N.A. Flu itself was a good enough interim thinning mechanism. We suffered our own losses here, but populations recover from mass diseases. Then they crowd and cramp themselves until terrible wars of expansion break out and thin things back. This is a fact, just like history has proven time and again.

"An ongoing reliable and workable population ratio is the only practical way to regulate fair shares for each citizen. And if we can't force legislation on them, then we need to take bloodless action on their own behalf—and that of this country's posterity."

The president blinked free of his trance. His eyes widened in somber disbelief. His words came slow and barely above a whisper.

"Just like that. You can reduce a horrific plan of conquest to a few simple mechanics?" President Warrington straightened with fresh resolve. "I am still going to petition that World Finance Council. I am going to ask their forgiveness and help, like I said. And I am going to surrender this illegal, secret project to their authority and bear personal consequences if that's what it takes to absolve my country of any involvement.

"In the meantime, I want a rescue party mounted and sent out to wherever that radio call came from, as soon as possible. I also want full particulars on this 'project' compiled and in my possession by tomorrow night."

Warrington turned from the now silent project director. Reaching for the door he paused, adding a last mandate over his shoulder.

"I want something else, too, Royce. The names of everyone involved with you in this—and your immediate resignation from your post."

Leaving the tape player behind, the president opened the door and was gone.

Corealis stood grim in the aftermath. He raked muscular fingers through his coarse graying hair, thoughts colliding at light speed deep inside his head.

Was the call real—or just some bizarre illusion? Had damage been done to the refining work? The plans? The product? Had any foreign legion posts heard the call and homed in on it? A serious push with ground-effect vehicles could put adversaries in range of the station within days.

Corealis did realize he had one single, large advantage. No matter how close anyone might get through sheer luck, only his people knew exactly where and what was going on. He also had the EM storm coming and a "react" team on standby.

An overdue switch closed in the director's mind. He grabbed at the phone.

"John, trouble. Wake up the agents and pilot. Doc Ashton, too. I hope Clausen's plane lives up to its billing, because I want it flying within the hour. But first, hook me up with Dick Welton."

CHAPTER 7

The sedan quietly took up station outside Trennt's bungalow. Idling patiently at the foggy curb, its sullen geometry was staked out in the cheerless red and amber smudges of its running lights.

Crushing out a smoke, Trennt took a final look at the place. Brief stays and unplanned, odd-hour departures were part of the job. Yet a strange facet about good lodging was always in the pang of hominess he felt on leaving—a peculiar wish that something could be taken along as a memento to sustain him later.

But again, this place as all others before it, offered no suggestions. So like the weary traveling salesman he'd become, Trennt dutifully flipped off the lights and set the door lock. Gear in hand, he stepped quickly into the stale night air, toward his ride.

The sedan deposited Trennt at the compound airfield, beside a medium-sized VTOL jet. Its dim cabin lights glowed a cozy saffron in the growing, bitter mist as Trennt stopped by its pilot and a ground crewman in the midst of exchanging signed receipts.

"I'm Trennt," he announced, surrendering his pocket badge to the pair.

"Okay," answered the young pilot. "About ten minutes more and we should be in the air."

The flier swung his pencil between a couple of technicians seen moving about the cockpit and a distant pocket of heat lightning.

"Apparently we need some last minute computer module adjustments before wading into that."

Trennt glanced beyond. The first blue and pink streamers of an EM storm were corkscrewing in, graceful and silent, from the predawn northeastern sky.

"Don't planes usually avoid magnetic storms?"

The flier grinned privately.

"This one is different, trust me. Go ahead and get settled in. Vittles in the galley, if you want."

Trennt looked about the drizzly taxiways. He sniffed the familiar, though much diluted, bite of ozone.

"Big inversion on the way."

"Already here," replied the groundsman folding his papers.

"Chicago took another big hit right after midnight. Level eight. Socked them in good. Sanitation boys'll have a busy time trucking stiffs to the burners after this one."

"Yeah."

Trennt gazed pitingly toward the invisible, suffering city, then back toward the parked plane.

"Seen anything of my partner?"

"Short guy? Already aboard."

Trennt stepped through the small hatchway and into the twenty-passenger jet. Ahead, the technicians glanced up from their control panel work. Midway back, Baker snuggled under a blanket. Business goods set in a pair of canvas satchels beside him, his peaceable grin was that of the world's best little boy on Christmas Eve.

In the rear sat a passenger Trennt didn't expect or recognize: an uncomfortable looking middle-aged man, clutching a bulky carry-on bag of his own. Trennt nodded hello, but the man only returned a bovine stare, preoccupied and unresponsive.

Baker, though, did mumble a closed-eyed, dozy greeting.

"Like going to work in a chauffeured Caddy, huh, Jimbo?"

"Yeah," Trennt answered, glimpsing about. "Pretty big plane for just a couple of us."

"First class, Pard. An' just a taste o' what's up the road, if'n we handle this job right."

The shooter's face lit to a broad, savoring smile.

"Say, you take up their offer of evenin' companionship?"

Trennt settled in across the aisle. "No."

"I sure did. Dialed me up that number and they sent over a couple tender young honeys eager to take me places I ain't been in quite some time." Baker's grin withered as he spared a critical eye for his associate. "See there, Pard. That's your trouble. Keepin' to yoursef' all the time just ain't natural. A man needs the right kind of relaxation now and again to keep things in balance."

Trennt ignored the advice and cocked his head rearward.

"Who's the stiff?"

"Doctor somebody," chuckled Baker. "Kinda peak-ed lookin' hisself though, ain't he?"

"You hear any reason for the sudden call-up?"

"Trouble in the hen house—paper cut, stubbed toe. Who knows? Figger it all out when we get there."

The shooter yawned, found that satisfied grin again, and drifted off, fast asleep.

Trennt marveled at the man's untroubled cherublike

glow. No lost winks over the horrors he'd survived. Or
devised. Not a care of what gruesome end might lay
hours ahead. Just turn it on, turn it off, like always.

Finally the technicians departed and the pilot
arrived. As if making up lost time, he initiated a
smart, two-handed drill in the cockpit. A brisk sequence of sharp clicking switches and toggles filled the
air. Outside, one, then the other, aft-placed turbines
awakened and stirred to life. Within seconds, their
mounting eagerness synchronized into a quivering
rhythm.

Waved clear by the ground crew, VTOL ducts and
tilt wing mechanisms hummed confidently to their
takeoff attitude. Amid a rising howl, the craft gathered
its strength and pulled from the ground. Seconds more
and it was above the hangars, slowly rotating about a
rising axis toward the west, on a merging path with the
growing flux of skybound magnetics.

From his lofty perch, Trennt imagined he could
discern the vague outline of distant Chicago. Drooped
beneath her sooty crown of thorns, the grand old lady
of the prairie hovered as a dim collage of askew roof
lines. Only the twin 3000-foot Nippon Towers stood
out. Then they too fell away. Supplicating arms
drowned in the newest quagmire of brown photochemical soup, soup that ruined lungs and birthed
killer pleurisies among its citizens—like that which
had claimed his own family.

Chicago. Trennt knew her all too well. Twenty-first-
century life wrapped in the tattered discards of the
Dark Ages. Its once magnificent boulevards now just
cluttered valleys to the fire-blackened stonework jut-
ting skyward like desolate mountain peaks. Deep in
its bowels, the old landmarks lived on as razed
abstracts: museums, planetarium, aquarium; the

scorched and chipped crematoriums that were once
Soldier Field and Comiskey Park.

Smothered in a roiling caustic fog tonight again, the
city stubbornly clung to life. With sunup the poison
would once more evaporate. Somewhere a church bell
would shudder to life and draw others to a throbbing
chorus of "all clear." Families would pull off their urine-
soaked rag respirators, parcel off their dead, and get
on with the business of survival.

Trennt had braved the routine many times and
earned his stripes as a survivor of the big city riots,
outliving the absolute madness, which drove off the
town's very soul one unforgettable scalding July night.

Dumped there by the millennium census, the Cee-
Dee population had lived jammed in each other's faces
for three years. Heated by lax supplies and inadequate
public care, their frustration finally exploded like a huge
boil, emptying its corruption far into the streets.

Wholesale slaughter flushed out, anxious to punish
the system which had abandoned its people. But what
remained of true authority was locked safely out of
reach. So the rage fell back on itself, setting neighbor
on neighbor and square miles to the torch. When the
insanity finally died, so did the spirit of the people.
Ever since, their only noise was the clamor of defeat.

The whole time he'd lived as her adopted son,
Trennt had hated the town. But now, cut free and
outside, he felt a weird rush of something like regret,
pity toward an abusive mother who simply couldn't help
herself.

Trennt dwelled on the horizon a long time after the
town was gone, awash in other memories: long ago
troop movements, drives against sworn enemies of his
country—supposed threats to his way of life. It had
mattered once. Or so they'd said. And he'd believed

them. America, right or wrong; the simple-minded
declaration of an old-fashioned bumper sticker validat-
ing it all.

Now, they were telling him again. Different words,
but the same old tune. Them and us. Conditional logic
that made even the bleak reality of total extinction seem
less a threat than the loss of national sovereignty. Not
that any of it mattered in the real world. Those living
in Chi-town would probably agree that the dead were
better off anyway. And to him it was all just part of
another job.

Trennt looked again at Baker. Beside the dozing
shooter sat two canvas duty bags. Trennt slid one over
and peeked in. As the old saying went, the trades-
man certainly was known by his tools. A pair of
holsters and well-oiled 10 mm automatics rested
inside. Beneath were two disassembled S-12 shotguns,
ready for a deadly mix of explosive and flechette
ammunition. A cased sniper rifle and enough other
ordnance to arm a determined infantry squad filled
the other bag.

Trennt shucked one of the clip-fed weapons free of
its chamois wrap. He clicked the barrel in place and
pondered the evil-looking result. Rubber grips, forged
aluminum receiver, extruded high tensile barrel. Lightweight, well-balanced. Coated in black oxide, it shined
dully in the cabin lights as both a familiar lover and
menacing servant.

Just holding the weapon awakened old and primitive feelings deep inside the handler. Power. And
shame. That grating mix cultured in the insanity of war,
where one sustained and the other tormented.

On a small, insulated tackle-type box, was a yellow
label printed over in a red ink. A tiny ball surrounded
by three wedge-shaped blades warned of its contents—
the A-bomb detonator Corealis had mentioned.

Trennt replaced the gear and left his seat for the mini breakfast buffet. He wasn't interested in the meager selection of self-warming rolls, but he plucked a sealed coffee from the courtesy rack. Popping its heat activating tab, he turned back for his seat when the pilot spoke.

"Someone back there free to hand me a java?"

"Sure." Trennt snatched up another of the sealed cups as the pilot reached out. Bright-eyed and friendly, he filled Trennt with the comfortable notion of his own younger brother.

"Thanks."

Trennt nodded and continued back.

"Say," the flyer added unexpectedly, "I've got an extra place up here. If you're interested."

Trennt paused. "Sure it's okay?"

"No problem. The bureau won't mind and this bird is bor-ring. Does everything itself. Just keeps me on like a kind of night watchman. Still comes with two seats, though. Have one."

Trennt shimmied through the narrow cockpit, mildly surprised to see the man absorbed in working a cross-word puzzle. He eased in the vacant right chair and browsed the flight deck. Some gauges he recognized, but others were strange. Scanning the tiny half dozen CRT screens monitoring systems' performance, he singled one out.

"'Core temp.' What kind of plane is this?"

The pilot grinned expectantly. "Nuclear."

Trennt blinked.

"Best thing to ever come out of Area 51," he declared.

"Point nine eight mach; tilt wing and vectored thrust. No fuss, no muss. No old-time fire worries. And never a thought of running out of fuel."

Trennt marveled. "No joke?"

"Serious as a heart attack," pledged the flier. "It could circle the globe nonstop for months, years. We'd give out before the plane would. The power plant is an extremely lightweight fusion-type reactor, made of something they call plasticized magnets. Very expensive and very limited. But you are indeed being powered by one."

The craft sounded and felt like a traditional jet. Trennt was naturally curious.

"Nuclear power normally means steam, right?"

The pilot nodded. "Kind of. A marble of isotope does all the work in a crash-proof container about the size of a watermelon. It superheats a propylene glycol and nitrogen mix that's routed from back in the tail through high-pressure plumbing to the aft-mounted turbines.

"Difference over other jets is in the hollow compressors. These radiate their heat into the outside air while spinning to squeeze it for thrust. That action both powers the plane and cools the propellant for its return to the atomic pile. Much like a car's radiator."

Trennt appraised the wonderful cockpit. "How'd they ever come up with something like this?"

The flier offered a jaded shrug.

"How'd they ever put sound and pictures on magnetic tape? Or anything else they do? Money. Where there's enough, there's a way." He continued, explaining, "The first nuclear aviation work was begun by the CIA Skunkworks in the mid-1950s. This prototype came about in the late '90s and was kept under lock and key at Groom Lake. Now, it's ours."

"A real nuclear airplane."

"Fly anytime, anywhere," reiterated the pilot, smugly gesturing at the controls. "And with its independent logic, it can be totally unmanned. Heads-up multicolored graphics if there is a pilot. Traffic avoidance.

Doppler. Even voice response. But everything is kept out of reach until you go through just the right access procedure. Synthetic intelligence doesn't want inferior humans mucking things up unless absolutely necessary, you know.

"Takeoffs, landings, and everything in between is run through its disinfected nanosecond brain. So for me, it's kind of like the sick old joke on rape: just lie back and enjoy the ride."

The pilot huffed a low, dark snort.

"But it is hard not feeling the occasional urge to yank out some transistors and make this crate earn its keep the old-fashioned way."

They shared a glance of solidarity.

"Drue Kosinski," the pilot introduced himself.

"Jim Trennt." The two men shook hands.

"You and the other guys work together?"

"Kind of. How'd you fit in?"

"Taxi driver. Besides spending a lot of shakedown time with this bird, I'm also familiar with your LZ. I've made the resupply runs out there now and again."

Trennt checked the heightened stream of twisting lavender pacing them.

"Any problem if those static bolts catch up with us?"

"They will, shortly. But no. They'll just pass around and continue on whatever path eventually gets them to the South Pole. Passpod and avionics on this bird are double insulated against magnetics and UV. Fuselage is graphite epoxy; strong stuff. We could handle some time inside the main weather cell itself, if we had to."

"Where's that?"

"A couple hours behind the light show."

"Enough behind for us to get in and out?"

The pilot chuckled somberly. "Sure hope so. I wouldn't want to get caught on the ground in its path.

A lot of old-fashioned lightning and hail still gets thrown around. And grounded planes don't handle that well at all. Not even one that does know its A-B-C's."

Conversation died away as the high flying jet raced with the dawn. Far below passed America's barren breadbasket. In less than a decade its once boundless wheat fields had faded from golden patchworks to a vast sea of dead khaki. Two centuries of chugging tractors, combines, and threshers were gone like the dinosaur, replaced with deep hollows and high dunes cut and piled by freak zephyr winds.

The great Missouri and lower Mississippi Rivers came into view. Redirected by the collapsed Madrid Fault, they now slammed headlong into a violent merge and flow which took a new river west. In the far distance a dim veil of gray-white plumes rose from the smoldering Pacific Plate volcano fields.

The jet navigated a path indifferent to the dead metropolitan centers far below. From its height, evident only as discordant flashes of dim and distant glass, were the cities: St. Louis, Kansas City, Omaha—all alike. Forlorn and abstract swatches sliding quietly beneath the autotinting windows of this climate controlled, private viewing studio.

Trennt looked on and wondered, How many innocent "displaced" families had found their end amid that distant silence?

The emergency National Census of 2042 was a desperate plan hatched by the withering federal government: a last organizational edict before decentralization finally knocked the blocks out from under Washington, D.C.

After several years of trying to devise a regenerative balance for its depleted urban areas, an injection of new bodies was hit on as the simplest approach. A special census, beyond the scope of any basic head count, ordered entire families to their father's birth city. This, it was believed, would redistribute needed skills and talents of the population and infuse fresh human resources into epidemic-withered areas after the devastating North American Flu.

Trennt and his family had traveled light. A two-bag limit was mandated for all refugee families, so few troublesome effects needed to be worried over. They were directed to the local post office to await transport on that early spring morning with little more than the clothes they wore. Of their entire rural township, they were the lone family to be sent so far away.

A few friends stayed with them during their wait that day, when hugs and assurances of a brief absence were exchanged. Trennt then led his family to one-way seats aboard a bus in a flotilla of commandeered vehicles and they took their place in an exodus not seen since biblical times.

After a week's living on wilted box lunches, they finally entered the hulking city by the lake. Trennt's wife and kids were asleep as their bus joined the angled rows of sooty Greyhounds and Trailways already parked at the Randolph Street terminal and Cee-Dee reception station.

Trennt woke Dena and helped bundle Jennifer and Andy against the late-night air. The family then spent three solid hours standing in a cold drizzle, awaiting their turn at processing into their new home.

Shortly after, four-year-old Andy became the first family member to develop the ominous Cee-Dee sniffles.

Kosinski's voice startled Trennt.

"We're about twenty minutes out."

Trennt offered a map folded to their landing zone.

"Can you hang just beyond range of the station while we give it a peep?"

The pilot reached for a swingout keypad.

"I'll ask permission."

"If things look sour you can set down in this secondary clearing about a half mile south."

Back in the cabin, it was Trennt's turn to do the waking.

"Baker."

The shooter came up in his seat same as always; instant on. No hint of normal human drowsiness. "How far out are we?"

"Few minutes. Get your goods around. We'll take a couple wide swings before deciding where to land."

"Grips, Pard."

Dismissing further courtesy, Trennt called back to the other rider.

"Hey, who're you?"

The man straightened to the gruffness.

"Doctor Thomas Ashton."

"You got something to invest in this, Doctor?"

"I'm to check over the station people."

"Whatever. If you're getting off, get ready. Otherwise, stay out of the way."

Changed to a transitional flight attitude, the jet swung a lazy wide orbit about the research station. From their height, a weave of hardwood trees and camouflage netting did obscure much of its surface. Yet all five research and storage buildings seemed intact—though uninhabited.

"No smoke or movement," declared Baker.

"Not good," Trennt concurred. He called to the pilot. "Drue, hit the alternate."

CHAPTER 8

The plane set down snugly in the designated clear-ing. Gear was quickly unloaded and readied. Trennt and Baker each took an S-12 shotgun, stuffing the magazines with explosive 10-gauge rounds. Pistols were likewise charged and holstered.

Lightweight speed packs followed, filled with Kevlar "sapper suits" for maneuvering through barrier vines, rappelling line, and assorted pyrotechnics. To allow freer movement, Baker discarded the awkward protective case housing their nuclear detonator and wedged the thin primer tube between the open straps of his pack.

After a couple of minutes orienting their map and verifying reference points, the pair was ready. The aerial light show had dimmed appreciably to the risen sun. But a somber gray void was beginning to fill the north-easterly distance. The air now also had the bitter-fresh nip of gathering ozone.

Trennt handed a walkie-talkie to the pilot as they stood in the heavy dank silence outside the parked plane.

"These should reach the short distance to the station, providing the magnetics don't get too wild. Keep an ear open. Your call sign will be 'One-One.' Ours, 'One-Two.' Anything special breaks loose, we'll call you. If the radios fail, just watch for a flare. Green means come; red, bailout. If things go good, we should be in place in three-quarters of an hour."

Baker extended a small-caliber pistol pulled from his waistband. "Can you use one o' these?"

The pilot regarded it uncomfortably.

"Hey, I'm no . . ."

"Don't have to be," interrupted the gunman. "Just keep it handy. Any trouble comes along, 'bang bang,' okay?"

Baker shifted his gear into a comfortable position. Pumping his clenched weapon, he rattled with boyish exuberance.

"Just like the old days, huh, Jimbo?"

Again checking the sky, Trennt didn't share in any nostalgia.

"Let's get it done."

They went back a long way. To the Peru-Ecuador scrap of the early new century. Dozens of long-range recon missions into enemy territory. Fighting side by side in the trenches of the Cordillera del Condor Siege. On a spot of ground named Hill 27, but forever known to the common grunt simply as "The Gnat's Ass."

All this time and it still rode fresh as ever in Trennt's mind while he hiked. Seventeen days in the spring of the year. Their firebase low on everything because of weather-fouled resupply lines. Food was a memory; hardly any ammo. Little cover and constant, driving rain. Nonstop downpours that brought on trenchfoot and those wonderful sucking leeches.

But weather that also helped smother the accuracy

of enemy mortar fire. And loosened the footing of three separate bayonet charges they fought off with entrenching tools and fire axes when the bullets finally gave out on both sides and taking that hill became a matter of honor for the bad guys. Like it or not, few blood ties could ever run deeper than the one Trennt shared with the lethal, slender man hiking beside him now.

Their pace was brisk. Heading off through a downhill mix of scrub and boulders, both the point of origin and their objective were soon lost from view. The terrain was brittle and oven dry. Left shriveled by years of drought, what life remained had even lost interest in catching fire. But it was easy to read. No signs of preceding travel took some of the edge off their pace and the agents made the butte well ahead of schedule.

Their first challenge waited there. Growing freely about the steep ramp were coils of a familiar and lethal hybrid thornbush. Developed in the old army labs by the very man they were here to rescue, the hellish parasite thrived as a living razor-wire fence.

A mesh of coal black, porcelain-hard barbs rose in flesh-shearing spirals taller than a man and fifty yards deep. Hooked like jagged crosscut saw teeth, the barrier waited to shred any creature foolish enough to dare enter. Blowing it away would have been time consuming—and noisy. The only alternative was to traverse it.

From the hill's base, Baker scanned higher levels while Trennt verified the location of booby traps.

"After we get through this stuff, there're a dozen tiger pits and dead falls. Beyond are electric mines and the Intruder Alert System, with the summit another couple hundred feet past that. The guns are stocked with twenty thousand rounds apiece in a corridor that varies in width from sixteen feet to five feet. Just as bad is a four-foot-thick bed of masonry sand, topped with concrete slabs and meant to avalanche if crossed over. So stay close."

The pair donned their Ninja-style Kevlar body suits. Acrylic face shields and mail hoods replaced their fatigue caps and they entered the deadly barrier. While the suits did protect their movements through the cruel growth, it couldn't prevent a drastic slowing of the pace. By the time they'd cleared the thorny, shearing tangle, twenty-five precious minutes had been lost. Above, an accelerating change in the weather was becoming obvious. The temperature was falling and an eerie green pigment began filling the sky.

"Deck's stackin' against us," noted Baker.

Trennt yanked off his sweated faceplate. "Let's make the most of it."

The pair cinched themselves together on a fifteen-foot tether and entered the steep wooded hillside. Against their better judgment they hurried the pace, advancing under hasty cover-and-movement spurts, while negotiating the lethal mix of exposed roots and loose earth.

Successfully rounding the tiger pits and deadfalls, Trennt led their way toward the primary bank of laser-activated intruder alert grids. He low-crawled in a wide circuitous route around the control box of the first camouflaged grenade dispenser. Clipping jumper wires to its power terminals, Trennt snipped the leads. With a finger slash across his windpipe, he sat tight as Baker sidearmed a root ball into the beam path. Nothing happened.

Four more positions were located, probed, and tediously neutralized in the same painstaking manner. Clearing the final station, the rescuers were just yards from cresting the summit itself, when Baker lost his footing and stumbled onto the plane of a hidden shear plate.

The reactive earthwork broke loose even under his bantam weight. In a blink all the dirt for sixty feet around was cascading downhill, carrying the shooter away in an engineered landslide and chewing greedily after his partner.

Trennt dove safely outside the broken shear plane himself, but he was still tied fast to Baker, and felt the slack umbilical between them rapidly paying out.

The low fork of an anemic sapling was his nearest hope. He thrust the S-12 between its tines, twisting the barrel and stock in opposite directions. Jamming and locking his arms through the web sling, Trennt braced himself and prayed it would hold.

Behind, Baker spun about as the last of his tether line went taut. He left the ground like a hooked marlin breaking water, then slammed back to earth, speed pack first. It cushioned the blow as he jammed hard against a tree stump, held stiff as a ship's prow to parting waves of cascading gravel and sand.

The avalanche roared on and away, crashing off far below. Trennt was left gasping and wrenched in its choking, dusty wake. He painstakingly freed a numb hand from his gun sling brace and grabbed at the tether line. All he found was slack. Somewhere hundreds of yards below he imagined Baker, torn free, crushed, and mangled.

Still clutching the locked weapon, Trennt pivoted slowly for a look behind. A heavy tan curtain of gently twirling dust greeted him. But his movement also dislodged a jammed rock. The snarled tether shot free and sprang back to tension. Trennt choked up a mouthful of muddy slime, hopefully testing his voice.

"Baker?"

Through the heavy swirling veil a muffled cough answered.

"Yo, Pard."

"You okay?"

"Think so. Speed pack took most of it, I reckon. Nuthin' feels broke. But I'd guess we lost any element of surprise."

Trennt slowly reeled the man up. Sharing a nod at their good fortune, they started the final yards to the summit, and the research station just beyond.

They could see the compound's five prefab buildings. Living quarters, greenhouse, lab, and storage boasted all the latest high-tech support system gizmos. Solar-steam electrical generators and chemical fuel cells sat in protective sheds, routed by thick overhead umbilicals, to a vast array of computers, air conditioning, and refrigeration units.

But aside from a growing rustle of static in the tree-tops, all was silent. No smells, no sound, no movement. The steadily thickening sky allowed no more time for caution. Shotguns tucked tight and hip-high, the pair split up and entered the camp fringes.

Now among its buildings, they found the first obvious signs of trouble. The compound's power plant was rent and buckled from an explosion. Its window vents were blown free, aluminum wall panels bulged and, in spots, were peeled back and flattened in the jagged flower-like petals of lethal shrapnel blooms.

Still, they saw no people. Taking cover beside the power station, Trennt leveled his weapon, finally calling aloud.

"Anyone in there, come on out! We're here to help you!"

Long seconds passed with no response.

"Do you hear me?" he repeated. "Come on out!"

Still nothing.

He was preparing to move forward when the barracks door burst open. Out flew a frazzled young woman. Wide-eyed and strung miles beyond hysteria, she glared in hateful silence for a moment, then charged Trennt, unafraid.

"Where have you been?" she demanded. "I've been waiting a whole day! What took you so long to get here?"

Trennt snapped his S-12 to port arms. He blocked her flailing advance and levered her off balance. But even knocked down, the woman regrouped and came at him again.

"Why did you take so long?" she growled, swinging wildly at his face with hands drawn into claws. "Where were you?"

Grabbing her wrists, Trennt forced her arms down. "Where are the others?"

The woman didn't answer, struggling on and babbling, until he jarred her senses with a rattling shake. *"The others!"*

She whiplashed in his grip. Then, suddenly frightful, she melted back to her exhausted senses.

"Inside," she whispered, wretched and spent. "All inside."

Trennt let her go, offering no apologies for his rough handling.

Doctor Keener was just beyond the radio room door. Piled under insulating blankets, he glistened in a bloodless white cast, doused in sweat and wheezing shallow, ravaged breaths. Beyond sat a row of blanket covered corpses.

"What happened here?"

The woman motioned vacantly about.

"I don't know. The powerhouse, it exploded. Blue smoke went everywhere."

She looked out a window, toward a tubular scaffold supporting weather monitoring gear and a small radio dish.

"Martin told me to climb, as fast as I could, while he woke up the others. The smoke was spreading all over by then. They were trying to cover their faces while they climbed. But they couldn't hang on. Martin couldn't pull them up either and fell back partway in it himself."

The woman broke into ragged sobs and sank to a dejected heap at Trennt's feet. He studied her for a moment, then checked the deepening cast of eastern sky.

"Baker. Call our bird over and help me take a quick look around. Let's find the goods and shut this place down."

"Grips, Pard."

But the gunman's radio was impossibly clogged with static. As agreed, Baker uncorked a signal rocket from his pack. A quick twist and smack of its primer cap sent the green starcluster streaking high into the ominous heavens.

Trennt, meanwhile, spared a few minutes to inspect the ruined powerhouse. Scattered hunks of spun metal littered the courtyard in silent testament of the blast's force. Inside the prefab walls he found the burst remnants of refrigeration and power units. Chalklike splatters of an odd yellow-green chemical precipitate were plastered about in dry, powdery streaks. And even now a faint bleachlike after-smell lingered.

Trennt was familiar enough with the bank of ruptured cylinders to recognize them as portable electrical fuel cells. Here, though, a double row of a dozen such bottles had been linked into a much more permanent and powerful arrangement. Thick braids of feed and return pipes were plumbed below to charging media and beyond to the pressurized chlorine separators and recyclers in an adjacent cubicle. Also sharing the space were refrigeration and air-conditioning containment systems.

Only token walls of a honeycomb insulating material separated one power medium from another. And a moment's study of the symmetric blast holes made Trennt aware of a peculiar and common orientation among the cubicles. He stepped back toward the doorway, realizing also that the power station was set slightly elevated to the entire camp—something military engineering strictly forbade out of normal environmental safety concerns.

Silently arrived, Baker gauged Trennt's scrutiny.

"Wha'cha see, Pard?"

Trennt shrugged, returning to the doorway.

"Maybe nothing."

By then the jet had settled in and its engines finished coasting down.

"I'll check the lab," Trennt said. "You salvage whatever might be of value in the barracks. And keep that bird ready for a quick start-up."

"Grips!"

Following Baker out, a final item caught Trennt's eye, something so obvious, he hadn't noticed it on entering. Mounted to the outside shed wall was an emergency panel box. Prominent yellow-and-black instructions were blazed across it:

FOR EMERGENCY SYSTEMS SHUTDOWN,
PUSH AND TWIST RIGHT.

It was a typical total-suppression unit, simply meant to govern all the power mediums housed within. Even now its safety pin and tamper label remained undisturbed, but left of the broad striped handle, a small stainless steel turnkey and beaded chain dangled from a tiny unmarked side lock. Trennt gently touched his fingers to the chain, then continued on, for the labs.

A different type of devastation awaited him there. A premeditated, man-made kind. But the manner in which growth chambers and related seedlings had been destroyed seemed no random act of madness, for DNA synthesizing gear, electron microscopes, and genetic particle guns hadn't been touched at all.

Further on, Trennt swung open the main storage vault. Lifting a flashlight from his grommet belt, he thrust it inside the darkened chamber and keyed its beam. A cruel halogen brilliance exploded before him. Playing about the blackness, it chased off the stark and irregular shadows of more ruin.

A collection of loose leaf binders, note pads, and computer printouts sat in a half scorched heap at midfloor. Further out was an empty gallon can of alcohol. Someone's attempt at kindling a fire had failed. Though no active extinguishing system was evident, Trennt reasoned the vault's dead air space may have acted as its own natural suppressant, quickly starving the flames.

Strewn about also lay a dozen or so small insulated storage chests. Looking as if they'd been cached here for shipment, the foot-square boxes now sat upended and scattered. Their intended contents appeared as numerous trays of thin glass vials suspended in protective wire racks. These had been stomped flat and likewise kicked about. Splashes of what must have been their contents glistened as straw-colored viscous liquid in the twisted wire and broken glass aftermath.

A new medium was also exposed to his light beam: the jagged crystal brilliance of shattered computer squares. Reminiscent of metallic sugar cubes, such squares had been the latest generation of data storage media before the arrival of Skylock.

Here, a few thousand of their fragments glimmered in a ruined bronzy sheen. But a smattering of cubes had escaped the rampage and dully reflected his light beam from distant corners of the room. Thinking they might still hold some useful information, Trennt knelt and began plucking them up.

CHAPTER 9

Outside, the wind was steady now. Saint Elmo's fire danced like erratic blue flames about the treetops. Static electricity tickled the skin and ever-thickening ozone blended an eye-watering nip to the air.

The young woman sat beside Doctor Keener in the courtyard, hand in his, head down. Her disheveled auburn hair shot randomly about her face in the spiraling wind gusts; vacant, victim's eyes idly followed the strangers in their sacking of the place she'd called home.

Moments later those same empty eyes flared. They locked onto the handle of the small-caliber pistol gradually working its way loose from the pilot's coat pocket. Each time he passed, it loomed a little larger. She checked the man's face and he didn't seem aware.

On his fourth trip, gun and pilot gently parted company. It tumbled away unnoticed, plopping in the twirling dust nearly at the woman's feet. When the pilot returned to help escort the two survivors aboard his plane, the pistol was gone.

Trennt had assembled his meager salvage as Baker returned. The shootist gazed forlornly about the room. He touched gentle fingers to a large smear of the golden syrup splashed on the door frame and came away uneasy.

"'Spose this here is the stuff, Jimbo?"

"I'd say."

"We too late, then?"

"Might be."

"Damn!"

Sight of a distant data cube prompted Trennt to bend lower. As he did, his light beam swept to the far underside of a storage shelf. He retrieved the cube, paused, then scooted closer.

"Pard," rasped Baker anxiously, "wha' cha see?"

Wedged beneath was another wire rack of vials. Like the others, it too had been stomped and must have squirted there, lost from view. But the steel mesh of this particular batch had deflected under, rather than flattening out, cupping over to partially shield the vials. Eight were lost. Yet twelve others had survived.

Baker jammed clenched fists skyward as Trennt held them to view.

"Hot damn!" he cawed. "Easy Street, here we come!"

"I'll handle this," said Trennt, grabbing at one of the insulated boxes. "You kick around and find the floor plate for setting that detonator."

Brisk steps filled the lab behind and Kosinski popped his head in the vault.

"Guys," he entreated, "we've got to go. Now."

Simultaneously Baker rocked back on his heels, making an equally dismal announcement from across the room.

"Something's wrong with this thing, Jimbo. It won't arm."

"What?"

Trennt forgot the pilot and scrambled over. He tried a hand at forcing the dusty mechanism. But his effort might as well have been wasted on twisting an anvil.

"Shit, it's locked tight."

"Musta jammed when it broke my fall in the land-slide."

Trennt gazed down the dim cylindrical hole.

"Think we can trigger it some other way? An external charge on top, maybe?"

Baker shrugged helplessly. "Shoot, Jimbo. I'm an old-time H and E man: primer cord, plastique. Don't know squat on nukes. Only what they told me on placin' this un."

"Guys," reminded the pilot.

Trennt glanced hastily about. He kicked at the empty can of alcohol used to start the failed blaze.

"This whole place is all aluminum and tinwork," he reasoned. "With the rising wind, a hot fire might be good enough to melt it all down. There must be more stocks of this stuff somewhere. Find whatever you can. Round it all up and set it all through the buildings. Then route a fuse. We'll have to hope the storm winds fan it hot enough to do the trick."

The shooter nodded toward the hole at their feet.

"What about the big one?"

Trennt set the dead primer tube in its trigger slot and slammed shut the floor cap.

"Not our problem. I'll finish gathering up here. You get started."

Baker sped off, yanking Kosinski from the doorway.

"Come on, Cuz."

A large cache of acetone, alcohol, and ether was stored in a distant point of the station. Fifty-gallon lots of the flammables were hastily parceled out among the buildings and primer charges set among each.

"Better get a move on," Baker warned Doc Ashton, routing a last fuse through the radio room.

The doctor fired a startled look from his vigil amid the corpses. "But the bodies."

Baker shook his head. "No time. 'Less you wanna stay, best get to the plane!"

The nuke's engines were howling to life as Baker yanked a friction fuse and hopped aboard. The primary wick split into five other trails, each snaking toward their target.

"Keep her just out of range for a while," Trennt told the pilot. "I need to make sure it works."

The frazzled young woman came to life at his words. She pushed up from her seat and through the loose heaps of research booty piled about the cabin. Her voice was numb and sluggish, but demanding as she arrived beside Trennt.

"What's happening? We're going? We can't. The others. We can't leave them behind. We have to go back!"

She ran to the hatch, clawing about its unfamiliar surface.

"We can't leave them! We can't!"

Baker intercepted and restrained her flailing hands.

"Easy does it, Sweet Thang," he whispered too closely. "No sense in all that ruckus. They ain't gonna feel nuthin', believe me."

The woman struggled on, but Baker kept her contained. Holding her prisoner in a kind of rough embrace, his flinty eyes roved approvingly over her shape.

Trennt interrupted from his place at a portal.

"You need to keep your hands busy? Then start packing all this loose stuff in for the trip."

The shooter assented, only slowly relaxing his grip.

"Okay, Jimbo. Okay."

Hundreds of feet below, the fuses reached their targets. A surge of purple-blue flame lit the jet's window glass as simultaneous ignitions stoked a massive blush of raw chemical energy. A fist of hard thermal air rammed the plane's belly and the camp dissolved in a roiling fire storm.

Nodding his satisfaction at Baker's work, Trennt motioned the pilot on. He then squeezed aft, to where the medic was busy tending the other survivor.

"What's he got?"

Doc Ashton rose, directing his words away from the stricken man.

"With all the gases which might've mingled, a diagnosis is difficult. But considering the skin necrosis about the eyes, nose, and mouth, I'd guess phosgene oxime poisoning."

Trennt frowned. "Phosgene? Like in the poison gas?"

"The same."

Trennt thrust his chin toward the woman.

"How'd she escape it?"

The doctor shrugged. "Phosgene, if it was that, is what they call a nonpersistent agent. It only rises to a certain height and breaks down rapidly by fog, rain; even heavy vegetation can restrain or filter it. Something as simple as a short breeze might've been enough to direct it away from her entirely."

Trennt studied the stricken man as he sucked feeble, wheezing breaths through an oxygen mask. "How bad is he?"

"He's through the latent period and into pulmonary edema. His lungs are blistered."

"Can you do anything?"

"Keep him on an IV, oxygen, and some codeine. If he makes the next forty-eight hours, he might have a chance."

"We'll get him to a hospital as quick as we can."

The medic shook his head. "Outside of a steady bed and an oxygen tent, it's as good here as can be done anywhere. The rest depends on him and luck."

The doctor's eyes hardened.

"None of this would've happened if they'd listened back home. And Heaven help me, everyone will know about it, this time. I don't care what the consequences are."

Before Trennt could question him, both men pitched sideways. The plane banged through a series of hard roller coaster jolts, shooting high one second, then slamming back the next.

The automatic cabin lights flashed on and Trennt realized just how black it had become outside. He spun about to see the plane's windshield filled with a tumbling cloudbank of cocoa and bone.

As previously advertised, the plane reacted automatically. Jolting the cockpit with a shrill warning buzz, a synthetic voice simultaneously confirmed their danger.

"*Event alert! Event alert! Emergency course heading correction to 90 degrees . . . 135 degrees . . . 250 degrees.*"

The voice fell off as the ship's logic and Doppler systems conferred on the broadening scope of danger. Moments later a last courtesy broadcast sounded.

"*Course abort warning! Course abort warning! Heading override; four-zero degrees relative. Full throttle engagement.*"

The craft began a hard, banking dive to the northwest. She screamed to full power and raced for all she was worth. Behind, the storm growled at its lost prey. Snapping frustrated at the nuke's retreating tail, it steadily fell rearward.

Kosinski fidgeted in his seat, helpless fingers working the empty air. There was no sense in grabbing at the controls. Shipboard intelligence would only wrench them away. Besides, the nuke's nanosecond feedback made his own best reaction time pale in comparison.

From his spot behind the pilot, Baker blew a low, measured breath and turned back for the cabin.

"Set up here if you want, Jimbo. It's all the same as elephants breedin' to me—somethin' I'd rather not watch."

He'd barely squeezed passed his comrade in the narrow passageway, when furious shouting erupted to their rear.

"*No!* You can't let him die! We have to go the other way! *Now!*"

The young woman was on her feet again. Only this time, clamped firmly in her hands was a .32-caliber pistol.

Baker glanced at the familiar piece and swept his eyes furtively toward Kosinski.

The pilot slapped a hand to his empty jacket.

"Damn!"

"You watch the plane," uttered the shooter contemptuously. "I'll handle this."

He started slowly aft, his best honeyed voice and thousand dollar smile leading the way.

"Come on, Sweet Thang, put that away. We got our hands full right now just tryin' to get outta here. We don't want you hurtin' yourse'f."

"I know how to use it!" she screamed. "And I don't care! We've got to turn around right now and get Martin to a hospital!"

Baker edged closer, offering upturned palms.

"We'll get him to one, soon as we kin, darlin'. Promise. But right now things're a little sticky. In the meantime, he'll be okay with the doc there."

"No!" she shouted. "I heard the voice up front say we were turning away. We've got to go back! Now!"

The woman sighted the gun barrel on Baker's chest

as he closed the last few feet, his hands still open in surrender.

"I mean it!"

"Oh, I bet you do." The shooter spoke with a touch of true admiration. "Pretty gal like you with spunk is a rare thang. And one I ain't about to argue with."

He watched the hammer creep back ever so slightly and froze.

"Easy there, sweety. We don't want that goin' off in here by accident. Holes in airplanes ain't a good thang."

"Then do as I say! Turn this—"

Her words were cut off by another slap of unexpected buffeting. She fell aside. Baker leapt forward to intercept the gun. Somewhere in between the hammer rocked and dropped.

In slow motion, it did so again.

And again.

One bullet screamed into the cockpit, blasting the control panel between Trennt and Kosinski. Two more went wide. One drilled a cabin window. The other pierced the left rear fuselage.

The cockpit squealed in pain from a control interference alarm as the guidance system tried vainly to make connection with its reserve backup. But the first shot had derailed the automatic bypass. Instead, the plane's CRT screens quivered and went dead in unison. A moment later an explosive *crump!* rattled the port engine.

The jet shuddered tail to nose and slumped left. A spray of metal shards erupted from its damaged engine housing. They paced the craft a moment as split-second bits of light then fell off in the slipstream. Peeling composite skin barked and shrieked, giving way to a high-pitched warble of uncoiling heat exchanger tubing.

A hurricane roared in from the blown portal. Everything not held down levitated, then swept threateningly about the punctured hull. Whiffs of propellant steam gushed inside. The heavy, sweet glycol immediately changed the cabin into a slimy, choking steam bath.

With an engine suddenly gone, the unbalanced nuke swung up like a pendulum. She found her tail and heeled over toward her wounded left side. There, with a gymnast's grace, she paused, then started to pirouette over on her back—again in line with the storm.

Capping off his breath, Kosinski locked his eyes on the speeding maelstrom. A hateful, living plasma of corkscrewing gray spires, thundering gunmetal columns, and jagged quills of pink/cobalt lightning roared toward him. It was cruelly beautiful and hypnotizing, even in its deadly peril. And only fleeting seconds away. But his eyes were frozen.

"Drue! WAKE UP!"

The pilot swiveled dumbly toward Trennt.

"Come on, man! What do we do?"

Kosinski blinked himself free of the windshield and ran inspecting hands over the damaged control panel. The bullet had entered a main breaker junction. A corner of the Bakelite housing was shattered. Beyond, he could see a couple of split capacitors. He yanked at them unsuccessfully.

"Give me a hand!"

Together, they pried at the warped unit. Slowly, their bleeding fingers dug it away. But not nearly as fast as the approaching storm narrowed the gap between them.

Another inch out. Another glance ahead. Both men took to peeking, squandering priceless seconds. Yet even Trennt found himself lulled by the horrific gorgon, wanting to stop and stare.

"Don't look at it!" he managed to order them both. "Keep pulling!"

Finally a satisfying click sounded. "Got it!"

Wedging the unit between his knees, Drue picked out the spray of loose brown splinters. Tucking a pen inside, he pried the grounded electronics back into a passable stance. Thankfully, the solder joints looked solid.

The block slid back on its runners. Mated with its waiting connectors, a joyous yuletide wash of LEDs and readouts flashed back to life. But they held no active logic. Just baseline warm-up grids and test patterns.

"What's wrong?" cried Trennt through the deafening wind.

Kosinski pressed the reset button, waited, and pressed again. A dismal message glowed on the control panel; robbed now even of its normal synthesized voice.

AUTOPILOT NONFUNCTIONAL.

Drue grated his teeth, pecking lamely at the jet's keyboard. Miraculously, the CPU processed and obliged his petition.

USER REQUESTS MANUAL AIRCRAFT CONTROL. ENTER PASSWORD AND USER ID, PLEASE.

"'Please'?" Trennt suppressed a nervous chuckle at the untimely courtesy.

Drue played tense fingers on the keys, somehow synchronizing his motions with the jarring turbulence long enough to sequence the proper strokes.

YM03468 ACKNOWLEDGED. CONTROL SYSTEMS RELINQUISHED TO USER. MANUAL FLIGHT MODE IN EFFECT. DO YOU WISH PILOT ADVISORY PROVISIONS?

The flier never had time to answer, as command of the plane was immediately dumped into his lap. Even so, the craft seemed to resent its forced surrender, wanting to continue on in its deadly aerial ballet.

Drue crammed the controls to their opposite stops, piling on a ton of body English when there was nothing more mechanical to coax. There he hung silent, like an exhausted terrier, waiting.

In a time scale measuring eons, the nuke finally came to her senses. She grudgingly slowed in her wingover and nosed obediently back around. But she felt different. Like a freshly broken horse . . . limp . . . dispirited and too slow to run.

The first real piece of storm cuffed them insubordinately. A hard rattle of gravel-like hail swept aft. Then came the boiling black gut of the monster itself, gobbling them whole.

An avalanche of mauling air pressure slammed down on the hapless riders. Their eye sockets boiled dry with pain. Flaming nails pieced their eardrums. Still, the nuke felt heavy . . . sinking.

Kosinski searched rear left. Outside, propellant continued gushing to green steam from her maze of severed wing arteries.

"Why hasn't that damn cutoff kicked in!"

He ran a hand across an overhead bank of mucky emergency switches. There was no backup response; electric or hydraulic.

"Autoservos must be gone!" he cried to Trennt. "Down between us is a panel and hand wheels. Got to turn it off!"

Trennt clawed open the access plate set low between them. Inside were a pair of common pipe valves. Five awkward turns to the left felt like a thousand. But the gushing vapor trailed off and stopped.

"That's it!" called Drue. "Okay, good!"

The nuke volleyed between hammering vertical gusts. Nearly rammed into orbit one moment, it was

slapped into a bottomless pit the next. In the driver's
seat, a dark part of Kosinski's brain screamed for him
to rabbit—jam in takeoff thrust and quick-burst the
reactor, gamble on the health of his remaining engine
to handle the overload. But he struggled above the
temptation. Even without gauges, he knew the coolant level must be marginal now. And even if the flash-
valving of the core lock-off still worked, there were sure
to be air pockets in the plumbing.

Fending off his instincts with strict procedure, Drue
cut his power back to maneuvering speed and rode
herd on the controls. He held tight as the nuke
whipcracked through one tooth-rattling blow after
another.

Snapping back from the deepest trough yet, the
cockpit lit to a sudden blaze of internal light. It was
the main flight processor screen, miraculously shaken
back from the dead. But like its crippled sister instru-
ments, it offered little more than the idle comfort of
its presence. The rolling data stream fluttered by as
a pointless jabberwocky of drunken, jumbled graphics
and erratic, haphazard numbers.

With the gauges' rekindling, however, Kosinski
detected something more. An obscure, independent
pulse was seeping back in the controls. And shortly he
realized the plane was reassuming its own command.

Drue squinted through the whirlwind of swirling
muck. Low left, flickering dimly through a muddy
splatter, it seemed the CPU control light had reanimated. He swiped a clenched fist against the bulb for
verification. Sure enough.

His actions alerted Trennt, who stretched over,
offering a hopeful thumbs-up through the churning
cockpit.

Instead, Kosinski shook his head.

"Either all this damn moisture has caused a short

circuit across some live bit of logic, or a command fragment is fading in from somewhere. This son of a bitch wants to turn back and climb!"

Trennt split a glance between the spastic control panel and angrily twirling storm fringes just beyond.

"Is that bad?"

"Yes, if I can't control it. And it's getting stronger by the second."

The jet entered the tempest. Fuselage windows flamed with sheets of eerie pink lightning. Static charges slithered in lime and amber boas over its nose and wings. Swirling arms of hail swatted the crippled plane, ringing off the fuselage in the ominous, discordant chimes of snapping guitar strings. Structural bundles of graphite fiber were beginning to fray.

The pilot watched long thin fingers of a bogus frost start their advance across his windshield. The glass was clouding over from a high-altitude sandblasting. He knew the same damaging grit was also being ingested by his lone, struggling engine. But worst of all, real ice was beginning to glaze in quick, shiny tiers over the wing surfaces.

Kosinski worked the controls, quietly gauging the situation for a few minutes. Finishing some private calculations, he finally leaned over with somber, flat eyes.

"This is no good, Trennt. We're icing up. With the vector controls locked, I have no way to divert bypass air to either clear the wings or try a vertical landing. Pretty soon we'll start losing lift and that'll be it."

Trennt huffed. "What do we do?"

"These storms have eyes like hurricanes. One's got to be somewhere near. If we find it and dump a lot of weight, it might lighten the plane up enough for me to shoot up and out the stack. Then I could try to figure a way down."

Trennt disgustedly spun his head about the cockpit.

"So what happened to the wonderful bird that could take 'anything'?"

"In good health," Drue apologized, "it would. Even with substantial power and control reductions. But not half crippled, like this."

Trennt knew anger was pointless.

"Okay, dump—dump what? You mean throw stuff overboard?"

Keeping his eyes on the windshield, Drue shook his head.

"Better. The passenger compartment is containerized in a full cabin ejection pod. It's actually a small survival shelter with rations, and a solar emergency transmitter. If we blow it free, it might make the difference in all of us surviving. You by parachuting and me by landing this bird."

Trennt frowned. "Why bother? Ditch with us!"

"Remember on the way out? I said just once I'd like to really fly this plane. I got my wish, didn't I?"

"So what? We all say stuff we don't mean! You said it was crashproof. Let the damn thing go!"

"Yes, but not meltproof. The blown left engine probably let air pockets into the coolant system. With no computer regulation to sift them out, they could start bunching up like an embolism. Someone'd have to stay onboard to screen them out manually. Otherwise, air locks might form in the high-pressure plumbing loop. That would mean ten-thousand-degree hotspots and a good chance of a full core meltdown."

Trennt snorted, pointing ahead.

"Are you serious? Look outside! What's it matter?"

"Here, maybe nothing. But inside the storm, isotope could come down hundreds of miles away. On people; little kids, who've got it bad enough already. I couldn't bail out knowing I let Avium 364 drizzle down on God knows who—could you?"

"Look, Trennt," Drue reasoned, "I'm no martyr. There's some last chance crew chutes stashed behind these seats. Once I get this thing steered toward the ocean, if I can't set it down I'll hit the silk myself and let her go."

Trennt conceded with a growl.

"All right! But just the others go. I stay with you!"

"Why?"

"Never mind. How do we blow the cabin?"

"At the four ceiling corners, there are access doors. Open them and give the safety pins inside a quarter turn. There's an electrical detonator up here that I'll cycle when that's done and everyone is belted in."

He started out. "Okay."

"Wait!"

"What?"

"Twist all but one key. That'll help keep the detonator circuit open until I can find the storm's eye. The chutes might not handle all this gale."

"Okay. Signal when."

Trennt groped his way aft. There, the other passengers were struggling just to stay put. The doctor was perilously out of his seat belt altogether, nobly disregarding his own protection in an attempt to cushion the ragged breathing of his critical patient.

To the side and restrained by Baker's hasty binding, the young woman smoldered silently, hate-filled eyes following Trennt's every move.

"We're icing up," he relayed to Baker. "The pilot says this whole cabin is an escape pod that we can blow if he finds the storm's eye. I want you to ride it in and keep everybody together until help finds you."

The shooter squinted in the ripping wind. "You ain't comin'?"

"Splitting up'll better our chances for one of us getting something back. We'll divvy up the data and vials once we get this thing ready for drop."

Baker nodded reluctantly. "Okay, Pard. If you say so."

Trennt pointed to the ceiling corners.

"Get in the rear and turn those safety keys. When Kosinski finds a clear spot, I'll do the same up front."

Precious minutes ticked by. Bolt lightning slashed ragged blue-white forks about them. Punishing hail continued peening the craft and its wings grew ever thicker with ice. The nuke's lift was decaying, trading itself for an awkward, pancaking sink.

Kosinski's heart filled his mouth as he searched the churning sky. A few snatches of light did materialize. But they were fleeting, gone before he could pursue them. Time was short, the moment fast approaching when he'd have to dump the passpod, regardless of their position.

Lateral gusts rammed the wounded jet. Determined head winds shouldered it back. Yet the pilot forced it on, a hapless mechanical sparrow caught in hell's total fury.

Then, ahead. Two o'clock low. A sliver of blue. Daylight. Maybe a mile out. Drue kept locked on the moving target as it blinked and re-formed; waxed and waned.

From nowhere, glorious sunlight exploded inside the craft. In a blink the gale winds were lost to a deafening silence and the clouds traded for a brilliant, flaring sun.

Kosinski waved a frantic, slashing hand toward the cabin.

"NOW, TRENNT! NOW!"

His voice was hoarse and grating in the sudden quiet. It startled Trennt, in the midst of divvying up the catalyst samples. He momentarily dumped them all back inside their box and set it ahead on the cockpit floor. Reaching above for the final turnkey, he never got to finish the job.

The lone *blat* of a single explosive bolt came too soon. It jarred the cabin and bunched the forward bulkhead into an accordionlike coil. The passpod slumped as an instant anchor in the murderous slipstream. About it the entire plane yawed hard left then back right, rocking on its belly. Salvaged files burst from their pouches and sluiced freely around the cabin walls. Passengers were rattled perilously about in their seats.

The bulkhead skin continued to buckle and flex. It gyrated through a full minute of such exercise before finally parting to a garish moan of tearing composite. A low-running gash spread across the compartment's entire width. Drawn on, ream after ream of loose research files skittered forward, exploding their precious information out into the gobbling slipstream.

Trennt sprawled against the animated bulkhead. Flattened spread-eagle between the ravenous fracture mere inches beneath his feet and the safety of the cockpit floor, just out of reach above, each new whipcrack tried bucking him loose. But he held fast in the brace of a tenacious spider. Behind him, though, the doctor and patient weren't as fortunate.

Trennt glanced helplessly over a shoulder as Keener was peeled through the slack web of his reclined seat. He joined the untethered physician and both men followed the descending trail of evacuating flotsam.

Eyes wide in horror, Doc Ashton doggedly fought to restrain Keener. He impossibly tried bracing his feet and grabbing handholds for them both on seat frames along the way. But his grasp slid vainly from one to the next, unable to prevent the slow descent of their combined weight. Just feet from the opening, Ashton's silent, fear-glazed eyes flew pleadingly up.

Risking his own uncertain perch, Trennt dared to intervene. He freed one hand, swung it blindly backwards and down. Desperate fingers strained up and connected. Palms locked tentatively against the sweat and grime oiling their flesh. But the cabin's angle and scouring decompression were stronger than the unwieldy grip. And slowly that grip failed.

Palms tapered off to fingers, then just hooked knuckles. The dead weight was peeling Trennt away from his own flimsy sanctuary; bending him ever closer to the gaping hole, himself.

Doctor Ashton's eyes flared in a last terrified look about. He volleyed a resigned glance between Trennt above and the torn fuselage ahead, then heroically yanked his hand away. In a blink, Trennt sprang upright and both other men disappeared out into space. Behind, the woman screamed in a long deflating peel. She strained at her bindings and sank from view in a dead faint.

Reeling with the sight of Ashton's terror-filled eyes, Trennt struggled to pull himself above. He battled the nauseating tempo boiling deep inside him and clawed up the steeply angled bulkhead. His hands made the cockpit floor and he tensed a leg for his final push. Just inches were left to go.

A quick triple pop erupted behind him. It was the tardy explosive bolts, severing all remaining cabin links in unison. Again, Trennt felt himself being twisted away. His fingers clutched vainly at the valise of precious catalyst samples ahead, but gee force won out. Doused in a brutal, quick wash of scalding exhaust, he watched as a helpless, flattened witness to the quick parting of plane and cabin.

A frenzied jet whine swiftly carried pilot and cargo

to higher regions while shoving the passenger pod rearward in its thrust. In another moment the double *chug* of additional pyrotechnics freed a trio of massive parachutes. A sudden decelerating yank signaled their safe deployment. Beneath, the passpod quivered and stabilized. Then, there was just the odd soft breeze of a gentle amusement park descent.

The two agents sat smothered in the misery of their ruined mission. Neither spoke and for a time, the only sound aboard the descending cabin was the peaceful moan of a plaintive wind.

Slowly, an odd noise disturbed Trennt's funk. Dead tired and frazzled, he dismissed what seemed a distant murmur to ravaged hearing and pure exhaustion. It persisted though; in fact, getting louder. He realized it was no fantasy when Baker's eyes met his from across the aisle.

"Jimbo? You hear that?"

A ragged look shot between the men.

"Sounds like the ocean."

CHAPTER 10

President Warrington was fuming and angry enough to have traveled the many blocks from his residence alone and on foot. The day was nearly over and he had still not heard from Royce Corealis about either his USDA resignation or the clandestine research program. Only recently had the director even bothered sending word as to where he could be found.

Arriving at the compound's garden facility, Warrington strained to contain himself.

"Is Director Corealis on the grounds?"

"Yes, yes, sir," replied the startled evening guard, fumbling with his sign-in sheet. "He came in at—"

"Never mind," interrupted the president, uncharacteristically gruff. "Get him on the phone."

The guard awkwardly obliged. But long seconds later he looked over sheepishly.

"Not answering, sir. Shall I have someone find him?"

"No. I'll go myself. Which dome is he in?"

"Number five, sir. You can use my patrol cart."

Warrington arrived at the furthermost structure and

parked beside Corealis' electric jitney. Entering the dome's sanitizing vestibule, he hurriedly donned the mandatory sterile paper coveralls and booties. He impatiently endured a flash of degerming light and spritz of sterilizing chemical mist. Each new second made the normally docile politician more agitated and reckless.

Properly decontaminated, the vestibule doors finally parted and the President of the United States entered the indoor garden plot, ready to do battle. Before Warrington, a hundred acres of lush terraced crops silently absorbed the frosty multispectrum light set high overhead. As if on cue, Corealis appeared, approaching through the ground level corn rows at a tourist's pace. A garden hoe was on his shoulder and filthy rubber boots covered his feet.

Warrington's rage grew hotter. Even now, the man could actually spare a moment's pause to study the forming corn ears, as unconcerned as though on a damned holiday stroll!

The president stepped into the musky atmosphere. He noticed the soil was oddly puddled in this pre-watering hour, but walked through it, unconcerned that he was muddying his highly polished shoes.

To the side, a lighting control panel was spread open, various repair tools laying about it. Disturbed by the prospect of an unwanted audience, Warrington took a quick glance about. Thankfully, no after-hours repair-men were in the vicinity. Maybe just off on their break—it didn't matter. This wouldn't take long.

Their privacy assured, he strode forward to confront Royce. But it was the director who spoke first, glancing innocently behind the president.

"Alone, Eugene?" he asked. "I expected at least guards and leg irons."

"You can damn well bet they'll be on their way,"

snarled Warrington, "if you don't do some quick and satisfactory explaining—starting with the truth about that nuclear airplane!"

Corealis raised his brows, mildly surprised. "Well, you've done some speedy homework. I am impressed."

His scornful tone bounced off the president.

"The truth!" he demanded.

Corealis repeated, glancing toward a distant clock, "The truth? Fine. I sent the plane out almost immediately after we talked last night. By now, it should have picked up whatever people may have survived their emergency—if there ever really was one. Agents onboard will have gathered up all the research work and files, leaving behind a small fusion device to erase any evidence of the base ever existing."

"When will the people be returned?"

Corealis reached over to consider a plant leaf and spoke bluntly.

"They won't. You see, a slight modification to the plane's intelligence system will have turned off its cabin pressure by now. All present will have gone into oxygen deprivation, nodding off gently to their eternal rest.

"As we speak, they and their research data are now onboard a fully automatic plane which will have climbed to a specific high altitude orbit over a predetermined locale of low EM penetration in the northwest territories. It will leave that orbit and come down for retrieval only when and where I have designated."

Warrington stared, incredulous.

"You have the gall to stand there and openly admit the consigning of innocent people to extermination like some litter of unwanted kittens?"

The director shrugged, unaffected.

"Thank yourself, Eugene. Your ultimatum forced the issue. Just yesterday, you said I was a bulldozer so badly needed to get difficult jobs done. And so I am. I was privileged enough to learn of a discovery like the world has never seen. You bet I'll guard it with my life—or anyone else's."

Corealis approached the president. His voice was sharp and hard.

"Are you too dense to grasp what the full regulatory power of an entire population means? Let me tell you. Religious declarations on birth control, individual decisions, and the complete magnitude thereof are forever under a practical governmental regulation.

"Economics is war, Eugene. Bloodless for the most part. But every bit as ruthless in direction and impact. And for a few soldiers to die in the name of the many who are not only spared, but reap its immense benefit, has all through history been a very acceptable loss ratio."

"Would," challenged Warrington, "you be willing to include yourself in that select fraternity of draftees?"

"To insure the program's success? In a blink," he pledged. "And I would not hesitate to ask the same of anyone else who might be required: co-workers, friends, family . . . even the president of these United States."

Warrington grimaced. "You monster."

The director pondered the comment.

"Really. Extending resources for unborn generations. Forever eliminating overcrowding. And doing it all with no real discomfort to those future-selected pawns?

"No one would get hurt. Everyone would have full bellies and those drafted into service would simply go through life with one biological function painlessly altered. If that wish makes me a monster, than I do stand guilty as charged."

Warrington shook his head with slow astonishment. "This very day you have killed people over the matter and can yet speak so flippantly? Such abuse of entrusted power is unpardonable!"

The director's eyes narrowed critically.

"If I've abused mine, Eugene, then you surely have neglected the proper issuance of your own. Be honest with yourself, my friend. You've lost your objectivity. You've crossed a line of professional restraint, which no leader can ever afford to. Admit it. Admit it and do the smart thing.

"Step down, Eugene. Let me convene the regional board of governors and find a proper replacement to wear your mantle of responsibility. Someone clinical enough to help get this country reunited and back on its feet once Skylock breaks. If you like, I'll disqualify myself from voting or even having any participation in its mechanics at all."

Corealis' face softened in Warrington's new silence. His voice turned personal and imploring.

"There'd be no shame, Eugene. Probably true admiration for a wise man's recognition of his own limits. Make the whole thing easier. Do it. Please. Or let me alone to finish handling this matter my way."

Warrington's eyes rekindled.

"No!" he bellowed. "No! Your Nazism is through. Do you hear me? I swear I'll see you convicted of every felony against humanity I can find!"

The director nodded remorsefully. Shuffling forward in his heavy gum boots, he stopped face to face with the president.

"Yes, Eugene. I hear you."

Corealis inhaled and raised melancholy eyes to the distant banks of grow lights. Unexpectedly, he drove the man back with a furious shove.

"You pragmatic oaf!" he screamed in Warrington's face. "You simple-minded fraud! Your kind and their ivory tower fantasies make me sick! You go through life with your heads in the sand or up your ass, dreaming your two-bit grand notions and distancing yourselves from the dirty work that constantly needs to be done, but always ready to accept the practical windfalls gained by the few of us willing to get bloody in the back alleys."

Corealis shook his head mournfully. "With enough time for proper grooming, you'd've done the same here, too."

"No!" Warrington defended. "I would never—"

His words were severed by another backward shove.

"I piecemealed that research station together brick by unallocated brick!" snapped Royce. "Sweated out three years' diversion of funds, equipment, and personnel. For my country. For *our* country, damn you! And now, a sudden fit of rookie utopianism is going to take it all away?"

Corealis stopped his pursuit of Warrington at the muddy vestibule entrance. Searching the man's face, his anger was suddenly replaced by frustrated resignation. He dropped his gaze, speaking to the thick mud between them.

"Your kind make for impoverished politicians, Eugene . . . and worse leaders. You're indecisive, weak-kneed in matters that count, and entirely too predictable.

"Before you ever arrived here I knew exactly what you'd say and that you'd come nobly alone to say it. Looking at you now I understand fully that your breed has only one redeeming fact at all, Mister President. And that is the sorry, ironic truth that you always do make such damn fine martyrs."

Warrington's mortified glow flashed to surprise as Corealis launched him with a harder, final shove. Muddy water splashed high on the man's pressed pants as he vainly tried to regain his balance. But there was no stopping his backward tumble into the live circuitry of the open electrical panel.

The lights in the agri-plot blinked only once. The 49th President of the United States went rigid, then crumpled away as the high voltage circuitry reset itself. In a few minutes Corealis stepped over the dead man and sloshed to the nearest phone. Clearing his throat, he dialed 911.

CHAPTER 11

Trennt and Baker yanked open the passpod's escape hatch and kicked it away. Churning flood waters rushed directly below, thrashing, deadly waves of cocoa brown, bobbed heavy with silt and lethal refuse. Menacing whitecaps pulsed stop-action-like in stark throbs of the pod's belly strobes.

Stunned, Baker rocked to his haunches.

"The hell?"

"Probably a flash flood from up country," reasoned Trennt.

"Whatever," replied the shooter glancing about. "I don't reckon this here is no lifeboat."

Trennt gazed further out the hatch. Some distance off, a broad dune of loose gravel swung into view as their sole alternative to a watery landing.

Descending gently, the passpod rocked in broad weighty swings between lethal rushing waves and hostile indifferent land. Undecided on which medium it should settle, the cabin swayed teasingly. One moment hard left to deep and treacherous seas; the next, toward the steep, uninviting hillside.

Trennt sided with Baker's logic.

"If this crate has life preservers, we'd better be finding them."

A quick search of the wind-trashed cabin produced inflatable optic-orange vests. Strapping them on and, in turn, about their catatonic remaining passenger, the two agents slung their guns crosswise over their backs and, with the woman sandwiched between, hovered in the doorway.

The vacillating landing zone rose up to meet them. Land, then water. Land. Then water.

Three hundred feet; land.

Two hundred; water.

Seventy-five; land.

Fifty; water.

Twenty; land.

"Jump!"

The trio exited the pod, crashing painfully in the loose, shin-deep stones of the steep hill. Short seconds later the pod mashed into the graveled shallows behind.

Safe.

They clutched the harsh incline, sucking raw, thankful breaths. But soon after, Trennt shoved himself erect. Stretching over the limp woman between, he called weakly to his partner.

"Were you able to save anything off the plane?"

Baker pulled at a corner of his ordnance sack then patted a coarse yellow notebook and limp clutch of random papers crushed inside his shirt.

"You?"

Trennt shook his head miserably. "All the juice stayed aboard."

Baker slumped back to the heaped gravel. "Damn."

Behind, filthy waves broke violently against the crashed passpod and into its open hatch. Stormy chocolate water swirled angrily about it in rough, tugging eddies, trying to dislodge and swamp the arrogant nuisance.

Trennt raised his face to the sky. High up, a friendly perimeter of calm blue was briskly shifting west. A gray arc of returning storm clouds was eagerly filling the horizon.

But between earth and sky was a more immediate concern—the still settling chute pack. Its garish orange and white striped blooms kited down like circus tents in the still, thick air. Shortly they'd splash out in the main current. Submerged, their brilliance would become a huge sea anchor, dragging the pod away from shore—and with it anything in the way of survival gear.

Without a word, Trennt was off, scrambling crablike over the slick, cascading gravel, back for the pod. Behind him Baker thundered in warning.

"No, Jimbo! Don't! There's no time! Let it be!"

But a second later the shooter himself was chasing after.

Trennt splashed through the already filling compartment, snatching up anything useable. In his wake, Baker did likewise. Between them a first aid kit, collapsible shovel, and ration water pack were salvaged. Self-heating coffees and loose courtesy snacks were being plucked up as the first chute touched down and was immediately sucked downstream.

Its shroud lines tightened briskly, telegraphing a hard jolt to the pod. Seconds later the next chute landed. A secondary jolt rattled in, sending the men sprawling in the frigid brown slush and their harvested goods flying about. The pod began a crunching backslide, sluicing ever deeper with the filthy, cold water. Only moments remained before the final chute landed.

Baker righted himself and stabbed quick, pecking hands at the precious flotsam.

"Jimbo, we'd better get a move on, pronto!"

Trennt underhanded him the folded shovel and drinking water pack.

"Go on!" he ordered, still grabbing up loose articles. "I'm right behind you."

A jerk of the last parachute was powerful enough to break the pod free of its anchorage. Slogging through the fast-rising slush, Trennt was pitched free of its sinking hatch. He scrambled away as a final moan of complaining metal vibrated behind.

The pod began a quick retreat from shore. Bobbing lower and lower in the main current, the brilliant roof strobes flashed dimmer with each new pulse. In seconds they were smothered entirely beneath the foaming, dingy waves.

There was no time for the survivors to mourn their loss. A sudden warning chill was in the air. The first tiny bits of light sleet drifted lazily downward, heralding a return of real punishing hail.

Trennt scrambled uphill. Trembling uncontrollably in his drenched clothes, he motioned to Baker.

"Take the shovel. Get her and you dug in as best you can. Use the survival blankets for cover!"

"What about you?"

Trennt spied a leeward undercut some yards off. "There!"

He charged ahead, fell to his knees at the hollow pocket and began clawing away clumped gravel with bare, freezing hands. His fingers were quickly skinned and bleeding. But he dug harder, managing a tiny den that he barely fit into. Trennt stretched his own survival blanket across its downwind opening and braced the flimsy barrier with forearms and knees.

In minutes a thundering gray colossus broke over

the landscape. Fueled with billions of frenzied horse-power, gale winds carved a deadly path across the open plain. Boulders were flung about like dried peas, gravel launched skyward as a trillion hunks of supersonic buckshot.

Scalding rain and shrapnel hail drilled the earth. Roiling sheets of lightning convulsed through the amalgam in searing flames of phosphorescent green and pink.

A deluge of boiling kettle water burst from the pregnant clouds. It clashed with the poisoned sleet and birthed tons of hard, black ice that slithered across the open desert floor, filling in hollows and pockets like quick-set cement.

His strength failing and wracked with chills, Trennt shuddered wretchedly in his den. Straining to hold up the thin fabric barrier, his muscles flamed, then went icy and numb. Somewhere in the struggle he heard himself scream.

Silence.

As quick as it had come, the cataclysm was gone. In its place settled a vacuum of abrupt, graveyard silence. The ravaged air sifted back. Coalescing pockets of damp heat and dry cold played out their last bits of dying energy in sodden, swirling eddies.

Trennt awoke to a stuffy darkness. The cold was gone, replaced by a curious steambath heat. Aside from the leaden numbness in his extremities, he was unharmed.

Shifting his arms for circulation, his knuckles rapped hard against his blanket. Trennt then realized the material was staying glued in place. Bewildered fingers touched it and felt a wall of ice, cast hard as the toughest iron.

Trennt fumbled about the obstruction. There were

no seams. No combination of hands or shoulders could lever the formfitting plug away. He managed to draw up a cramped foot and pump out some anemic kicks. But they had no effect.

The other foot joined, together ramming the bizarre cold glass. Ten, fifteen, twenty times gave no result. Trennt sucked more of the thin, heavy air, capped his breath and fired out twenty more. Still nothing.

Another rest.

Another twenty.

Again and again, until he could do no more.

His leg muscles gone to potter's clay, Trennt leaned back. Little oxygen remained in his pit and no more strength to draw from. But he also felt an odd womblike tranquility in the smothering den. Here, no decisions were required of him, no need for plans or worrying about others.

A gentle, timeless sleep beckoned. He glanced drunkenly about the darkness. Not such a bad way to go. Just doze off and fade to black. Only thing remaining was permission.

"Is it okay, Dena?" he asked of the gloom. "Have I paid enough to be forgiven?"

Trennt surrendered, ever to remain lost in this forsaken and unmarked tomb.

But once again, it wasn't to be. Through the fog of his clouding mind he heard a distant snap. Dense and brittle, it collected another. Then another. Again, and once more. Slow and irritating, a series of faster pops gathered in a random, grating chorus. The moan of something heavy giving way filled his tarlike hearing.

No, he thought. Go away. Leave me be.

But the racket grew even more determined. A staccato of *pops* and *snaps* rose up, pelting Trennt with icy, biting chips.

A final, brittle shudder vibrated about him and the ice wall tumbled away in shattered foot-thick chunks. Freezing, bothersome air invaded the tiny den. It swirled painfully around Trennt, stealing his hard earned solace and driving him out.

He understood. It wasn't okay after all, was it, Dena? No, more payment was required.

Trennt staggered out like a slug rousted from hibernation. His body sweated steam with the lazy resolve of a fresh-skinned carcass. What awaited staggered him fully erect, for all around was a landscape devoid of color or life.

A metallic, monochrome wash of gray stretched earth to sky, as far as eye could see. Still dangling about his neck, the limp blaze-orange life vest stood out in absurd contrast to the overpowering desolation.

Trennt cast dumbfounded eyes above. There, a zinc-colored vault hung speckled in the tattered woolly mantle of post-storm clouds. Low on the horizon, the sun existed as a hazy white orb; dim and distant, offering no warmth or comfort. The universe vibrated with quiet.

Trennt absently touched his fingers to the smattering of scalds and freeze burns dotting his neck and face. He shook out the cobwebs, filled his lungs with the iron cold air and stooped to retrieve his metalized survival blanket. Snapping it free of clumped ice, he draped it about his shoulders in a shawl-like fashion. Then it hit him.

"Baker!"

No answer.

"Baker!"

Trennt ran to the area he remembered the gunman digging at. But any identifying tailings were lost to the gale. And more black ice set plastered over the ground like nothing had ever taken place there.

Trennt dropped to a crouch. He swept spread fingers back and forth over the hard, frigid earth. But his hands found nothing and were soon numb with cold, stiff enough to miss a slight depression in the ice. Only a skidding knee betrayed the tiniest fret in the glassy, adamantine surface.

Trennt dropped to all fours and blew. His breath revealed a solitary crack. It led a tracing finger to other tributaries and to the web of a circular fracture. At dead center was a flattened spring of familiar silver blanket. Yet another plug of the impossible black ice opposed him.

He grabbed the sparse lever and pulled. Beneath, wedged tight as a shotgun wad, the bunched fabric began tearing away. He gathered the scanty outcropping as careful as he could, gingerly rocking its metalized fabric as a kind of handle while jabbing his boot heel into the flinty area around.

Slowly, a ragged, milky white seam leavened in the crust. He kicked harder and maneuvered bleeding, numb fingers between it and the anchoring surface rock. A thick black slab yielded, rising slow as an obstinate manhole cover.

One hand got through. Then a forearm. Scalding every inch of open skin, the frozen, heavy obstruction might have been embers hoisted from a raging fire.

Razored ice slashed Trennt's flesh ever deeper. But he dismissed the pain, forcing both arms downward. Then, at bicep depth his fingers finally rounded the ice block. He clamped its underside and his weary back struggled it free. Beneath were two motionless forms.

Trennt dragged the woman out first. Dazed and gasping, she blinked in owllike confusion as he wrapped her in the ice-speckled bedroll. Then, equally stunned, came Baker. Lifting him from the hole, Trennt never remembered seeing the gunman look so oddly vulnerable.

He quickly set to work, alternately rubbing the chilled, stiff hands and gray face of one, then the other. Switching back and forth many times, Trennt quickly warmed his own chill away. But the asphyxiated people were slow in responding. So he broadened his efforts to include their shoulders and legs, working harder and more determinedly.

Ironically, something long absent stirred uneasy and deep inside the man as he tended the limp female. From the outset he'd suspected what service she offered in the new social order. But she wasn't at all like the thin-lipped, hard-eyed whores he'd seen prowling the world's late-night streets. Nothing like the shot-carded and licensed bubble brains laying tech village high rollers these days.

Neither cheap, nor simple. Instead, a notion of certain grace flooded his senses. High and starkly undercut cheekbones blended with a delicate jaw line. Tiny ears merged with an elegant, sculpted neck. And her reddish brown hair carried a texture and hue much like his own Dena's.

Trennt tore free of the disquieting notion. He didn't know her name, nor did he want to. She was just another hunk of cargo placed in his care for proper disposal. Regrouping, he continued her massage, but with less force and direction.

After many hard minutes the pair regained their rudimentary senses. Trennt got them seated upright and dug the few cups of self-heating coffee from their pit. He popped the tab of one. Its bracing aroma conjured a much needed sense of hope as he guided sips between them and himself. The brew made a half dozen rounds, until its few ounces of precious warming liquid were gone. A second cup was opened and worked about likewise.

While the pair regained their strength, Trennt set to work enlarging their foxhole for nighttime accommodations. They'd spend the evening inside, their combined space blankets and shared body heat sealing out the cold. Tomorrow he'd consider their long-term options.

Baker sat wrapped in his foil blanket, watching the customary emerald and sapphire hues born on each Skylock dawn.

"That pod's emergency transmitter musta got a lick or two out on the way down," he declared. "It musta. Think any friendlies heard it?"

Trennt stood nearby, searching the far horizon.

"If the air was still clean enough, maybe the competition. At the moment, though, I'd say the odds of us winding up in anyone's hands aren't the best."

The shorter man joined Trennt's quiet scrutiny of the western distance. Leagues of piled gravel stretched as far as either could see.

"Damn, Jimbo. The hell you figger we are?"

Trennt kicked at the loose oval pebbles.

"Somewhere in the Barrens. From all the ocean bottom stone, I'd say probably the southwestern tidal wave area. Nevada, California, maybe."

"That far west, ya reckon?"

Trennt shrugged. "Our plane was caught in one strong storm."

Baker nodded, looking skyward. "Yeah, our plane— wherever the hell it went off to."

He dropped his head in a wagging flush of remorse.

"Boy, we sure mucked this one up, start to finish."

"Maybe not."

"Wha'cha mean?" Baker asked.

But Trent's reply was hindered by the young woman's appearance. Emerging from behind a nearby rock pile, she made brief eye contact with the men, then looked away, straightening her belt.

A suggestive grin darkened Baker's face.

"Hey now. Sweet Thang. I plum forgot her. At least the trip wasn't no total loss."

"She's freight," reminded Trennt sternly. "And our job is to get her back, unmolested."

Baker made special note of his tone. "Don't care for her much at all, do ya, Pard? Now that is truly a shame."

Trennt didn't reply. Instead, he knelt, sifting through the pathetic clutch of survival rations and gear gathered at his feet: a spare foil blanket, tube of skin cream, ball caps, and cellophane UV goggles. One two-kilo pouch of freeze-dried trail mix, a few survival crackers, and an eight-pack of canned water.

The meager lot had been designed for people marooned in more civilized times and places. Folks lounging around some temperate zone before their quick and imminent rescue, not ones left to their own designs at mid-desert.

Trennt kept silent as the mathematics of long ago survival schools sifted through his brain. He weighed and adjusted fluid and caloric values for terrain and climate, tossing in a couple of variables for the unknowns of time and distance.

Working with the weather at an easy pace, the larder might stretch to fuel a week's travel, but the water limitations were critical: eight pints—little more than a quart per person—for a realistic daily expenditure easily quadrupling that.

Standing beside him, Baker's silence supported the poor odds. Neither spoke as Trennt lifted the metalized blankets and began making X-shaped cuts at their centers.

"These will double as serapes against the sun and cold," he said to no one in particular. "We'll make a signal in the stones here then start west. Travel in early morning and late afternoon light. Depending on the terrain and heat, we might make ten, fifteen miles a day."

For the first time, looking composed and rational, the young woman approached.

"How many days?" she asked.

"As many as it takes," he replied with obvious disdain.

"And where do we go to?"

"Follow the sun toward the ocean. Then north, along the coast to whatever town we find."

"Then what?"

Trennt stopped his knife work, fast annoyed.

"Then, we get you back to wherever it is you belong."

"Well," she declared, regarding the still raging mud-flow. "I say we stay right here and wait. Or follow the river south."

"You're cargo," Trennt replied bluntly. "You don't get a vote. Now start gathering rocks for that signal."

CHAPTER 12

Royce Corealis halted in adjusting his necktie. His eyes glinted hard off the dressing room mirror.

"What do you mean," he said confronting his aide, "they don't have it?"

The young man shrank a bit.

"All reports received by courier to this point claim the plane has neither landed, nor been seen at its planned rendezvous."

The tie remained untouched as the director narrowed his gaze.

"You're saying that three whole days after it should've been well in hand, not one of our field men has yet even spotted it?"

The aide flushed. "No, sir. There's some feeling that it may have been destroyed, torn apart by the storm itself."

The director cinched his tie roughly, then plucked his suit coat from the bed.

"Fabulous. What interval are the updates coming in at?"

"Every fifteen hours."

Corealis shook his head. "Too slow."

The aide dared defend the timing.

"Considering the reports are trucked and hand-carried for almost two thousand miles, that's really not bad, sir."

"Too *slow*," Corealis repeated, looking him in the eye.

The aid dropped his gaze.

"There is no other way at the moment," he offered meekly. "Each group is prepared to link up for a multistation radio relay. But we won't have a rudimentary transmitting window for another two weeks."

"Two weeks of wasted time," snapped Royce. "Besides, I don't like either option. I think it's time I took a much more proactive role in this matter."

The director finished straightening his suit coat.

"At the moment I've got a state funeral to attend and a eulogy to deliver. But immediately afterward we need to start arranging our own transportation out there. We'll make a visit, like Eugene suggested—something in the way of a goodwill tour. We'll announce our beloved president's departure, but assure our isolated countrymen that our hearts are still with them and that we are working toward the country's reconstruction.

"In between, we'll just have to manipulate travel to suit our true purpose."

The aide felt his stomach sink. Travel into the heart of what was almost enemy territory? But he knew if anyone could pull it off, it was the man before him. He swallowed anxiously and turned for the door.

"Yes sir."

Trennt's assumption was right. They'd landed dead center in the Great American Barrens. Three people afoot, amid a thousand square miles of desolate, stony dunes.

Torn from the ocean bed when the entire San Andreas and contributing Newport-Inglewood Faults gave way nearly a decade before, loose ejecta had been rammed far and wide by a series of colossal tidal waves, resulting in this forsaken wasteland.

Though christened by West Coast survivors, little was actually known of the Barrens. But on foot, the three refugees quickly gained a firsthand intimacy of the place and its cruel, callous beauty.

A post-storm sun was rekindled in the desert skies. Raking the brittle landscape with a vengeance, it ignited captured starfire in a trillion gleaming flecks of silvery mica and pink quartz; scalding the castaways' skin and vision alike with its brutal dawn-to-dusk majesty.

At night the same sky hung heavy as the blackest iron, awash in a smothering and frigid silence. Temperature swings between were furious. For the three travelers, daylight was spent hiding in meager shade like insects driven from the sweltering blast-furnace heat, while nighttime hours were endured shivering through a grating, rawboned chill.

No sounds of other life were carried in the low moan of an infrequent, roasting wind. Only occasional dust devils materialized to chaperon them. Gentle thermal mammoths spawned of midday heat, the little whirlwinds contentedly played out their brief lives in games of tag among themselves, passively vacuuming the oppressive desert floor before disappearing again.

Rations disappeared, too. The trio sipped three ways at a single daily pint of water and nibbled handfuls of survival granola. Throats were rasped sandpaper dry from sucking the thin, oven-parched air. Dust-caked mouths drooped in heavy rows of split and oozing heat blisters.

Travel itself was risky. The ankle-deep amalgam of
flint and granite slashed razored daggers at their boots
and worked to twist ankles with every step. Going lame
out here was an all too real possibility.

Through it all, Trennt kept his pledge and their pace.
Leading the way from first light to midmorning and
again from early evening to nightfall, he dragged his
people on. But his own determination was flagging to
new forces loosed deep inside him; ones every bit as
threatening as the terrain he crossed.

From the thickening whirlpool of instinct and logic,
yellowed memories distilled and took form. A collage
of transparent images gathered to play off the stark,
empty sky ahead like a huge reel of silent movie foot-
age. Dusty alluring phantoms, which drew him on, like
a suicidal moth lured to the flame of its own demise.

Few believed it would work, Dena being a big city
girl and all. The transformation from L.A. to Eureka
was a trip across galaxies; two spots in the same state,
light years apart. But the city gal who'd come to love
the up-country seclusion through summer vacations
with a rural aunt, came also to love one of its men.

Dena surrendered a college degree, city comforts,
and big league career chances to raise her own children and vegetables in the big sky country. Designer
denims to flannel work shirts was a leap she made with
the grace of a gazelle. Never a word of regret. Never
a look back.

Her only complaint ever had been in the absolute
contempt she held for the government's neat little title
hung on her and her children. The same name bolted
to its new legions of transplanted Americans with the
dog tag-like holograph necklaces they'd been forced to
wear: Cee-Dee—Common Displaced.

❖   ❖   ❖

"These are your ID badges," an unsympathetic processing clerk said to Trennt on that long ago night. "From now on, they have to be on you and your people in plain sight. Get caught without and it means jail—shit work. Burial details, sanitation stuff. Understand?"

Trennt's heart still ached remembering the faces of his wide-eyed, terrified children and disbelieving wife.

"Yes, we understand."

"Good. Now follow that yellow line. You'll all be given inoculations and deloused. Afterward, you'll go to a marshalling area for assignment to a housing sector."

Jennifer, who was deathly afraid of shots, began to whimper. Her fear aroused Dena's fierce maternal instincts.

"When will this be over?" she demanded, breaking free of her own stupor to confront the clerk. "When can we take our children and go home?"

The clerk stamped a paper and shoved it toward Trennt.

"Lady," he answered scornfully, "you are home."

Trennt lost his footing and stumbled. He snapped back to the present and stared ahead. Wrapped in a wavering heat haze, his weeklong destination seemed no closer. Sheathed in solemn purple hardness, unnamed peaks glittered like newly made arrowheads. They were not true mountains, but thick, jumbled slabs of shale, slate, and granite. Burst and buckled in dazzling mountainous heaps, tiers of shorn bedrock had been brought up from staggering depths by the quake. Piled on edge and toppled over like the back plates of a huge fallen dinosaur, they were every bit as dead.

Considering the terrain, Trennt guessed they'd averaged a steady eight miles a day. An extraordinary effort. Survival school trained, he'd taken Baker's and his own stamina for granted. But he grudgingly admitted a new respect for the woman, for through it all she maintained a stoic silence, keeping their pace without complaint. Head down and mouth shut, she trudged on, mirroring his own best effort.

Yet fifty miles pared from the hundreds undoubtedly waiting ahead was barely a sliver. And that hard truth was driven home just before dawn of the seventh day, when Trennt had a full-blown hallucination.

From far overhead, a faint throbbing rumble reached his ears. At first he smiled with the thought of a thirst-quenching rain. But the canopy was the same clear wash of brilliant, uncaring stars as each night prior . . . and neither of his companions reacted to the sound.

Trennt almost spoke, hoping his voice might give the mirage substance, make it real—or at least convince the others of its existence. But there were no flashes of distant lightning to offer him hope and he finally admitted the truth. There was no prospect of rescue, none of survival. And never had been. Pushing further was a fool's pointless quest.

The event also made Trennt finally admit to the fever he'd felt growing since yesterday. The routine was becoming textbook. Exhaustion and dehydration would soon fuel a mix of chills and delirium as the body's biorhythm fell out of synch. Then the deadly visions would set in—and mouth-foaming insanity.

Each in his own time would go mad. They'd wander aimlessly in the full sun. Brains would slowly shrivel to jerky; tongues swell to choking purple wads. Nature would so claim them, finally tanning their dead hides with excruciating disinterest.

Already a touch of fatal giddiness was tickling the edges of his mind.

"Ladies and gentlemen, I present you the lesser mummy of James Trennt, Esquire. Please note the similar skin texture to Ramses the Second—or—an old pair of work boots."

He motioned a stop and they silently bedded down in the thinly shaded hollow of a crescent dune. It was there that Trennt invoked a rusty oath taken between Baker and himself in a long ago battle zone. Gazing across the pitiless horizon, he hoped himself finally worthy of the deed as he drew enough breath to speak.

"Tonight," he hissed through split and peeled lips, "you take the point, Baker. I'll close off the drag."

Cradling his weapon like a toddler ready to nap, the shootist swung heavy-lidded eyes over and gave his comrade a solemn nod. Between them the girl drowsed already, not understanding what decision had been made.

The commitment fell heavily on Trennt. Best for it to come now, in their sleep. He needed only to stay alert and keep his mind clear enough to make the hits quick and clean: the girl first, then Baker. Didn't matter how ragged a job he did on himself. Just a couple of minutes until they nodded off. He clicked the safety off his weapon and gazed skyward.

Royce Corealis shot up, nearly crying out in alarm. Jolted from his sleep aboard the cruising jet, the interim president clutched the arms of his seat, tensely swinging his head about the light-dimmed passenger cabin. But everyone around him slept on, and after a few seconds reassurance, he, too, settled back.

The man gazed out his window at the darkened landscape below. Nothing but empty desert blackness filled the horizon. Yet the sensation was as certain as if someone had impossibly reached out from all that distant shadow and pressed an icy accusing finger to his very skin.

Corealis shook off the thought. He glanced at his

watch and contemplated the stop ahead. Another few hours and he'd be at his first shoreline California conference. Taking the deceased president's place on what had been changed to a perfunctory goodwill tour, he'd leave the jet seaplane to meet the various towns' elders along the coast. He'd make some public appearances before meeting up with the scout detachment leaders under camouflage of the upcoming Freeville rendezvous. With luck it might all soon be over.

Corealis settled back and rested his eyes.

CHAPTER 13

The sensation faded in and out. Sound or vision? Trennt wasn't sure. Humming engines? Voices?

Blinking awake, he bolted. Dammit, dreaming! He'd fallen asleep, too! A chilling gauze dangled in his face and whirled with heavy eddies. Fog. Night fog. He'd been out all damn day! Beside him, the young woman and Baker also stirred. Now it was too late to mercifully conduct his business. They'd have to endure another day.

Trennt swiped angrily at the grainy veil. Then he heard the sound again. Voices. But unlike his prior hallucination, this time both his companions shared the sensation. The same electric thought flashed simultaneously through all their minds.

Rescue.

The woman dove to her feet, coughing as she struggled to rise above the dune.

"Here! Over here! Help!"

Trennt grabbed at her belt. But she twisted away, calling hoarsely, again and again. Baker pitched in, finally jerking her back and to her rump.

She squealed, slapping in disbelief at their hands. "What's the matter with you? They've found us! Help has come!"

"Shut up and stay down!" Trennt ordered. "We don't know that!"

She glared incredulously, shouting all the louder. "HELP! HELP! OVER HERE!"

Trennt snapped out a backhand and cuffed her mouth. She grabbed her face in stunned silence and sat back. Then, stiffly gathering his own feet, he cautiously peeked over the dune.

In the thick fog beyond, rectangular blotches outlined several all-terrain trucks. Interspersed among them moved the shapes of a dozen or so people.

A form suddenly appeared to his side. Swathed in desert BDUs and heat-imaging goggles, it thrust an automatic weapon at Trennt's face and slowly circled closer. The soldier jerked his gun barrel upward, signaling them all to raise their hands while approaching cautiously.

"*¡Mira!*" he called to those behind the dune. "*¡Aqui!*"

The prisoners flinched at a burst of sudden shots. But the slugs weren't for them. Heavy calibers were barking from several directions behind the dune.

Rifle grenades and light rockets tore at the air. Quick yellow-white ripples of high explosive cut stark blossoms in the viscous fog. Their captor forgot his prisoners and scampered back toward his own people, never to return.

In minutes the gunfire was over. Then sounds of different machines neared, the rushing wind and spraying sand of small turbines. Ground-effect vehicles coasted to stops and cautious new footsteps crunched about. There was rustling and the sounds of inspections being made.

Sentences were exchanged. New and syrupy,

rapid-fire consonants replaced the Spanish. Slavic—
maybe Polish or Russian.

Eventually the GEV engines stirred back to life and
moved away. In their wake, a few groans lingered.
Then the cold night returned to a foggy silence.

Next morning the mist was still thick. Ordering the
woman to stay put, Baker and Trennt circled outward
from opposite directions of their dune, starting toward
the night's action.

What awaited was the product of a classic ambush:
quick and intense, brutally launched from point-blank
range. The victims' four-wheel-drive trucks lay knocked
over, tires were blown and shredded, jagged fender
chunks peeled back and strewn about. Even now parts
of wreckage still smoldered.

Then came the bodies. Most were whole; some
though, like the vehicles, in pieces. The look of mass
murder never changed.

Baker drew up beside Trennt and joined in a grim,
if fleeting, appraisal.

"Bastards never had much chance, did they? Sure
hope some water is left."

The dead wore common issue fatigues. All had thick
black hair, high cheekbones, and square, even teeth—
Indian heritage and Spanish blood mix.

Their skin had gone blue-purple since night. In this
early hour, the blood painting their wounds was com-
mingled to a burnt gravy and chocolate syrup appearance. A lucky few had died outright and lay closed-eyed
where they'd fallen, almost orderly and at peace. But
the majority rested in splayed, rag doll heaps. Dead
eyes wide in a snapshot of fright and horror.

Facing the reality of his own thirst, Trennt absently
reached down to liberate a dead man's canteen.
He knocked back several deep gulps of the stale,

lukewarm fluid and swiped at the gratitude watering his eyes.

Trennt saw the victors had spared time enough to hunt souvenirs among their victims. Side arms, holsters, and personal items were gone. He spied the out-turned pockets of a particular corpse and winced at the indignity, remembering.

Once, in the Amazon, he'd done it himself. Robbed an enemy lieutenant he'd killed in a firefight, taking the man's pocket watch as a battle memento. Later, he'd had the inscription translated, to find it a present from the dead man's parents, a gift commemorating his commission date in the service.

Trennt had stalled a dozen offers to buy the keepsake, at the same time, feeling its dead weight grow to tombstone size in his pocket. He finally dropped the watch in a hole scooped out along a shallow river while on patrol, giving the morbid trophy an ironic burial not afforded its discarded owner.

The woman's voice interrupted.

"I suppose you'd like an apology from me for calling out last night like I did."

Trennt glanced over. Too tired to lecture, he recapped and handed her the canteen, offering a simple caution before walking away.

"Don't drink too much or too fast. You'll heave your guts out and only need more."

Ahead, Baker returned from his own battlefield appraisal. Unaffected as always, he munched on a liberated ration meal, already getting a spring back in his step. To him the whole matter was viewed with the jaded indifference of an old-time mall shopper. Wiping a daub of grease from his fever-blistered mouth, he pointed a spoon as he gave Trennt his assessment.

"Break and drop rocket tubes up yonder. Shithouse fullo' spent Eastern Europe shells. Fanned patterns in the sand show three, maybe four midsize hovercraft headed northwest."

"Bandits?" asked Trennt.

"Wouldn't think so."

Baker exhibited his food can as proof.

"Vittles and water cans ain't been touched. Only well provisioned soldiers would settle for combat trinkets and leave everythin' else. Damn lucky for us."

Trennt concurred. "Recognize the trucks?"

Baker touched fingers to a nearby fender with the acumen of a horse trader.

"French design made under license in Argentina."

Geri's shout clanged across the battle site like cold iron.

"Hey! Hey! This one's still alive!"

The wounded man was dressed in unmarked fatigues, same as the others. Yet something in his bearing seemed a bit more refined: higher class—possibly an officer. His skin was pallid and loose. Eyes hung half open, locked on some desolate, private vista which was fast approaching.

The soldier's clothes were blood soaked from midchest to his knees. The desert fabric was split by shrapnel, which'd turned his intestines into a bulging sieve of shiny blue-red coils. Pain seemed beyond him though, mercifully displaced by the body's own opiate of shock.

Trennt knelt beside the soldier. Capping his breath against the man's overpowering stench, he asked, "Who are you?"

The black eyes drew back from their trance. They touched on Trennt, then dropped to the brown pudding pooled in his own lap. The soldier's face twisted with confusion. He seemed suddenly bewildered and annoyed, uncertain of it all.

He raised his eyes and closed them. Tears squeezed

from their corners. With great effort he half whispered, *"Este es el dia de los difuntos."*

Trennt recognized the words as Spanish. But his own smattering of functional phrases was long behind him.

"He says, 'Today is the day of the dead.'"

It was the woman. Though obviously distressed by the soldier's wounds, she also knelt and placed a comforting hand to his cheek.

"Como se llama?"

He groped for a missing name tag, then plopped back. His lips fumbled with a tongue grown too thick to meet the task.

"No importa," he said, shaking his head with feeble despair. *"No importa."*

The woman poured a warm trickle from the canteen to her fingertips and moistened the soldier's scorched lips. She lifted his head and touched his mouth with more. But it dribbled pitifully off his chin, raising new smears of crimson in the brown crust of his belly wound.

Her effort did raise the man's consciousness, though, enough to listen and comprehend as she whispered slow and gently. Words soft as a new mother's loving coo gave him strength. In return he offered a few slurred phrases and chanced a gaze about.

The soldier saw the nearest corpses and some emotional words spilled from his lips. His hard sobs became a raging cough that sent him rapidly spiraling back toward shock.

She rested his head gently against a truck tire pillow and stood.

"He says he has failed them all."

Trennt studied him. "Any chance of finding out what they were doing here?"

"Maybe looking for us," she replied tersely, then added, "I'm going to find a compress to cool his head."

A touch of sarcasm flared as she paused beside Trennt. "It is okay to waste a little of his own water on him, isn't it?"

Trennt didn't answer, granting her permission by merely stepping aside to let her pass.

The pistol shot startled them both.

Before them the soldier sat artificially erect, as if someone had just called his name. In the next moment he softened and gracelessly toppled over. To the side, Baker casually viewed the man's shattered temple, reholstering his gun.

The woman charged back and bulled her way past him. She froze, utterly horrified by what lay at her feet.

"He was gut-shot," Baker reasoned pragmatically. "No fixin' it and no time to spare on somethin' that kin take a long, painful spell to get over. Now he don't have a problem and neither do we."

Her face crumbled in total revulsion and disgust.

"You killer!" she screamed in Baker's face and turned to include Trennt. "Both of you, killers! Don't you feel anything? Care for anything?"

Trennt looked at the dead man, then shared a glance with his bewildered partner. Though oddly annoyed himself, he also knew the reality of the situation and didn't criticize the remedy.

Instead, he grabbed the woman by an arm, again confronting the deep, emerald green of her hating eyes.

"He's right, lady. Our problems here are both over. Now walk around and gather up all the food and water you can find. Baker, let's see if we can make one good truck from all these pieces."

The shooter nodded. "Grips, Pard."

An hour's work yielded a bounty of supplies. Fuel to stoke a few hundred miles hard travel. Top-notch desert sun garb. Water and rations enough to last a week. Spare tires and containers were transferred and lashed down to the most roadworthy vehicle.

Pausing as they prepared to leave, the woman cast a final glance at the carnage left behind.

"After taking what was theirs, I don't suppose you'll make time to properly bury them, either."

Trennt fired the truck's engine, shifting into gear and looking straight ahead.

"Nope. Now climb in."

CHAPTER 14

Equipped with adequate transportation, Trennt pushed even harder. Moving dead west, they drove almost nonstop. Five full days elapsed. Then there she sat.

Stuck before them as an abstract sculpture was an oceangoing freighter. Erect and alone in a vast sea of gravel, she rested like a giant toy boat left high and dry after its bathtub ocean had drained.

Her hull plates were black as obsidian, polished by gritty desert winds to a dark gloss. The ironwork of her upper decks shone like powdered cinnamon. Any name plates or registry were long gone. She was simply there.

Dunes had piled against her port side. They were packed into a steep, natural ramp that rose and spilled onto her broad angled deck like a great walkway. Assorted tracks and trash about her marked times of periodic habitation. But further investigation was broken off by a disembodied voice.

"Kinda blows your mind, huh?"

The dumbstruck trio looked about. Cloaked in the

161

stark shadow of the ship's stern was the dim stick figure of an old man. Grizzled as a prospector, he stood beside a makeshift teepee tucked in the cool leeward side of her broad rudder.

He wore a tattered pair of old military fatigue pants. Around his wrist was a hammered copper bracelet, gone dark green with age. A dull beaded chain hung around his neck, sporting an oval medallion that framed a crude, three-pronged member, one reminiscent of a long-tined fork.

The old-timer started toward them. A well-worn Chinese SKS rifle hung loose and low in his grip. Dangling the mummified claw of an ancient rabbit's foot, a bleached-out bush hat was crushed firmly over his terrain-hardened eyes. Even in this barbaric land, his torso was bare.

"Yeah, kinda blows your mind," he repeated. "Big ship like this, here in the middle of nowhere. Freaked the hell out of me when I first came across her, too."

Baker snapped his shotgun up, halting the man's approach.

"Who're you?"

The old-timer carried on another couple of steps before stopping near the ramp. He regarded Baker's weapon, sweeping quick, appraising eyes to the people and vehicle behind them. He then raised the forked medallion at his throat.

"Peace, friend. Easy on the trigger. No one's looking to rumble."

Trennt approached the man. Up close, he looked glazed a walnut brown, almost flame broiled. Once he must have been muscular, but his build now was eroded and waxy with age, yet still exhibiting plenty of wiry vitality.

Faded blue outlines covered much of his skin like a rash. Tattoos ran in a sprinkling of stars across the

backs of his hands and the Statue of Liberty spanned
the inside of one forearm—all impressive artwork and
evidence of certain toughness. But the real statement
was chiseled in a clump of ancient shrapnel wounds
shining across his upper chest and a dim snarling
bulldog adorned with four powerful letters: USMC.

A long, coarse ponytail of pure white hung down
over the old man's spine. He pulled thoughtfully at a
matching white Pistol Pete moustache as he stared
back.

One crusty old turd, thought Trennt. A desert
crazy? Maybe. But there was no lunacy in those
piercing eyes. And something valuable translated from
his body language—a scent of experience mixing with
the powerful sweat dousing him now.

"My name's Trennt," he offered, feeling a quick
gut-level kinship with the man. "That's Ivory Baker.
And this is—" He realized that he'd forgotten her
name.

"Geri Litten," she declared.

The old-timer grinned tentatively, working to make
a connection between the odd trio and their out-of-
place truck. He turned first to Baker, still with his gun
barrel leveled.

"I asked you to put that away once, dude."

"Baker!"

The shooter glanced at Trennt, only lowering the gun
with much reluctance.

"Noah Snipes," said the old man plainly.

"Wha'cha doin' out here?" questioned Baker.

"Wha'cha doin' out here?" he fired back.

"We were in a plane crash, nine days east," said
Trennt. "We need to make the nearest town and get
the woman back to her people."

"My people are dead!" Geri snarled.

The old-timer pulled a drawstring bag from his cargo

pocket. Still regarding the bunch, he thoughtfully ground some pale leaves into a thin twist of paper. Lighting it, he drew heavy on smoke that carried a nip of burning twine.

"Lucked out there," he continued. "Rendezvous starts in Freeville a few days from now. Headed that way, myself. Pickers will start meeting up here tomorrow. We make up one big wagon train and cover each other's goods for the last push to town. Then one whole week of partying like rock stars."

The old-timer spared a moment to smile in anticipation. He then raised his carbine to the brazen military stenciling brushed on the truck behind them.

"Won't have no trouble over it with the people gathering here. But I'd ditch that ride before you ever think about pulling into Freeville. Otherwise you'll find yourself trying to answer beaucoup questions you can't answer—or walk away from."

"How's that?" asked Trennt.

"Detachments from half a dozen countries got claims staked thereabouts. They kind of run the place and make law as they see fit. You show up in a beaner truck loaded with bullet holes and you might just disappear."

"What should we do with it?"

"Plant it. I'd strip off those extra fuel cans. That loose ammo is a premium item, too. Pile the stuff on my truck to sell off like trade goods. Then take that machine a couple of dunes over, peel off those rims, and bury it in the sand."

"What'll you give for the salvage?" Trennt asked, opening the door to a bargain.

The old-timer smirked, half annoyed. "Hell, dude, I'm no trader. I'm a scout."

Trennt looked him hard in the eyes. "That's what I mean."

"Ride to Freeville is on me," he huffed. "No charge."

"No, I mean later."

The old-timer settled back, regarding Trennt head to toe like some odd, fresh-caught specimen. "You do, huh? Where?"

"Wherever I might find the plane we were on."

"Thought you said it crashed."

"We did. In a passenger capsule. The rest flew off on autopilot in that big EM storm. You must've seen some of that, even out here."

The old-timer nodded.

"That I did. But there's also beaucoup square miles of boonies for a plane to crash out here."

"This one is different. If we find it or not, just say 'yes' to helping us try and all that gear is yours. Here and now. Don't even need to start off until after Rendezvous."

The old man thumbed his hat back amiably.

"I admire your sense of character, Cap. You've known me for all of ten minutes and make an offer like that? I could lead you off somewhere and cut all your throats in your sleep."

"That you could do tonight," Trennt countered. "Because we're going to spend it here, with you."

The old-timer shouldered his carbine and after a final study of Trennt, motioned up the sand ramp. Like so many other alliances forged from necessity, the rugged "picker" fraternity had become a clannish bunch, protective of their own. And a key to their acceptance of an outsider was to arm that person with their nickname.

In a picker camp you might ask around for someone by name and never find him. But set with his "handle," you were on the inside track. And in that regard, a very powerful connection was about to be made.

"We'll ditch your rover later," said the old man,

leading the way. "Come on, I got some ration chow making topside in a solar cooker. And that's what they call me, 'Top.'"

"This old girl was from China," he continued without breaking pace. "Loaded with TV sets. All rotted now. So a little stink comes up from below deck after dark. But once the sun goes down and that desert night sets in, all her iron stays warm as an electric blanket."

Trucks began appearing on the horizon around noon of the next day, drawing in from the southwest and east. In groups of two vehicles, or five, or eight, their riders were every bit as shabby and trail-worn as their scarred and dented machines. But to a person, all shared the same infectious happy mood—spirited and ready to spend the next seven days on some heavy-duty R and R.

They were nearly fifty trucks long by the time they made the primary trade route. Once a main coastal artery, it was now a nameless run of packed clay, scabby blacktop, and buckled concrete. Following its track north, the formidable column made the stark coastal ledge a day later.

Centuries from now there'd be no mistaking what had happened here. Originating northeast of Los Angeles and fifty miles beneath the Palmdale Bulge, the Quake had snapped off a full third of the land mass clean as peanut brittle and replaced it with a sprawling new sea.

No trace remained of the hundred or so miles of ground swallowed up due west, nothing of the millions lost that day in May, 2036. Just the haunting call of wheeling gulls, echoing mournfully above the silver-flecked cobalt depths.

Yet, even a place of such immeasurable tragedy

was given a notion of grandeur. For Nature held no remorse, only change. And in her ruin, she was already remolding, smoothing the stark and sculpting the dull. Waves and wind were hard at work, chiseling beautiful arches and stacks, carving majestic blowholes and offshore tables.

Three more days up the coast and Freeville came into view. The small community left itself open for inspection from a distance. What you saw was what she was: a sun-washed, clapboard-and-tented bay town, crowned in a benign halo of rare diesel exhaust and blue cook smoke. Her pearls were the polished chrome blossoms of innumerable solar collectors. Her cologne, the scent of hot engines, sweated canvas, and simmering stews.

Further beyond stretched a hazy sapphire backdrop belonging to the treacherous Wilds. A foreboding mix of forest and desert, it was home to untamed tribesmen and crazies.

Here though, everything was under a fierce guardianship of the Russian foreign legion. Even now their blatant claim to the area rested in a giant atomic cargo submarine. Surfaced and anchored just offshore, it rode the gentle swells like a contented metallic whale. As the convoy neared, a ten-man hovercraft left the dock for her, boiling a grand rainbowed spray in their wake.

The picker campsite was a quarter mile from town, a measured distance prescribed by the Soviet landlords and one meant to keep everything contained and observable. Already a couple hundred trucks preceded them. But there was still room enough for hundreds more.

Even under the fierce afternoon sun, Freeville reeked of life and vigor. All about could be heard welcoming shouts and the flow of good-natured obscenities. One of those gazing hopefully at that glorious site was a grizzled soul called "Fibs."

His was a nickname earned for being the wildest storyteller in the corps of pickers. A handle and knack that kept him in drinks and smokes during the infectious mood of Rendezvous and supplied him with modest travel donations when he started back for his solitary months in the field.

Maybe forty years old, Fibs looked eighty. Personal neglect and abuse had left him battered and toothless; a man hardly taken seriously, except of course, by himself. In his early days, Fibs'd made some respectable finds. But a robbery and near-fatal beating changed that. Reduced him to a brain damaged kind of hobo existence that he somehow managed on alone.

Unable to afford any transport of his own, Fibs hiked everywhere. Bedroll, canteen, and walking stick made him a recognizable and sympathetic Johnny Appleseed kind of figure. And though having him around for any length of time rapidly wore thin, he was considered something of a lucky piece among veteran pickers, one meant to be touched and quickly passed on.

Fibs had developed a routine of culling the same exhausted treasure grounds time and again for overlooked bits of value. His efforts rarely gained him more than a handful of profit. But his needs were simple, so he survived.

Outwardly, this time was no better. He had a few ounces of electronic silver gathered over months of solitary campfires. Some curiosity pieces that might interest jewelry smiths. But one thing Fibs had found he knew was his best treasure ever . . . and it was where no one could steal it away—overhead.

Later, Fibs would begin his ritual of wandering from tavern to tavern, begging drinks in exchange for his

usual blend of wild tales. Now though, the charitable
meal offered paupers by the Freeville Christian Organization beckoned. So he took a place in its serving line,
just ahead of two other men and a young woman.

Top had deposited Trennt, Baker, and Geri at the
same aid station. Their reward for enduring a consid-
erable wait would be chipped bowls full of a perpetu-
ally simmering, nondenominational stew: cabbage
hunks, runted spuds, and bitter carrots mixed with
tough cubes of jerked meat, beans, and random corn
kernels. Afterward, an offer of tattered blankets and
a place out of the weather would be extended, with
a few pages of scripture, for those who cared to spend
the night.

"If anybody is looking for you, sooner or later they'll
know to stop here," said Top, depositing his pack of
grateful strays.

"I'll see what I can hock your goods for. If you need
me, come out to the truck park. Otherwise, hang loose."

"Peace," he said, flashing an odd, split-finger hand
sign and was gone.

The old Marine's words proved cruelly prophetic.
For the trio hadn't even finished their meals, when Geri
stiffened and came electrically erect at her place across
from Trennt. He followed her gaze, astonished as well.
For there stood Royce Corealis himself, appraising
them from across the broad dining tent.

CHAPTER 15

Corealis left the safety net of his security people to approach the trio alone. His eyes flared like glowing embers as they touched on each grimy face, then he leaned forward on the table between Trennt and Baker. He spoke in a much restrained, though cutting whisper.

"All right, gentlemen. What the hell happened?"

In shabby contrast to the fresh-scrubbed face hovering over him, Trennt sat with travel grit caked deep in the pores and creases of his own skin. He still wore the clothes he'd put on weeks before and sported clownlike dollops of first-aid cream on his collection of heat blisters and peeling skin. But he was unrattled.

As in their first meeting, Trennt again matched stares with the man. He glanced up from his nearly finished stew, put his spoon aside and settled back to answer for all.

"Just about everything you could imagine," he began. "The only thing that went as planned was the ride out there. We found the research team dead and

170

the lab ruined. Your Professor Keener was poisoned and barely alive. To make a long story short, our plane got loaded down with storm ice and dumped us dead center in three hundred miles of desert."

"Keep your voice down," Corealis ordered.

"Bullshit!" Trennt snapped back. "After what I've been through I don't care who hears me!"

Nearby heads turned at the outburst. That included a young Russian corporal monitoring sidewalk traffic through the open street-side doors. Baker and the corporal touched gazes through the distance and Baker came up from his chair to intervene.

"Why don't we all go get a little air out back, fellahs?"

But outside, the atmosphere was no more hospitable.

"No researchers. No catalyst. No data, no airplane," itemized the director. "I presume you at least carried out the proper destruction of the research station."

"We torched it."

"Torched? As in fire? Did you not have a device specifically designed for more than just that?"

"It wouldn't arm."

Corealis swung a demeaning glance between his two agents. "Unbelievably sloppy and totally unacceptable work from people I understood were the best at their trade."

Trennt was unrepentant. "Believe whatever you want. But I'd say we did damn well, under the circumstances. Survived a storm and plane crash. Made it across a few hundred miles of desert by sheer luck. Almost died from exposure and almost got killed by foreign legion troops. But we're here to tell of it."

Corealis considered the point. "All right. I do appreciate your survival skills. That's what qualified you for this work in the first place. Discounting all the sloppiness, your primary task was to retrieve chemical samples developed at the site. I'll write off everything else if you'll just turn them over."

Trennt sighed. "I didn't get them off the plane in time."

The director leaned closer. "Excuse me?"

"They were with us until the very last moment before bailout," defended Trennt. "Then something happened and the ejection charges blew early. I fell one way and they went the other."

"Lost?"

"Back onboard the jet. We did save some research papers and computer cubes that might have value."

Corealis snorted. "Something, at least. Well, let's have them."

Trennt turned back for the dining hall. But before he even stepped inside he could see Geri's empty chair. The satchel of documents was gone with her.

"I'll get them back," he declared. "But as far as I'm concerned, the real issue here is an unselfish pilot who stayed aboard to try and get that crippled wreck down in one piece. He's alone out there somewhere right now. Maybe hurt bad. And for his sake only, I say if that plane can be found, we're still the ones to do it."

Corealis slowly shook his head.

"Spare me the inappropriate chivalry. Your failed task will be assigned to more capable persons. As of this moment, you are terminated from any further employment with our organization.

"Against my better judgment, I will allow you a degree of compensation for your inept work. You can choose between a ride back to the streets of Chicago, or a measure of undeserved severance pay in the trade dollars of this place."

The director waved an ominous finger in Trennt's face.

"But do not get any ideas of intervening in this

matter—for humanitarian reasons, or otherwise. Because if either of you are seen interfering, in any manner, you will be shot out of hand. Now, which payment is it to be?"

Trennt hissed and turned away. "You know what you can do with either."

Corealis nodded curtly to his aide.

"John, pay them here."

The aide nervously stepped out from between the guards. He offered a fold of bills that neither Trennt nor Baker reached for. After trembling with the outstretched money a few long seconds, he dropped it at their feet and made off with the departing entourage.

Baker scooped up the coarse paper only after they were out of sight. Regarding the clutch of scrip dollars, he looked glumly to his partner.

"Closest I ever been to grabbin' the brass ring."

Trennt thrust an arm after Corealis.

"I told you not to join this circus from the start! Now he walks off and tosses out thirty pieces of silver like we're a couple rookie street walkers. If you want more of that treatment, then go, chase him!"

The shooter blanched. Uncharacteristic distress clouded his face. In one of the rare little-brother moments he allowed for no one else in the entire world, Baker's words flowed in an uncommon, wounded tone.

"Ain't no call to talk to me that way, Jimbo. No call! Business is business. That's all. You know I'd take a bullet 'fore I'd ever crawl to anyone. You know that!"

Both men went silent. Baker made another doleful examination of the money he clutched, then looked about the new town.

"Well," he said rhetorically, "If 'n the old goat don't up and run off with our trade goods, I s'pose I kin make a new start herebouts."

Trennt sighed. Disgusted with himself about the whole chain of events, he plopped a fist on Baker's drooped shoulder in something of an apology. When he spoke again his words were a vow, his tone a threat.

"I don't care who Corealis is. Or what he says. I don't plan to just let myself be washed out of this thing. If there's any way at all, we'll find his plane. Just to shove that damn stuff down his throat."

Baker straightened to a dose of regained pride.

"Good enough, Pard," he declared. "But how do we start?"

Trennt swiped at his exhausted eyes. "Something that control voice said in the cockpit's been eating at me."

Baker looked over optimistically. "How's that?"

"It called out four course corrections just before the storm hit us. The third was for 250 degrees. But the very last was for 40 degrees relative. Because of the pole shift, all compasses are celestial-mathematic. With no magnetic variation, that would make an actual heading of 290 degrees, or somewhere northwest and right this way."

Baker desperately wanted to side with his friend's logic. But he saw too much daylight.

"Jimbo," he reminded, "we were all over the sky in that wind. And 'member, when that engine cut loose, we got turned clear back the way we came."

"Yeah, I know. But part of what made Kosinski decide to drop the passpod came from something automatic taking away control of the plane. He said it felt like a bit of stray logic was fighting him to turn back and climb."

Baker shrugged. "That still leaves a lotta ground to cover. How we gonna know for sure?"

Trennt nodded toward the distant truck park.

"First thing tomorrow, we find Top."

✧   ✧   ✧

It was nearing sundown. The lull between daytime trade and nighttime hellraising was almost over. Soon a din would spill from the town's saloons capable of muffling gunshots. But now it was still placid enough to hear the rising night breeze tug at loose shingles of this particular gaming tavern—and magnify a familiar shuffle of slowing feet just outside its door.

The bartender recognized the familiar sound and stink, and mumbled under his breath, "Oh shit."

From his place at a distant table, Top waited to play some poker. But for now he sat alone. With a portion of his wagon master's fee, he'd bought himself a hot bath and shave, clean clothes and a room. Absently shuffling a deck of cards, he watched the familiar, ragged picker tentatively scout the sparse gathering of early patrons.

The picker's weather-beaten mug lit to the vacant grin of a friendly old dog as he dared step inside.

"Hiya, bro," he said through a slur of missing teeth and advanced state of inebriation.

The barman hissed and shook his head.

"When I'd heard you'd made it back, I figured sooner or later you'd work your way over here."

The picker shrugged. "Youse know me, bro. I keeps plugging."

"So, what can I do for you, Fibs?"

"Well, sell me a drink, ah course."

"Sure thing. Just show me some credits."

The old bum shuffled his filthy boots, studying them for a time. "Truth is, I'm a little short."

"Already? Or didn't you have anything to begin with?"

"Hey," objected the bum, "I had me some silver."

"But you drank it up."

At that, Fibs might have blushed. Yet under his filthy skin, who could tell? He simply stood quiet.

"Yeah," complained the barkeep. "Like always. Just once, I'd like to see you start at this end of town while you still had some money."

The old beggar shuffled again. Sweeping his eyes among the few other patrons, he saw no invitations and finally conceded defeat.

"No hard feelings," offered the barkeep to his back. "Maybe later some of the guys'll start feeling generous."

Fibs paused and turned. His voice livened.

"Hey, wait. I do got somethin' to trade. Well, not all of it. But a little piece."

The barman conceded. "Dammit, Fibs! Okay! One shot, that's all! Then you gotta move on, understand?"

The picker nodded vigorously and hopped aboard an ancient bar stool.

"Uh-huh. Oh yeah, sure."

Measuring out the drink, the barman pushed it over, careful to stay beyond his patron's noxious bouquet. He watched Fibs sip the sour mash graciously. Then, bobbing his head, wanted to get the usual aftermath over quickly.

"So okay, Fibs. What is it this time? You see space aliens out there again? Ghosts in some graveyard? Maybe L.A. rising up from the sea?"

Fibs settled back in a regal motion, which instantly transformed his threadbare stool into a throne. From it he grinned in kingly amusement at the barkeep's pitiful lack of insight.

"Heck no, bro. None of that junk. You could never guess."

He paused to regard the glass.

"But, gimme another of these and I just might share a little something special with you."

Like what?"

"Well, like an airplane, flying around with a big hole in its belly."

"Uh-huh."

"Not only that, this one can stop, go to the side, and back up, even."

"Yeah."

"I tell you!" The bum defended, thumping his chest. "I seen it, myself."

"Oh, well, that makes it true for sure."

A couple of nearby customers chuckled pathetically, bringing on a flash of rare anger in the usually docile bum.

"I did!" he charged aloud. "I seen it; more'n once!"

"Right, Fibs. You've seen lots of things."

Fibs frowned in heavy concentration, working to draw some reasonable analogy. He glanced about and fidgeted, as if he were betraying some great trust.

"Just about sunup, it'd come round every few days and do the same thing every time. Like, like it was lookin' to set down an' nest. Only, only, it'd act like it changed its mind and come back next time, a little farther on down and do the same thing again, just maybe a tiny bit lower in the sky."

"Right. And where's all this been happening?"

Fibs leaned across his drink with a tone of grave confidentiality.

"North and west, all the time. North and west. Seen it do the same thing for the last two solid weeks comin' here."

"And that's where you've been? Northwest? When everyone knows the treasure fields are all south and east?"

The barkeep leaned back expectantly.

"Next thing you'll say is you were in the Wilds and met up with a nice bunch of crazies, who made you their king. And I'd believe that first. You probably didn't have any trade goods at all when you came to town this time, did you?"

The barkeep swept a dismissing thumb toward the door.

"On your way, Fibs. You suckered me for the last time."

His welcome used up, the derelict's throne turned back into a commoner's stool. But from deeper inside the saloon a charitable hand intervened.

"Go ahead, dude. He's worked hard. Give him one, on me."

The barkeep looked over in admonition.

"Top, you know this guy. Start now and you'll not get rid of him. And neither will I."

Top shrugged off his generosity. Buying a half pint of bootleg whisky, he led Fibs out the door and to a sidewalk bench. In a few minutes he sat as the private audience to an impossible tale of a beat up airplane that repeated its appearance and maneuvers every few mornings.

CHAPTER 16

Rendezvous. Town streets swelled with tradesmen, rough necks, and gunslingers. Like any other frontier town through the ages, vendors and outfitters hawked trinkets and hard goods from quick-set sidewalk stalls. Further down, kitchens, repair shops, and brothels offered their own brand of service from more stationary locales.

In between hovered the league of returned pickers. Gunny sacks of excavated electronic booty and bric-a-brac hoisted securely atop their shoulders, they milled about in vast herds, considering which traders might give the best deal.

This place called Freeville was the post-quake metropolis of the modern West Coast, the hub of major commerce, which all other new-shore towns longed to be.

Christened for the notion of openness it wished to portray, the Ville drew its life blood from an economic system regulated by its warrior landlords. Since the Soviets were its primary benefactors, it had surrendered its identity to one assumed more pleasing to them. Cooking and dress hinted at a Slavic flair and East European phrases found growing acceptance in the local tongue.

The effort, however, did little to appease Major Josef Dobruja, one of the transplanted Soviet officers living here. This morning he crossed the crowded street on his usual prenoon policing round. A dour tech sergeant walked at his side.

Josef raked powerful, tanned fingers through his still-damp hair and reset his limp duty cap. A freshwater shower aboard the cargo sub was one of few real luxuries offered military personnel in this pitiable locale. Yet, just the short walk here from the dock had made both men nearly as sweaty as the pathetic vagabonds pressing about them.

Dobruja was a fighting man grown long bored with this caretaker's assignment. He'd come across twenty-two months earlier from Saint Petersburg. There, an admiral-uncle had kept him sequestered as a tactics instructor, safely stashed away from the filthy North American Flu epidemic.

But once the disease was stemmed, Josef wanted out. He volunteered for the most exotic post he could manage and accordingly found himself on the California frontier.

The post-quake shore states had taken on a separatist mentality that encouraged foreign legion occupation. Inhabitants willingly traded outpost space for the supplies that their own country could not afford to give—not that any occupying force had much to spare, either. But the combined benefit reaped from billeted East European, South American, and limited Asian militaries actually allowed a better standard of living here than was granted most of the States' urban countrymen.

Josef's nation was the only one determined enough to invest seriously, and he resented the high price imposed on those left back home for whatever obscure futures might exist here. Expensive petrol, hard goods, and food reserves were diverted halfway around the world to bribe frontier officials and fuel the efforts of treasure hunters who combed the old Silicon Valley ruins for high-tech odds and ends.

A few scientific finds had been noteworthy. The economic mainstay, however, was mostly a trade cycle of rendered electronic gold, silver, and platinum; for which Mother Russia traded dearly—and witness to it all was the impatient major.

Dobruja had originally been promised command of an expeditionary battalion. He was to be given free rein in the extermination of those northern crazy bands and convict tribes liberated from asylums and prisons when the Great Quake hit. Such a policing action had been planned to endear the peasant population to a growing Soviet presence. And the combat experience was certain to assure Josef a prominent role in establishing a string of Soviet forts across the new West Coast.

But there was always one bureaucratic delay or another preventing Josef from starting the crusade and establishing his name. Some in government even questioned his enthusiasm and methods. It made him angry and long for a return of the old Communist hardliners—people who would understand and approve, not reprimand his efforts like the indecisive weaklings now in power back home.

The wait had frustrated Josef enough to dare some unauthorized search and destroy missions into the northern Wilds and eastern nonpartisan sectors. Most were paltry victories over bands of wretched woodland crazies, but one recent patrol had proved worthwhile.

He chuckled grimly. How pathetically easy; textbook to a fault. A classic X-shaped ambush of five South American search trucks drawn to a brief and questionable S.O.S. call. Dobruja had considered a more in-depth search of the call, afterward, himself. But the signals were far distant and had long faded. So back here, to the drudgery it was.

The major shouldered his way through another gaggle of American rubes. Walking along, he sighed. Military Governor Dobruja. The title carried such a nice ring. But the wheels of the gods moved so pitifully slowly. He'd long realized that his only hope in expediting his career would be the orchestration of some grand maneuver. But what of any consequence might ever happen in this dung heap?

Josef's instincts were suddenly roused by an unformed flash of alarm. His hunter's eyes darted about the vagabond commoners and zeroed in on two approaching men. They too shared the notion, for they eyed him in return. The taller one offered a deferential nod as they passed. But the other stayed coolly neutral, a hawk's raw keenness in his face. Josef made a mental note of the pair.

Further down the crowded street Baker spied Geri. Standing on an opposite corner, she quietly watched them.

"Well, lookie there."

Trennt did look. But he kept his pace, making no effort to communicate with her. In moments, though, it was she who came jogging up behind them.

"I can imagine what went on last night," she spoke with a hint of respect to their backs.

"Too bad you weren't there to share it," answered Trennt over a shoulder. "I wouldn't say they're real happy with you, either."

Coming alongside, she offered a dismissive shrug.

"That doesn't matter. What does is your decision on me going along."

Trennt stopped. "Where?"

"To find what's lost," she replied.

"What makes you think we'd look?"

Her green eyes slashed between the pair.

"Because nobody sends your kind packing. And because I've got as much right to be part of a search party as either of you."

"How do you figure?"

"Squatter's rights," she declared. "I spent almost two years with some decent caring people, ones who deserve more from their labors than a cheap race to their findings, while lying forgotten, burned to ash and shredded."

Trennt frowned.

"Where's the satchel of papers?"

"I have it. Say 'yes' and you can have them back."

"What we've been through might be nothing compared to what's ahead."

"I'd carry my share."

Trennt hissed cruelly. "How? On your back?"

A hand swept toward his face, which he caught and twisted aside.

"Those papers!" he demanded.

Her green eyes met his with an equal glow of contempt.

"Break both my arms if you want, tough guy. Either I go along or you'll never see them."

Trennt held his grip for seconds more, but she matched his stare, unafraid and every bit as unyielding. He finally flung her hand away.

"I go along?"

No answer.

"I go—or no papers."

"Yes, dammit," he growled. Without saying more he walked off.

Behind, Baker flashed Geri a wink.

"Welcome aboard, Sweet Thang."

The old man was making some under hood adjustments to his truck as they approached. He greeted them in the old-fashioned slang he seemed to enjoy.

"What's shakin', dudes?"

Trennt nodded. "You?"

"No complaints."

The old man set down his wrench, wiped his hands, and motioned the trio aside. He dipped a couple of fingers into his shirt pocket. Out came a hefty clump of folded scrip money, which he handed over.

"From your goods."

Trennt took the cash and peeled off a handling fee to stuff back in the old-timer's pocket. Top accepted it with a nod of thanks. Before he spoke again, he glanced about, then shook his head in disbelief.

"I got something else, too. A wild-ass story, that's so far-freakin' out it just might be true. If you'd want to waste your time listening, I can tell it."

"Top," confided Trennt, "we've got nothing but time."

Leaning back against his truck, the old Marine relayed his previous night's encounter. When his audience didn't laugh, he advanced a proposal.

"From what Fibs said, this plane is working its way to the northwest, just about what you figured should be its direction of travel. Don't know where it goes to or comes from. But if it keeps on flying and we could spot it every couple of days, simple dead reckoning should get us close enough on its trail for shits and giggles—providing it doesn't keep on and wind up out in the drink."

Baker was skeptical. "Jimbo, you don't really think . . ."

Trennt puffed his lips. "It does match what Kosinski told me about it."

He offered back the remaining fold of trade money.

"You up to leading the way?"

Top waved it off.

"Let's take a ride out first and see if Fibs' story is real. I'm curious enough to scope that out for free. If we boogie all night, we could make a good vantage point by dawn tomorrow. We'll talk trip and pay later. In the meantime, burn some of those Commie bucks and get yourselves a hot shower and change of clothes. They'll be the last you'll have for a while and you cats need 'em. Be back here and ready to book at sundown."

The group disbanded. Nothing in their brief exchange appeared any more noteworthy than would any other discussion among pickers over the next few days. But even so, their talk had been specifically observed and noted by a familiar young Russian corporal casually trailing behind.

Top fired up his truck at dusk. Slipping on a priceless set of visual-display-monitor glasses, the old-timer deftly adjusted their 3D and latent heat imaging sensors. Resetting the truck's compass from solar to celestial, he spoke over a shoulder.

"I know the terrain. I'll handle the drive. We'll still be way inside the safe zone. So you dudes zee-out if you can manage."

From his place in back, Baker leaned forward between Top and Geri, riding shotgun up front.

"Say Sweet Thang," he offered in his best Okie twang, "if y'all get chilly up 'ere jus' 'member you kin share my blanket any ole time."

The woman smiled grimly. "I'll be fine, thanks."

Top intervened, glancing over a shoulder with an exaggerated drawl of his own. "Where'd you-all buy that accent, Tex?"

"I'm not from Texas," Baker declared. "I'm from Oklahoma."

The old-timer winced. "Hmm. Guess we all got our problems in life."

Top and Geri shared a smile as he shifted the truck into gear.

The night's travel passed uneventfully. The truck's confident motion and monotonous engine drone lulled its passengers into a bouncing, fitful doze. At first light, Top hung a broad, sweeping turn. He aimed them toward the approaching dawn.

"Up and at 'em troops! This is the place."

Trennt sleepily searched the sky, rubbing his stiff neck.

"Any idea when?"

"According to Fibs, any time now."

The wait began. A fingernail paring of spent moon and cold dot of the morning star gave the only sky-ward reference points. The sooty horizon slowly yielded to an indigo bruise. Healing lines of pink and gold invaded and bloomed. Minutes ground on. The first rays of a new sun pried brutally between earth and sky.

Then came a presence—no sight or sound, but an approaching sensation that brought Baker's field glasses up.

"There!" He pointed, coming to his feet. "Just below Venus!"

Heads raised to look at a faint dot in the distant sky. A growing sound confirmed it: the flat, low whistle and steady blowtorch "whoosh" of a jet plane.

The dot lengthened, then sprouted wings and a swept tail. It entered their view battered and streaked

with grime. Its once brilliant white airframe had gone
to a shocking gray. A moderate list to its damage side
was obvious, as was the broad dark square of a jetti-
soned panel on its hollow belly.

At its nearest point, the craft passed just a thousand
feet overhead. Free as a child's lost balloon, it glided
high and truant, answering to no one but itself.

Then it slowed and began the odd hovering maneuvers as Fibs had described. Wings went to a raised
angle of attack and the craft made a series of difficult
one engine lateral moves, as if indeed pondering a place
to settle. But something in its guidance system wouldn't
allow a landing and it awkwardly returned to normal
flight. Shedding its wings, it receded to the same tiny
dot.

"Hot damn!" proclaimed Baker, breaking the group
trance. "I'd never've believed it! But it's gotta be her,
Jimbo! Gotta be! How long yah reckon she's been up
there?"

"Three weeks, maybe."

"Shoot, all that time without landin'. You don't think
the pilot's still onboard?"

Trennt slowly shook his head, eyes yet chasing after
the departed craft.

Behind the steering wheel Top chuckled, orienting
a map.

"Freaky as hell," he said in wonder. "But for once
old Fibs was telling the full truth."

He turned for Trennt in the back seat.

"You make the call on chasing her, Cap. But if we
go and there's anything of value aboard, I say Fibs
deserves some cut of the action for even getting us this
far."

Trennt nodded. "Agreed."

The old man lingered.

"Something else. The travel alone will be enough

of a ball-buster. But know this, they don't call them, the 'Wilds' for nothing. And I'd guess we might be going deep inside before we're done.

"Bunch of strange stuff boiled up that way since the Quake: hot springs, quicksand, and mud flats that're straight poison from all the chemical dumps that got opened up and mixed in. Just the fumes'll blister your skin a mile off.

"Even worse are the tribes—crazies and killers. Hundreds, thousands, were all freed when the jail and asylum walls caved in, and just the worst are left to deal with these days."

His eyes skewed toward Geri. "Only prisoners they take are better off dead."

Baker scoffed, leaning over the front seat. "Don'cha worry none, Sweet Thang, I'll protect yah."

Top answered without looking over.

"I've been out there before, Slick. Going is the easy part. It's getting back that's always hardest. What I need even less is bad karma on my case from somebody a little too anxious."

He looked to Trennt, speaking flatly.

"For anybody else, I wouldn't go. But I think you're a righteous dude, Cap. So for you, yes."

"Is there money enough?" asked Trennt.

"I'd say so. Enough volunteer farm crops grow wild to keep us from starving. Those scrip bucks should cover the hard goods we'll need. We'll divvy up a shopping list, so no one person draws heat from the man. Just hang loose and be cool if someone shows interest in what you're buying."

"Any chance that guy Fibs might shed more light on the matter?"

Top frowned. "With him you never know. I can try."

Reaching for the truck's ignition, the old man offered a last warning.

"Understand, I won't guarantee anything. Not even getting out empty-handed. Everybody be sure this is what you want."

"It is," declared Trennt, speaking for the group.

"Okay, then. Let's rock."

CHAPTER 17

Royce Corealis settled back comfortably in his meager hotel suite, watching his evening caller depart. He now glowed with success on all counts. His hasty goodwill trip west was working out far better than he'd ever hoped. His medicine show approach of simply drumming up folks on street corner stops about Freeville provided him with an audience far from the hostile lot he'd anticipated.

To the contrary, they gathered eagerly to hear his news of the struggles endured back east. They seemed vexed by their former president's untimely passing and sympathetic toward stories of what their less fortunate city-bound cousins contended with. Royce's vague proposal of a future election stirred their craving for a return to normalcy and he enjoyed free movement through the crowds, offering optimism and hope.

He now smiled. Snake oil and democracy, one and the same.

The local Red military contingent was understandably reserved at his presence. But they did not hamper his entourage and stayed as pleasantly tolerant as their stiff-necked military courtesy would allow. Even this, Royce felt, could be put to eventual use.

Corealis' true purpose was also netting results. Agency scout teams had easily infiltrated the Rendezvous crowds and were probing for information on the lost plane. Better yet, he was now armed with confirmation that his previous agents had indeed disregarded his warning and were aggressively pursuing leads of their own. Things couldn't be working out better.

The director watched his aide pouring cups of Russian coffee.

"It's rewarding to know that values such as integrity and propriety are still very much the fabric of dedicated people like our freelancers. I'm certain our task shall be made much easier by their vengeful efforts."

The director's grin tightened as he took a cup.

"We'll continue following the northern coastline on our goodwill junket and let our crusaders proceed. But maybe at an appropriate moment, we should also play the role of good neighbor and leak word of them as possibly dangerous insurrectionists to the local authorities. A little extra driving force, if you understand my meaning."

Aboard the anchored cargo sub, Major Dobruja was listening to a status report of his own.

"Corporal Lansky saw this himself? The very same two men we passed in the street yesterday also spoke to this bunch of visiting dignitaries?"

The sergeant nodded. "Yes, sir."

"He's absolutely certain?"

"He has no doubt. He was on sidewalk duty when the American dignitaries went past on a tour of the town. They were shaking hands with everyone like politicians do. But at the soup kitchen they singled out the pair as though they knew them.

"The corporal couldn't hear what was said. But shortly tempers rose between Corealis and the taller of the pickers. The group went outside to finish. By the time Lansky managed to work his way around, they'd split up.

"There's been no further contact between the two groups, but Lansky made a point of trailing the pickers on his own for a time yesterday, and they have since hooked up with a woman and an old man. They drove off together last night and were seen again today. This time they split up and spent the entire afternoon bartering for travel goods and fuel enough to go a long distance."

The major pondered the matter. It did strike him exceedingly odd that random pickers would be singled out for such contact by the politicians. And the two men in question did raise his own suspicions, just by their presence.

But otherwise, their actions spoke of nothing different than any other pickers would ultimately wind up doing. Even provisioning so early into Rendezvous usually meant something as minor as simply getting a jump on the competition for some newly rumored treasure field.

Still, Dobruja sensed more. And it bothered him.

His sergeant voiced the obvious. "Extremists?"

"Maybe," Josef answered wryly. "We are, after all, not loved by everyone. Might at least make our own lives more interesting, to deal with some actual radicals. Public trial and execution, maybe. But we've been reminded time and again, by superiors back home, to watch our manners."

Dobruja's thoughts returned to the recent arrival of

the American diplomats. He regarded them with typical disdain.

"Our new guests appear to be just more stuffed shirts on a phony goodwill tour, gravely surveying damage they can't possibly correct and making promises of public aid not worth the breath to say them. Still, what could be the connection between two such groups?"

"This Corealis does have a way about him," remarked the sergeant. "Seems to be a good talker. People listen."

"Like all good politicians," assured Dobruja. "Hoping only to handpick a replacement favorable to himself for their empty throne back in Washington, or wherever their self-serving capital is these days. I've seen it happen over and again in their hypocritical two-party system."

The major dismissed the dignitaries. "Well, let them pretend and talk; pass out party favors and shake hands. In a few more days their band will move on, and take their empty promises with them. In the meantime, we're reminded by further orders to offer courtesy, hospitality, and not hamper their movement in any way. This is, after all, still their country."

In a few moments the major's eyes narrowed.

"It might be prudent to continue having someone watch our other group, though. They do seem to be quite the industrious bunch."

"Yes, sir."

Dobruja came to one last point.

"The camp fool Lansky reported as seen talking with the old man. Bring him around for questioning."

"Anything else, sir?"

"Have a squad of our infantry on standby. If our guests do leave again, we may trail after for a few days to see exactly what they have in mind."

Dobruja looked to the sergeant, a feisty jut to his square jaw.

"Regardless, any excuse would be another nice break from more of this old occupation drudgery. Stretch our legs out on patrol. And so soon after our latest victory, eh, Sergeant?"

"Yes, sir!"

Travel commenced with first light. It was easy at the outset, northwest through the gentle run of roller coaster hills and saddles bunched up by the gathering surface action of the Great Quake. The following days would be spent crossing hard-packed pumice sandbars and waist deep streams of distant mountain runoff. Further on uneven ground and sheared faultland steps started, then it was pure desert.

Supper that first night was canned rations, which the group ate in near silence. Geri was done before the others and walked off, disappearing for a time behind the truck. Next to the small campfire Top had rolled an after-dinner smoke. He lay back, head in hands, to enjoy it. Baker, meanwhile, began what would become a nightly ritual of weapon cleaning.

His tools were set out in a preordained sequence. Auto-shotgun, pistol, and custom-boxed sniper rifle were gently disassembled, wiped and rejoined. Oddly, something in the gunman's precise actions and doting care generated a certain hypnotic peace for Trennt. Those nimble fingers racing over familiar latches and pins lulled him to a near doze as he sat cross-legged, spooning up the last of his own hash.

Something blurred past Trennt's face and plopped heavily in his lap. His trance shattered, he shot up, straight-backed. But gazing down, he found ample compensation for his lost woolgathering. There, yellow firelight flickering off its battered cover, was the missing satchel of research papers.

Above and behind him stood Geri, eyes brimming with her standard flush of disdain.

"You haven't asked lately," she reminded, "but I won't welsh on my part of the deal."

Picking them up, Trennt eagerly gave the clutch of papers their first in-depth review; though shortly, he knew it was pointless. Only a hodgepodge of random sheets had survived: partial chemical and enzyme reports, temperature and pressure charts, plant growth evaluations. Nothing that made any sense to him. Maybe a botanist could wring something of minor value from them. Yet even that seemed doubtful.

Just that odd pad of cheap yellow paper held any continuity among its faded and smeared pages. Yet it was in a queer foreign language, lacking the clutches of numbers, degrees, and equations truly valuable information was certain to have.

Trennt flipped through the sheets. Spanish? No. Italian, maybe. What did it matter? Not much to show for all the effort and risk invested. Frustrated at the poor lot of salvage, Trennt gazed across at Geri, now quietly feeding sticks to the fire.

His voice rang coarse and demanding.

"What the hell happened at that station?"

She raised silent eyes as the others looked over.

"Why did you live and nobody else?"

The amber flames painted the young woman's face with a wash of distress. She answered simply.

"I have no idea. It certainly should've been me who died, instead of all those wonderful people."

"So what happened?" Trennt repeated.

She directed her eyes back toward the flames.

"The project was almost over. And I couldn't stand

the thought of being separated from Martin and the group. So I took things into my own hands."

"How?"

She stared even harder into the blaze.

"I had a key. One I was supposed to use to shut the power systems down only when things were done and we were ready to be evacuated."

Trennt remembered the tiny chrome key and obscure lock at the mangled power station.

"Why would a housekeeper be trusted with something that important?"

Geri looked him frankly in the eye.

"How should I know? I was told it was one of the things I had to do if I wanted to go along. And to get away from where I was I'd've bitten the head off a snake. All I know is that the project was ending. And I didn't want it to. I didn't understand much of the work, but I did know enough to realize that a constant temperature was critical in the greenhouse. I figured if I turned off the power systems, the experiments would be spoiled and things would have to be started over."

Trennt offered the papers. "Have you looked at these?"

She nodded. "Some."

"Understand any of it? Anything make sense to you?"

"No."

Trennt clenched the text, close to simply pitching the whole lot into the flames—but he held back.

"Any more questions?" she asked with scorn.

He replied sullenly, "No."

Geri stood and brushed off her knees. "The fire needs more wood," she said and walked off.

Top nodded his approval as she left.

"Buttercup is one strike troop. She's got sand enough to go the distance on this gig, no sweat."

Baker forgot his weapon cleaning as she walked by. A switch suddenly closed in his own head.

"Hot damn!" he said, offering his personal seal of approval. "I bet she could at that."

Trennt gazed over irritably. "What?"

Baker scooted closer.

"I make her now, Jimbo. Why sure, she was one of the special vintage dollies reserved for visitin' muckety-mucks at the tech village. It was her I 'member seein' on the lap o' some big army brass at one party a year or so back."

Baker rocked delightedly with his insight.

"I knowed she didn't look like no housekeeper. Private squeeze for the brain trust—all makes sense now."

Trennt's silence brought a familiar criticism from the shooter.

"Now there you go again. So high'n'mighty. She's trained as a good-time girl. Ain't nuthin' wrong with that. And I for one say it's exactly the kinda trainin' that shouldn't go to no waste."

He glanced over a shoulder. "Ain't that so, Whiskers?"

When the old man also reserved comment, Baker dismissed him with a sweep of his hand.

"Yeah, you're probably too old to remember."

There, Top did reply.

"What I do remember is what we start crossing in a few days, Slick. Hard ground. Tough going. So save your energy."

The old-timer's word was gospel. Everything remotely tolerable was shortly traded for a place as bleak and barren as the homestretch to hell. They crossed a desolate range of spotty hardpan born from a marriage of thick volcanic ash, killer rains, and merciless sun. In some spots it set hard as the best

concrete; in others, it was like as a powdery blanket
that rose in a talclike fog with the slightest breeze,
lingering forever and smothering every fabric weave
and fold of skin.

Temperature swings were equally savage. Daylight
blasted to triple digits, while nights hovered in the
low teens. Nothing except the lone truck struggled
through the vicious environment. No mammals or
lizards of any kind were seen. Not a solitary bird
crossed the sky.

Each of the group took turns clenching the skillet-
hot steering wheel, fighting its torturous twists and
jolts with muscles long frayed and spent. Swaddled in
layers of loose clothing, they sucked quick breaths of
blast furnace air through bandannas kept moist
with small doses of precious water. Exhaustion and
monotony became dangerous companions. The inevitable consequence awaited not far off.

Dawn of desert-day four approached. The last gray
of night was mingling with the first flecks of daytime
blue as Geri finished up her turn at the wheel. Her
shift had been through deceivingly gentle terrain.
Riding shotgun beside her, even Top, the trip's ram-
rod, had finally succumbed to a doze.

Awake alone, Geri drove on like a marionette. Her
limbs, gone over to the jerking strings of fatigue,
seemed to work outside her control. Cresting yet
another gentle hill, she took a breath and closed her
eyes for just the briefest moment.

A bloodcurdling scream split the crisp early air. A
frenzied, wild-revving engine joined the clamor as the
truck cut hard aside and came up on two wheels.
Equipment and sleeping bodies were flung out into the
darkness.

The truck continued on full circle, flipping a huge
glut of sand over itself like an elephant dusting off.

Then, with a moment's pause, it fell back, bouncing hard before going silent.

Stunned, Baker, Trennt, and Top climbed to their feet. All fired wild-eyed glances at each other.

"Everybody okay?" shouted Trennt gazing into a dark precipice just yards away. "Have we got everybody?"

He bit off a sharp breath and rushed screaming to the truck where Geri still sat, hands welded to the steering wheel and skin as white as the rock dust settling about her.

"What the hell's wrong with you? Trying to kill us all?"

"My fault, Cap," blushed Top, intervening from behind. "I eff-yewed just as much from zee-ing out with a rookie at the wheel. I should've been awake to keep an eye on her."

Trennt raged, jabbing an accusing finger ahead. "It wasn't you driving! It was her!"

Finally able to catch her breath, Geri wheezed through terrified sobs.

"I'm sorry. I was so tired I didn't see it until the last second. I'm sorry."

But Trennt had no room for sympathy.

"Tired!" he repeated in a scalding tone. "That makes it okay? We're all tired! And damn right, you're sorry— a sorry excuse! All the big, tough talk and now all you can do is sit there and cry!"

"Jimbo," interrupted Baker, "she did make one kickass recovery. Kept us from goin' over the edge altogether."

Trennt booted a loose piece of gear.

"With half our equipment gone, we might be better off down there!"

Geri buried her face deep in the backs of her filthy hands and continued to cry. Trennt loomed beside her, then issued a low spiteful hiss. He stomped up the loose tire ruts to the deceptive rise that crashed off into a nearly vertical shaft. In its shadowed bottom was a twisted dark jumble of balled-up gear. The two other men arrived and, side by side, all three pondered the depths like inquisitive little boys over an open manhole.

"Long freakin' way," Top granted.

"Aint no lie," added Baker.

Trennt glanced back to the truck.

"What did we lose?"

"All but one water and two fuel cans," replied Baker. "Rations, most everything else went over."

"Dammit," Trennt groaned. "Any water stops out here, Top?"

The old-timer ran a thumbnail over his chin stubble in thought.

"Farther ahead than we'd want to try. If we turn around now, we could probably make it back okay. But that'd be the end of it as far as you bankrolling this trip."

"Alternatives?"

The old-timer gazed far in a different direction.

"I can't be sure about the water table. But I do remember some sandstone lowlands a few days east."

Trennt moaned. "East."

"Best I can think of, Cap."

Trennt gazed over the edge again.

"Either way, we need to get down there and save what we can. Baker, rig me a harness."

"I should go," offered Geri meekly, from the side.

"You?" he mused. "Ever walk a line—rappel?"

"No. But I still think . . ."

"No, thanks. You've done more than enough already."

The truck was brought right to the cliff edge. Trennt latched himself to the dusty spool of braided winch cable and hooked a flashlight to his belt. Straddling the cable spool with heels planted astride the truck's channel-iron bumper, he turned his ball cap around and readied for his descent.

"Watch yourse'f," cautioned Baker from behind the idling throttle. "Shaft walls look tricky as a porcupine's crotch."

Trennt pulled a bandanna over his nose and set goggles against the abrasive dust waiting below. He flashed a somber thumbs-up, then leaned back, testing his weight on the cable once before pushing off. A quick shove and Trennt was out in the chilly, black space of the dark well.

The shaft walls offered a treacherous checkerboard of brittle, razored spikes that had to be met flat-on with boot soles. A twisted rebound and an ankle might be slashed; a knee split to the bone. Several times Trennt nearly lost his footing to the loose rock face. But he also rediscovered the forgotten exhilaration of a clean descent, the comfort found in the familiar rattle and sway of rapelling gear and his ability to use it.

The winch paid out line with a confident hum. Slack fed easily between Trennt's broad downward hops. Old sensations familiar and reassuring took him away, back to his days at Forts Benning and Bragg, to times before right and wrong seemed so tangled, before there were people in his life who would love and depend on him . . . those he'd love back—and hurt. A dreaminess settled in his motions that Trennt wished would go on forever, straight down and out the other side of the universe.

A clap of thunder broke above. The cable snagged and stopped. For an instant Trennt bounced weightless, a floating bit of milkweed idly waiting for the next breeze to give him direction.

But a second later he was an anvil, screaming in hot from low earth orbit. Far overhead a muffled cry sounded.

"Cover up, Jimbo!"

The cable snapped taut. Trennt recoiled like a yoyo, shooting ten feet straight up, then spinning off into the shaft wall. He barked a shin, barely shielding his face with a forearm before an elbow and cheek impacted, splitting open.

Down came a hail storm of rock chips. A table-sized boulder flashed by like a jet fighter. A volley of bowling-ball hunks whistled passed. Pounds of gritty shrapnel trailed after. A piece nicked his ear. Another slashed between his protecting forearms, lancing his scalp.

The avalanche rumbled past, dragging its thunder toward the crevice floor. In its wake Trennt clutched at himself, swaying gently like a silent pendulum.

Again, he heard Baker's voice.

"Jimbo! You okay, Pard?"

Trennt shook himself off and capped his breath against the heavy settling dust.

"Yeah," he coughed.

"The whole cliff face gave way up here! Damn near took the truck with it. You want back up?"

Trennt squinted up through the last dust stringers separating him from the others, 100-plus feet above. For a moment he had the overwhelmed feeling of a lost little boy. Touching fingers to the split in his scalp, they came away smudged with pink mud.

"No! Finish it!"

He flipped on his flashlight and the cable started again. This time it delivered him flawlessly to the taffy-like darkness of the narrow crevice floor.

The bottom had surrendered most of its definition to the rock slide and powdery blanket. Beneath, their lost gear was reduced to an amorphous, twirled heap.

Trennt pulled at some loose ends, liberating fresh gouts of the heavy talc-like dust. Amazingly, their hard goods appeared mostly salvageable. But dread flashed through him when his boots squished through a mucky low spot. A muddy rainbowed ooze, mixed of water and fuel, glinted like metallic slivers in the dusty light beam. Trennt yanked at the first can.

The morning's salvage sat piled beside the truck. Their insulated medical kit and much of the fuel had survived the drop, but a substantial amount of rations and nearly all of the water was lost. Off to the side, Top meticulously picked rock splinters from Trennt's scalp. He made a dressing that he set the man's fingers to.

"Keep it there while I try to find a butterfly for that cheek."

Geri cautiously approached from the side.

"Feeling any better?"

"Wonderful," Trennt hissed, squinting through a headache.

"I just want to apologize, okay?"

He framed her with hard eyes.

"Apologies won't bring the water back, will they? Or replace the lost food. Now we've got to waste time trying to find more. And hope it doesn't cost our lives."

Top returned with a fresh bandage as the woman wretchedly brushed past. He glanced after her with a touch of compassion, then tilted his patient's head to clean the gash. Clearing his throat tentatively, he began to speak in Geri's defense.

"You know, Cap. It's none of my business, but. . ."

Trennt flinched at the bite of disinfectant.

"Keep it that way, alright?"

The old Marine nodded and dropped the subject.

"What about getting water?" Trennt asked of Baker, studying maps on the truck's hood.

"Terrain agrees with Whiskers. This rock tapers

down to a central low spot eighty or ninety miles east. But there's also some showin' straight north and a lot closer."

Top shook his head vehemently. "No way, dude. I know the place and it's dead water, man."

Baker squinted. "Dead, like stagnant? We got filters."

"Worse. Shaky ground poison; real number ten bummer. Pockets of that stuff run in a straight line all through there. I'll tell you about it when we got time to spare. But for now, just know to stay clear."

Bathed in the morning's first true rays, Trennt pulled the gauze from his scalp. He studied its bloody smudges like a palm reader.

"Ninety miles; might as well be a thousand. And off in the wrong damn direction."

He stood pensive for a moment then flung the gauze aside and stood.

"Pack up. We're going for it."

CHAPTER 18

Josef Dobruja wiped his knuckles clean of blood. Flexing his fingers against their swelling, he read the note sent over by the departing American goodwill tour.

"You say the dignitaries left this?"

Sergeant Karelian stepped from the shadows behind the prisoner. Normally indifferent to interrogations, even he was amazed by the major's brutality toward this simple, witless creature.

"Yes, sir. It was given to a returning street patrol not long ago."

Dobruja frowned inquisitively.

"Interesting that complete strangers should feel the need to report suspicious activities of their own countrymen—especially ones they themselves have been seen in the company of."

"If the said direction of travel is true," reasoned the sergeant, "they could indeed be rendezvousing with a freedom fighter band out in the Wilds. And that is something we should prevent."

Dobruja glanced at the bloodied, quietly sobbing

imbecile before him. With eyes blackened, nose broken, and lips split wide, he still clung to his ridiculous story. Tied to the interrogation chair, Fibs' mouth gleamed with a glossy mix of spittle and blood.

The sergeant dutifully lifted his superior's blood splattered blackjack from the floor. "Finished, sir?"

Josef nodded. "The simpleton irritates me. No one clings to a lie like that. But I can't force myself to believe such a fairy tale, either—an airplane that reappears and never lands."

The major again regarded his swelling hand.

"Mount up our infantry squad and draw a couple week's rations," he ordered. "We'll see for ourselves. And take this one to the cliffs. He won't be missed."

The sergeant opened the door and beckoned some soldiers.

CHAPTER 19

Three days were lost moving due east. Following sporadic tracks, it was obvious that if there was water out here someone else knew of it—and was there ahead of them.

Baker shifted his weapon about and looked disgustedly at the limp white flag slumped between them.

"Don't mind sayin', I don't care for goin' in this way. Might as well have a damn target painted on us."

Trennt swiped a clammy hand against a pant leg and brought it back to the heat-slick steering wheel. His own eyes darted uneasily among the rising canyon walls.

"So you've been reminding me. And like I've been saying, I'm betting the only reason anyone else would be out here is if they were travelers like us. Or settlers. No bandits would have the patience to hang around, hoping to ambush somebody."

"Maybe nobody's out there at all," offered Geri optimistically.

"Oh yeah," replied Top. "Been watching us for the last half hour, at least."

"Why not show themselves?" growled Baker.

"Probably don't know what to make of us," said Trennt. "So don't give them any reason to be hostile."

Their eyes met and Baker looked away, making no promises.

"Two hunnert meters."

"Less," corrected Top.

The voice boomed down from the near hills almost simultaneously.

"Stop where you are, white men!"

A smattering of Bedouin riflemen sprang from easy concealment in the rocks. They wore loose-robed, handmade desert garb, neck-veiling caps, and split-skin goggles. Sun glinted off the worn gun barrels they aimed at the convoy.

A lean spokesman in ancient, wire rimmed mirror shades stepped daringly into the open. Carrying the lone automatic weapon in the group seemed to impart some authority over the others.

His thundering voice added more.

"You have violated the territory of New Africa! Surrender your arms or die where you are!"

Baker kept his eyes low and forward, leaning slightly toward Trennt. An evil I-told-you-so smile cracked his dry lips.

"All I see is that one auto, Jimbo. If we move quick, me dropping him and Whiskers fanning that flank, you kin throw'er in reverse and make some cover."

Trennt's reply was firm.

"No. They've got the water we need."

The group sat still as the black riflemen filtered down to encircle them.

"Throw out your weapons!"

Even behind the mirrored glasses, their leader's expression was intense: rabid and hating. His prominent cheekbones glistened with the raised keloid braids of ceremonial scars as he screamed further, gesturing menacingly with his rifle.

"Out of that truck! Hands on your heads!"

Gun metal speared hot sand in gritty *chugs*; ammunition bandoleers clattering in fallen heaps like dead metallic snakes.

"You people are prisoners of New Africa!" he announced proudly. "Invading our borders has labeled you as enemy spies, who will be tried and sentenced accordingly!"

Trennt raised his voice.

"Our truce flag means we've come here in peace. We mean no harm, but need water for our travel."

The headman cuffed it aside.

"That rag means nothing to us!"

"To bandits, no," countered Trennt, "but to honorable men, it would."

The headman glared at his prisoner, yet he said no more. The group was shoved into a single file, flanked by his soldiers. Top walked first, then Geri, Baker, and Trennt. Their commandeered truck led the way, its horn blowing vigorously in triumph.

The blistering sand shallowed out near a hillside and firmed to sandstone footing. A narrow path led to the deep groove of a slot canyon and a series of naturally concealed passageways set low among the towering overhangs.

Here, hidden from the merciless noonbake, was the heart of a settlement. Women and children clustered in the refreshing cool of the sudden heavy shade. Nursing mothers tended their young. Other women worked at meager meal preparation, slicing cave mushrooms into chunks and carving out the pithy yellow meat of dwarf desert gourds.

The adults gazed at the paraded captives with lackluster eyes. Ancient hatreds had been long dulled by the harsh reality of their spartan existence; but some of the smaller children, having never seen a white person, ran brazenly forward to touch and cuff at them, then scamper aside, giggling.

The distractions kept both prisoners and guards moving at a jerky, irregular pace, one that Baker measured. Catching his subtle glances, Trennt watched the shooter's fingers loosen their weave against his head. The inevitable came seconds later; so quick that even having read his mind, Trennt was hard pressed to react.

Baker's hand darted to his belt. A small-caliber gun flashed up and targeted on the parading headman. Trennt sprang from behind and dove forward. Gun and men pitched ahead. A wild shot echoed in the canyon.

A moment later rough hands were on them, rifle muzzles pinning both men to the ground.

"White devils!" snarled the headman. "We should kill you where you lie!"

Looking into that pool of frothing wide eyes left no doubt. On his own, the man would've done just that, but Trennt saw his livid hovering face respond to some standing order even more powerful than his own flaming emotions. After a tense breath, he withdrew his skewering gun muzzle from Trennt's chest.

"Into the pit!"

The foursome was marched on and shoved headlong into a deep, natural cistern. Thick sand at its bottom was all that cushioned their dark, twenty-foot fall.

Baker immediately heaved himself up and away from the group. He kicked up a hard spray of frustrated sand, storming off to the far side of the dim hole where he scowled disbelieving at Trennt.

"Dammit, Jimbo! Why'd you do that! I could've dropped Scarface, no trouble! Now what chance do we have?"

Trennt, too, shoved himself up.

"A whole lot less than if you'd listened from the start!"

Baker dropped to his rump and slammed back against a different spot of the flat sandstone wall. Folding his arms, he sank into a deep self-indulgent sulk.

Sometime later, Geri's voice rose tentatively.

"Any idea who they are?"

"Does it matter?" challenged Baker.

"Maybe. Remember back before the crash? That black TV evangelist who called for a separation of the races? The reverse apartheid thing?"

Trennt dimly recalled headlines. "That guy they called the new Moses? You think this bunch is them?"

"Or what's left."

"As I remember," Top added, "he had no great love for the white man. And I don't think we've made it any better."

The ledge above them lightened. Torches flickered a greasy orange radiance down on the captives. Two guards and the headman appeared. The guards carried hand-crafted swords and the headman had traded his carbine for a brutally honed machete.

"Who is your leader?" he demanded.

"Me," said Trennt squinting up at the invading fire-light.

A rope ladder plopped in their midst.

"Come up, then. And the rest, behind you. But no one talks, unless told so."

They started up the ladder.

Another series of even deeper passages led to a large cavern divided into several adjoining cubicles. Inside one they glimpsed a group of dour faced tribespeople hovering about a form set prone and motionless. At its feet Trennt saw their own appropriated medical kit spread wide for a detailed examination.

Their particular destination waited further, a sort of meeting chamber, not far beyond. Thick homemade candles illuminated it; years of spent wax cascaded in tall dusty cones on the rock floor. A number of carved sandstone boulders served as chairs. Against one wall was a collection of shields, spears, and ceremonial long bows, painted in brilliant reds, yellows, blacks, and green, tied with graceful clumps of eagle feathers.

Seated before them was an imposing figure. Late middle-aged, yet muscular and trim in the wrap of a loose fitting garment. Oddly, he was unarmed. But his coal black eyes burned with an inquisitive intelligence that said even so, violence was not beyond him. His voice issued bell clear.

"From what our soldiers say, you have invaded our borders—a charge worthy of immediate execution."

"We came under a flag of truce," declared Trennt. "We didn't see any off-limits signs."

"And why should we?" chimed Baker. "New Africa, my ass. Ain't nuthin' but old California desert out there!"

The remark earned him a shove from behind.

"Shut your mouth, dog!"

The seated man raised a calming hand. But the headman circled between him and the captives.

"Leader, why waste time on these pigs? They're no better than others who've tracked us. Execute them and show our people a grand victory over the white devils!"

The pair of guards closed, clenched sword handles showing agreement. A quick damning silence rose about the captives like a sudden crest of rushing flood waters.

"*Machu!* Take the guards and leave us!"

The headman recoiled. "Alone? With the prisoners? White men can't be trusted!"

The chief rose. "In this case, I suspect otherwise. Now go."

Ushering his reluctant guards from the room, the chief passed within easy attack range, offering his back.

"Would you try to overpower me?" he asked. "Take me hostage to free yourselves?"

"No," answered Trennt.

The chief paused beside him. "I believe you."

He went quiet for a time. When he spoke again, his voice held an abrupt change of tone, almost cordial.

"Who are you people?"

"My name's Trennt. We're here looking for water to continue on our trip northwest."

"For what purpose?"

"To find a lost plane."

"Lost where?"

"In the Wilds."

"Your style of weapons say you're prepared to kill."

"Not here. We came in broad daylight with holstered guns."

The chief's gaze shifted to Baker.

"The slim one thought otherwise."

Trennt sighed. "He's not always quick to obey."

His point seemed to touch home. The chief appraised Baker and nodded.

"Hotheads, yes. I know the problem myself."

His admission opened a door to neutral ground. Suddenly a different man stood before Trennt, a man much burdened.

"I appreciate your honesty. Permit me to return something of the same. The sad little band you've seen here is the lone remnant of a grand idea—an exodus from the cities that was to build a free-standing state of honor and respect for the black man."

"You're Freeman Whitney," declared Geri bravely. The chief allowed himself a bittersweet smile.

"Yours truly, miss," he replied kindly. "Thank you for the recognition."

A bit of tarnished pride lit Whitney's face as he looked at the torch-blackened rock ceiling. His eyes misted over, remembering a day from long ago.

"It certainly started out grand enough. Me, the TV preacher, leading my people from the yoke of their urban self-oppression, to the misguided vision of my own dreams.

"What a glorious day it was. Thousands of the faithful gathered behind me for an unknown spot of desert where we'd settle and build our own Jerusalem. Tired pickups and new Cadillacs, vans and flatbed trucks— all lined up with headlights blazing. Everyone singing hymns and going to the Promised Land.

"But that place proved to be a sour reality. The lowlifes and hot bloods had no commitment, no pride in industriousness; saw no point in hammering sheet metal into the solar collectors and methane generators we'd need. They bullied and stole; broke off in splinter groups that fought among themselves before dying off.

"In the end, even our grand city betrayed us with poisoned water from the wells. Many died. More left. Myself and barely a hundred others were all that remained. And as you have seen, even that has been reduced by the nomadic hardships of our seasonal wanderings, between here and our hunting grounds, in your own direction of travel.

"Now, in the room beside us, my other son lies sick from such a journey; he may be the next to die."

Whitney nodded at Trennt's sudden realization.

"Yes, the hothead who captured you is my eldest, Machu."

Sudden pain snared the man's face. For a time it looked as though his composure might crumble . . . but it held firm. His eyes hardened and his mouth tightened in proclamation.

"Like so many tons of ore needed to refine the purest nugget, we have survived. What remains is the pitiful essence of our genesis, yes. But also our legacy, the start of a new generation. Children raised out here know nothing but total commitment, self-reliance, and pride. And for the first true seed to flourish, I would not even consider my son's death as a waste."

Trennt concurred. "I wish you success."

Whitney didn't reply. He suddenly looked beyond them all, to the unguarded doorway and a tearful little girl standing there.

"Lahkia." He spoke her name with great love.

His tone gave enough encouragement for the girl to run inside and crush herself in his embrace.

"My daddy is no better, Grandfather."

The chief caressed her thin, small back. "I know, my dear light. The pain is great. But we must be strong and know that whatever happens will have its reason."

The little girl nodded tentatively, still sobbing. Their moment became one of a grandfather and granddaughter. No more time was left for talk with outsiders. Guards reappeared to escort the prisoners out.

Headed down the dim stone corridor, Trennt took a better look inside the sick room. There, a pallid young man lay on a stone billet. His smell hit Trennt first: the strongest kind of urine stink, flushing right through his skin. It sent Trennt back to a dying horse in his uncle's barn when he was a boy.

"Whew," Top puffed in a low breath. "The smell coming off that dude is mudflat toxin, no lie. Must've been got caught out in the chemical bogs."

Trennt studied the fearful little girl looking in from outside the room, then to the young man within.

"What's wrong with him?" he dared asked.

"Nothing, dog!" barked Machu, issuing another shove.

"That's our medical case in there," Trennt reminded. "Even if you've stolen it, I still deserve an answer for it having been taken."

"We steal nothing! It is a spoil of war!"

The chief again intervened.

"He was on a lone pilgrimage across the western plain, on the last phase of his Ooh-Tah, his rite of passage. He found himself caught by the fumes in a daylight crossing of the poisoned flats, as the old one said. It is a miracle he had the strength to make it back."

Having listened to Trennt, the little girl walked bravely among the strangers. She paused before him, searching his face with hopeful, trusting eyes.

"Can you help my daddy?" she asked softly.

The chief set a hand to her head.

"My son's wife died when Lahkia was born. They have only each other."

Trennt studied the little girl a moment, then knelt and gently took the precious oval face in his hands, tenderly wiping away her tears with his thumbs.

"Once I had a little girl about your age. I loved her very much and lost her when she got sick like your daddy. I couldn't do anything then. But maybe I can now."

The message was years beyond her. Yet Trennt's tone brought a thin smile of trust. Choking off his breath, he entered the infirmary and set a cautious hand to the unconscious man's cheek.

The head, hot as an iron and greasy with fever, rolled mushily at his touch. Everything about the sick man felt jointless, muscles gone to jelly in a sinewy body where nothing but cabled strength should reside.

The young man pulsed with a dry, sweatless heat. Raised splotches like fifty-cent pieces covered his skin. Fever blisters crowded for space on his lips. And through lids split like half-healed cuts, brown eyes were lifeless and flat as a doll's.

His pulse was far too prominent. Trennt could feel it thumping through every spot of his skin, double-action pumps of a weakened heart working overtime.

"He's got it," asserted Top. "Seen it happen to a couple dudes on one mapping run. Kidneys are filling with poison that they can't flush."

"What'd you do?"

"Gave them the usual citric-zinc detox pills and piled them under blankets to try sweating it out."

"And?"

"Watched them die."

"You can't give pills to an unconscious man." It was Geri, in a bold tone of voice that surprised both the men.

Trennt glanced over. "Any suggestions?"

"Shock immersion. An old Plains Indian way of breaking fevers."

She folded her arms at their amazement, offering curtly, "Once upon a time I was a college junior in American History studies. I learned that tribes would soak the ill person in hot water to raise his temperature even higher. Then they'd dunk him in cold. The snap between could jar his system back in synch."

Trennt stared mutely. Even with his authority eclipsed, he felt a sudden and strange reliance growing for this troublesome woman. But it was the chief who gave voice to the drawbacks.

"This same immersion might not also be fatal?"

Geri nodded honestly. "Yes."

Whitney regarded his unconscious son for a time, then studied Geri and his own people beyond.

"If we learn something, we all gain. Do what she says!"

The tribesmen reluctantly stepped back, ready to follow Geri's orders. Her manner was bold among the warriors, and had a professional confidence they responded to.

"The big thing we need is water. Five, ten gallons— as hot as a person can stand; again as much, ice cold."

"The solar collectors might still catch enough afternoon sun," declared Whitney. "Get them turned! What else?"

"We'll need a tub to soak him in, one that can be quickly drained."

"We have no such thing!" barked Machu, stepping forward. "This is fool's work, Father! Let me remove these dogs!"

Geri faced the repugnant man. "Your brother has quit perspiring. Before long his brain will cook like a hard-boiled egg and you'll lose him for sure. Is that what you want?"

Trennt offered a suggestion. "The canvas top off our truck might work if tied at the corners."

"Get it!" Geri ordered.

The brother stepped forward, blocking Trennt. "You stay here, dog. My men will get what is needed."

The canvas roof was stripped off and lashed by ropes into a tub shape. Gallons of precious water were set to heating aboveground in an assembly of tiny solar collectors. More was sunk to cool in lower crevice depths. A difficult wait began.

Geri marked time acting as an attending physician, daubing the stricken young man with cooling alcohol and rubbing salves from the medkit. The spirits and ointment beat back his rankness with a smell of hope.

Then, a sullen tribesman appeared.

"We've lost the sun, leader, and the water is barely warm."

Machu shot to his feet.

"This white devil foolishness is done, then! Send them out and let our own healers return."

The chief sighed in accord. "If we have no other means of heat . . ."

"Our truck," said Trennt, "also has fuel. Use it."

The chief motioned to his men.

Distant pockets in the stone floor were filled with lit fuel oil and cans of water strung across to finish their heating. Geri readied the soaking tarp and motioned. "Bring him."

Machu set aside his spear and strode forward to raise his brother, but before he could lift, Trennt was on the other side. He locked eyes and wrists with the warrior, not allowing the man to budge unless they did it in unison. Machu's eyes flashed with surprise, then grabbed Trennt back. Together they hoisted the ailing youth toward the makeshift tub.

The patient looked even worse than before, moving through the thin passageway light. His skin was mottled and lumpy, almost seeming to cringe in the flickering torches. Trennt felt his own flesh crawl as they lowered the sick man into place.

Some distance off, Top and another tribesman stood ready as the hot water brigade.

Her patient set, Geri called. "Top!"

"Yo!"

"Water ready?"

"Guns up!"

"Bring it!"

The pair threaded hardwood spears through the

sooty, five-gallon cans' carrying lugs and shuffled over. The hot load was heavy: eighty-plus pounds swinging like huge unwieldy anchors.

Trennt and Baker met them with shirts off and bunched into oven mitts. At Geri's nod, the first can was slowly blended into the room-temperature water. The sick man's eyes fluttered with the new heat. His shallow, racing breath hiked up to a higher notch. Tribespeople glanced about uncertainly, but Geri drove them on.

"Keep it going! Don't mind him!"

The man's skin shimmered. Veins in his throat and temples began to bulge and throb. His eyes swelled against their drawn lids.

Geri shouted again. "Cold water!"

Two tribesmen supported the sick man while she yanked a corner knot to dump the first wash. But the weary, sun-bleached fibers snapped as she moved to tie the rope. It was too short to reattach, so Trennt grabbed the sheared end and drew the cord snug by hand. Geri's eyes met his.

"Do it!"

The cold water was administered. At first the patient hung unaffected and still. Then he began to tremble. Slowly gathering power from somewhere far outside himself, the young man started quaking like an addict gone hours beyond his last fix.

The frigid water about him came alive. It bubbled and fizzed to a counterfeit boil. Yet he couldn't seem to shed the sudden bolt of energy fast enough, and drawing back, finally exploded in a ghastly eruption.

Head and shoulders flew out. Arms shot wide. Icy water sprayed far in a great silver blast. From its depths the youth rose as a high-arched piece of newly cast granite.

Machu shouted, barging ahead.

"The devils are killing him!"

"Keep him away!" countered the chief. "And hold this one down!"

Hands of tribesmen and prisoners alike joined to grab and suppress both men. Shocked at the indignity of his arrest, Machu melted in their grasp, but his unconscious brother fought them all. His case-hardened body corded and bunched with runaway power, until ligament and muscle seemed drawn beyond all possible limits.

Just when it appeared he'd tear himself in half, the patient paused; then softened and crumpled—gone full circle, mush to monster and back.

Geri caught him as he settled into the trough. She gently propped his head while the cold water drained.

"That's all we can do," she said, handing over a thick medkit envelope containing a mix of sugar and salt. "Dry and wrap him up. Tomorrow should tell if he'll live. If he can drink, mix this in two gallons of water and give it to him. It'll replace all the body salts he's lost."

The crowd hovered, numb in the aftermath. Though the patient was still unconscious, his breath now settled into a relaxed, easy rhythm.

The chief granted Geri a bitter smile. He then moved aside to speak a time with a pair of warriors. Shortly after, the prisoners were led from the cavern. Behind, only Machu broke the silence, calling out a final warning.

"If he dies, dogs, you will wish you had first!"

This time the captives were directed to a new, ground-level cell. A boulder was rolled over the opening and the four sat again, cast in darkness.

Sometime later, Top got to his feet.

Trennt looked toward Top's rustling.

"What's wrong?"

"Something's weird in here."

"How?"

"Don't know. Too—too . . . cold maybe, for this far inside the rock."

The old-timer shuffled across the cave. Sweeping his hands slowly in the air before him, he stumbled over Baker, stopped, and doubled back.

Baker growled, shoving him away. "The hell you doin'?"

"I felt something, man."

"What, spiders?"

"No." He continued his motions. "More like, yeah! There it is again."

"What, already?"

"A breeze."

Baker climbed to his own feet. "Oh, you're—" The shooter caught his words. "Jimbo, I think the old coot's right! You kin smell bits ah' fresh air, too."

The rest came over.

"Spread your fingers and sweep them slowly," Top directed. "Move too fast and we'll never find it."

Their hands worked the dark ether in the fashion of sluggish mimes. Then, stooped low, Geri called out.

"Here!"

Top got to a knee. "Right on, Sunshine! It's coming up from low in this wall." He reached in and pulled away some corroded sandstone.

"Oh, yeah. There's big time air coming in! And maybe enough room for a dude to squeeze through."

"Then step aside, Granpaw," called Baker. "Don't wancha' gettin' your old hide hung up in there and blockin' my way out. I'll skinny on through."

He was gauging the opening when Geri objected.

"No. I'm smallest. I made a promise to carry my weight. This is a chance to prove it."

The shooter paused. "Jimbo?"

"Let her try," answered Trennt.

Baker moved aside and Geri shinnied bravely into the narrow crevice. Her head and shoulders disappeared. Slowly, chest and waist vanished, thighs and knees; ankles were last and she was gone.

The gritty sounds of her movement dulled and moved steadily away. Finally they stopped.

Top called in a harsh whisper. "Sunshine! You okay?"

Long seconds passed without a reply.

"Sunshine!"

"Yes," finally came her far-off voice. "Come on through. You can make it. And you won't believe what's out here."

Baker went next. Then Top. Steadily upward, thirty feet and more. It was a snug fit, but manageable, like a passage which had been used before. Last in line, Trennt wriggled through the final yards. He exited into a bone-grating chill.

The path had taken them sixty feet through the settlement's rock walls. It was long after dark now and, compared to the relative in-ground warmth, the starry late night air was brutally cold. Chilled flesh joined frayed nerves as the group stood shivering, in the unexpected presence of their truck.

It sat loaded, just as it had been taken; roof tarp back in place, weapons stacked across its hood. Even the medkit was closed and secured. In addition, their water cans were patched and filled. More brimming skins had been lashed aboard, as well. Inside rested a larder of dried gourd hunks and parched strips of lizard meat.

They stood silent and grateful—except Baker, who broke the spell with a brusque grab at his guns.

"Hot damn!" he yipped, stuffing them back in his belt. "Felt bare-ass naked without 'em."

Geri soberly examined the food cache.

"A lot given by those who don't have much to spare." Trennt motioned toward the medkit.

"Take some out for us. Leave the rest here."

Geri did as instructed, but coming upon more of the thick sugar and salt electrolyte packs, her fingers paused. After a moment, several were eased out and slid deep into a cargo pocket.

CHAPTER 20

They'd passed through the town's chilly fringes for the better part of a damp afternoon. Weaving a trail through the flattened roofs and buckled, weed-grown streets of some extinct blue collar burg, they toured yet another quake victim—one more left with its neck wrung and its name forever lost in the growing bitter drizzle.

Rising from beside the truck, Trennt swiped mud and pine needles from his knee as Top jumped into the chill beside him.

"Now what?"

"Loose rim."

The old man scowled at yet another in the irritating rash of recent mechanical ailments.

"Damn, Jack! Never, ever had this many gremlins hit me in any one trip. Next thing'll be a flat in the puncture-proof tires. Lugs okay?"

Trennt rubbed them again. "Yeah. Just in time. Threads were starting to fret. A couple miles more and they would've begun to pop."

Again, it wasn't anything grave; merely another quirk in the chain of loose nuts, bolts, and assorted fittings, which had sprouted in the week since their return to the woodlands.

Trennt surveyed the dismal swirling mist. Sodden tufts of shredded house insulation drooped from surrounding treetops like grotesque wads of filthy pink moss. Splintered lumber, twisted sheet metal, and tumbled brick walls cast foreboding shadows as far as he could see. There wasn't any night cover that didn't appear inadequate or risky.

"No sense pushing on and chancing a wreck in this soup," he declared. "Let's tighten up the rim and pull over in that tree stand for the night. Seems like the best we can do."

It looked to be the miserable start of another chilly evening, napping upright and digging deep for warmth inside their foul clothes. But drawing up her collar, Geri spied a dim flash of color and pointed.

"What's that?"

Top swung the truck's spotlight over. In its damp glow a broad amber-glazed shape rose: the shiny brick of a wall nearly smothered in wild brush and vines. Above it flashed a crazy glint of shattered tinted glass.

"A church," Geri gushed, answering her own question.

"Could be a jail cell for all I care!" squawked Baker. "Tonight it's home an' dry. Let's scope it out."

A quick examination revealed a partially collapsed, though stabilized wall and roof; a complimentary drive-through entrance for the truck and natural vent for an indoor fire.

First inside, Top played his flashlight about the moldering brick and fallen plaster. Aside from its scattered pews, crackled marble altar, and random artifacts, the sizeable building was a shell.

His light bounced harshly off a stainless steel baptism font, then tracked up a bird-stained wall to a clump of uneasy pigeons roosting in the rafters. The birds bunched uncomfortably against the invading glare, but did not fly.

Top dropped his beam happily.

"Far out! If someone wants to wrestle that stew pot from the wall and start a cook fire, I think we just found supper."

Windfall branches were dragged in and water added to the remaining gourd meat. Mixed with soup stock from the half dozen hapless birds Top and Baker clubbed and plucked, the first hot meal in many days began to stew. Its simmering aroma and bright hearth imparted a certain, quick hominess to the dank and abandoned building.

The group split up to gather wood and explore. Top, having taken up station as self-appointed chef, brought out his private stash and plopped down comfortably by the fire to indulge in a predinner smoke.

Beside him, Baker unloaded his weapons. He set the edge of a rough, whisking hand to the marble altar top before shamelessly pouring out his cleaning tools. He noticed the stone surface didn't seem as dusty as it might have been, left alone for who knew how long. But he continued on and soon the clinking of tempered steel parts jingled through the deserted sanctuary.

From his spot at the fire Top took a deep hit off his smoke, shifted to a side, and curiously scouted Baker's exacting movements.

"You go through that same bull on every piece, every night, even if you don't use them?"

Baker answered without looking up. "It relaxes me. Besides, precision goods need care. Not like that old steam driven piece of yours. Where'd you find that muzzle loader anyway, the Civil War?"

Top affectionately nudged a dirty boot against the SKS carbine beside him.

"My daddy brought it home from the Nam—place you probably never even heard of. Dinks knew how to make them last without all the crap you go through."

"Well, just stay downwind if yah ever have to pull the trigger. Don't want that blowin' up around me."

Top drew another hit from his smoke and surveyed Baker.

"How many dudes've you greased, man?"

Baker shrugged. "Quit keepin' score."

"Bet you've bagged your limit."

The slender gunman disassembled his custom-made sniper rifle and lovingly reset each piece in its form-fitted case. "The Good Book said when you find a talent, you should let your light shine on through. Army gave me the trainin' and job opportunities. The rest is all natural ability."

Across the church, Top saw Trennt disappear up a run of dim choir-loft stairs.

"You two been tight a long time, huh?"

"Me 'n' Jimbo? Like ticks."

"Meet up in the Army?"

"Yep. Doin' LURP work down in the Amazon war—long range recon stuff. He was an 82nd Airborne trooper and me, a sniper. Had us spots in a nice ole Special Ops squad.

"We'd go up past the DMZ. Snoop around. Blow a bridge here. Wax some enemy official there. Mebbe plant laser homing devices for our planes along high-traffic guerrilla routes. Mess with 'em. You know."

The gunman paused in his chores, smiling fondly. "That was good duty. No questions, no rules. Just do the job. Kinda sad when it ended. We got disbanded and the Army went back to all its silly-ass stateside regulations. Me 'n' Jimbo, we lost track of each other

until just a year or so ago. And here we are today, doin'
almost the same thing, together again. Funny how stuff
works out."

"Deju vu," Top concurred.

Then it was Baker's turn to critique and he glanced
down with a discerning eye.

"Musta dropped the hammer a time or two yourse'f,
Whiskers. Why the questions?"

Top sucked another deep hit from his roach. He
blew a smoke ring and regarded its rise toward the
cracked ceiling.

"Old-fashioned I guess. War or self-defense is one
thing; a gun for hire is another. I don't care to be
somebody's amigo today and their dinero tomorrow."

Something caused Baker to pause, but he didn't
speak.

"Back in the desert," continued the old-timer, "you'd
have taken on that whole black rifle platoon right there
out in the open, wouldn't you?"

Baker replied without hesitation.

"In a blink. I'm still disappointed I didn't kill ole
scarface. He'd better hope we never meet up again."

Top rocked his head in sour amusement.

"You are one certified trip, Jack. I only hope if we
ever do get in a firefight on this gig, you're half as good
as you make out to be."

Baker grinned privately. "Time comes, watch me
work."

"Whatever turns you on. Just don't trip out and blow
your mind like back at the tribe. That's a number ten,
baa-aad scene."

Baker looked at the fire from under heavy-lidded
eyes. A dark chuckle filled his throat.

Geri took in the church's ruined grandeur as she
gathered kindling. Pausing before a huge shattered

window, she studied the random shards of leftover color still clinging determinedly to its weathered leadwork. Even in this advanced dilapidation, a certain nobility remained here that she admired.

Her study was interrupted by a flash of movement up the dim adjacent stairway. It was Trennt, involved in a more practical investigation of the ruins. Minutes later, he descended the choir loft steps to find Geri, kindling under arm, blocking his path.

"Must've been beautiful here at Christmas," she commented idly.

Trennt slowed, yet he didn't answer as he came down, set to begin a search of the far side. But Geri wasn't about to be put off—or let him alone.

"What is it with you?" she demanded. "What exactly are you supposed to be? No one out for kicks, like your friend over there. He lights up every time he fingers a gun. But there's no cheap thrill like that for you. So why? What was it with that little tribegirl back there in the desert? Or in getting me 'back to my people'? In your mind, are you the great twenty-first-century crusader? Some rough and ready, new generation Don Quixote, rescuing damsels in the second millennium?"

Trennt hovered in an ill-at-ease stop. When he tried starting around her, the woman swayed with him.

"Well?"

So cornered, he told her, "You ask a lot of questions that are none of your concern."

A wicked smile crossed her face. "Humor me."

"Okay," came his even-tempered reply. "Why not me? Somebody's got to do it."

But Geri stood with eyes dull, already having passed other judgment.

"As long as it pays."

"Yeah." Trennt smirked. "That's right. Big money. I'm saving up for my new Corvette. Of course, I don't know that the factory will be taking orders any time this century."

His flippant answer didn't put her off.

"Crusader or not, down deep inside you're still no better than Baker. You're dried out and used up, Trennt. You've become some kind of sick monument to your own pain and that makes you even more dangerous than he is."

Trennt coolly regarded her, head to foot and back. His own gaze narrowed as he took the offensive.

"Lady, you don't know a thing about me or what I do. And I wouldn't get in line for a halo just yet, if I were you. But if you want to ask questions, ask yourself something. What was your sainted Doctor Keener thinking the whole time he was working on whatever dark project it was back there? It didn't seem they were exactly holding a gun to his head for results."

He'd touched a nerve. Geri straightened, yet she held her ground. "Maybe I deserve that. But he doesn't. You saw him. Was he the picture of a power hungry madman? Or just a simple, misused and innocent genius?

"You say I don't know you. Well, you didn't know him, either. But I did. And he was a good, gentle man. Giving Martin a task was no different than handing a jigsaw puzzle to a very bright child. No politics or practical reality entered into it. Just finding a solution. But you're not the type to—"

A thundering voice bellowed down from the choir loft.

"This place might be in ruins, but it still deserves respect for what it once was!"

Trennt shoved the woman away. His sidearm was out and on target with Top and Baker; all simultaneously trained on the darkened voice as it continued, unafraid.

"Any of us travelers who take shelter here should treat it with proper respect—by keeping our voices down and not defiling its altar with guns!"

Even at this distance, Trennt could sense Baker's trigger finger constricting and he raised a belaying hand.

He called beyond. "Who are you?"

"Someone spending the night. Like yourself."

"Step out so we can see you."

From the shadows a tall and haggard man of scarecrow proportions appeared. He said no more, but crunched down the grit-covered stairs of the other loft, walking fearlessly into their midst, and headed directly for Baker.

The stranger stopped at the altar. He gazed appalled at the obscene streaks of dirty gun oil glistening across its web of fine marble veins. When he did speak again his voice was restrained, as though addressing an imbecile, forever beyond understanding the profanity of his actions.

"Do you have any idea what this place is?"

Lowering his gun hand, Baker tossed his head nonchalantly about.

"Yeah. A mess."

"It never occurred to you that it might be a house of God?"

Baker shrugged, appraising the newcomer.

"Well, by the look o' things, Cuz, I'd say He done moved away."

The stranger lunged at the clutter of parts. But Baker was quicker, yanking the man's shirt across the dingy marble block and jamming the pistol squarely in his forehead.

From behind its cocked hammer the shooter's tone issued cool as the grave. "Don't ever try somethin' like that again, Cuz. Never."

Though frozen at mid-stride, the unarmed man didn't buckle.

"You've obviously never been in a church before."

"A time or two. But I found me a better religion. The one stuck to your head. Care for a hollow-point baptism?"

Still, the man didn't flinch and even Baker yielded a respectful grunt.

"You don't rile easy. I'll give yah that."

More so, Trennt felt something refined and unthreatening in the stranger's bearing. He stepped up.

"What's your name, friend?"

"Wayne," came his reply. Nothing more.

"You alone?"

"Yes."

"What're you doing here?"

"What's it matter?"

" 'Cause Jimbo says so," chimed in Baker.

Top looked up from his stew tending. Also seeing no apparent danger in the man, he smiled and shook his head.

"Don't mind Slick. He's always quick to make friends."

"Screw you, Whiskers! I don't trust nobody I don't know!"

Trennt motioned Baker's gun away and obliged the stranger with a provisional nod.

"We can leave it as your business—provided we're not in for any surprises. Because then, my enthusiastic friend there would have my full permission to deal with you as he sees fit."

Baker settled in behind a broad smile.

"In the meantime, Wayne, you're welcome to share our fire and meal . . . if you don't mind it being made from some earlier members of tonight's congregation."

The stranger's initial antagonism flickered out.

"Thanks." He then looked to Top. "I happen to have wild onions and carrots found fresh today. Some dry seasonings too, if you'd like to add them to your pot."

Top swung a welcoming hand. "Outta sight, dude! Shake 'em in!"

The stranger knelt to pull at his knapsack. "In answer to your first question, my full name is Wayne Truax. As far as I know, I'm the only member left of this parish. I stay here every so often. Wild crops supply the little I need and I spend my time traveling alone, trying . . . to make some sense of things."

"Good luck," snorted Geri, punctuating her words with another armload of dropped branches.

"Pretty big place for just one person," said Trennt. "Nobody else from town weathers here?"

Wayne shook his head. "None left. The Quake took some. The Flu, others. The rest moved on."

The new man said no more as he began peeling and slicing up his meal contributions.

The stew rose to a delicious simmer. After dinner, the banked fire burned down to a cozy heap of pink and sapphire coals, guaranteed to warm the travelers until morning.

Again occupying his idle time in a pointless rehash of the satchel's contents, Trennt glanced toward a crunch of approaching boots. It was Top, returning from patrol.

"Anything going on outside?"

"Negative." Top unslung his carbine to squat by the fire. "Made a few laps around the perimeter. Even the owls are sitting tight in this soup."

"Bring in the guard, if you want. I think for once everybody can share in a decent night's sleep."

The old Marine nodded and went for his bedroll.

Baker casually trundled over as soon as Top had left. After a few moments spent superficially gauging the flames, he crowded beside Trennt, speaking in an odd, off center tone.

"You know, Jimbo. I been in for doin' this from the start. But what happens if'n we don't see the bird again? Ain't once since we got back from the desert— four days now. Or what if we see it crash out in the ocean? Then what good's all this been?"

It took Trennt a moment to realize what he was hearing.

"Well? What if?" Baker asked.

Trennt leveled a condemning glance.

"I don't know what you're saying. But who got us into this? Quit now if you want and take everybody with you. But until I personally do see that plane go down in the ocean or find it plowed in somewhere, my part isn't done."

Baker nodded emphatically. "Yeah, I know. And you're right. The professional code and all that. But, shoot, Jimbo. Y'all heard ole Corealis hisself fire us. What's the sense in doin' him a job we ain't apt to finish?"

Trennt zipped his jacket with a perturbed swipe.

"I said it once, I'm not doing it for him. If anybody, it's for Kosinski. Finding the chemical samples or any data still aboard will be a bonus."

Yet, Baker dogged on. "Okay, even then. So we get the plane. What's the odds of him bein' alive or even aboard? He coulda jumped or fell out anywhere in a thousand square miles. Besides, he was just another bus driver runnin' his route. Prob'ly wouldn't even 'member, if you two met on the street. Who cares what happened to him?"

"I said, I care." Trennt paused, sensing an alien

gulf spreading rapidly between them. "And why the different tune from you all of a sudden?"

Baker swung a fretful hand about. "Well, lookit us, Pard. We been at this for what—three, four weeks now? Doin' it from our own pocket. Livin' like bums on whatever nuts and berries we find. Sweatin' to death one day, freezin' the next. Always thirsty and turnin' into a traveler's aid club for any charity case we find along the way.

"All's I'm sayin' is it just might be time we call in the dogs and piss on the campfire. Cut our losses on this goose chase and get to worryin' 'bout ourselves.

'Member, from here on out, we're independent contractors. We need to get back to Freeville and make contacts to start payin' for groceries."

A passing shadow paused. It was Wayne. He seemed to linger, listening to their exchange, and after a few seconds Trennt glanced over his shoulder: "Problem?"

Wayne answered as if shrugging off a trance. "Sorry. I didn't mean to eavesdrop. It's just that I haven't seen Latin script in quite a while."

Trennt straightened, pointing to the frayed booklet sitting forgotten in his lap.

"You recognize this stuff?"

"Only as far as a language requirement of higher education. Not a personal favorite. But something I muddled through." He motioned to the folder. "May I?"

Trennt gladly handed it up. "You bet. What's it say?"

Wayne leafed through the coarse and faded pages. "It's a diary of sorts, I'd guess."

With a last look at Trennt, Baker dropped the other matter and departed, but Wayne remained, studying the sheets. Something distressing suddenly clouded his gaunt face, then passed away. His eyes swept cautiously down.

"Mind if I ask whose this is?"

"A man who died being rescued. Why?"

"Besides me being more than a little rusty, its author was a lot better at the language than I could ever hope. A little background might help me understand his intentions better. But even so, this could take a while."

"Whatever you decipher tonight would help," said Trennt. "We're on a tight schedule."

Obligingly taking possession of the booklet, Wayne settled in yoga-style, directly across the fire. Watching him for a time in its orange wash, Trennt dozed off noting how the moment and man combined, to project the fitting likeness of a scholar extracting lost knowledge.

CHAPTER 21

Trennt bolted upright in the dark. He drew quick, shallow breaths as the ragged tatters of his nightmare swirled and thinned.

The same. Always the same. Buried alive. Unable to free anyone from the strange quicksand, but himself. Him rising; them sinking, being pulled away, slipping through his grasp. The faces of Dena, Andy, and Jennifer, glowing with incandescent anguish as they cried out to him in terror.

But in the thick molasses of that horrible dreamscape there never was any release, except his own. No way to turn. Or hug. Or even say good-bye. Just feel the clawing pain of his own survival as he was drawn away; left to endure the ghastly echo of their dimming cries.

Trennt strained for breath, amazed even in his terror. It had been such a long spell since his last haunting that he foolishly believed he might have finally been freed of it for good. But, fresh as ever, the old wound was still there. Lurking in the shadows like some untiring demon, it was simply deferred to just the right moment in which to strike out and harvest its greatest pain.

Riding out his slowing chugs of breath, Trennt stayed glued in place, erect and mute; still as a trapped rabbit, until he was certain of his surroundings. Through fading beats of a thundering heart, he dared slide his eyes about the still-sleeping forms. There was no motion illuminated in the firelight. With luck, he'd been quiet enough.

Damn.

Yards away, a shadow separated from that of the truck. Of all people, it was the woman, gazing over at him like some unwitting voyeur.

Trennt shifted about. He hoped his feigned nonchalance would conceal him, but, as soon as she spoke, he knew otherwise.

"You okay?"

He sucked in a quick, self-conscious breath. "Yeah."

"No one awake but me," she added in an odd, reassuring tone.

They faced each other for a brittle moment. Then Trennt snatched up his weapon and climbed to his feet. Shouldering the cold shotgun, he started off through the dark.

He stopped in the crumbling church vestibule, staring out at the dense fogbank as tentative footsteps trailed up behind.

"You loved them a lot," Geri declared without preamble.

He answered in the first civil tone he'd found for the woman.

"Not enough to keep them alive."

"I'm sorry," she offered. "We've all lost people we've loved, all of us powerless in one way or another to prevent it. The best we can do is keep them alive in our hearts."

With those few words he felt a quick and obscure need to uncover his grief and, for the only time he could remember, Trennt spoke of himself.

"We were logging people, from right here, upstate. My family got dragged to Chicago with the census because I'd been born there when my folks passed through one time. So, like in the Bible, it was where we all had to go when the government decided on that national head count and 'skills redistribution,' after the plague.

"What a nightmare. Buses arriving from all over the country with us outsiders. Not wanted by the locals, not liked by arrivals from different states—and blamed by everyone for starting the N.A. Flu. Might as well've blamed us for causing the Quake.

"All us West Coasters were packed into one downtown reservation like the worst kind of outcasts. Little sanitation or clean water; everybody catching everyone else's germs and, with the ozone inversions, coughing and hacking all the time. Those really sick barely stayed alive on public medicine and rations illegally reduced, just because of who they were.

"Then one day a rich kid wandered into our sector, a stupid-ass, punk, rich kid out for kicks or a dare from his buddies. Maybe looking for cheap sex from one of the widows desperate to make ends meet. A pigeon served up on a silver platter. And right in front of me."

Trennt's eyes brimmed with tears. He continued slowly.

"So easy. He was lost and scared. I wouldn't've even needed to hurt him, just shake him down and turn him loose. But a fool like me let him go. Even then, with my whole family sick as dogs, I couldn't even steal from someone who had more than he deserved. I dragged the dumb ass out of there and didn't let anybody touch him. And my reward was to have everyone turn on my family because of it.

"Better if they'd killed us. But they didn't. They shunned us, instead—and that was worse. In the middle of all that city we were locked away by a wall of silence like we were the only ones there."

Trennt let out a long, deliberate sigh.

"Probably nothing could really have been done for my wife and kids, anyway. I don't know. But knowing no one would lift a finger to help me tend them made it worse than you can imagine.

"They all died on the same night, burning up with fever and choking on their own phlegm. Next day the sanitation department bagged them for that week's cremation at Soldier Field. Everything I loved was mixed with old tires and cooked away in that black greasy smoke drifting out over Lake Michigan."

He chuckled mirthlessly. "Funny thing. Through it all I never got so much as a sniffle. Afterward, I begged God to kill me. When He didn't answer, I asked the devil. Finally, I gave up on them both and everything in between.

"I thought hard about different ways of doing myself in. But they all seemed too easy, compared to what my family was dealt. So, I came to this work, somehow hoping it'd offer me a way to hurt slow and long in payment for failing them."

Trennt drew a wretched breath.

"The worst thing a man can do is outlive his children."

Another silence sprouted between them, one as heavy and labored as any of the hateful, intolerant moments they'd shared since meeting. But this time, it was different. Here was a new silence, one under-scored with patience, one punctuated by a hand that stretched through the cold darkness and came to settle, warm on his arm.

Trennt wheeled slowly toward it—to thank her, maybe to apologize for everything prior. But she was suddenly too close for any of it. Wanting to speak, he could only focus on the rubied highlights of her auburn hair. And even now, after so many hard days on the move, he was starkly aware of how fresh and sweet she seemed.

From nowhere Trennt felt a bloom of desire spark and smolder deep inside him. He shuddered before its unsettling, abrupt heat. It was preposterous. And wrong—all wrong. Wrong for the time and place. Wrong for the memory of what he'd had with Dena. Yet those very facts only made his need more urgent.

Trennt fell back on his trusted defenses, but the fabric of logic and restraint which had so long sustained him began to quickly unravel. A critical glue was giving way inside that was both frightening and wonderful. Like a suicidal moth, he dove headlong into the flames.

Trennt grabbed Geri by the shoulders and reeled her back to him. He layered the woman in fierce, greedy kisses; desperate to smother and absorb every spare inch of her warm, soft flesh.

But there was no response in Geri. She merely stood fast in the moment, isolating herself from the too-familiar method of handling. Mentally leaving shore, she began the slow and protective backpedal into deeper, secluded waters.

Yet for the first time, she found that dependable harbor gone suddenly shallow. With no warning, she was left aground on something rare, energizing, and all-terrifying. A storm of raw craving blazed to hot life within her as well. Tested old battlements swayed drunkenly to the man's determined caress.

Geri drew a sustaining breath. She struggled to

remember that she utterly detested him. But the notion withered pitifully in his grasp. And with a final gush, she abandoned herself and plunged headlong into Trennt's embrace.

Her arms lashed tightly about his neck. Her lips met his with equal passion. Thrust together in this dark and indifferent arena, man and woman clung to each other and the fragile moment. Their fury was a balm for all the cold and lonely nights ever spent alone.

But the gears of an indifferent universe ground quickly onward and fast-rising floodwaters were loosed against them.

Trennt blinked first. The mechanism setting him aflame sputtered and starved, and as quickly as it had taken flight, his racing system laid on the brakes. In an instant, an unstoppable flow of molten lust was quick-frozen in the heaviest shame.

Geri felt the stumble, but denied it. She stretched across the sudden crevice, willing to bridge and compensate, yet driving herself harder into his arms was a lost effort. The spell had broken and the moment crumbled to one of mutual embarrassment.

Arms were disengaged and retracted; lips parted, heads bowed, eyes swept aside. Trennt retreated, back inside his tempered core. Geri withdrew into familiar, secluded waters.

They stood again as strangers. For a ragged moment, the damp air between them was thick with disgrace. But hurriedly regrouping, Geri dismissed the matter, beaming her best, practiced smile.

"Don't worry about it. A working girl needs to stay in training. Thanks for the refresher course."

She started back, head high. Only the glimmer of distant firelight betrayed a lone tear bunched in the far corner of her eye.

❖　　❖　　❖

Baker kicked out the fire's last coals with eager motions.

"Well, Cuz," he asked, "you done? It's sunup and we got miles to go."

Wayne shook his head, glumly regarding the curled pages.

"The best I could do are snippets here and there of what does seem a kind of diary."

"And?"

Trennt approached, listening as well.

"There are notes and personal thoughts on the progress made developing better food grains. But too much time away and the lack of a dictionary has put most of it beyond me without a longer study."

Baker snatched up the book. Unimpressed, he returned it to Trennt.

"Thanks, anyway. See y'all later."

Wayne smiled thinly. "Sorry. But like I said, I'd need time."

"Wish we had it to spare."

Trennt looked to Top, just returning from outside.

"Where to next?"

"Due north," said the old grunt. "Pit stop a couple days out. Then the Wilds—if we still got a reason to boogie."

Trennt gazed up through the shattered church roof.

"How's the sky?"

"Fog's burned off good enough to hear and see your bird—provided she's still up there."

"Don'cha worry none, Jimbo," said Baker. "She'll be by. Clouds been thick enough to muffle a tank column for the last few days. We'll see her today. You bet on it."

They shared a fraternal smile. Behind, Wayne cleared his throat.

"I do have a suggestion to offer. If you don't

mind me riding along, a few days more might be time enough to make some real headway with the diary."

From his spot packing the Upland, Baker's grin deflated.

"Sorry," he declared. "Few more days'n we'll know what we need, with or without it. Thanks anyhow."

"Drop me wherever you'd want," continued Wayne. "I know my way back and I've got no place better to be. In the meantime I'd decipher what I could."

Still clenching a tiedown rope, Baker eyed the man suspiciously.

"What d'you care what that stuff means, anyway?"

The stranger shrugged, a little self-consciously.

"I don't get much intellectual stimulation these days. Write it off to a welcome challenge. You know, like a good crossword puzzle."

Baker only narrowed his gaze. "Always hated them things. You a teacher or somethin'?"

Wayne nodded. "I was, yes."

Trennt considered the offer.

"Okay, you're in. A couple days, anyway. I can't guarantee anything more."

Baker stomped behind the truck, scandalized and muttering. Yanking frustratedly at a cargo strap, he jerked up a length of excess cord. Beneath, a sliver of brilliant white was dislodged.

The gunman scuffed a boot toe at the color, then stooped to retrieve it. Bunched and jammed beneath a tire were several empty packets. Though dirty, their crumpled paper was new, with sharp, fresh-torn edges.

They were identical to the eight-ounce electrolyte packs found in the medkit. Straightened and upended, residual crystals trickled freely into his hand. Salt—or sugar.

Baker contemplated the packets a moment, then stepped to the truck's fuel door. A tiny spill of more crystals rested there, ones someone had tried to hastily sweep away. Baker did so with his own fingers as Geri's call split the morning chill.

"She's coming!"

He slipped the empty packs into a shirt pocket and hurried outside to where the rest gathered, looking skyward.

Though four days tardy, the nuke dutifully kept this morning's rendezvous. Now, however, she loomed huge and low. Lumbering and ungainly, she listed rakishly and smeared the treetops with her broad, crooked shadow.

Her lone engine moaned in a labored and cycling whine as she struggled past. No longer was there any effort at vertical flight maneuvers, just a tortured struggle to remain aloft.

Nobody spoke until her sound was completely gone. Then it was Baker who again gave voice to the obvious: "That ole mud hen won't last the day."

Trennt didn't reply. Instead, he looked hopefully at Top, who gazed up from working his solar compass.

"Same direction, Cap. Straight toward the Wilds."

Minutes earlier and several miles south, another camp was breaking. Major Dobruja sifted his fingers through the spoor of dried tire tracks. Rising from a crouch, his range-tough eyes chased wearily along the meandering truck path. After a week of trailing, he'd grown bored with the hunt; disinterested in the capture.

"Not far ahead," he said mechanically. "Their trail remains easy to follow. Still north. We could close and ambush them at our leisure. But their determination troubles me. What can such vagabonds be after? Certainly not meeting with radicals this far out."

Sergeant Karelian followed the officer's gaze.

"Whatever it is, another few days will put them—and us—in the tribelands."

Josef bowed to the logic.

"Yes. We are short on supplies as it is. Without more troops, it might not be prudent for us to follow. Maybe we've wasted time enough on the matter."

He flung down the mud clod and decided: "Let the fools be. We'll find easier game to sport. Gather our men for return to base."

The sergeant was circling a raised arm when the morning sun dimmed in the flash of a huge, screaming shadow.

"Son of a bitch!"

Top angrily yanked open the truck hood and scoured the broiling engine compartment. In the spotty shade where they'd coasted to a stop, he ran testing hands about the hot components. Yet, everything appeared intact.

Trennt slid from behind the steering wheel to join in the survey. "See anything?"

The old Marine straightened. "No loose injectors or ignition wires. But it shouldn't have just cut out like that."

From inside the trunk, Wayne spoke, "Does that rotten egg smell have anything to do with it?"

Trennt also caught a whiff. It was a swampy kind of decayed stench, though heavily sulfured. "What is that, raw fuel?"

Top didn't answer. He forgot all about the truck. His eyes flashed with quick and sober raptness at something both in the terrain and the air about them.

Baker dismissed the brief, faint stink. He wandered

over and spoke with a casual tone of certainty. "Way she was surgin' at the end there, I'd lay money on a plugged fuel system."

Top frowned. "Don't know how. Been using strained G.I gas up to now. Won't have any old stuff until we fill up at the junkyard. Even then, it'd take a mondo load of crud to plug both the tank and engine filters in a multi-fueler hog like this."

Trennt eyed the silenced engine. "Do we have much choice but to check?"

"Guess not." The old-timer rolled up his sleeves. "At least they're cleanable mesh cartridges. I can drop and flush them without too much hassle. Trouble is all the daylight we'll waste before making the gas station and getting the still set up."

Trennt swatted at a line of perspiration from under his fatigue cap and readjusted his sun specs. Beyond their scrubwood shade, the heat-scorched horizon danced uninvitingly.

"How far is it?"

"Few miles. Why?"

"I know how to work a membrane still. Would it be worth the effort for me to hump the gear in and get things ready?"

Top followed Trennt's gaze across the distant, splintery terrain. Turning back, he cast another strange glance at the cut of ground immediately about them.

"Yeah. That might be best. Can't do it alone, though, Cap. You'll need rappelling line to start a path down the hillside and someone to lower gear. The still alone weighs a good thirty pounds empty."

Geri's eyes swept toward Trennt. "I'll go."

"Me too," added Wayne.

Baker spread his arms across the open engine compartment.

"You go ahead an' take 'em on, Whiskers. I kin handle these filters myse'f. Ketch up when I'm done. Ain't no big deal." Baker started wrenching at the fuel system.

Top glanced about the eager troops. He snuggled up his UV goggles and bowed toward the open.

"Straight north when you're done, Slick. About five klicks."

Baker didn't bother raising up from under the hood. "I'll find yah."

"Okay then, dudes and dudette, let's book."

Neither time nor age had dulled the old-timer's up-country abilities. The Corps' best training flooded back, making Top's motions purposeful and exact. Fueled by a younger man's juices, he set an unrelenting cadence over the miles of scorched, powdered scrub, onward toward the distant wash of dull green.

The hillside rolled off deceptively easy at first. Then it fell away so steeply that the only thing holding Trennt back was the rope link itself. Hand over hand, his gloves cautiously paid out the tough, braided nylon line.

He made a secondary level. Sunlight filtered in dusky green rays through the tight weave of suckered trees above. A musty deep forest scent rose up from even further below. The sap and bark smells were refreshing after all the dry, open country of the last few days and Trennt paused a moment to draw in their vitality.

"Should be near the drop-off," warned Top, invisible above him. "Take her real easy, Cap."

"Roger."

Trennt shook the last coils of brilliant orange rope out behind him. A half dozen more rough bounces and he broke through a tangle of willow saplings and lush fern, ten feet over the sandy canyon floor. A sudden, tremendous heat warmed his back. Brilliant spears of white light cut raw slashes at the foliage about him.

A final bounce and he was on level ground. Undoing his harness, Trennt came about and froze. Nestled in the valley basin, a blaze of fractured light erupted from acres of compressed glass and chrome. Before him, rank after rank of cars and trucks sat tucked fender to fender, running on forever. Some on the edges were upended or piggybacked, but most of the sun-faded assemblage tracked in orderly rows— like a moment of rush hour traffic quick-frozen on the freeway.

High above, Top read his silence.

"Blows your mind, huh, Cap?"

"What is it?"

"Not sure. Interstate ran through here once upon a time. Might've washed out or fell away during one of the early tsunami evacuations."

The still was up and running by the time Baker rejoined the group. Cans were distributed and every car, truck, and bus holding the barest promise of fuel was siphoned off for cleaning. By dusk ten gallons had slowly been strained free of moisture and contaminants. But forty more would require the same tedious treatment through all night babysitting.

Geri ran a cleaning twig under her fingernails. She'd spent a hard afternoon, lugging dirty fuel the one-hundred-plus yards to their portable strainer. Now, she raised her face to the welcome coolness sifting gently down the canyon walls.

"I'm going for a walk," she announced.

Her eyes met Trennt's as she passed, but he quickly shifted his gaze back to the slow trickle of clean fuel.

From his spot quietly cleaning guns, however, Baker followed her departure with a singular interest.

Yards away, Wayne stood alone, packing up a bounty of wild onions and potatoes he'd harvested from a nearby hillside. Some had been baked in mud wraps for the night's supper; the rest would supplement whatever might be foraged tomorrow.

Finished with his task, he was engaged in a leisurely study of the broad night sky as Geri happened along.

"Make any more progress with the notebook?"

He gave her a discerning glance. "Some. You were with those people for a long time?"

"They were my friends."

Wayne studied her further.

"In a couple more days we should find time to talk."

Geri caught something grave in his tone, but didn't press the issue. Instead, she joined his overhead search.

"Watching for paratroopers?"

He smiled. "Kind of a hobby. Looking for old satellites."

"You serious?"

"Takes the place of television," he mused. "A lot of old stuff is still orbiting up there. Some from before we were even born. All junk now, of course."

She squinted through the wash of distant white embers. "How do you find one?"

"They look like dull stars—except they move. Kind of an off-white or yellow color from reflected sunlight. The one I'm waiting for is pretty good-sized and due . . . there!"

Geri focused on a tiny ivory-colored pearl passing through the star field.

"I see it!" she said eagerly. "Which one is it?"

"That one's no satellite. That's the Phoenix II."

"The space station?"

"Yes."

She recalled the headlines. Eleven men and women astronauts died onboard, fried by the first heavy rush of solar wind almost fifteen years earlier. They sacrificed their lives remaining to measure radiation and send back manual updates, rather than bail out on the failing automatic systems. Their reward was to parade by nightly, the corpses of America's last heroes.

"Circles every ninety minutes, like clockwork," said Wayne.

"How long will they stay up there?"

"At a one-thousand-mile orbit, maybe forever."

The evening air took on a new chill as Geri watched the stellar tomb move away. She left Wayne and slowly proceeded deeper into both private thoughts and the night shrouded valley.

Beside the fuel still, Trennt rapped an impatient knuckle at the condensing trickle of precious sepia-colored fluid.

Propped against a nearby stump, Top chuckled.

"Watched pot never boils," he offered. "Always starts out slow with a new batch, Cap. Don't worry, she'll speed up. Come morning we should be real close."

Trennt cracked a dim smile. Snickering softly at himself, he started to rise.

"Maybe I should go check on the truck."

Holstering his cleaned pistol, Baker cut him off with an eager tone.

"Been workin' harder than all us combined, Jimbo. You stay put. I'll tend to it."

With that, the gunman was off.

Top considered Trennt for a time after Baker had left.

"Cap," he finally asked, "what'll you do when this is all over?"

Trennt shrugged. "Haven't thought that far."

"You cats really crossed swords with some big guns."

"Yeah."

"How'd a line grunt like you ever hook up with someone like that Corealis?"

"Real bad planning."

The old Marine grinned approvingly.

"You're a righteous dude, Cap. I dig you and I've been thinking on it. Once this is over, why not throw in with me? Full time. Wagon-mastering isn't so bad a gig. Lead 'em out, bring 'em in. I can teach you the trade routes. Hell, I might even let old Slick come—"

The sudden racket cut short his offer: a handful of rapid and sharp reports followed by a dying echo of deep, vibrating bangs. The clamor seemed to emanate from points all around the valley and the horizon flashed in unison with an eerie, phosphorescent pulse. In seconds the night returned to silence.

Trennt—and Wayne beyond—perked up curiously, but Top sprang to his feet, peering intensely at the horizon.

"What is it, Top? Heat lightning? EM storm?"

The old man didn't answer right off. When he did, his voice was slow and mechanical.

"Yeah. Probably nothing."

As they sat back down, Trennt noticed another whiff of that odd swampiness tainting the air. Across from him, Top said no more, but his eyes came back to the horizon time and again for a long while afterward.

Alone on her walk, Geri also paused at the strange pulses of noise and light. Soon, though, the night settled back and she strolled on through the icy blue moonlight; lost in private thoughts and unaware of just how far she'd wandered from camp.

Oddly, even among the cluttered ruin, there was a feeling here akin to what she'd known at the research station—freedom. It relaxed her.

Geri still longed for things other women had known: one man to love and one to truly love her. Family. But all that now seemed as possessions removed by too many business miles on designer sheets.

With her father chewed up by the Corealis juggernaut and history teachers in low demand, a "hostess" slot was all a pretty girl could find in the new order. It seemed innocent enough at the start—smile, talk, be nice. Then came the roaming hands . . . and threats from management.

"Hey there, Sugar Britches."

She flinched at the nearness of Baker's voice. A moment later he stepped from the shadow of a tipped truck.

"Dangerous walkin' 'round these wrecks unescorted. Good thing I happened by."

Geri regained her composure and started off again, but Baker stayed close.

"Yah know," he declared, "a gal could get herse'f into real deep trouble—mebbe even shot—for committin' acts o' sabotage."

Geri squinted tediously. "What're you talking about?"

Baker paused and grinned.

"All those breakdown coincidences we been havin' lately is what I'm talkin' 'bout. Loose fittin's, wire connections, and rims might've just happened, sure"— he reached into a pocket and let the empty medkit packets sift through his fingers—"but plugged fuel filters from sugar in the gas is somethin' that don't just come along."

The quiet shock in Geri's eyes sharpened his smile.

"Not very smart, jammin' them under a tire, like ya did. Better to just've tossed 'em in the fire. But mebbe you didn't have enough time or chance, huh?"

Baker's smile turned hard.

"Now, I personally don't much care how this posse

makes out—findin' the plane or not—but you truly do. So the way I see it, we got two ways to handle this: 'A,' we find some nice quiet spot to get acquainted. Or 'B,' Jimbo gets told and you get shot."

Geri tossed her head indignantly and tried to turn away, but Baker clamped her by a wrist. His eyes were suddenly fierce and predatory.

"Don't cold-shoulder me, girlie. I ain't askin' no permission. There's lots o' places a body could just plum disappear out here, too, ya know."

His grip held tight as a short, wide, push dagger popped out from his western belt buckle. Its stout blade touched under her chin, then levered persuasively against the hollow of her throat.

"I see us a nice little spot up yonder. That delivery truck'll do just fine."

Geri's belly flooded with ice. Ushered to the truck's clammy, weed-littered floor, she plopped backwards. Baker was on her in an instant. His hot searing lips dragged across her soft throat and below. His hips ground urgently against hers.

"Off with that top," he ordered in a cruel whisper.

She obeyed slowly, mechanically undoing the buttons. But it wasn't fast enough and he grabbed the collar of the khaki shirt, tearing out all the fasteners in one yank.

His blade left her throat. It came up between her breastbone and soiled bra, drawing a few beads of blood in his haste. A quick twist parted the tired garment and he eagerly sank his face in her warm, salty flesh.

A hand wedged between them, yanking at her belt. Geri choked off a resigned breath as her cargo pants were roughly peeled away. She tried conjuring up that old protective shell, but somehow she just couldn't manage anymore. Instead, she clenched her teeth and eyes, waiting for the inevitable.

"Baker!"

The gunman spun fiercely off the woman. Like a tiger rousted from its hard-earned prey, he was lost in a quiver of mindless animal rage, one which saw Trennt's unexpected presence only as that of a competitor.

Baker hovered, wide-eyed and tight-skinned, ready to lunge. Cold starlight rattled off his poised blade.

But the next instant the beast was gone and the man returned. His savagery flaked away, leaving the shooter grinning with the innocent shine of a school-boy prank.

"Caught us a saboteur, Jimbo," he announced proudly.

"So I see," Trennt replied. "Why don't you head back? I can handle the matter from here."

"Yeah, sure, Pard. Sure."

Baker gathered himself up and hopped down from the truck.

Inside the van, Trennt found yet another version of the troublesome woman. This one was drowned in a miserable silence, eyes glistening with the pain of someone made tragically vulnerable.

But his eyes couldn't avoid the obvious, either. And in the dim light her skin shone smooth and unblem-ished—just the right shading to illustrate fine muscle tone as she strove for breath.

Trennt was startled at his own surprise. Embarrassed and at a loss, he suddenly wanted to scream at her; call her all the filthy names he could think of, slap her senseless and take a turn between her thighs, just to teach her a lesson.

But a different door opened in him and, instead, he helped her up. Setting his own shirt about her bare shoulders, Trennt had only one question as they started back through the sharp settling chill.

"Why?"

She spoke through sniffles.

"Because everything that happened at the research station and since has somehow all been caused by Corealis. I hate him for the way he uses people up then throws them aside.

"My own father was a prominent administrator in the Crop Research Division, an honest man who wouldn't bend to Corealis' style of bookkeeping and whose presence was somehow threatening. So he was reduced in rank, demoted, and shuffled about in more and more demeaning roles until it finally cost his sanity and life.

"And because of him and Martin, I'd do anything to stop Corealis from getting whatever it was they discovered at that station—no matter what it might cost me."

Trennt stooped to retrieve the discarded sugar packs.

"You know," he confided, "Baker would've told me, anyway."

She dismissed it with a shrug. "I'd still have paid his price."

"So why the tears?"

Geri looked away. "You wouldn't understand."

CHAPTER 22

They stood anxiously below as Top leaned forward. High in the tree's dead branches with binoculars screwed tight to his eyes, the old-timer was quiet. A few more seconds and the specs came away. He soberly climbed back down.

"We're being followed, all right. There's dust in the air."

Trennt looked to the trailing horizon. "How far?"

"Not close. Mile or two, at least. Keeping their distance, but on our trail for sure."

"Tribes?" asked Wayne.

Top shook his head. "Still too far outside their country. Besides, gooners'd be on foot or using trucks. I'd guess these to be GEVs."

"Ground effects vehicles?" Trennt thought back to Freeville. "The Reds?"

"I'd say."

"Why haven't we heard them?"

"Newest stuff. High velocity, low pressure fans. Very quiet. But still dusty."

Baker looked on with his usual skepticism. "You sure, Whiskers?"

Top pragmatically offered the tree.

"Climb up there and wait, Slick. You can ask when they come by."

"How'd you know?" asked Geri.

"Just been having some bad vibes the last few days."

"What could they want?"

"Maybe nothing in particular," reasoned Top. "Like I said back in town, they're one nosy bunch. Too much time on their hands and way too much fire power. Bullies with guns and no one to keep them in line. And bet your stripes, if they followed us this far out, it's not to rap."

"What do we do? Turn back?"

Baker guffawed. "Heck no, darlin'. We find a good ambush site and put the hurt to 'em, X-style."

The old Marine chortled. "The quick answer to everything for you, huh, Slick? Pop 'em; drop 'em; smoke 'em; grease 'em."

The shooter stroked a rough hand over his autoloader. "That's right. Any grunt worth his salt would set up ah trap and waylay 'em from the corners, pop, pop, pop!"

Top smirked. "Sure, dude. Easy money." He considered Trennt and Baker. "I can believe you trying something like that alone, too. But in our case, figure on just a Vee-style ambush. Against a couple of squads, that leaves a big-time open door for counterattack."

"Besides them, though," he added, "we might have bigger problems put us in the hurt locker."

The old-timer looked at each face. "Guess none of you were up close and personal for any of the quakes, huh? New Madrid, Wabash Valley, Carolinas. Or the super shake out here. Well, those of us that were learned a lot about your basic seismic event,

ricky-tick. See this nice little gully we've been following the last few days? Anyone notice how fresh-cut
the side walls look? All the new-dead brush around
it? The ground leading straight toward your bird is
a fault line, Cap. Not long ago it shifted and I bet
it will again."

Their nervous eyes flashed about in sudden
awareness.

"I first noticed it when the truck last went down.
Wanted to be sure before I said anything. But that
on-and-off rotten egg smell is a good indicator. It's
sulfur gas from way down deep, like the stuff in oil
wells. Only comes up if you drill into it or a big crack
lets it free.

"Those nighttime bangs and light flashes back at the
gas station wasn't any heat lightning. It's what they call,
'brontides.' Noises of ground moving, way inside. Like
a clockspring slipping.

"Sometime, maybe soon, there's gonna be a shake.
Might be a mondo load or a bunch of tee-tee small
timers. Hard to say. But if we stay tracking your bird
on this line, we'll be walking the edge, straight into
the Wilds. And if it lets loose, the Reds or any gooners
might be the least of our worries."

Trennt surrendered to Baker's reasoning from back
at the church. "Maybe we should do just what you said
the other night. Throw in the towel, cut our losses, and
head back to Freeville."

Top pulled out his map and spread it across the
truck's hood.

"There's one big time shortcut," he declared. "Guaranteed to save travel time. But it is a ball-buster."

The team crowded silently about as he swiped a
grimy finger across the chart. It came down amid a
wavy hourglass shape marked, POISON FLATS.

Baker frowned sarcastically. "You forget the sick

tribesman? If you think we'd do any better, you're crazier'n I thought."

The old-timer offered upturned hands while Trennt gauged all the miles to be saved.

"Explain," Trennt demanded.

"The stuff in there is a mix of chemicals from old-time electronics and plastic manufacturing. The Quake slopped it all together and pooled it like one bad-ass cocktail. It runs another thirty or so klicks north-south and five or six east-west. But it necks down to only a mile or so not far ahead of here. The truck's too heavy to get over, so a crossing would have to be done on foot. Rickety-tick and after dark."

Baker laughed scornfully. "On foot and at night, huh? You happen to pack chem/rad suits for everybody? And boats?"

Top shook his head. "Don't need 'em, Slick. It's what they call photochemical. Boils like Old Faithful in daylight and will kill you a hundred yards off. But it calms down with sunset. Or cold, or rain. Mellows out to form these kind of . . . sandbars along the shallows, almost like a crusty ice. They're hard enough to walk on.

"We'd smear our clothes and skin with axle grease, burn jelly, anything we can find that'll stick. Rig up some snowshoes and dust masks. After dark, when the fumes settle, we tie everyone to a safety line and guide-stake our way across."

Baker continued his disbelief. "A mile of that crap on foot, in the dark? Why not just blow our brains out now 'n' save the agony?"

Unconvinced himself, Trennt swung aboard the truck. "Top, show me."

They were still a couple of miles upwind when the first scent reached them. It was deceiving. A faint touch of brimstone was carried in the air, almost like a Fourth of July perfuminess. But it gained, steadily mounting into a cheesy stench.

Still closer, the ground itself warmed, gathering in new and truly hostile odors. Hints of creosote and asphalt, chlorinated solvents, and heavy oils added their lot to the distant, poisonous stew.

Soon the air reeked with the noxious stink of a midsummer railyard. Even a half mile off the stench was eye watering. They broke out goggles and tied damp bandannas over their faces before proceeding.

An entire spent forest came into view. Brown as old tea bags and uniformly sucked dry of life, the once robust stand of majestic pine boughs now drooped like great arthritic claws, stripped of all greenery and poised as if to snatch up any witless trespasser.

A scattering of animal rib cages and yellowed skulls littered the place in firm testimony. Nocturnal foragers, disoriented and trapped at sunrise, rested as they'd fallen. No scavengers seemed foolhardy enough to pursue the hapless carcasses.

Top steered a crackling path through the brittle deadfall, finally stopping on a hill still hundreds of yards off. Even upwind, there was no getting any closer.

The air beyond swelled with a thick, roiling fog. Dense billows of the purest white, almost metallic, mist twisted away from its churning taffylike source. Cumbrous, high-rising corkscrews climbed to a hundred feet, then coalesced and sifted back on themselves like snowflakes which had been deboned and sent back for recycling.

Even at this distance, soaked masks were barely enough to restrain the diluted fumes. Every bit of exposed skin tingled and stung. After only a few minutes, Top slapped the truck hard in reverse and beat a hasty withdrawal.

The matter wasn't brought up again until back at the camp, as Trennt put the finishing touches on yet another willow branch snowshoe. He looked over, still not entirely convinced. "You're sure it will die down?"

"Come nightfall," Top pledged, "all that slop'll settle off to a mill pond. Won't hardly water an eye after midnight. If we give it extra time to scab up and start over at two or three in the morning, it'll be no worse than crossing a sand dune. With a good starry night you might even see all the way across."

His voice did find a hard, final note as he reiterated an earlier point. "But we've got to be across by dawn. The soup doesn't need much to start up again. Soon as any direct sunlight hits, she boils up fast."

They made for the narrow fording spot at dusk. The truck was parked in a gully and hidden with loose brush. Crossing gear was readied and set out. A night guard was posted and the wait began.

A rough hand jostled Trennt in the dark.

"Cap, it's time to grease up."

"Any more sounds behind us?"

"Not a peep," said Top.

They traded their fatigues for spares doused in a mix of axle grease and medkit jelly. Open flesh was slathered in more of the stuff. With cuffs tied off, snowshoes and face masks in place, Top issued insurance policies in the form of foil pill packets, explaining:

"Zinc detox. Down 'em with your whole canteen on the other side. They'll help pass any vapor or dust you absorb. Save the other pack for the trip back."

Trennt paused beside Wayne and Geri as they finished suiting up. He spoke to neither in particular. "No one expects you to be part of this."

The rookies shared a private glance. Wayne spoke for both.

"You need help carrying enough stakes to make a guideline."

Trennt nodded. "Okay."

Top hooked each person to the next with rappelling line. Everyone fell in single file, shouldering loads of sharpened willow sticks for trailblazing. Their other gear and weapons were divvied up and the group moved ahead.

The darkened flats awaited as calmly as the old-timer had prophesied. No vapor issued. No stink tainted the air. The madly boiling witch's brew of that very afternoon now sat starkly tranquil. Cast in an innocent and almost inviting white frostiness, the plain appeared no more threatening than a snow-blown prairie.

With the northern lights silently marking time overhead, they ventured across the bizarre caustic flat. Its crystalline surface snapped and crunched in brittle protest beneath every step. But it held solid.

As usual, the old-timer set a determined pace. His guide-stake trail was completed without incident and daybreak barely a suggestion as they set foot on new ground.

The unfamiliar shore was a replica of the one left behind. Another splintery and long dead grove led away to the high grass of a savannah-like plain. Beyond, the terrain quickly thickened, becoming the heavy cover of a semitropical woodland.

Though broadcasting a deceptive rural peace, the Wilds had earned their name for good reason. Here was an eerie, doleful region dosed heavily with full-spectrum sunlight and torrential coastal rains. Smothered in rampant weather swings, it had become a bizarre tangle of vines and lush wild scrub straight from Edgar Rice Burroughs.

Just steps inside its boundary, the familiar dry-roasted sky was traded for a dank olive canopy. Gnarled ropey climbers and waist-deep ferns crowded every spot of earth. An avenue of dense lacquered boughs stretched as far as anyone could see.

The clammy new air hung sickly sweet with the liberated sugars of plant decay. And interspersed was that same faint stink of rotten eggs.

Only a fraction of old forest giants had survived the quake path and harsh new times. The majority of ancient timber littered the ground in rotting hulks or jutted skyward as mangled parent stock for quick-growing suckers: new generation mutants better able to cope with the extreme and fitful weather.

Insects ruled the landscape. Enormous dragonflies darted about the thick air in their banded white and black, D-Day markings. Boiling clouds of pestering gnats and biting deerflies retreated before the invaders, then circled back to dive-bomb and torment at every step.

Various zoo animals liberated in the Quake had also migrated to this overgrown sanctuary. Some of the flourishing transplants now preceded the explorers in overhead squawks of alarm. Occasional parrots flashed through gaps in the canopy, thumping the heavy air with labored wing beats. At lower levels, monkeys chattered their babble of warning and scampered off through the branches.

They heard a distant cry that warbled in a hard rise from bass to falsetto and back, then vanished. Eyes flashed right.

"Man-eater," dismissed Top. "Lion. Tiger. Moving away from us."

Occasional failures were discovered, as well. The

huge domed rib cage of an elephant lay as it had collapsed, and its skull tall as a man. Splintered yellow tusks jutted forward in the dirt. The edges of its bones were well gnawed by scavengers and its empty sinus cavities were now draped in the silvered gauze of poisonous spider webs.

Deteriorating cars and trucks punctuated the green landscape like bizarre mod-art sculptures; derelict hulks left split and twisted by ancient blasts now set on tireless rims, washed in licks of fading soot and growing long feathers of rust.

A welcome sight broke into view during one of Top's infrequent rest breaks. A sprawling freshwater pond, sweet and inviting, loomed dead ahead.

But while everyone uncorked empty canteens and gladly started for its soothing crystal brilliance, Top barred their advance.

"Stay back, people. Let it be."

The group came up short, questioning both the command and the oasis beyond with a zombielike silence. Top's order held.

"I know it's there," he declared. "Just stay back."

Baker flatly disregarded the admonition and stomped forward. When Top snagged him by a sleeve, he yanked away.

"I know springwater when I see it, Whiskers. And that stuff's crystal clear!"

The old-timer nodded. "For good reason, Slick. Look it over. You see any minnows or water bugs? How come there's no frogs or cattails at the shore?"

"Who knows? Mebbe it's too cold."

"More like too dead."

Top pointed his carbine at an irregular stream of fat, lazy bubbles tumbling at the surface, farther out.

"Those ripples aren't springwater coming up. They're gas: monoxide, methane—worse."

Baker sniffed suspiciously. "I don't smell nuthin'."

"You won't. That's what makes it more dangerous. The water filters it."

"So, what is it?" asked Trennt.

"Sinkhole. Not unusual for them to follow a fault line, like the one we're on now. When the ground caves, everything around slides in and gets buried. Most just stay empty craters. But sometimes they clog and fill with floodwater. The stuff below rots and gasses off, sterilizes the water above with poison.

"Drinking that would boil your guts out. But even worse can happen if the bottom plug gets stirred up and breaks loose. All that bad air can fart out, ASAP, and smother everything downwind. There's no warning smell to let you know it's coming. Get caught too close and you'd die on your feet. We'll find safer, dirty water to refill the canteens. Right now just take five and look the other way."

Another hour's travel brought the first up-close warning of trespass: a clutch of weathered human skulls impaled on a corroded steel rod. Sun-bleached cheeks bore obscene red tears from the rusted spikes driven through each eye socket and their crusty brain vaults carried the deep, jagged, hack marks of scalp hunters. The group passed the grisly totem in silence.

The old Marine led them ever deeper, a proficient machine, confidently tracking a path through the dense bush. But the first day waned with no sign of the jet. Night was spent crammed together, fending off mosquito hordes in a tense and sleepless camp.

CHAPTER 23

Travel began anew at first light, more hours of fighting difficult terrain unsure of what or who might wait. Then, at midafternoon, a tick of something unnatural rattled Top's instincts. The old worminess crawled over his neck that said contact was near.

He motioned the rest to stay put and stretched his point slot to draw off any awaiting ambush fire. But there wasn't any. So he continued alone, homing in on the sensation.

Experience refined it to a smell, then reduced and isolated that further, to a new crispness in the muggy forest air. Finally, Top recognized it as the scent of freshly crushed plant matter.

Ahead dangled a large spider web. In it glistened bits of shredded lime confetti. Beyond, random clumps of whole leaves lay draped atop ground level foliage and the dense canopy was ruffled. Still further, bold spears of sunlight jabbed randomly through the top cover at stark, wide angles.

Then dead ahead sat a broad and nearly vertical sheet of metal.

❖   ❖   ❖

An hour had passed when Baker spied the approaching rustle of brush. He drew a bead on the motion with his weapon, holding back only when a harsh whisper sounded.

"Marine coming in!"

Top broke into sight. Carbine low in hand, he nodded vigorously, face flushed and tight with excitement.

"Found her!"

Everyone clustered about as he gasped between long, heaving breaths.

"She's straight on. A few klicks out."

Trennt squeezed the old-timer's shoulder.

"Good work, Top. Any signs of life?"

"Not from where I was. Just a tail section sticking up like a church steeple. And dead quiet, man. Watched her for a good ten minutes. Not a sound. But she does look to be in one piece."

The nuke was waiting as described. Its vertical stabilizer rested only a few degrees off center, smeared green with minced leaves and cabled in thick loops of severed vines, but upright and suggesting an intact airframe.

Trennt felt galvanized in its presence. A dreadful molasses of anticipation filled his chest as he issued orders.

"Top, you circle left. Baker, go right. I'll wait five, then take it straight in."

Allowing a few minutes for his flank men to advance, Trennt scrutinized the miracle craft. Even from this distance, its flying days were obviously over. She sat buried like an undignified sow in her eighth mile trench. But random swatches of still-shiny paint gave the forlorn notion of a child's best Christmas toy, misused and abandoned long before its time.

Her leading wing edges were battered and flattened. Smashed from their scything descent, the engine intakes were choked with drying mud and leaves. All her running lights were dead, the cockpit glass, a shattered opaque web.

A thin twist of green propellant steamed lazily off the still-warm engine. The air about her hung low with a hot stink of scorched oil and charred metal. But aside from the random metallic clinks of cooling engine parts, she sat wrapped in a haze of disquiet.

Trennt agonized during the delay. When he could no longer contain himself, he started cautiously ahead. Yet, in the span of only a few steps, he was overwhelmed with a new sense of urgency, flooded with a dumb need to know. After all this time, reaching the plane had become something he could no longer restrain himself from. Disregarding all his reconnoitering experience, he charged recklessly ahead.

"Cap, wait!" cautioned Top, dangerously breaking silence from the side.

"Jimbo, no!" joined Baker from the other.

But there was no stopping him. Trennt drove on and lunged through the twisted arch of a missing cabin door.

"Kosinski! You there?"

Only dead silence answered from the buckled and mud-crammed interior. The plane's hollow belly had acted as a plow, scraping up all the slimy earth it could manage to jam inside. In that dirt Trennt saw the reason for all their warnings.

Footprints.

Heavy steps thumped up outside. Baker slammed back-first into the fuselage. Still guarding outward, he caught his breath, scolding over a shoulder at the same time.

"Jimbo, why didn't y'all wait! There's been . . ."

Trennt finished from within. " . . . someone here already."

Top ducked under a wing. Irritated with Trennt's recklessness, he spoke only to Baker.

"You get him squared away. I'll pull security on the roof."

The old-timer shouldered his SKS and in a second was deftly poised atop a rent wing. Baker entered the buckled fuselage, himself uncommonly flustered.

"Jimbo, I ain't never seen yah do somethin' that careless before! Me, mebbe, yeah. But never you. And the worst place ever!"

Trennt only gazed vacantly about, unconcerned with his actions.

"No one." He mumbled as though in a daze. "Nothing. Maybe Kosinski walked off hurt somewhere. We need to find him."

"Shoot, Pard. There wasn't no pilot left on this here crate." The gunman fired a quick, dismissing glance about the wreck. "Well, that tears it then, Jimbo. Let's get on outta here while we still got our scalps."

The shooter spun on his heels and went back outside with the others. But Trennt remained. He emerged long minutes later, spent and dazed. Glancing at each face, he sought out his scout, perched silently above.

"What do you think, Top?"

Still miffed with his breach of security, the old-timer eyed Trennt sternly.

"I think we're really deep inside some tribe's back-yard. Either a scout or hunting party happened by this before us. Tracks say they're on foot. Probably headed out to join back up with their main body, somewhere."

"How far ahead?"

"Hour, maybe."

"What else?"

"They look to be traveling loose and sloppy. So the

gooners aren't expecting anyone this far inside their turf. That's big time in our favor. If we boogie right now, we can blow this pop stand with no hassle."

Trennt persisted. "How many?"

Like an oracle, Top gazed down, reading his thoughts.

"Ten, fifteen. Bad news is they got a couple dogs."

Trennt looked through the treetops. The sun was starting its nightward slide.

"I've come too far, Top. I've got to know for sure. You and the others wait down the trail or start back. I'll take it from here on my own."

Silent until now, Geri spoke up from the fringes.

"It's two days back, any way we look at it. I say wait here, until you do know."

Wayne nodded in accord, Baker didn't reply. Top went with the group decision, but he offered a final caution: "One last thing. Anybody notice the birds? Flocks been moving inland since we got here. Same with the game—all sounding to our east. It's not the time of year for anything to migrate. They know something's going down."

Baker clicked the safety back on his weapon, and squinted up at the old man. "You still talkin' quake?"

Top looked back. "Yeah, Slick, I am."

Even that possibility wouldn't put Trennt off. He snatched up Top's VDM specs and started out.

It was a tough hike. Trying to scout the gooners before dark meant a strenuous double-time pace. With his automatic shotgun carried at port arms, Trennt was breathing deeply after the first half mile. His slack mouth mechanically sucked at the thick air, choking down waves of suicidal gnats in raw gulps, fighting to ignore overheated muscles that throbbed and burned.

Near dusk Trennt broke into a clearing and came upon the hard-packed earth of a speed trail. He dropped to a knee, scouting the pathway. Sharp gouges and recent blood spatters were mixed with footprints and evidence of an animal kill. They also joined the cleated tire marks of at least two trucks.

Trennt raised his eyes at the buzz of overhead cicadas. Beyond, the turquoise heavens were thickening to an early bruise. For the first time in years, he felt a little boy's fear of the dark loosen deep within him. He swallowed hard, and, with the night goggles snugged in place, continued.

Traces of wood smoke were in the air . . . and voices. He heard them faintly, approaching the cola stained waters of a wide shallow stream.

Trennt sank to a crouch and crept the last yards through thick clutches of tall concealing reeds. It was dark enough now to hide his movements. But his mouth was full of bitter metal as he closed the final meters.

Top's estimate was right on the mark. Trennt counted fourteen gooners in the clearing. They looked to be a mix of Anglos and Hispanics, tattooed up and hard-core savage. Thankfully, no women or children were among their number.

The campsite appeared to be a familiar gathering point. As Trennt watched, a few members nimbly butchered a young boar. Others stoked the beginnings of a roasting fire. All were armed with machetes, guns and hand blades of varied nature.

The pile of miscellaneous loot sitting heaped at midcamp suggested the group to be a routine scavenging party. In its stack Trennt saw everything from scrounged cookware to pioneer tools. Also, there were tan-colored seat cushions and assorted trimwork from the plane—stuff destined to be creature comforts and gift trinkets.

A bolt of recognition flashed hot through him. There, among the spoils, was a familiar box: the same one he'd set inside the cockpit just moments before the passpod drop. All those rough air miles and it had somehow stayed aboard. He wondered if Kosinski might have preserved it in some selfless maneuver, which had ended up costing his own life.

Trennt's pulse heightened as a warrior, possibly the leader, walked over to open and examine the box. Another man happened by and the pair casually regarded the wire rack of stainless steel tubes suspended inside.

Each removed and evaluated one of the bullet shapes, before pressing the side detents and exposing the straw-colored glass ampoules held within. They raised the vials to the firelight, shook, and examined them. Deciding the fluid was of no immediate significance, they disregarded the box and walked off to check on the butchering.

Already Trennt could smell faint wisps of pot smoke in the air and some of the warriors appeared to pass about jugs of homemade hootch. No one seemed concerned with security tonight.

Then he saw the reason for the camp's nonchalance: dogs—huge, burr-covered monsters. Scar-faced and mangy, they presented the biggest obstacle to a camp incursion and his own most immediate danger.

From his spot in the reeds, Trennt counted three of the grim brutes. As he watched, they roughly competed for castoff hunks of raw boar fat and bones. Even so, one paused, suddenly drawing a bead right on the spot where Trennt hid.

The beast stared with bone-chilling, murderous yellow eyes. Its lips slowly curled, as if considering a charge. But a new scramble for a slab of freshly discarded gristle distracted the mutt and, before he might reconsider, Trennt slowly backed away.

CHAPTER 24

"Quarter loads," declared Baker, shining a light at Trennt's diagram in the dirt. "Quick 'n' quiet. With the silencer, hardly a peep."

"It'd only take one pooch to hear you and have the whole camp up," cautioned Top.

Baker shook his head definitively.

"Uh-uh. Them dogs'll be all together and near the carcass. Camp dogs're always hungry. When they get a rare chance to gorge themselves, they sleep like babies. Won't matter no how. They'll all be down before anyone can blink an eye. Guaranteed."

"Either way," interjected Trennt, "come morning they'll know we've been there. So we've got to move fast and hard as soon as we take the first step."

Baker glanced back to the diagram. "Gonna come upstream?"

"Best way. Enough water flow to mask our movement. Firm sandy bottom, barely shin-deep. Plenty of cattails to hide in." Trennt added more lines to the dirt.

"About fifty yards out it curves off to a straightaway. There, we'll set trip flares. If we're being chased, we'll hit them first and light up the area behind for Top, who'll be waiting with cover, further up here. As soon as the flares light, we dive off to the side and let him sweep the stream with suppressing fire."

The old timer rapped a thumbnail thoughtfully against his nose. "If you saw only two trucks, then it's got to be some kind of rendezvous spot for a still bigger group on its way."

Trennt had just one question. "Can we pull it off?"

The old Marine nodded judiciously. "Rock on."

They came in the early morning hours. Top took up station on the rise just around a sweeping bend from the camp. He matted down a good rest in the straw grass and clicked a 30-round banana clip in his SKS. Three other clips were set beside. The pair of non-combatants were left in his charge and safely tucked in behind him.

Top watched Baker happily assemble his two-piece sniper rifle, attach the long silencer, and quietly chamber subsonic .308-caliber rounds.

"Okay, homicide. Show us your stuff."

Baker's eyes twinkled as he and Trennt worked swipes of creek bottom mud over their faces. He put Top's night goggles on and started out in the lead. Clicking the safety off his S-12, Trennt tugged a loop of the gunman's pistol belt.

"Don't get carried away," he advised.

Baker's mud-streaked face parted to a brilliant white span of even, square teeth.

"Aw, Jimbo, quiet as a church mouse. Scout's honor."

But starting off, the shooter felt that sweet old rush mount up deep inside him. Leagues beyond the wildest passion, the nearest drug high paled in comparison. Be it for a country, kingdom, or square yard of earth, it didn't matter. This was his calling.

Once they'd disappeared, Top gauged his field of fire. He swept his rifle sights back and forth between the dim reed tops, then began prepping a couple of Baker's frag grenades.

Behind him Geri suddenly called in a harsh wheeze. "Wayne! Where're you going? Wayne!"

Top was stunned to see the man already well away, briskly trailing after the sappers.

"Rookie!" he added hoarsely. "Get back here!"

But the man continued and Geri got to her own feet, ready to start after him. Top took her arm and shook his head.

"Let him go. Just hope he don't blow things."

Baker and Trennt followed the streambed as planned. At its bend, Baker stood guard while Trennt paused to set out a pair of trip-wire flares. They then made for the camp itself.

The air still carried a maddening scent of roasted meat. But the area was graveyard quiet. The cook fire had burned down to a smoldering night light's glow, with the barbecued hog all but a memory. Gorged on wild pork, stoked with herb and jungle hootch, the gooners slept on.

As Baker had declared, the dogs were as complacent as their masters. Glutted on scraps, they were sleeping off their good fortune in a heap near the butchering site.

Trennt nestled low against the wide stump of a rotten elm. He nervously clenched the rubberized grips of his weapon, while Baker wormed through a clump of cattails another fifty feet upstream.

In a couple of minutes, Trennt saw the first hound buck in its sleep. A second rose groggily, going down

likewise a split second later. The third came fully
awake, drew breath to bark, but never got the chance.
In under four seconds Baker had neutralized the camp's
early warning system.

The sniper climbed from the stream bank. Cautiously
slinging the long gun upside down across his back, he
replaced it with his S-12, raised a thumbs-up to his
partner, and motioned ahead.

They entered the camp ninety degrees to each other,
automatic shotguns again held tight and hip high;
charged with a staggered mix of explosive shells and
10-gauge shot.

Baker scouted the two parked trucks. Both were well
worn four-wheel drives, foreign makes beat to hell and
decked out in tribal markings and gruesome curiosi-
ties. Scalps and frayed women's panties dangled from
the bodywork. Also, strings of human teeth and what
at first seemed to be dried garlic bulbs, but were soon
evident as mummified testicles. Luckily, both trucks
rode on old-fashioned pneumatic tires. With a cautious
look around, the shooter dropped to a knee and worked
his dagger into their muddy sidewalls.

They entered the camp further. Stepping over and
around stoned warriors, they made for the booty pile.
Astonishingly true to character, Trennt watched Baker
actually spare time enough to rummage through a plate
of leftover boar meat and select a hefty slice for
munching.

Both men snapped their weapons toward a sudden
movement at their rear. There Wayne froze, hands
raised. Exchanging a bewildered glance with Baker,
Trennt vigorously motioned the new man to stay put
and he continued the camp probe. But in seconds
Wayne ignored the order, and trailed after them.

Trennt found the ampoule rack still dumped atop
the booty pile. Its contents were filthy, but intact.

Unsuccessfully trying to one-hand the awkward mesh carrier into a cargo pocket, he paused when Wayne arrived beside him.

Wayne raised an empty canvas bandoleer and motioned for the vials. Still questioning his presence, Trennt obliged, gently handing over the device and freeing both his hands to cover their withdrawal.

They were backing away when Trennt heard one, then another, distinct clicks. He recognized a third as coming from behind and spun Wayne hard around.

Incredibly, the man was casually snapping off the glass necks and dumping the liquid as he walked along.

Trennt ripped the bandoleer away.

"Jimbo!"

Trennt ducked to the gray blur of a whirring machete. The thunderclap of Baker's S-12 flattened his ears, its explosive shell liquefying an attacking warrior's head poised just beside him. The men were showered in a gray-green mist of warm tissue and bitter, fleshy droplets.

A second gooner sprang up. Trennt dropped backwards, firing his own 10-gauge from the hip. Its round caught the man's midsection, cleaving him in a mince of shredded blue-pink organs and hunks of yellow backbone.

Trennt scrambled back to his feet. He shoved Wayne ahead and joined Baker, backpedaling toward the stream while dousing the awakened camp in a rain of shells. In an instant the simple incursion had become a full-fledged orgy of murder.

Wayne clenched anguished hands to his face at the water's edge. Screaming at the carnage, his words were lost to the searing thunderclap of heavy gunfire.

"*No! My God, please! No!*"

But there was no turning back. Explosive shells and buckshot fell heavy in crisscrossed, overlapping patterns.

They scattered the campfire and dropped several more gooners in midstride. Yet the ravenous automatics hurriedly gobbled up their magazines and the infiltrators were left clicking on empty chambers while still yards from the protective stream.

They broke for the water as the first return shots burned hotly after. Bullets slapped tree limbs and trunks, whining off the gravel at their feet. Splashing like madmen, they juggled spent weapons and dragged the wretched, sobbing anchor Wayne had become.

Not daring to slow and reload or even glance back, they pounded twenty yards through the pitch-blackness. At a dead run, the sand made each new step an escape from living taffy. Thirty yards; thirty-five, forty. Pounding full speed through the night, their lungs burned with exertion.

Hate and rage now poured after the bold invasion. Lathered profanities bloomed in their wake. Return fire narrowed the gap. A bullet whizzed over Trennt's head. Another cracked in the water at his side, singing off with an angry hum.

He felt the trip wires give way to his ankle. In a millisecond the blackness flared to a silver-white spray of erupting magnesium and phosphorous.

Top, where are you? he thought.

"Hit the deck, Skipper!"

The trio dove straight ahead on command, landing hard and skidding on their bellies in the astringent mineral waters. A second later, the old-timer's vintage carbine was growling its rage at the approaching enemy.

Fanned in its muzzle blasts, Top dispensed ancient 7.62 mm rounds with surgical precision. Textbook fire raked the enemy charge: side to side, and back again.

His cover bought Trennt and Baker time enough to unholster their 10 mm pistols and rejoin the fray.

Savages dropped in heavy splashes. Attacking footsteps soon became retreating ones. They were free.

Top hefted the smoking SKS in a defiant shake.

"First time, every time! Semper fi!"

The celebration was brief though, just long enough to catch their breath. Then it was a mad dash, through the moonglade at breakneck speed, back to the distant poison flats.

After four hours they could go no more. With bodies numb and senses half dead, the group tumbled in an unceremonious heap. They gasped for breath, rubbing at faces and limbs left slashed and burning from their headlong charge through the dark miles of razored sedge and thorned vines.

But from the moment they stopped, Trennt's eyes were hot on Wayne. Gulping jagged breaths, he struggled across to stand over the stranger in silent loathsome appraisal.

Trennt grabbed the man's shirt and hauled him up, eye to eye.

"You caused a lot of death back there for no good reason. And it's not over. You can damn well bet the survivors have gone straight for help."

More words failed him and Trennt fired a punch into the man's stomach.

He followed with a slap to the face; a backhand and another punch.

Top and Baker looked on, silently neutral. But Geri watched in obvious distress.

"You lousy bastard! What I should do is tie you to a goddam tree right here and leave you for them! Give you what you deserve and slow them down for the rest of us!" Trennt shook the man and slapped him again.

Then Geri lunged, grabbing his arm. "He's had enough, Jim! Leave him be!"

Trennt shucked off her hands. "Lady, I'm just getting started."

He yanked the sagging man erect.

"It might not matter now. But I want to know what the hell were you trying to do back there, huh? What?"

Blood welled up on Wayne's split lips.

"My job."

Trennt squinted. "What the hell's that mean? You work for Corealis? You do, don't you!"

He rattled the man with another shake.

"No. For no man. That was my church back there. I didn't mean for anyone to get hurt. Above all I didn't want that! I just wanted to destroy that stuff." Wayne's voice fell off in convulsed sobs.

But Trennt's rage grew even hotter. He throttled the man again. "Dammit! What is that stuff? Tell me or I swear I'll beat you to death right here—priest or not!"

Geri's voice stopped him cold. "It's a grain catalyst."

Wayne slipped through Trennt's fingers like so much forgotten sand. Trennt turned slowly around.

"And just how do you suddenly know so much?"

She looked down at Wayne. "He told me. He's known from the moment he set hands on Martin's diary. And because he knew how much I loved Martin, he wanted me to know. So, if you need to leave someone behind, tie me up as well. I'm just as guilty for keeping quiet."

Trennt sucked in a hot, threatening breath. "I just might!"

Geri knelt beside Wayne. Gently wiping his bloodied face, she continued:

"That stuff is a chemical and enzyme concentrate developed to get more grain production from crops— wheat, rice, whatever. It worked well enough to give a threefold harvest in half the growing time. But in it they also found something else. Made a certain way, it can permanently sterilize young adults: male and female both."

To the side, Baker croaked in a weak chuckle. He retrieved the muddy bandoleer, sarcastically hoisting it like a mock banner.

"That's a good one, Jimbo. All we been through to get us a birth control prescription!"

Top surged with his own exhausted snort.

But Wayne shook his head vigorously, talking passed his broken, swollen lips. "No! No, it's more than just that! Don't you see? They can use it in food distribution to control the population. To limit races or ethnic groups—anybody they want! Doctor Keener saw this for what it was and it destroyed him! That's why he ruined the lab and tried committing suicide. In his diary he outlined it all."

Wayne drew the tattered journal from a hip pocket. "Listen to his last entry. Then you decide."

Wayne squinted at the dim, faded script.

"I have never intentionally hurt anyone in my life. But I am guilty just the same through my many acts of omission. Wanting only to help my fellow man, I have instead, again and again, been pressed into service against him through words of false patriotism, and hollow pledges by Corealis and those of his kind.

"Too many times I have turned a blind eye to the true implications of my work. And once more I am confronted by a product I've developed which can serve no purpose, beyond an even greater manipulation of humanity. But no longer will I allow it to continue. And if that means a sacrifice be offered in substitute, then let it be me."

Wayne raised his face to Geri.

"What I haven't even told you is what I suspect was your planned part in it. The key you were given was a crucial link in tying up any loose ends for the people behind the program. It had to have been meant to trigger a mechanism that would gas everyone there. Then those in charge could have what they wanted with no evidence to worry about. But in trying to turn off the power systems, you only made it happen early— and that probably saved your life."

Trennt fell against a tree in anemic laughter. "With all the death from the quakes, N.A. Flu, ozone inversions, and everything else—someone is actually worried about birth control?"

"Yes!" nodded Wayne vigorously. "Exactly! They know Skylock will break. And when that happens they want a guaranteed, secret way to control the population, without political or religious interference. Think of what a powerful tool it would be!"

Trennt shook his head.

"Who cares? It's the same stuff people have been glad to have for the last ninety years—have wanted for the last nine thousand."

"It's more," defended Wayne, "the absolute power to render full involuntary control over anyone!"

Trennt raised a questioning hand.

"Is that so bad? In Chicago, I lived near the Zone D abortion clinic. Any idea what went on in places like that? I saw it on a regular basis. All the unwanted commoner babies were flushed out once a week and dumped in clear specimen bags for sanitation pickup. Dozens and dozens of pickle-sized blobs, in their own little zippered, plastic shrouds; poured in trash cans at the curb. Only, the sanitation pickup schedule wasn't as regular as it should have been, so they piled up quite often. Then they'd spoil in the heat and the starving dogs would come."

Geri turned away.

"This is worse than even that!" Wayne argued. "It dehumanizes the very core of mankind."

Trennt dropped his gaze.

"I'm not sure I even know what that means. But I do know how I stood helpless as my own babies drowned in their snot one night, because there wasn't enough proper help to tend them. That was pretty dehumanizing. If I can spare other people that kind of pain, maybe there is some good to be found in that stuff."

Geri took exception. "And what of the joy they'd also be denied? The same store of fond memories you've hung on to, even through the pain?"

Trennt licked his parched lips. "Baker?"

"Yeah, Pard."

"Go ahead. Smash them and be done with it."

The gunman hoisted the bandoleer to eye level and regarded the dirty vials. He cocked an arm to dash them as ordered, and Wayne vigorously entreated him:

"Yes, Baker! Do it! For God's sake, break every single one! Right now!"

His tone caused the shooter to pause.

"Bustin' these little glasses means that much to you, Cuz?"

Wayne faced Trennt. "I'm begging you. Do it and you won't have to tie me here. I'll walk back toward their camp. I give you my word as a priest. Just destroy that evil here and now!"

Baker lowered the vials. "If this guy is so set against this stuff, mebbe it's worth more than we know."

Trennt threw his hands out, divorcing himself of the entire matter.

"I've got no more time for this. It's another full day's travel back to the crossing. And the path we're leaving might as well have road signs."

"No!" protested Wayne. "Don't keep them! In the name of God! Don't!"

But Baker only clenched the bandoleer tighter.

CHAPTER 25

The day festered on. Drawing from a threatening sky and saturated earth, humidity grew in powers of ten. The soggy forest air became a smothering near-solid, something needing to be bitten off and chewed, rather than simply breathed. But Trennt never let up the pace.

Another four hours passed. Six. Eight. He drove his people through thickets and deadfalls; across marshy sandbars and gut-slick, rooty stretches. Fleeing unseen yet certain pursuit, they banged shins, barked elbows, and skinned hands: fumbling zombies plodding along in a waltz of fatigue, gulping bugs and rank swamp water with every step.

But even Trennt's adrenaline surge was fading, flaking off from the raging hunger, thirst, and pure exhaustion it had smothered in fear. Their steps slowed, then dragged. There was no choice but to rest.

The group plunged to the swampy ground for only the second time. Their clothes hung like soaked burlap. Runnels of foul sweat cut stark, weblike tributaries across their soiled faces and throats.

On his rump, Trennt kneaded stiffening calves. With eyes that came back to Wayne again and again, he found strength enough to once more confront the man. Only this time, it wasn't to punish, but to challenge.

"What you said back there, was that exactly what you read in that booklet?"

Closed-eyed, Wayne merely bobbed his head, huffing thin, swift breaths.

"Even if that stuff is what you say, how could they pull off such a thing? Why would they want to?"

Between more gulps of air, Wayne explained.

"Technology is the one thing which hasn't been lost. Even now, its precious secrets are locked away somewhere, ready to resurface when needed by those in power. And a large, unnecessary population feeding off that technology is a draining burden. Why have millions of people to deal with if you only need a percent to function? A country with that control has the ultimate economic weapon."

Trennt swiped at a trickle of sweat on his nose, debating the scope. "It'd be impossible to coordinate something like that."

Wayne licked his dry lips. He offered a melancholy record.

"The Nazis once worked out a pretty efficient system for something similar. So did a less polished and totally insane force in Cambodia named the Khmer Rouge. They tried restructuring their country by eliminating every educated person they could find. Not foreigners, either. Their own teachers, doctors, engineers. Countrymen they needed. What sense was that? This new method allows attaining the same end by a much less complex mechanism."

Wayne focused on Trennt.

"Remember how our own government tried legislating the two-child family law before the crash? That arose from something as simple as the call to decrease aggravated petroleum usage. But there was too much political 'due diligence,' religious interference, and minority backlash to get it moving.

"Now, they could pick and choose—manipulate behind the scenes as they pleased. As for getting it organized, don't forget the nice tight little groups they managed countrywide for the millennium census. Who says it couldn't be arranged again?

"They could blend special flours and breads at will. An empty stomach is always the best magnet. In times like these, food handouts are never questioned. Even in good times, soup kitchens . . ."

Wayne's voice fell away. His eyes swept toward the mucky woodland fog, recalling a personal failure just as gray.

"There was a time when I prayed for soup kitchen work. Fresh from college, I heard the Lord's call and headed straight for the seminary. Came out all set to be the new Saint Francis—roll up my sleeves and go to harvest for the Lord. I put in for a poor neighborhood, no nonsense stuff."

His head swayed mournfully.

"Instead, I was assigned to just the opposite. Made assistant pastor to a huge wealthy parish. Three thousand families with big bucks. Brand new church. Best of everything. My dreams of a dirt floor and cot were derailed by a multilevel rectory and private bedroom. Intercom, cable TV, housekeeper. A freezer loaded with T-bones. Amenities galore and no real responsibility. Pretty heady stuff for an apprentice saint.

"Amid all that, my life drifted away from shepherding and into the role of a dinner guest and cheerleader; all banquets and meetings. It got to the point where I was more concerned over a scratch in some parishioner's new Buick, than if they'd made their

Easter duty or not. Slowly, the world started seeming to need less salvation and more understanding.

"Then came the collapse. Suddenly there was no money, barely any food. The church was filled with a new kind of people—the frightened, praying kind. It was time for me finally to be their shepherd. Only by then, I was no different than they were. And putting on the team uniform didn't make a difference. So I left them all behind and ran away.

"When I finally returned, I found just what you did—nothing. I stayed there by myself, on and off. Alone, until you came."

"So why get in on this hassle?" asked Top.

"The old church was big on acts of atonement. I read the diary and saw my real chance to make a personal reparation."

Tears cut sharp trails down Wayne's filthy cheeks. His head sagged.

"But I fouled up even that."

Trennt studied the man with a new sense of commiseration.

"I guess we're all running from some ghost or other."

The clatter interrupted. A sharp, triple rap of wood on wood. Distant, but man-made. Seconds after, another responded far to the right. Then likewise a third, far left.

The three veterans shared a knowing glance.

"They got our number," mused Top, "and by now they know we're not many."

Trennt scanned the distance. Everything appeared deceivingly serene.

"Do they use any kind of organized fighting tactics?"

"Cut you off and pin you down," said Top. "Then the young bucks come—pilled-up and head-on, eager to improve their tribal standing with the scalps they take."

Baker already was working his dagger into deep X-shaped notches on a handful of pistol rounds. "Gonna pay dearly for this ole boy's pelt."

"How far to the crossing?" Trennt asked Top.

"Too far. They'll catch up."

Trennt gazed about the forest. This spot was a decided liability. "Anywhere's better than here. Let's move."

They clawed their way back to exhausted feet and forced themselves on. Their pursuers did likewise, dogging signals echoing every so often. Moving about, one flank ahead, then the other; falling back and shifting leads with an unnerving tempo. But the main thrust stayed solidly behind, driving them on to a final convergence and ambush.

A leaden grayness settled across the woodland. It bled off the steambath fast enough to actually chill the air. High up, a wind began to dip and ruffle the forest canopy. Cresting a brush-cluttered run of hilly saddles, a drizzle was loosened on the escapees. There and then Trennt made a decision. Turning to Baker, he rapped his knuckles against the man's ordnance bag.

"Bring your stuff."

The gunman brightened.

"We gonna make a stand, Jimbo?"

Trennt didn't expound. Instead, he led the shooter to a first thicket-crowned hillock.

"I'm betting the main force will come head-on, through there, like we did. The two flanking groups might converge about there and there. That would give this spot a direct line of ambush over all three. What can you rig up?"

In his swift appraising manner, Baker scrutinized each avenue and hill. He gave a quick litany of assessment.

"Double trip-wire grenades at all three approaches. Head on, two frags. Both short-fused with the zero-zero primers traded from smoke grenades. Each off-set to the other to maximize the blast area. Flanks get one napalm grenade each. The fire should light both approaches up for us and hold 'em back 'til those in front are dealt with."

The shooter swung his hand in the arc of an imaginary gun.

"We take out as many as possible from the first station, pop a smoke and fall back to the next, and the next. Same, same. Same, same. All the way out.

"A bonus comes in play at the last bunker. It's a pit that's full of wash-out gravel. Nice an' cupped, an' facin' out forward. We bury my kilo brick of plastique dead center, hook it to a friction fuse and you got the world's largest claymore set to clean house. Then skedaddle out the back door and it's home free."

Trennt nodded his approval. "Get to it."

Baker switched fuses and hooked them to thin filament trip wire. He straightened and loosened the pins for easy removal, then set his grenades low between concealing rocks. At the gravel pit he dug a V-trench. Nestling in the C-4 block, he tamped a heap of stone atop, in the fashion of a shaped charge.

Finished, he returned with a broad smile.

"All set, Jimbo."

Trennt nodded again.

"Good work. Now, gather up the rookies and move out."

Baker's jaw fell. "Pard, you ain't gonna . . ."

"My call. Get going."

"No," Baker protested. "I ain't leavin' you here alone."

"Uh-uh," joined a new voice. "Neither of you stays. Nobody's pulling this detail but me."

Top stood behind them, carbine slung over a shoulder.

"Those newbies need two grunts to get them back. Besides, Cap, you've got more important things to tend." He nodded at Geri, fitfully napping yards behind.

"Up to now I've been minding my own business, like you said, back in the desert. But I'm calling this rap session, if you like it or not. Wise up, Cap. You've been fighting long and hard. But down deep inside you know Buttercup and you are meant for each other. And that's the one solid thing to come from this whole mess. I'll mop this up one-handed. You get her safe and don't ever treat her bad."

The signals echoed again, this time much closer.

"Better boogie on out, now."

Trennt woke Geri and the four gathered up as Top decreed.

"Noah," said Geri, using his proper name, "you be careful."

The old-timer flashed his best smile. "Later, Sunshine."

Baker approached.

"Sure you wanna play this hand alone, Whiskers?"

Top huffed indignantly.

"One Marine is worth a squad of dizzy army pukes any day. The Corps didn't fold at Iwo, Khe-Sanh, or Desert Storm, sonny. It won't here, either. Now sky out. Ricky-tick!"

Baker drew a five-shot, snub-nose revolver from his belt and tossed it ahead.

"Hollow points bolted to 'Plus-P' loads. They'll get'cha home."

The old-timer snatched the backup gun in midair, setting it in his own waistline.

Last to leave, Trennt placed his S-12 and spare clips against a nearby tree.

Top appraised the gesture. "Might need that yourself."

Trennt tapped his holster. "Got enough."

They shared a fraternal, brothers-in-arms nod.

"Dee-dee on out, Cap. I got this gig covered. No sweat."

"We'll wait at the truck," Trennt declared.

"Right on. I'll dazzle 'em with some hard core fire and movement; then book myself. Be right behind you."

The old Marine looked Trennt firm in the eye.

"More important, you remember what I said. Hear me?"

Trennt nodded. "Watch your six."

Top flashed his odd, split-finger hand sign, same as the first time they'd met.

"Peace, dude. Keep on truckin'."

Trennt stepped away. The brush between them swished closed brusquely, like the curtains on a play's final act. He glanced behind after only a few steps. But even then the barrier was already back in place, as if nothing existed there.

Alone, Top set out his banana clips. After last night's skirmish, he had barely enough shells to fill one and half of another.

He loaded his SKS, setting it and the spare clip on the first rise. Beside it rested the pair of smoke grenades. He'd follow Trennt's plan: primary ambush site here, the secondary would be one back with the automatic shotgun and its stuffing of double-aught buck. Last stop would be the gravel sump and sand hill, where he'd bail out and let the magic of chemical energy take over.

Sequence fixed in his head, Top settled in behind the snarled weave of camouflaging branches and waited. In twenty minutes, the drizzle became a

shower. Fifteen minutes more and he saw them
coming. A lot of them; a platoon-sized group, maybe
more. Cutthroat faces were ritually blackened with
charcoal and painted for war in signs of the zodiac.
Even from this distance he could see drug-stoked
flames of murder glowing hotly in their eyes. Not a
smiling face in the bunch.

The frontrunners had guns; those behind, a mix of
spears and axes, machetes, and skinning knives. Top
clutched the ancient SKS, set his eye to its shallow
V-sight and waited for the trip wires to start the ball.

The left flank erupted in a greasy orange mushroom.
A pair of human torches burst forth, filling the air with
ghastly feral screams.

One of the frags blew at twelve o'clock. Then the
other. But nothing triggered on the right. The gooners
had somehow gotten past Baker's final trip wire.

Top spun that way and cut loose with his carbine.
The soaked brush split and sprayed from his impacting rounds. Deep in the green foliage a silhouette
bucked and fell. Three others jerked and slumped.

Now, though, the main force was regrouping and the
first probing shots of return fire sang wildly toward
him. Top squeezed off a handful of answering rounds.
Again, his marksmanship was superior. Unfortunately,
the heavy wet air was throwing in its lot with his
adversaries. It condensed and collected his powder
smoke in a twirling signpost overhead, drawing gooner
slugs ever closer.

Seconds more and Top's weapon clicked empty on
its first magazine. He yanked the sizzling clip free and
jammed in its only replacement. Fifteen more precious
rounds and his faithful SKS would be silenced for good.
Time to pop his smokes.

The gooners started to advance under daring,
one- and two-man charges. These Top dispatched as

the curtain of orange smoke merged and settled protectively about. Too soon though, his final 7.62 mm round left the skillet-hot carbine. Affectionately regarding the useless weapon for a moment, he scampered to the next fighting hole.

The old Marine snatched up Trennt's S-12 as new footsteps charged after. Firing point-blank into the heavy orange wall, 10-gauge loads punched quick holes toward more invisible attackers. The ground thumped with additional enemy dead. Yet still more were coming. And faster.

Shotgun in hand, Top scrambled for the plastique charge. Cresting the hill, a lucky gooner round ricocheted off a rock at his feet, spun up, and slapped him in the shoulder. He twirled at the bite, nearly dropping the weapon.

Damn, another heart! he thought.

Top bounced into the gravel sump and grabbed at the waiting friction fuse. But the sweat-slick fingers of one hand struggled futilely to mate with those gone icy-numb in his other. The starter slipped though his grip again and again.

A raging scream sounded above him. Top jerked up from his work and looked straight into a snarling, warpainted face of sharpened, snapping teeth.

He thrust his shotgun at a chopping machete. The killer blade glanced off the S-12's receiver, dislodging a thick curl of shaved aluminum. Top instinctively countered with a butt stroke into the savage, chomping mouth.

The attacker collapsed, broken-jawed, at his feet. Yet a bolt of scalding pain also tore through the old-timer's injured shoulder and the shotgun slid for good from his ruined grip.

Top took a deep breath and refocused his attention on the friction lighter. Setting the matte-colored cylinder between his teeth, he clamped tight and yanked the pull ring with his good hand. A "tick" of igniting primer compound sounded, followed by a lazy satisfying hiss of smoldering fuse. Twenty seconds now.

Top drew Baker's five-shot revolver as a new gooner face appeared before him. In a moment another was alongside. The little Colt dispatched both with a pair of hot .38-caliber slugs.

The shower was becoming a cold rain. It started to beat serious pockets of visibility in Top's smoke cover. Enemy bullets landed closer by the second. It was time to scoot.

He tucked the revolver in his belt and set his good hand to scooping a quick path over the hill. Near the crest a second round bit the old Marine, tearing deep in the back of a thigh.

Two, make an oak leaf cluster, Top thought, awarding himself another medal.

Top strained impossibly at cresting the hill. The leg was trashed. Cleaved through the hamstring, it folded under and he slid helplessly back into the pit.

Barely reaching its bottom, he faced a new pair of daring attackers. With honed machetes cocked and wanting his head for a trophy, they dove ahead. Two more shots ended their threat.

Top stoked a deep breath and tried evacuating again. It was no good. More than a couple of feeble steps up the incline were beyond him. He looked to the charge's shortening fuse, then drew back his shattered arm and leg to sit beside it.

In seconds, more heathen faces flashed over the hill. Aiming his final slug, the old Marine shouted defiantly above their war yells; something none of his attackers would understand.

"Three hearts means a trip home! SEMPER FI, YOU MOTHERS!"

❖   ❖   ❖

They'd listened to the pulses of grenades and staccato of distant gunfire. No one spoke. Yet everyone kept track of the shots, marking each new silence with Top's retreat to the next foxhole, and the next.

The impatient *Ker-Chug!* of detonating high explosive grumbled hopefully across the landscape. But the utter silence afterward confirmed the dismal outcome.

They paused, all silently facing the unseen carnage.

Geri slapped filthy hands to her face.

"Oh, Top! You too!"

Trennt felt his own stomach knot in loss. He sighed a grievous breath and set an encouraging hand to her shoulder.

"He did it for us," he urged. "Come on, let's go."

Geri dragged dirty fingers across her eyes and continued.

CHAPTER 26

Between catnaps they forged on, continuous rain blending day and night into a single erratic blur. Fighting the terrain and their own spent bodies, instinct had pushed them beyond all caution.

The rain finally stopped. Night was slowly graying to day. Ahead was a break in the forest and beyond the savannah loomed, broad and inviting. With time enough to still cross the chemical flats, they rushed wildly ahead.

The ambush was sprung before they could stop.

"Halt!"

Soviet riflemen appeared. The escapees were nailed dead to rights and numbly raised their hands in surrender. Red infantrymen disarmed the captives. From behind Major Dobruja approached, patiently examining each face.

"Surprised to see us, eh? Understandable. But the camp fool—Fibs, I believe—shared thoughts similar to your own, on crossing these very flats; along with the wild tale of that automatic airplane. I realize now that he was more intelligent than people gave him credit for. Probably should not have been so hard on him myself."

The major appreciatively examined the captured heap of handmade crossing gear.

"Quite a determined undertaking for a handful of civilians," he complimented, pausing specifically to eye Trennt. "If that is what you really are."

He next stopped at Wayne.

"And here is a new face. But I don't see the old one. Where—ahh! You stirred up a hornet's nest among the tribes and he remained to deal with them. I see."

Dobruja tapped a pensive finger to his lips as he swaggered.

"I've speculated much over what your purpose in such a resolute trek might be. But whatever, I'm certain the low northerly passage of that damaged jet aircraft figures in prominently. Now, I want to know how and why."

No one volunteered and the major nodded curtly.

"Honor-bound. I do appreciate the notion of valor and camaraderie. But the dawn is near and there is no time for bargaining."

He casually drew a sidearm and stuck it between Trennt's eyes.

"If three are dead, the fourth is guaranteed to talk."

He blinked apologetically and cocked the hammer.

"Sorry, my friend. You are first."

"NO!"

All faces swung toward Wayne.

"It's my project," he declared boldly. "These people are merely working for me. I'm the one you want. Let them go."

Josef lowered the pistol and approached curiously.

"And you are who?"

"Doctor Martin Keener."

"No!" Geri shouted. "Don't!"

Trennt barked as well. "What the hell are you doing?"

Wayne looked over mournfully.

"There's no use pretending. Let me be."

The major looked about, then shook his head.

"The name means nothing to me. Doctor of what?"

"Bioengineer," explained Wayne. "North American Chief of Studies for the Manna Project. You will find it all verifiable."

Josef gazed derisively about.

"I must apologize, but I am currently without any such method of doing so."

Josef's men chuckled darkly and Wayne offered the limp, crushed journal.

"Here is the diary I've kept on the matter," he explained, then pointed at Baker.

"He carries the finished product about his shoulders."

Dobruja hooked a finger, silently beckoning for the bandoleer. Baker slipped it off and flung it at the Red, who snapped it up, trying not to flinch at the loose and flailing ends.

"Another silly such action will be your last," he warned courteously.

Slipping one of the stainless vials from its grimy elastic band, Josef separated the scratched metal halves. A crimped, tempered glass ampoule slid into his palm. Raised to the beam of a flashlight, it shone as deep, 24-karat amber. The major's eyes ignited in its presence; not so much comprehending its value as basking in the glory of its possession.

He pointed at Wayne. "Take this and him with us. We will figure things out later."

Returning to Trennt, he snapped a magnanimous, mock salute.

"Thank you for your efforts, my friend. Mother Russia thanks you as well, I'm certain."

Dobruja's smile stayed tacked in place as his gun hand again raised. But his grin fled at the sound of a sudden, gathering groan.

The land began to growl, then shift. Soon the earth all about was quivering; swelling and surging. Surrounding trees were animated with a leaf-shaking palsy; their trunks popped and splintered. Captives and captors alike were pitched off their feet.

Disregarding the rest, Dobruja grabbed Wayne and hurried his men aboard the deflated ground-effects craft. It rose quickly and in seconds was cushioned safely above the gyrating landscape, gaining speed back toward the chemical flats.

In seconds more, the tremor ended. Trennt, Geri and Baker climbed back to their feet. Where level ground had been just moments before, now was a network of shallow, jagged furrows and rent earth.

They stood dumfounded amid the settling dust. Their lives had been spared, but they were disarmed and totally abandoned on hostile, unfamiliar ground. Once more, it was Baker who broke the spell. He threw a frustrated fist high after the departed GEV.

"Lousy bastards!" he growled. "Take a man's guns!"

He stomped about in maddened circles, kicking up muddy grass and frothing on, until Trennt calmly spoke.

"Dawn's still got to be at least a half hour away. The ground is soaked and cool from all the rain. If the overcast holds . . ."

Geri blinked dumbly. Baker forgot his rage.

"Jimbo. They took our suits, 'member? Besides, Whiskers said fog shot forty feet high as soon as sunup hit. We get stuck out there if that sky breaks—"

Trennt cut him off. "Then stay here, dammit!"

"He's right, though," added Geri. "What could we even use for skin cover?"

Trennt kicked at the mucky, rent earth.

"That!"

They clawed out wads of the tacky, foul-smelling clay and slapped it to their faces. More was slathered over their skin and clothes. Doing so, Baker spared time enough to quizzically regard his friend.

"Jimbo, what d'yah figger that ole boy was up to— givin' over the juice like he did, but lyin' to them Commies that way?"

Trennt sighed. "No personal good, that's for sure."

Sergeant Karelian paused as he finished climbing the rise. Ahead, the major was busily sweeping brush from Top's truck. Noticing his longtime comrade, he offered a disarming smile, but continued in his chore.

"Have we learned anything of value from our prisoner?" asked the sergeant, a bit mystified by Josef's actions.

Dobruja nodded judiciously.

"Much! From the good doctor's explanations, I believe we have captured a fine and valuable prize."

Sergeant Karelian grinned in accord. But something in the major's tone also struck him oddly—as did the gag over Wayne's mouth and his hands cuffed to the truck. Simultaneously, he noticed two grenades set loose on the ground.

Karelian never was able to ask why. A second later he found himself gazing down the silenced barrel of Dobruja's pistol. And into the officer's ruthless eyes.

The sound of the shot was barely that of a grasshopper taking flight. The stunned sergeant grabbed at his chest, slumping dead without a cry.

Dobruja smiled diplomatically at his shocked prisoner.

"My regrets for having to view that. But, you see, great promises were made to me early on in my career, yet they remain unfulfilled. All my hard labors have gone unappreciated and promotions been denied me for one vexing political reason or another.

"I've long needed something to expedite my career. But now, with the article in hand, I realize it just well may be time for me to put further allegiances aside and strike out on my own. There are other legion settlements further up the coast. We will proceed there and trade you and your product to the highest bidder." Josef's eyes ignited. "Back to your own people, perhaps!" He shrugged impishly. "But, I cannot leave witnesses behind. So, please excuse me one last time."

Dobruja retrieved his grenades and smiled thinly, stepping around the body of his longtime comrade. He walked above the remainder of his men, seated at the hill's base. When a few looked up from their rest break, they saw only their trusted major waving from above.

Josef gazed upon them with a deep and burning pride. Such fine soldiers. Genuine tears of love gathered as he slipped his fingers through the grenade pull pins. They would understand.

The salt flats had a much softer, spongier surface than during their night crossing. To this point it still held, but with less and less authority.

To protect the others from a breakthrough, Trennt had spread his point lead twenty yards. They were three-quarters of the way across when he heard Geri's frightened call.

"Trennt!"

He saw the danger immediately. Just yards behind, their trailing prints were filling with lazy coils of dense smoke. Like freshly seared branding-iron marks, each new impression was dissolving, linking up to the others in sullen, weblike fractures.

Advancing from its center, the salt flat itself was gradually passing back into solution. Sluggish, misty waves burped from the awakening stew and radiated outward like a leavening stage fog.

Trennt checked the sky. The cloud cover still held, but had much thinned to a shade of burnished pewter. The air was warming and, through his boots, he realized his feet were likewise starting to heat up.

But in the distance he could also see the other shore.

Baker swiped a hand at his mud-clogged eyes.

"Mebbe if we slow down some, Jimbo. Our steps'd be lighter then."

"And slower," he argued. "No. We've got to be over the shallows by now. Way passed the deep stuff and above the last to thaw. Don't slow down. Speed up! Faster! Go!"

But for the first time ever, Trennt saw Geri shake her head in surrender.

"Let's go!" he repeated.

She didn't move. Instead, her eyes swelled with tears. She sobbed and reeled perilously on her feet.

"No more. I can't. Just leave me be!"

Her words cut through Trennt at gut level. He felt a genuine sense of fear burn through him; a great notion of lost purpose and direction.

He walked back and growled in her face.

"No! You're not going soft on me now! After making it through a plane crash, desert, and all that other bullshit, you're going to quit when safety is only a few hundred yards away?"

Trennt grabbed Geri by her shirt sleeves and yanked her to face him.

"Lady, you were the tough one through this whole

nightmare! Thirsty, freezing, you never once complained and I admired that. It was you who kept me going, because I was too damned ashamed to quit first! Now, you just want to sit down and die? All right! Quit if you want. But so do I!"

Trennt swung his hand at Baker, some yards removed.

"Go on, man! She and I are stopping here! You go!"

Geri's stupor bled away to shock. Her eyebrows furrowed and flexed in disbelief. Yet Trennt stayed put. For the first time ever, he matched and held her stare.

His eyes filled with wonder. What a deplorable specimen she was—comically plastered in a foul-smelling mud wrap, speckled in goose bumps and red bug bites, puffy and swollen with cuts and scrapes, feverish from exhaustion and thirst. But in the entire world nothing more beautiful existed for him.

No contrition could possibly earn forgiveness for all the wrong he'd done. So Trennt merely stood there, hovering before her like a pathetic dunce.

Then, from somewhere far away, the true and right words gathered and finally came.

"What happened back at the church was real. I love you, dammit!"

Geri's bloodshot eyes flared. She didn't speak, but slowly, a hand gently rose to touch his filthy, beard-stubbled cheek. His arms, in turn, went tight around her.

"I don't care anymore about this," he declared. "I just want you."

Her gaze thawed. A trusting hand went to his and they joined Baker in making for the home shore.

The trio shuffle-walked side by side, keeping a double-time pace as growing whiffs of the chemical mist skittered determinedly after.

It reached their ankles, quickening toward their

shins and knees. The white fumes probed vigorously among flex cracks in their flaking mud cover. It found fabric and wicked its way inside, toward unprotected flesh.

Their skin began to tingle. First, insectlike tickles coursed up and down their legs. Then determined pinpricks, and finally legions of scalding bee stings.

They struggled on as a unit, forging through the last yards of caustic sands and toward the first spot of true earth. Never losing their contact with each other, the threesome bulldozed through the waist-deep, dead pine boughs, pulling and pushing. With their strength reserves at the absolute lowest, they gathered for a clumsy near-run toward the distant safety broadcast in a faint wash of green.

In their wake, the first probing rays of a new sun lanced the failing cloud cover. Mini white twisters sprouted in each sunbeam. Teetering uncertainly at birth, they eagerly gained their balance and launched skyward. More bloomed and joined the dance, until dozens of the ghostly entities whirled about in a frenzy.

Finally the sun burst through, flooding the caustic plain in one single blast. All the solitary flares raced toward its center and detonated into a single, mighty thrusting column of boiling silver-white.

But safe from its reach, the survivors stumbled, clothes and all, into the welcoming, algae-green waters of a well-shadowed marsh. They gratefully splashed through its shallow acreage, dousing themselves with soothing muck and splashing its scummy waters across their seared flesh, before simply plopping down.

Dipping her fingers in a shirt pocket, Geri withdrew a familiar and battered foil packet. She wordlessly rattled it before the others—Top's return-trip ration of detox pills.

They all choked down their last dose of the

astringent zinc and citric acid pellets, adding hand-fuls of brackish water, as well. Stomachs long empty and numb were violently awakened by the sour medicine and it stayed put only with the greatest effort.

Trennt spied a tree-lined ridge not far off. Later, they'd spend the night sheltering at its base. But for now, he just wanted to soak in this cool bath and relax.

CHAPTER 27

Major Dobruja shoved himself painfully away from the truck's oversized steering wheel. Ahead, shattered windshield glass was flecked with his blood. Through the cracks and spatters, a mauled reflection gazed back.

The scalp above the major's left ear glistened with a tarry sheen. Matted hair fed sluggish tributaries of ooze that forked about it and rejoined in the coarse weave of his shirt collar.

He looked to the handcuffed man slumped beside him.

"Are you hurt?"

Wayne put uncertain fingers to a bloody nose but did not answer.

Josef touched his own smashed cheekbone and his universe swayed suddenly with pain. Then he froze, realizing it was indeed doing just that.

Gazing passed his fractured image, the major settled on a slowly bobbing emptiness just beyond. The truck was seesawing on a rocky ledge. Beneath, a dim rugged slope plunged off to a shadow-choked bottom.

Josef cursed his haste. Winner's euphoria had clogged his better senses. Flying down the quake-leveled trail, he hadn't anticipated the hard jog cleaved into the fresh ridge. Only his catlike reflexes had prevented both vehicle and men from completing the full ride down. Now they were trapped.

Dobruja dared raise his eyes to the rearview mirror. Burned into the greasy bunchgrass, a pair of muddy skid marks disappeared beneath him. Only some knobby root ball or fickle boulder wedged under the truck was even now keeping it from completing the ride.

The Red settled back and took stock of their situation. His weapon was jammed, butt first, against the far door. Just his motion of reaching toward it made the old rover sway menacingly. Likewise, stretching for Wayne's locked wrist did the same.

The catalyst vials and diary were a better bet, though. Still wedged behind his seat, Josef touched both with no threat to their balance. His sidearm, too, remained securely holstered to his hip.

While messy and painful, his injuries were not life-threatening. The truck, though, was a lost cause; the odds of salvaging his captive, not much better.

Josef slowly retrieved and draped the web belt over his head, necklace-style. The journal went inside his shirt. His rifle and passenger were forgotten.

The major then shifted himself about. Left hand and foot went to the door frame. Right, on the steering wheel and brake pedal. The truck seemed to register his preparation, absorbing and magnifying the furtive motions into a single ominous rhythm.

Coiling in his powerful athlete's legs, Josef drew a full breath of thick forest air. He glanced at Wayne, stunned and edging toward unconsciousness.

"Sorry, my friend," he offered. "I can only manage so much."

With that, Josef erupted from the truck. But leaving, the major felt himself jerk aside as his holster snagged a spoke of the steering wheel. Its leather flap popped open and his precious pistol squirted out, taken in quick trade.

An assured landing also vanished and Josef fell short, impacting on the ledge face. His boots kicked frantically for footholds. Feverish hands tore at the gnarled clumps of exposed roots.

Behind, there was a simultaneous groan of complaining metal, as the unbalanced truck shifted about its fulcrum. It dipped left to right, up and down, in ragged seesaw motions.

Still aboard, only now did the situation register to Wayne. Tugging his manacled hand, his eyes briefly flashed about like a trapped animal. Then inexplicably, they stopped. The arm was lowered and the man assumed an oddly serene posture. Father Wayne drew a breath and gazed upward in surrender.

Momentarily righting itself, the vehicle teetered. Josef looked back in sudden hopes it might actually find a stable center. Yet the laws of physics were impatient and the truck upended smartly, and slipped off for the ragged, shadowed depths.

From his uncertain roost, Dobruja realized that his doomed passenger never uttered a single cry. But plastered nearly vertical against the crumbly sand and root-bound ledge, Josef's own survival was still very much in contention.

He felt the loose journal spin and slip dangerously low, inside his untucked shirt. Its mangled wire spine scraped down against his belly, slipping between it and his fatigue pants. The metal coil then snagged the lip of his cotton belt and dangled full weight, in the open.

Dobruja chanced a look below. Both he and the diary hung precariously over an eight-story drop. But securing the book was important enough to risk the effort.

The major loosed a hand. He edged it downward, between cliff and belly, tediously inching toward the notebook. His balance held. Even so, there wasn't clearance enough to quite touch and Josef gently exhaled to make room.

The action also allowed greater movement for the dangling manuscript. It took up a gentle walking sway, ratcheting over the belt's rough cotton weave, one loop at a time.

Now just inches away, Josef thrust his hand down. Snatching fingers scrambled over the text. They skipped hopelessly about its ragged cover and the journal squirted out into space, joining the man and precious truck already lost below.

The failed effort also compromised the major's balance and he felt himself start slowly drawing rearward. From the shadowed depths, however, a fickle breeze stirred. It issued up the stark chasm wall and twirled curiously about the soldier. It caressed his battered cheek and probed the fine muscular tension of his compressed back. Already given so many generous offerings, Fortune smiled.

The breeze nudged Josef toward safety.

An eternal silence hung through the gauzy prehistoric dreamscape. Day again. The remaining night fog was thickening to a coarseness that hinted of retreat. But not soon. And what had thus far condensed only made them more miserable with a heavy, soaking dew.

Arms wrapped wretchedly about himself, Baker trembled with chills as he searched the indistinct woodland. All about, the forest lines were dark, oblique slashes.

"Where d'yah figger the old man's truck is?"

Tightly holding Geri, dozing in his arms, Trennt shivered too.

"Seems like we came across further north, maybe. Might have to backtrack to find it."

A rattle sifted down the fog washed hillside. Geri tensed, waking, but they all remained silent, waiting for a repeat of the sound and hoping it was just a passing animal.

Seconds later the brush clattered again. And with it came the noise of loose footing. Working at a determined pace, the steps were thoroughly human. Thankfully, the noise was moving away. Its source would soon be gone.

But a final slide of gravel cascaded down toward them. At its apex a lone, hobbling shape broke through a clear spot in the fog. Grabbing at jerky handholds in the snarled weave of branches, a figure noticed them and paused.

Dobruja.

His feet slipped badly in the mushy hillside. Limping along with a gait every bit as lame as their own, he struggled to keep his balance. Half his face seemed smeared with mud or darkened by a large bruise.

Trennt's eyes found his immediately. A quick twist of surprise flared on his ruined mug and the major was gone. New effort drove him back the way he'd come and higher into the heavy mist.

Geri felt a quiver radiate through Trennt. His shoulders tensed, then he slumped beneath the crushing yoke of restored duty. Her fingers gently restrained him.

"Let it go," she urged in a whisper. But the stiffening of his body said that could not be.

Trennt's eyes eluded her. They raised, instead, to the fog, training on the whirling thick curtain blending shut in the Russian's wake.

Geri's continued silence remained a plea for him to stay. Yet even so, her grip relaxed.

Trennt climbed to his feet and issued a final directive.

"Baker, head straight west. To the shoreline and south. I'll check this out, then find the truck and catch up."

He raised Geri to her feet, gently kissing her.

"You keep her safe for me," he ordered and, not looking back, started off.

Three hours had passed. Trennt broke through a snarling tangle of fireweed to the base of yet another tremor-fresh scarp. Twice since starting, he'd heard brontides. But nothing more had happened and he moved along.

The air, which had earlier been a chilling nuisance, now offered soothing comfort to his frazzled leg muscles. He rubbed them a time while scouting the line of determined footprints still leading him on.

Again, Trennt forced his body ahead and his misgivings behind. Still upward and after. Pulling at bare root braids and rocks, his corded arms slowly drew him ahead. Bad enough, having traded a sweet dream for a filthy chore, but not a quarter mile back, an aching question had also been answered.

He'd found Top's mangled truck, belly-up. Beneath it, a virtuous man, crushed to death and left discarded. And once again, there was no time to spare for a burial—only time enough to remove his own safari shirt and place it over the silent bloodless face.

Trennt pushed upward. The weary tendons propelling him caught and skipped like frayed cables, one excruciating step after another.

Finally, he crested the scarp. But having arrived, his aches gave way suddenly to a quick flash of even more powerful hunter instincts. With eyes gone huge and flat, Trennt cast a scouring glance across the hundred-plus feet from this ledge to a lesser twin.

He knew his quarry was still ahead. Yet his scalp pricked in warning from a new and invisible presence off his flank. He saw nothing though and returned to scout the silvery-green path of trampled grass before him.

A change of wind brought new smells. The sea, very close now, loomed brisk and refreshing, leavened with vitality. But his ill-timed distraction cost Trennt a misstep and he buckled under a twisted ankle.

The joint flamed and gave way, dropping Trennt to his rump in the sandy cliff-top grass. He clenched and kneaded the ligament and flesh—fast growing stiff as a hunk of old statue.

Damn it! He couldn't fold now. Had to keep going. Get to his feet before the leg swelled and left him lame. He straightened halfway with certain difficulty.

"American!"

The shout curdled Trennt's blood and brought him fully erect. From the breeze-stirred treeline stepped his adversary. The web belt of mud-caked vials hung about the major's shoulder in plain sight. But the man possessing them was no longer the steely-eyed hunter of yesterday. Now, just a survivor. Damaged goods, same as himself.

Dobruja's left cheek was shiny purple with swelling. His eye, changed to a sunken black slit, was set in tight billowing flesh. He moved into the open, favoring his right shoulder, yet obviously inflated with a certain exhilaration at this ultimate confrontation.

Speaking took him some effort. Still, Josef's English remained impeccable.

"I see you are alone, as well."

Trennt nodded. "I am."

"I have a proposal."

"I'm listening."

"It is not proper for two professionals such as us to waste time and strength chasing each other. Let us finish the matter here and now, on a field of personal honor." Dobruja grinned appreciatively. "Looking at our equally deplorable conditions, I would say neither of us has the advantage. Would you not agree?"

Trennt didn't answer. "I found our truck," he said instead. "And the man you took from us. Just so you know. He wasn't a researcher. He was a priest."

The major shrugged pragmatically.

"And the unfortunate casualty of an automobile accident, I'm afraid. But let us pursue more important things."

Josef removed the bandoleer and offered it enticingly. With a quick snap, he flung it to the flinty dust midway between them.

"To the winner, go the spoils."

For a time the men merely regarded each other. Reluctant combatants hunched over in the teetering sway of weary apes, stale air worked through their slack mouths. Neither possessed strength enough for a long fight, but both were matter-of-fact about the prize set between them.

The Russian lunged forward. Trennt met his charge. They collided with the awkward ferocity of grade-school wrestlers in a flurry of bared teeth and labored grunts. Greasy hands flailed for a grip. Their exhausted struggle took on the appearance of a sloppy, pathetic dance.

Aware of Trennt's weakened ankle, Dobruja focused on it. He pulled and twisted, craftily widening his adversary's stance. Finally, he felt the proper shift in weight and levered Trennt around and down in the dirt.

Trennt kicked his good leg straight back into the

major's gut and scrambled quickly out of reach. They separated and regrouped.

"Good move," congratulated the Red. "Perhaps the next round won't go so well."

Taking stock of himself, Trennt knew the man was right. His ankle was unreliable. His vision, blurred. And his skull throbbed with the fevered beat of temple-high drop hammers. He gazed mournfully at the bandoleer and Josef's cold, wolfish grin.

"Come on! Come on now, Yankee man!"

Trennt realized the only way to end this matter was through total and absolute abandon. But his heart ached. What for so long would have been welcomed as a rightful penance, now crushed down on him in excruciating loss. His soul filled with a new anguish— the bitter irony of an unrealized and forsaken dream.

Trennt drew his breath slowly and tightened his stance. There was no time for rehearsing. Just get it done. Head down, he came on.

The major read his charge and braced for a simple kick and shove. Yet at the last second, Trennt's courageous rush became a cheap dive for the prize.

Dobruja threw his eyes wide in realization and alarm. His shock erupted in a rolling scream of denial.

"NO!"

Josef chased after his retreating foe. Just steps ahead, Trennt scrambled determinedly toward the ledge. Bandoleer clutched tight, he mule-kicked at the hands struggling to restrain him. A half dozen flailing snaps landed on Dobruja. But the man endured them all to snag a pant leg.

Down went Trennt.

In a moment the major was on him from behind, one arm about his neck, and the other grabbing at a loose tangle of bootlace, working the injured foot painfully backward.

Trennt managed a wild, roundhouse elbow to the man's swollen eye. The major spat a lizard's hiss in pain, but kept his grip. He fired a retaliating punch into Trennt's kidneys. A second, third, and fourth.

Trennt had no further intention of fighting back. He'd committed every last ounce of strength to making the cliff edge and struggled on tortoiselike, dragging both men slowly forward.

Josef's unobstructed punches landed harder and faster. A karate chop to the base of Trennt's skull finally dislodged the bandoleer. Trennt felt it leave his hand as his face plunged forward into the grit.

In his exhaustion, he hoped vainly that the belt had somehow fallen over. But its broad coarse weave soon dragged down across his face. It skipped off his chin and clamped viselike about his throat.

Behind it, Dobruja levered in a maniac's grip. Trennt could feel his neck bones pop and his windpipe flatten. The edges of his sight dimmed. His consciousness bled off and retreated to a wobbly orbit somewhere high above. Oxygen-starved brain cells went wild, fast-forwarding through snapshot glimpses of his life.

Paying out like slack chain through a runaway pulley, random slices of boyhood times flashed by. The army. His life as a woodsman, husband, and father.

A bittersweet image of Geri materialized. Then even it faded as his mind whirled helplessly toward the inevitable rush of approaching black.

Trennt felt his body surrender, his arms go limp. He knew he must now die.

His ears filled with a snake's sudden and angry hiss. A sharp crack, like leather on leather, slapped hard in the sullen air. Trennt heard the sounds of thrashing feet, gurgles and snorts, the bellowing cough of a hog clearing its throat.

The strangling noose abruptly relaxed. His

executioner's grip fell away and glorious scalding air flooded his gullet.

Trennt managed a feeble roll to his side. Through blurred, tearing vision he saw the Russian major fully erect and on his toes, ballerina style. The man waltzed drunkenly sideways, his hands worrying insectlike at a hardwood arrow lancing his neck.

Confused, Trennt struggled to his knees, as Dobruja continued past. The web belt dropped from his grasp and to the ground. Stumbling on, the major paused at the cliff edge and glanced back.

Dumbfounded, he toppled gracelessly off into the rift.

A blaze of colors on the fatal arrow caught Trennt's eye. It was a curiously familiar fletching blended of red, green, black, and yellow.

On hands and knees, Trennt painfully raised his head. Across the divide he saw two black men. Hunters. One was lean with gentle features. But it was the well-muscled archer, standing with fired bow still in hand, who captured his attention.

No expression showed on the face bearing long keloid scars of nobility. Yet a hand did raise the bow a notch, indicating a direction of travel.

Trennt dropped his head and struggled to work his voice. Rising again, though, he found the other cliff empty and his benefactors gone. His only companion was the filthy belt.

CHAPTER 28

Trennt dragged up the forfeited prize and climbed back to his feet. Shuffle-walking along, he proceeded in the direction indicated. Not certain why, he didn't know for how far or how long.

Then from nowhere hovered the apparition of a soldier. Baby-faced and dressed in crisp G.I. fatigues, he stood with weapon low, watching.

Trennt hunkered on past, close enough to touch, but certain it was just his spent mind conjuring a mirage.

His attention, went instead, to a broad shining lagoon just yards ahead. It was water as clear as any he'd ever seen. Sweet and deep and long. He remembered once learning to swim in just such a place. Maybe the owners would let him take a dip now.

But the phantom persisted. It addressed him in a respectful, almost apologetic tone.

"Sir?"

Trennt walked on, tugging at his belt as the ghost spoke yet again.

"Sir. This way, sir. They're waiting for you."

Trennt finally stopped and wheeled painfully about. In much the manner of a doorman, the soldier swept out a hand, indicating a path to follow. But doing so, he made no attempt to either force Trennt or disarm him of his hard-earned prize.

Trennt inspected the youth head to foot and back. For reasons completely unknown, he complied. Turning from the lagoon, he limped into the broad mouth of a sloping gully and descended a narrowing chute leading to the small shoreline encampment set at its end.

Through a clutch of trees Trennt saw the ocean. It rolled gently on with peaceful green swells, but to his disappointment, shared none of its cooling breeze. Rather, it selfishly drew the stale land air seaward, instead.

A pair of high-speed, inflatable rafts sat on the rocky shore. Maybe a dozen people moved about. None looked familiar, save one.

Dressed in a crisp blue jumpsuit stood Royce Corealis.

The director waited expectantly in the open, hands astride hips and handsome face struck in stone-cold respect. His voice rang bell clear as Trennt approached.

"Look what stands before you, people! The very definition of valor itself!"

Corealis raised his head in something of reverence, shaking it with slow and absolute wonder.

"This man took on all odds and comers to fulfill his duty. My god, Trennt, what a noble specimen you are!"

Trennt did not reply.

The silent moment also brought a pause to the director. In it he found time to express his contempt for all those of less virtue.

"I remember seeing mountains of grain when I was

a boy. Vast golden hills lying out in the rain because there weren't enough bins to hold the harvest. And still, my farmer father struggled, scraping up enough money to buy us kids shoes.

"I saw surplus potatoes dumped in the ocean; milk poured in sewers, cattle shot rather than sold for low prices. And, the supreme idiocy, land shelved to lie fallow. All inefficiencies and theft perpetrated by the white-collar criminals in their high tower city lairs. Patronizing those they feared with welfare handouts, encouraging the free breeding of drug addicts and psychotic criminals, just to insure their own rank."

But this reverie held no significance for Trennt. "I have what you want," he proclaimed. "Good people died helping me get it and I want to know why."

The director took no offense at the interruption, nodding amicably.

"As a soldier in your country's service, you have indeed earned the right. We are at war, Mister James Trennt. Without guns or armies, we are still very much fighting for our very survival. And what you hold in your hand is key to our victory.

"Skylock has reduced all world powers to economic square one. And those same powers share a common denominator in the bulk of their unserviceable populations.

"In years past that problem was exercised with real war. It thinned the people, rebuilt industry, and strengthened the currency. Throughout history, all that shooting has ever amounted to was a chess game of mutual consent. An economic cure-all, fueled by propaganda and patriotism to make it honorable.

"But nuclear proliferation ended those easier days. And no workable alternative was available. Until now. Painful as it's been, Skylock has provided us with that alternative. But it is breaking, diminishing even as we speak. The solar storm is losing strength and once the poles complete their reversal, there will be a full return to geologic and atmospheric stability.

"Yet under those new friendly skies and solid ground will also be the stark potential for at least fifty years of a cashless, bartering society. We know it and the Manna Project steering committee knows it. Whoever gets their currency to the table first will call the shots. And no one wants it to be us. So the question becomes a personal one for you.

"Would you deny your country its chance to set the bar? A chance also to rebuild its cities without slums? Recreate a stronger America, whole and proud, instead of one owned by foreign dollars and run on cowardly welfare programs?"

Corealis took a step forward and spread his arms.

"Don't mistake my presence as the result of a love for being in charge. Rather, more because of its curse. But I learned long ago that no one can legislate morality. That all decadent societies need to be extinguished in order to be rebuilt. And someone needs to step up and brutally take the reins in order for that to happen.

"In the last decades, the United States had become the same as the old Roman Empire; beyond its golden age and on a pathetic slide away from the sanctity of family, hard work, and proper codes of conduct. It dove headlong into the unbridled dregs of sexual excess, drug abuse, and mollycoddling legal systems.

"Then, just like the Bible, with its Old Testament plagues, Skylock arrived to provide a practical spring-board to regeneration. It cleansed our ranks and left a nucleus of righteous people to take up the yoke of their society, people willing to sacrifice and deny themselves in order to ordain its proper destiny. And you have just proven your mettle as one of them."

The cold beacon of his logic was blinding. Trennt was being sweetly lulled by values dear and concepts valid. And he found himself wanting to agree, nodding idly in accord.

In body, as well as now in mind, Trennt was too weak to resist further. He had to take full and swift action.

With a quick twist, the ampoules were underfoot.

"I hope you have a reserve plan!"

Royce suspended his argument. His face clouded with genuine distress as he nodded. "Of course I do. But your choice does disappoint me."

Trennt hovered, poised to crush the vials as Corealis motioned behind.

"Let me introduce a new factor to help you reconsider."

A soldier appeared, leading Geri, hands bound, behind her.

Trennt felt the raw comfort of his rage desert him. He stumbled back and gawked.

Yet even free to beg, the woman refused. Instead, her green eyes burned as fierce and determined as ever.

"*Do it Trennt!*" She commanded. "*For God's sake, do it!*"

Her cry wasn't what should have passed between lovers and for a fleeting moment the balance of power tipped with Trennt. But it fell immediately back with Baker's appearance, a second later.

"How long've you been working for him?" Trennt heard himself ask.

The gunman shrugged. "All along—same as you. I said it before, Pard. This ain't nuthin' but business. And nuthin' in business stays a secret. What we give to Uncle Sam today, he might well trade away or sell off tomorrow. But then that's his privilege. In the meantime, we're just givin' somethin' back to the people who own it, anyway. And whatever happens later will or won't, with or without us."

Baker stepped closer.

"Think on it, Jimbo. Our profession's like ball players. Ain't much call for middle-aged couriers or mechanics. And that's where we're headed. But here's our brass ring and there's room enough for us both to grab a hold. Take it with me."

"Listen to your friend," Corealis encouraged. "He makes good sense. And don't be too hard on him for being practical. He made the only logical choice. In the meantime, look at yourself. Dead on your feet and nothing to show for it."

Trennt disgustedly flung the belt ahead. "Eat 'em!"

Corealis, in turn, motioned to his guards. Geri's cuffs were unlocked. She ran to Trennt's frail embrace, touched fingers to the fresh blue and purple strangle marks on his throat; kissed his filthy cheeks and lips.

Royce gently removed the surviving ampoules and inspected each one. Carefully resetting them in a larger insulated box, he took a moment to sadly regard the lovers.

"A supreme disappointment," he murmured to Baker, beside him. "After such a fine vocation, he folds for what?"

The gunman shook his head.

"Don't. Don't hard talk my friend."

Royce shrugged off the matter.

"As you wish."

Royce then called out.

"I've accepted your flag of surrender, Mister Trennt. And I am not out to make this episode into anything personal. So, we'll be on our way. And you can be on yours."

Geri sneered, looking back.

"Always so easy for your kind, isn't it? Just use people up and move on."

The director offered her a small, benign smile.

"People make their own choices, kitten. You've made yours."

Royce motioned to another soldier, who brought up a haversack.

"For understandable reasons, I can't allow you a firearm. But inside the sack you will find rations enough for a week. It's the best trade I can make. You're free to go."

His eyes never leaving Corealis, Trennt lifted the goods. He offered no thanks, but took Geri's hand and started a slow, deliberate march back up the gully.

"Jimbo!"

They didn't look.

"Jimbo!"

Still no acknowledgement.

Finally, Baker jogged up, stopping at their backs.

"Jimbo, wait! Hear me out."

There, Trennt did stop. But facing away, he still didn't speak. Remaining behind, the shooter mewed uncharacteristically.

"It's all just a silly game. Companies, countries—everyone wantin' to be in charge. Bigger 'n' better. First in line. So what? Sooner or later they get ours and we get theirs. Why not cash in on the deal?"

Trennt slowly came about. His quiet stare made the man squirm.

"Don't look at me that way, Pard. Like I'm some two-bit chicken thief."

But Trennt didn't condemn. Instead, he praised.

"That was some pretty convincing talk you gave at the church. 'Maybe we should quit, Jimbo. Turn back.'"

Baker's face tightened.

"At the time, I meant it. With all my heart."

Trennt gazed protectively at Geri.

"Not keeping her safe, you broke a bigger trust, to me." He nodded behind. "Go on. Your master's waiting."

The couple moved off.

Baker didn't follow, but continued his plea.

"Pard, we been through too much to quit like this. I'd rather take a bullet than see you just turn away. Say somethin'. Please."

"If you mean to shoot us in the back, be quick about it."

"Aw, Jimbo, nobody's gonna . . ."

Baker's voice tapered off. A lump of grief slid down his throat and he walked away, as well. Even though hurting, his opinion didn't flag: "He's a good man."

Corealis looked up at the shooter walking toward him.

"Trennt? The best I've ever seen. But he's acquired an Achilles' heel and that makes him risky."

Royce glanced toward the departing couple, then to the shore.

"The first raft is set to leave," he said. "Take it to the plane and relax."

Baker nodded and ambled on. But halfway, Trennt's last words twirled uneasily in his head. He paused.

"Nuthin's gonna happen, right?"

His reappearance startled Corealis.

"We're breaking camp. What's it look like?"

"No. I mean with Jimbo."

Corealis repeated. "The raft is leaving. Be on your way." His dodge only filled the dank air with more peril.

"Somethin' is goin' down. Ain't it?"

When Royce didn't answer, Baker grabbed a sleeve. "I asked you a question."

Corealis yanked away, annoyed, but still silent. And Baker shook his head.

"Uh-uh! Ain't nobody gunnin' down Jimbo Trennt like a dog."

The director nodded to several zealous security men.

"You don't have much to say in the matter."

"We gave him our word!"

Royce drew a burdened breath.

"No. You did. And, you're keeping it. Besides, he's no longer a friend, remember? Don't force me to start questioning your value, as well."

Baker dropped his eyes and voice.

"That's better," said Royce. "Now go on."

Baker again turned for the shore. But a second later, sprang back around. His belt buckle dagger was out and up against Corealis' throat.

"*You fool!*"

Baker nodded vigorously.

"Yeah, that's me. But now, we're gonna make sure nuthin' happens to Jimbo."

"You've just lost your ticket out!" threatened Royce.

"Uh-huh. And you just might have yours punched. Now, get a move on, Cuz!"

The couple had left the gully's narrow stretch and mounted its steep, wide mouth. Ahead loomed the beautiful lagoon. A breeze continued across it, passed them, and down the cut, out to sea. But it wasn't cool or sweet, just a fetid, sloppy lick.

Then he stepped into view.

It was the same young soldier who'd first guided Trennt to the camp. Now though, his courteous face was hard, his weapon leveled with purpose.

Geri lost her breath at his appearance. But Trennt only regarded what he'd expected all along. He cradled the woman to himself. With a resigned stare, he looked over her head, straight into the calculating hazel eyes of their executioner.

"Shoot straight," was all he said.

The youthful rifleman slowly raised his sights.

"JIMBO! *Hold up, Pard! Help's a-comin'!*"

The young assassin paused, suddenly uncertain and puzzled by the commotion.

Then there was Baker and his entourage, coming up the draw with all the fanfare of a carnival pulling into town, with Royce Corealis in tow, and the entire landing party circling threateningly about.

He grinned up at Trennt with his typical schoolboy shine.

"Guess I stirred me up another beehive, Pard. Never been much good without yah to keep me in line. Well, your thinkin' was right again. Just never can trust upper management. Lie through their teeth."

They shared that familiar, renewing smile—friends again.

"When you see your chance," ordered Corealis bravely, "shoot him! Shoot them all."

Baker smiled.

"Yeah, boys, you do that. And I guarantee a hole in Mister Cee's neck big 'nuff to spit down."

He frowned at the young assassin.

"Whatcha waitin' for? Toss that piece over. And be quick about it!"

The soldier flung his weapon out as ordered. But the barrel skipped off a rock and the gun twirled just out of Trennt's reach. As Trennt stepped to retrieve it, his weak ankle folded and he went down.

Baker fired a worried glance around his prisoner. "Pard?"

For a split second the blade loosened.

Corealis jerked aside. A gun exploded.

Baker's grip relaxed and Royce Corealis shoved

himself free. The shooter plopped low against the gully wall. The director indignantly brushed himself off and looked over.

"Simple-minded fool."

Giving the prisoners a dismissing glance, he turned back for the boat landing. "Finish it."

Trennt gazed mournfully at his dead colleague. Baker's ultimate, blood-soaked end had long ago been ordained in the stars. But even so, it seemed over too quickly, without the grand flaming finale those knowing him had come to expect. No matter, that chapter was now forever closed, as soon would be the entire book.

The grumbling began. Another brontide. A mild tremor rose expectantly with it, up through the cut of gully walls, then quickly petering out, barely a shudder.

After a moment's pause, the landing party reassembled for their return. The executioner was left to finish his task.

But facing him again, Trennt blinked at something beyond. Out in the lagoon was a motion, a quick surface fizzing about a third of the way across. In moments, it flashed through a simmer and into a furious boil.

Clutching Geri again at his chest, Trennt pressed his mouth to her ear.

"Start breathing hard," he whispered. "Hold your breath, when I say. No matter what, don't let it out!"

Yards ahead, the soldier again focused on the couple. Now though, Trennt gauged his mettle and timed the creep of his trigger finger against a new flatness in the seabound breeze.

Across his sights, a sudden, mystified look came over the young killer.

"Now!" Trennt ordered Geri and chugged a last breath himself.

The soldier's own respiration hiked. His trigger finger flexed and reset. He blinked and drew a fresh bead.

Abruptly, the rifle wavered. It fell away as stunned hands grabbed instead for his throat. The young man toppled, mouth and eyes wide in terror, not comprehending his quick unheralded end.

Dragging Geri along, Trennt charged for the ridge. He push-pulled her higher, higher. With his own lungs ablaze, they made the crest and a hopefully, safer level. But he didn't dare test the air, and instead buried her face tight against him.

Below, the lagoon boiled and pitched, rapidly venting its gush of lethal gas into the seaward breeze. The churning also gnawed at the soft loam-filled shore. It surged and rocked, easily sawing a quick, ragged gash at the lower, gully end.

Driven on, the lethal waves themselves burst forth and flooded down the narrow canyon like a miner's sluice; gas and water quick on the heels of the now retreating shore crew. Trying to outrun it, terrified men dropped their weapons, stumbling over the uneven ground, surging rollers, and each other.

But, heavier than the air it displaced and kept in check by the narrow gully walls, the lethal mix of carbon monoxide, methane, and ammonia flushed freely among them, asphyxiating man after man in the span of mere steps.

Royce Corealis had enough presence of mind to cut a right angle to the flow and start against it, toward the ridge. His only mistake was in crossing over the dying Ivory Baker.

Baker's eyes reanimated with the director's approach. In a last act of defiance, he grabbed the man's ankle and hung on. Understandably, his grip was weak, and in seconds, Corealis easily stomped and kicked himself free of the gunman.

Yet doing so caused Royce to squander the extra breath he needed to clear the steep gully wall. And halfway up, he rattled with an air-starved hiccup. His esophagus burned and he coughed, sucking in a throatful of gas.

Royce spat it back immediately. But the floodgates to an unstoppable cycle had been sprung and he coughed and breathed again. And again. His chest tightened. His vision blurred. The ridge danced and twirled teasingly just out of reach.

Royce Corealis was angry. All those years of working so hard at staying in shape, only to have his body betray him like this!

He willed it on. Yet his steps became staggered, rubbery. His limbs wouldn't obey. Nor would his foolish lungs be still. Out of control, they pulled madly at the searing witch's brew, cramming more and more poison deep inside.

His grip loosened and the interim president fell away.

CHAPTER 29

In minutes the event was over. The pond had emptied, its water and poisons both flushed out to sea. Trennt and Geri still hugged the ridgetop, nearly unconscious themselves from the effort of holding their breath.

Climbing to their feet, they tested the air with quick gasps and looked about. Below, all signs of the landing party were gone. What the gas had stilled, thousands of tons of water and mud had flushed away. Neither Corealis nor Baker were anywhere to be seen.

In the bay, the jet seaplane still rode at anchor. Roughly jounced about, it now settled back into a lopsided buoyancy, regaining its threatened confidence. But no activity registered aboard it, either. Any crew left there had likely succumbed, as well.

Trennt spied a few inches of metal jabbing rakishly from the heavy sediment. It was the filthy barrel of an M-16, which he rocked free of the dense, foul mud. He also managed a clutch of floating MRE pouches and a few remaining odds and ends.

The couple transferred what little they salvaged to the lone surviving raft and climbed aboard. Trennt fired up the 2-cycle outboard motor and pulled some yards from shore, where he stopped and sat idling.

Here, the breeze was exhilarating. After so many weeks of dirty land travel, the couple lingered gratefully in its welcomed embrace.

Then Geri pointed to something floating further out. Barely breaking the surface, it was green-brown and lacquered to a shine by the waves. At first Trennt thought it a turtle. Drawing up, however, he realized it was the insulated box of catalyst vials.

Trennt gaffed the box with the M-16's flash suppressor and brought it aboard. There at their feet, the amber fluid looked so innocent. There was no indication of all the hard miles it'd traveled. No tally of the lives it had cost, nor the millions more it could prevent from ever beginning. Trennt handed the ampoules to Geri and she quietly finished the task begun by Wayne those days before.

Trennt then idled further into the current. There he realized, for the first time, that he had no new sense of direction. His hand absently worked the tiller, unsure of where to proceed.

Again, it was Geri who had the answer. Reading his mind, she reached for the motor and deftly killed its ignition. They'd let the current decide.

She gently kissed her man on the forehead, then settled to the floor at his feet. He, in turn, set a loving hand to her shoulder.

Slowly, they drifted north, up the coast.

DAVID DRAKE RULES!

Hammer's Slammers:

The Tank Lords	87794-1 ◆ $6.99	☐
Caught in the Crossfire	87882-4 ◆ $6.99	☐
The Butcher's Bill	57773-5 ◆ $6.99	☐
The Sharp End	87632-5 ◆ $7.99	☐
Cross the Stars	57821-9 ◆ $6.99	☐
Paying the Piper (HC)	7434-3547-8 ◆ $24.00	☐

RCN series:

With the Lightnings	57818-9 ◆ $6.99	☐
Lt. Leary, Commanding (HC)	57875-8 ◆ $24.00	☐
Lt. Leary, Commanding (PB)	31992-2 ◆ $7.99	☐

The Belisarius series with Eric Flint:

An Oblique Approach	87865-4 ◆ $6.99	☐
In the Heart of Darkness	87885-9 ◆ $6.99	☐
Destiny's Shield	57872-3 ◆ $6.99	☐
Fortune's Stroke (HC)	57871-5 ◆ $24.00	☐
The Tide of Victory (HC)	31996-5 ◆ $22.00	☐
The Tide of Victory (PB)	7434-3565-6 ◆ $7.99	☐

The General series with S.M. Stirling:

The Forge	72037-6 ◆ $5.99	☐
The Chosen	87724-0 ◆ $6.99	☐
The Reformer	57860-X ◆ $6.99	☐

Independent Novels and Collections:

The Dragon Lord (fantasy)	87890-5 ◆ $6.99	☐
Birds of Prey	57790-5 ◆ $6.99	☐
Northworld Trilogy	57787-5 ◆ $6.99	☐

continued

DAVID WEBER

<u>The Honor Harrington series:</u> *(cont.)*

Flag in Exile

Hounded into retirement and disgrace by political enemies, Honor Harrington has retreated to planet Grayson, where powerful men plot to reverse the changes she has brought to their world. And for their plans to succeed, Honor Harrington must die!

Honor Among Enemies

Offered a chance to end her exile and again command a ship, Honor Harrington must use a crew drawn from the dregs of the service to stop pirates who are plundering commerce. Her enemies have chosen the mission carefully, thinking that either she will stop the raiders or they will kill her . . . and either way, her enemies will win. . . .

In Enemy Hands

After being ambushed, Honor finds herself aboard an enemy cruiser, bound for her scheduled execution. But one lesson Honor has never learned is how to give up!

Echoes of Honor

"Brilliant! Brilliant! Brilliant!"—*Anne McCaffrey*

Ashes of Victory

Honor has escaped from the prison planet called Hell and returned to the Manticoran Alliance, to the heart of a furnace of new weapons, new strategies, new tactics, spies, diplomacy, and assassination.

continued (☞